A KIND
OF
JUSTICE

Also by Renee James

Transition to Murder

A KIND
OF
JUSTICE

A NOVEL

RENEE JAMES

Oceanview Publishing
Longboat Key, Florida

ISBN 978-1-60809-213-0

Published in the United States of America by Oceanview Publishing
Longboat Key, Florida

www.oceanviewpub.com

10 9 8 7 6 5 4 3 2 1

PRINTED IN THE UNITED STATES OF AMERICA

*Dedicated to Katie Thomas,
friend, mentor, role model*

ACKNOWLEDGMENTS

WRITING IS SUPPOSED to be a solitary profession, but as I contemplate how this story progressed from a first draft that only a friend would read to a manuscript a prestigious publisher would consider, there are enough people to fill a crowd scene in a Hollywood blockbuster.

Many thanks to my esteemed beta readers: Mary Whitledge, Katie Thomas, Brenda Baker, Lisa Coluccio, and Jonnie Guernsey.

Thanks to consulting editor Chris Nelson and my wonderful agent, Tina Schwartz. Thanks also to Windy City Publishing, for getting me started in this business, and Oceanview Publishing for daring to read this book in the first place, then for taking on the challenge of publishing it.

Thanks to the many writing groups who helped me on the way, including especially the Wisconsin Writers Association's Novel-in-Progress Bookcamp, the Chicago Writers Association, and the Off-Campus Writers Workshop. Thanks also to John Truby, whose seminar on plot structure was incredibly helpful.

And many thanks to the transgender pioneers who have delivered us to a time when we can be heroines and heroes in books and movies. A special thanks to the National Center for Transgender Equality, and to the many groups in Chicago who have made our city so livable for transgender people.

A KIND
OF
JUSTICE

1

THURSDAY, JUNE 12, 2008

PEOPLE MILL AND mingle and bathe in Chicago's moment of late-spring perfection, a last touch of Eden before the heat of summer sets in, a sun-drenched, breezy, shirtsleeves and sandals day. Pedestrians walk with a bounce. Motorists have their windows open. People caught indoors look out and curse their captivity.

But for Wilkins, sipping coffee at an idyllic sidewalk café, it's just business. For Wilkins, sunlight is only the appearance of happiness and the flower-scented air is only a sugarcoating for the stench that lies just under the sweetness. Murderers and rapists and psychopaths and thieves walk the streets on days like this, just the same as when the snow's flying or the summer sun is turning exposed skin into melanomas.

He's on business, but not official business. Yet. More a get-reacquainted visit. He wants to learn everything he can about the queer in the shop across the street. See who goes in. Get a sense of the area. Get a sense of the quote woman unquote who got away with two violent crimes and made a fool out of him in the process.

He finally has the time to make things right. That's the one good thing that came from the divorce. No more restrictions on his time. There's only an empty apartment to go home to, a dark empty place that feels like a mortuary and smells like dust. He hates the place.

Dreads it like he dreads dentists and doctors. He loathes it like he loathes crooked politicians and soft judges. The only good thing about the fairy queen is, she gives him a reason to keep out of the apartment.

He had forgotten about her until the divorce left him standing there with a suitcase full of shattered dreams, wondering what to do with himself. It was when he reviewed his open case files, looking for cold-case projects for his spare time, that he saw what the investigators missed in the Strand investigation, the ones who came after he'd been pushed off the case. They never connected the other crime to the Strand murder, the strange case of a small-time thug getting savagely mugged but not robbed.

A motion at the edge of his peripheral vision takes Wilkins' attention back to the street. A youngish man, midtwenties, dressed wrong, moving too fast on the sidewalk. Way too fast. He pushes people aside to pass them. He is almost running. His face is so tense Wilkins can see the sinew of his jaw muscles. He's wearing filthy jeans with holes in them. Not designer trash, the real thing. Junkie clothes. His t-shirt has dirt smudges and hangs askew. He's crazy thin. Like a speed freak.

Wilkins drains the rest of his coffee and leaves as the junkie bursts into the beauty salon across the street. Something interesting is going to happen.

* * *

Marilee is chatting about her first grandchild, a doe-eyed waif who is nearly as cute as Marilee thinks she is. I'm doing a curling iron set on her hair and enjoying the social hour. It's like a vacation, a leisurely service filled with easy conversation, time with someone I love. My friend. My surrogate mother.

I'm coming off a brutal week. Ten-hour days in the shop to tend to my clients' needs, then four days at a hair show, doing breakfasts with sponsors every morning, platform shows all day, and the mandatory party circuit every night. Eighteen-hour days.

It's not fun anymore.

And I have other things on my plate now. I've been managing this salon for several months while Roger tends to his partner who is in chemo for pancreatic cancer. He wants to retire and have me buy the place from him. I've done the due diligence, talked to the bankers, hired an attorney, but I'm dragging my feet. This is no little ma-and-pa business. It's a big, upscale hair salon in the high-rent River North neighborhood. It carries a price tag that makes my heart pound. I try not to think about it, the debt, the risk, the pressure. Dealing with the flighty personalities of our hairdressing staff. Handling bitchy clients. Getting sued.

And I worry about not having time for my niece. The child I have been talking to since she was an embryo in her mother's womb. The child whose face often appears in my mind before I fall asleep each night and whose happy smile and infectious belly laughs bring a gladness to my world beyond anything I can imagine.

"What made you finally decide to give up platform work?" Marilee asks. She's a shrink and my mother confessor. I've been talking to her about it for a while.

I tell her about an exhibitor party last week. "It was late. I was beat. I started seeing things that were terribly depressing. The drunks. The false gaiety. Then a couple of models staggered out of the bathroom with cocaine eyes, and I just got this overwhelming sadness about what's ahead for them. A wasted life. A bad death. All of a sudden it wasn't glamorous anymore. These were not beautiful people, the partying was desperate, and I was so tired I could sleep on the sidewalk."

I lock eyes with Marilee in the mirror. "You know, I had to ask myself, what do I love about this? And the answer is, doing hair. Which I can do here."

Marilee begins to say something when a terrible crashing sound fills the salon. A wiry, crazed-looking man has flung open the entry door and crashed into a display case, sending bottles and cans of hair products flying through the reception area. The receptionist is frozen in terror, standing with hands to mouth, eyes the size of pancakes.

The man stands at the threshold of the work area, his eyes wide and lit up like demonic coals. His soiled jeans and t-shirt suggest street person, but street people don't terrorize beauty salons. His face is twisted in pain and hate. He looks like death.

"Where's my bitch!" he shrieks. "Where's my fucking bitch!"

All movement in the salon stops dead. A wave of horror fills the room, sucking the oxygen out of the place. Hairdressers and clients alike gape. I can't move any part of my body and I can't get my mind to comprehend what's happening. Who is this person? What is he doing in a beauty salon?

"Trudy! Get your cunt ass out here! Now!"

His voice thunders through the room, powered by a high-pitched desperation. Murderous desperation.

Trudy is a junior stylist. She's only been here for a few months. She comes out of the break room. A hair dryer clicks off, then another and another. The last sound. Silence and stillness grip the salon as though we are all frozen in ice.

"Joey, go away!" Trudy's voice is taut. It sounds far away. Her face is a road map of fear and mourning, a picture of someone caught in a terrible vision they can't get out of.

The power of movement comes back to me in small bits.

His face is a portrait of some distant human emotion boiling in a pot of bile. He is seeing her through the veil of his own demons, a hideous lens of chaos that crazes his eyes and shreds his features with silent claws that turn his skin into deathly folds and creases.

What do you say to someone burning with a rage that is not of this world?

"Sir, this is a beauty salon."

Brilliant.

I step toward him, putting my body between him and Trudy. Stupid. I'm a transsexual hairdresser and even though I'm six feet tall, I'm less intimidating than a poodle. My hands are shaking and my heart is fluttering. My mouth is so dry I can barely make words.

He looks at me, confused. Like he can't believe what he's seeing. I get that a lot, even from people who aren't on some kind of chemically induced trip.

"Who the fuck are you?" His tone is caustic, taunting. A warning. I'm a bug about to be crushed.

"I'm the manager of this salon. I'd like you to leave at once." My tongue is sticking to the roof of my mouth as I speak. It sounds like I have a speech impediment. I want to say more but I can't.

It doesn't matter. This man is listening to a different voice. Maybe lots of them. His lips curl back in a vicious sneer. His muscles flex. He is outraged that I would speak to him at all, let alone order him from the room.

I call to the receptionist. "Samantha, please call the police." She already has the phone to her ear and is speaking in a furious whisper into the receiver. To the man I say, "The police will be here in a few moments. Please, let's take this outside so you can avoid trouble." It's not the Gettysburg Address, but I manage to say it without squeaking, without my tongue getting stuck to the glue that coats my mouth.

"I want my bitch, you ugly freak!" he says. His face is as red as a stoplight.

He yanks a pistol from behind his back and starts toward Trudy, raising the gun as he goes. I step into his path. My curling iron cord pops out of the power socket as I reach the end of its length. Another male figure appears behind him, just entering the salon. Something about the new person looks familiar, but I don't have time to think about it. The maniac swings his pistol in a backhanded motion toward my face. It's an arrogant gesture, meant to break my jaw and knock me senseless. He doesn't need to waste a bullet on a sniveling queer like me.

I would have agreed with him about that, but he didn't ask and my reflexes take over. I bob under the arc of his hand the way a boxer dips under the wild hooks of an amateurish opponent. Before he can recover to swing again, I stab him in the solar plexus with my curling iron.

It's hard enough to take his breath away and as hot as a branding iron. He wants to scream but can't because he can't breathe. As he tries to suck air, I gouge my left thumb deep into his eye socket. Years of self-defense training in action.

The madman drops like he was shot and writhes on the floor gasping for air with lungs that are frozen shut, both hands held to his eye socket. For a moment I worry that he'll die, then he takes a short breath. A new problem. He'll recover in a moment, and we'll start all over again.

I kick his pistol in the general direction of the receptionist and bind his hands behind his back with the cord of the curling iron, then tie a salon cape over his face. The cape thing is bizarre, but it works with some wild animals, maybe with him.

We don't find out. The police arrive before he recovers enough to resist. Two uniforms tend to the maniac, another asks me what happened. As I answer, I see the mystery man just over the shoulder of the cop. A thick, powerful black man who is staring at me with palpable malice. He looks vaguely familiar.

I give my statement and the cop moves to Trudy, then other witnesses. Other cops take the maniac away. Trudy is in shock, gray-faced, blank-eyed. She moved out on him a week ago, sick of the drugs, the beatings, the low-life friends. Stayed with one of the other stylists and kept a low profile. Joey is dangerous. Slugs, slaps, punches. Scorns. Mr. Wonderful. His brutish personality is blended with the intellect of a carrot. It took him a week to figure out he could find her at her place of work.

It amazes me how often a beautiful girl like Trudy gets involved with a doper or pusher or gangster or one of the other breeds of low-life men. My friend Cecelia says it's a low-self-esteem thing. They only respect men who don't respect them. A lot of them get into drugs themselves, or booze, or dehumanizing sex. It kills me. I'd give anything to have been put in Trudy's body. I'd pay any price and I'd do anything to keep body and mind whole. And here she has it all and pisses it away on a scumbag like Joey.

Slowly the salon evolves back to doing hair. I instruct the staff to comp all the clients in the salon during the scene and I personally apologize to each of them. Some of them look at me like I'm some kind of hero. John Wayne in a miniskirt. It's kind of funny, but the humor hides a more somber truth: I'm one transwoman who doesn't play the victim anymore.

The police finish their interviews. The last one to leave pauses to talk to the mysterious black man who is still in the reception area, sitting now, still staring at me. Even from a distance I can see the anger on his face. Not quite the mask of hatred Joey brought in, but the same genre.

He looks familiar, but I can't place him. He can't be a customer. What little hair he has is cut almost flush with his scalp. Whoever he is, whatever his issues, I decide to confront them head-on. I approach him and ask, "Can I help you, sir?"

He stares at me as though I have insulted his wife. He stands, his face inches in front of my face, scowling, breathing through his mouth. His breath reeks. He holds a badge in one hand, beside his face. That and his hate-filled eyes, his wide nose, his powerful shoulders bring back the memory. The badge reads "Detective Allan Wilkins." I remember him as Detective Hard Case. He wanted to implicate me in two violent crimes in the transgender community when I was transitioning. He hated me because I was a man with tits, a freak, a simpering queer who wouldn't acquiesce to his bullying tactics.

"Great work."

He's talking about my takedown of the crazy man. But he's not really admiring it. He speaks in a voice only I can hear, but he manages to convey hatred and anger with great efficiency.

"You know how to handle yourself," he says. "You act like a big fairy who wouldn't hurt a fly. But you showed who you are just now. You're a violent pervert and you get off on hurting men. You did that poor sap in the alley and you did John Strand, too. You thumbed him in the eye, just like you did this asshole, and then you slit his throat. I'm on your trail, Cinderella, and I will get you this time."

The poor sap in the alley had raped me. He and a buddy. A bloody beating followed by a first-class rape. Wilkins was one of the cops who figured I had it coming. Fingering me for the mugging the rapist got months later speaks eloquently about where transgender women sit in his legal priorities.

"Get out of this salon right now. Don't ever come back, or I'll report you to the DA's office again." I say it in a furious whisper, my eyes boring right back into his. Getting lip from a transsexual drives him stark raving mad, but I couldn't care less. He's not fazed by my little reminder that the last time he tried bullying me, he got censured by the LGBT advocate in the DA's office. No matter, that was my promise to him, not a defense mechanism. I'm not on this earth to take crap from bigots.

"I just responded to a call with my brothers in blue," he says, flashing a mirthless grin. "That's my job."

"I insist you leave immediately." I say it loud enough for the receptionist to hear me. She has been watching since I approached him.

Wilkins' lips widen into a menacing leer. He nods. Leaves. I'm supposed to be scared and intimidated. I am, but I have news for Wilkins. I've gotten rid of him before and I can do it again.

The first morning of the rest of my life. An omen.

2

THURSDAY, JUNE 12

THIS WORKDAY ENDS in a unique way. A cluster of hairdressers linger to talk after we close, not like us at all. In our shop, when your last customer leaves, you do a station cleanup and get out the door. Tonight, everyone wants to talk about the wild event of the morning. And the aftermath. They vent their emotions, recall where they were when it happened, what clients or other stylists said or did. They replay my heroism, especially Samantha, our receptionist. "You may not be a man anymore, but you sure know where to hit one, Bobbi," she says.

I'm transsexual and my friends' lighthearted repartee and joking about it in the shop keeps the edge off. Many of these people went through my transition with me. It was a difficult time for all of us. They had to get used to me in a dress and makeup, and not looking quite right, a woman in male proportions. I had to get used to me, too. It was hard. I'd like to think we're all better people for having gone through it. I know for sure we're closer.

Sam's remark brings murmured assent. The girls may be taking some comfort from having an oversized transwoman in the place. I'd rather be five-five and 120 pounds, but this morning, it was nice to be six feet tall, 160 pounds, with enough leverage and heft to drop a piece of bad news in his tracks.

My mind notes the fact that Sugar Ray Robinson was six feet tall and 160. Dad's favorite fighter. But Dad wouldn't see much similarity between his son-turned-daughter and the great Sugar Ray. Even before he got to my white skin, he'd blanch at my plump breasts and my almost-feminine butt. And Dad would puke.

My father was homophobic when I thought I was gay. He would have been transphobic, too, but he died before I got to this part of my life. Whatever. I've come to realize that, with or without a dick, I'm a better person than he ever was.

As I modestly proclaim mine a lucky punch, Roger unlocks the front door and enters. He is the owner of the shop and one of the finest human beings I've ever known. He stuck by me in my transition, even when customers and stylists alike were making his life miserable. And he wants me to own this shop with the kind of passion a patriarch might have for keeping the business in the family.

Roger walks directly to me. He is a smallish, slim man whose walk and mannerisms are more effeminate than mine, even though I work at it and he doesn't. His movements are fast, like there is a fire burning behind him. His face is stressed. He stands on his tiptoes and throws his arms around me and we hug like siblings who haven't seen each other for years.

"Are you okay now?" he asks as we break the clinch. He is almost shaking with pent-up anxiety. He doesn't wait for an answer but moves among the others, asking the same question, hugging each one, apologizing that his salon was the scene of such a violent event. He can be a very tough boss and a hard-nosed businessman, but deep down inside he's as mushy and sentimental as any of us.

As the staff starts trickling out into the night, Roger and I retreat to his tiny office. When I'm in here with him, the ghosts of my transition always lurk on the edges of my consciousness. This is where Roger didn't fire me for coming in as a woman, out of the blue—yesterday a man, today the worst sort of queer—a transsexual woman. This is where he told me to quit apologizing for who I was and just get to making women beautiful. And this is where he introduced me to the SuperGlam people and recommended me for their hair show staff, the start of my platform career, which led to me becoming what Roger calls a rock-star hairdresser.

Even though there is no one left in the shop, Roger closes the office door before sitting at his desk. I'm in a hard plastic chair facing him, with just enough room to cross my legs.

Roger clears his throat, looks at me, drops his gaze, clears his throat, looks at me. On the third cycle he bursts into tears like a broken-hearted child. This is not hair salon histrionics. This is pure grief. I rise and come around the desk and throw my arms around him. He stands and we hug, me stooping so our bodies match up.

He sobs for a long time, until his torrential grief subsides to a throbbing ache. I know what that's like and I wouldn't wish it on anyone.

"He's not going to make it, Bobbi," Roger says as I sit down again. He's referring to his cancer-stricken partner, Robert. They have been a dedicated, loving couple for decades. They had dreamed of someday getting legally married, but Illinois is still wrestling with the twin bigotries of homophobia and religious hatred. How they manage to face each day upbeat and cheerful in the face of such injustice is beyond me, but they do. At least, until now.

"They're saying three months, maybe less. I asked him what he wanted to do with the rest of his life . . ." Roger tries to smile but sobs. He is in such pain I want to give him my tears to cry.

"He wants to finish his days watching the sun rise and set in Florida."

Roger and Robert have both done very well in business and bought a beautiful home in Key West. I haven't been there, but several of the hairdressers have and they rave about it.

"I need you to buy the business right now, Bobbi. No more dawdling.

I need to get Robert to Florida, and you need to own this salon. Believe me, Bobbi, you will make it even better and owning this place will help fulfill you. You're made for it. These people look up to you . . ." Roger pauses a beat as I raise my eyebrows in surprise. I'm an unlikely icon for leadership in the beauty business. "No, they do. They admire you, Bobbi. You're smart and fair and you are one of the greatest hairdressers in the city. They'll stay if you take over. You'll all do well."

"I'm worried about the economy, Roger." I am. The financial crash ushered in a recession. We've always been able to handle them, but this one is ominous. Economists keep forecasting a recovery, but it keeps getting worse, like a wound you can't stop from bleeding.

"You're getting a fabulous price on this business," says Roger. "Believe me, I could get more from other sources. I want you to have it. If things get really bad, we can redo my part of the deal." Roger owns a high percentage of the business. The bank's share isn't much more than a line of credit, which is why I can make this purchase without putting up much in the way of cash or assets.

I nod but don't say anything. He's not done yet.

"I need you to do this fast, Bobbi. I have another offer, and I'll have to take it if you aren't ready to move."

I shouldn't be so intimidated about taking on hundreds of thousands of dollars of debt. I worked in the corporate world as a marketing type, so I've been involved in mergers and acquisitions, some on a grand scale, but none involving my money.

Words don't come to me. I want to tell Roger that I'm thinking about it, but it scares me. He's heard it before.

"Bobbi, I've wanted you to have this salon ever since I saw you standing out in front of buildings freezing your ass off in the dead of winter handing out leaflets for your services. I've never ever met anyone who wanted to be a hairdresser so much and who was such a good person. I love you. Robert loves you. Do this!"

Roger's timing is impeccable. The adrenaline rush from taking down that junkie has wakened my inner warrior, and Roger's words have caressed my heart.

"I love you both, too, Roger." I want to say how heartbroken I am. For both of them. But the words seem too trite to say out loud and so I stare at him and let my tears come. Roger regards me with the greatest sadness, powered by his loss and also by my grief.

"Okay, Roger," I say finally. "I'll have my attorney contact yours."

So ends months of procrastination, me trying to reason the whole thing out, not able to rationalize making the move, plunging ahead now on an emotional whim. I'm not going to think about it anymore. No second-guessing, no buyer's remorse. I said yes and now I'll see it through. I'm scared, but the truth is, Roger is right. I can make this work, maybe better than anyone else. And if I fail, I'll be brave and I'll start over.

Roger and I hug again, a long embrace baptized with tears. When we finally leave the shop, we blow kisses to each other on the sidewalk and go into the night in different directions.

* * *

WEDNESDAY, JUNE 18

"Of course I will," says Cecelia. She glances at me, a wry smile playing at her lips, as if my question was silly. She has just agreed to come to the closing on the salon with me.

We are puffing and sweating along the Chicago lakefront, engaged in our weekly Wednesday power walk together. Cecelia is a retired investment banker. She was at the top of that pyramid back in the day, back when she was an alpha male. Now she's a leader in the Chicago transgender community and my best friend. She's big and loud and defiantly transsexual, unwilling to countenance bullshit from anyone about it. We met when I was first beginning to explore my hidden transgender reality. My first impression of her was unkind. I thought she was a loudmouthed jerk.

But when I began my tortured transition, I discovered a different dimension to Cecelia, a deeply compassionate side that she keeps mostly hidden. She shared that part of herself with me during my transition, when I was hit by a tidal wave of societal waste that stripped away my self-esteem and left me alone in the world. She gave me hope and courage and a role model for the parts of transitioning I was worst at. She got things from me, too. I gave her a different friendship than she had with others. I needed her but didn't take her crap and she liked having an equal. And we both found in the other someone who had similar intellect and came from the white-collar business world. She has counseled me through this whole acquisition scenario, especially holding my hand as I fussed about all the debt and responsibility.

"Here's the funny thing," she says, nudging me playfully with one elbow. "When it's all done and you're walking around with a debt bigger than the sky, after you learn to live with the fear of failure, you start to feel powerful. Special. How many people are successful enough to carry that kind of debt?"

I can't picture the power trip she describes. All I can see is the sheer horror of coming up short, losing everything, seeing my colleagues have to scramble for new jobs. Destroying Roger's retirement.

The conversation ends as we pick up the pace to an aerobic level and focus on the burn. Twenty minutes later, we shift to a cool-down pace. As my pulse and breathing return to normal, I look Cecelia in the eye and blurt out a question that's been on my mind for five years.

"Cecelia, where were you the night Strand was murdered?"

She stops cold and stares at me. Her eyes are blue, her brows rounded in surprise. Shock maybe. This is something we don't talk about.

"I was with you until eleven or so."

As if I could forget. The worst, longest night of my life started with a beat-down Bobbi group therapy session with three of my best friends and my transition psychologist. Afterward, my friends insisted I have a drink with them. I have never so desperately wanted to be alone as I did then. I had a rendezvous with Strand planned for that night and I was so wracked with tension about it I could barely make conversation.

"Where did you go after that?" I shouldn't ask, but I can't stop wondering. My nightmare is, she admits to being the one who slashed John Strand's throat and later the police try to coerce that information from me by offering me a deal I can't refuse. Give up my best friend, or give up the rest of my life. You'd like to think you'd never do that, but who knows until you face the reality of it?

"Where did *you* go after that, Bobbi?" Cecelia's voice is sharp. We stare at each other in silence for several long beats. She isn't asking a question. She's making a statement.

"I heard that detective is back on the case," she says. "If he asks me, I'll tell him I went home after I left you. But, Bobbi, none of us wants to know where the others were that night. We all went home after we left the bar. What if someone told you they killed Strand? What would you do with that information? If you talk about it with anyone, you could ruin that person's reputation. If you tell the police, you could get that person arrested. If you just eat it, what's the point? Nothing good can come of it."

My thoughts exactly. Sometimes I just forget myself and blurt things out. Like when I asked Strand if he murdered my friend Mandy. A stupid thing to do. It told him point-blank what I was up to. Of course, it also produced my first glimpse of the malice that boiled just below his amiable facade. Up to that moment he had been seductively charming, but as the question rolled from my lips, a shadow passed over his face, and I could see the demons of hell in his eyes. Just for a moment. I wish now I had given more credence to my instincts that night and just walked away from the whole thing—Strand, the murder investigation, everything. Strand would still be alive and terrorizing people, but I would have avoided a horrific conflict, and I'd still be able to sleep like the innocent today.

"Do you understand what I'm saying, Bobbi?" Cecelia knows I zone out sometimes. She wants to make sure I'm in the here and now for this message.

"Yes, Cecelia." I nod my head in the affirmative. But my question dangles unanswered in my consciousness like an itch you can't scratch. Might I someday be locked away in a place worse than death for something she did? Would I be able to live with that?

* * *

FRIDAY, JUNE 20

Don Richards stands and smiles as Betsy shows me into his home office. He is a decent guy. He's good to Betsy, almost everything I would want in a man for the woman I have loved both as a husband and a sister. He's not quite tender, but he's considerate. And kind. And reliable. He will always be there for her, and for my niece, little Robbie.

He had already won my respect when he and Betsy married, but he cemented it when Betsy miscarried the first child they conceived. Betsy was devastated, not only from the loss but also from feelings of guilt that she must have done something wrong. Don felt the loss, too, I could see it in him, but he put his pain in the background and invested himself in nursing Betsy's shattered soul back to health. To me, that's courage, love, and decency—most of the good things I can say about anyone.

The other thing about Don is that he has allowed Betsy and me to continue our relationship. We who were once man and wife became sister and sister. Betsy was the prime mover in our reunification. We had drifted apart after the divorce, mainly because I was ashamed of who I was. I felt that I'd betrayed her, not being the man she thought she had married. She reconnected with me when I started my transition and insisted we do things together. We shopped, had coffee, I did her hair, she and Don had me over for dinner.

Don went along with all that, even when most men wouldn't, even when it probably gave him the creeps, seeing his wife's ex-husband as a transsexual woman. Because of all that, I can forgive him for being a Republican. And for having to pretend that he likes me instead of actually liking me.

Don is a pleasant-looking man. Neat, well kept, a hint of middle-age spread. More scholarly than athletic. Serious. I can't imagine him telling a joke. The computer screen behind him is filled with spreadsheet data, glowing like a beacon in a dark room where the only other light is a curved-arm desk lamp with its beam focused on a neat stack of papers and a neat stack of files on the desk.

The desk is cleaner than an operating room. More organized than a Japanese factory.

We shake hands. He manages not to recoil at my dainty fingertip offering. He's not comfortable with me being a woman. He tries to hide it, but I recognize it in him just as clearly as I feel ill at ease in such an unnaturally tidy room.

We sit down, the desk between us, and he straightens the papers in front of him. He has been doing due diligence for me on the salon's books. He passes me the written report and starts on the verbal. "Roger's books are in order, his annual audits are thorough, and the business looks to be in good shape," says Don. "Cash flow is excellent, receivables are small, bills get paid on time. The net profit isn't going to make anyone sell their Google stock, but it's solid and consistent, and from what I've been able to glean, has a good margin for a retail beauty salon."

He continues on for another ten minutes with only a few pauses. The bottom line: the business is in great shape and probably worth more than I'm paying for it. Don doesn't see any obvious places to expand sales, though he hastily adds that he doesn't know the salon business at all.

I'm not feeling all that knowledgeable myself.

"You like to have an idea when you buy a business like this about how you can grow it or cut costs to pay for it," says Don. He painstakingly takes me through the byzantine logic of how company selling prices are based on multiples of gross profit, and how bigger companies command higher multiples than small ones.

For me, the multiple I pay will be an estimate for how many years it will take to pay off the business. I can reduce that number by increasing profits, either through organic growth or higher margins on existing business, or both.

I comprehend the concept but find the weight of it oppressive. The closer we get to the closing, the more I just want to do hair. In fact, as Don goes on, my mind is filled with the image of a beautiful up-do, my hands can remember how the hair looked and felt when I worked it. Its color is deeply dimensional, a mesh of tones and shades that invite the eye inside its density, like a cavern of beautiful colors that streak and blend and lead you ever deeper into the mystery below.

Don asks if I have questions.

"Is this a good investment for me?" I ask.

He grimaces. "That's better answered by Cecelia. What I can tell you is, it's a well-run business and its paper value seems to be higher than what he's asking. If there are hidden debts or problems we don't know about, that could change everything. But from what you've said about Roger, those things aren't likely."

We adjourn to the kitchen. Robbie rushes to greet us. She is a merry cherub, three years old and taking full pleasure in a world that sees her as sweet and cute and denies her nothing. I help Betsy carry dishes to the dining table, trying to quell my inner panic. My acquisition of Salon L'Elégance is down to one last step: a sober session with the lawyers, at the end of which I will take on a debt that is worth many times more than my life.

*   *   *

FRIDAY, JUNE 27

Being a transsexual woman is like living in a four-season climate: your environment is constantly changing. The difference is, for the trans-woman—for oversized ones like me, anyway—the changes come fast and furious and not in any natural order.

I'm bathing in a springtime moment as we leave the law offices of Roger's attorney. I have just closed on the purchase of Salon L'Elégance. It's Roger, Cecelia, me, and my attorney, but it might as well just be me. I am the nominal owner of one of Chicago's most prestigious salons. I'm swimming in a bottomless sea of debt and I have just taken on an inhuman degree of responsibility, but as Cecelia predicted, part of me is giddy with the realization of how far I've come in the world.

When we step out onto the street, my springtime moment gives way to a winter storm.

As we take the LaSalle Street Bridge over the Chicago River, I see Wilkins on the other side of the street. He's leaning against the bridge structure, staring at us. I can see the sneer on his face from here and I feel the menace of his thick body.

I point him out to my attorney and convey to him in a private voice a brief history of my run-ins with Wilkins, including the restraining order the city put on him five years ago.

"Can I bring charges against him for this?" I ask quietly. "I'd like to get him off my back."

"I doubt it." The lawyer says it regretfully. "I doubt the order is still good, but even if it is, he has a right to be in a public place. Truthfully, I doubt they'd arrest him unless he physically assaulted you. There are just too many hard-core criminals and too little jail space."

"So I just have to suck on it?" I ask. Probably not a good analogy for a transwoman to use. Especially not one as perpetually unfulfilled sexually as me.

The attorney nods.

But I'm not in a mood to be bullied by a rogue cop or take a contract attorney's word for what my rights are. My mind drifts back to the last time I was being followed by someone who was a threat to me. That ended in a flash of violence that left a nasty thug permanently retired from the intimidation business. Wilkins isn't a thug, but he's a hateful bigot and a threat to my freedom. We'll see what the DA's LGBT advocate has to say about his lurking return to my life.

3

I BREEZE INTO the cozy café in Logan Square like I own the place. It's a queer-friendly neighborhood, but I still draw a few glances. Fewer if I pay no attention.

That's easy to do tonight. It has been a brutally long day that followed a short, stress-filled night of little sleep. I'm tired. I'm ravenously hungry. I want a glass of wine so bad I could burst. But more than any of these things, my pulse is pounding in anticipation of meeting the man who invited me to dinner tonight.

Officer Phil's call came in the middle of the usual salon mayhem, like a perfect rainbow arching from my most delicious fantasy into the reality of today.

Phil used to be a beat cop in Boystown and an envoy to the Chicago queer community. He picked me out as a contact in the transgender world. His goal was to reach every segment of the gay, lesbian, and trans communities with the message that the Chicago Police Department cared about them and could be trusted. He did his job very well, though I never bought the proposition that the huge Chicago PD had much institutional interest in the welfare of transgenders. Phil did, though. On top of which, he was a very sexy man. He was the talk of the gay male community and just as alluring to transwomen, at least the ones who were attracted to men.

Since he got promoted to a cushy job downtown in community relations a while ago, I haven't seen him much except for his monthly haircut. Then today, like a bolt out of the blue, he calls me at the salon. Can I make dinner tonight? Catch up on things?

Do bears love honey?

Officer Phil is seated at a small table, a quiet spot perfectly chosen. A bottle of wine graces the tabletop, two glasses of red at the ready. Even at a distance he still makes my heart beat a little faster.

He stands as I approach and steps forward to kiss my cheek and exchange hugs. He is tall, an inch taller than I am in two-inch heels. He's dressed casually, khaki slacks, polo shirt, loafers. His hair is fashionably short, perfectly groomed. A speck or two of pepper gray is visible, and there are a few faint lines on his handsome face. He's in his forties now, and the signs of age make him even more attractive.

"Bobbi, just look at you!" he says. "You are absolutely stunning!"

"I get that a lot," I say, "but it's not usually a compliment."

"Stop that," he replies.

My heart flutters for a moment. He holds my chair and slides it beneath me with the casual precision of a gentleman. I am overwhelmed by the way he makes me feel like a lady. Girls like me don't get treatment like this very often, so I allow myself to luxuriate in it for a moment.

We drink a toast to each other and go through the usual conversation foreplay. I ask if he's got a serious love interest yet. No. He asks me if I do. No. This is a topic I won't allow in my salon services, partly because it's good business, and partly because we transsexual women get bombarded with really inappropriate questions. Have you tried out the new plumbing? Did it work? How does it compare to being the one with the penis? Are you into anything kinky? The questions come easier to inebriates in bars, another reason I don't frequent them. Officer Phil would never indulge in such stuff, but others do, men and women, so I have a hard and fast rule—we don't talk about sex or politics in my chair.

"How is the hairstyling business?" he asks.

I tell him about buying the salon, giving up platform work, sweating the loan payments. I ask him about working at headquarters with the suits, dealing with the public. He's fine with the brass, loves working with civic groups, small businesses. He misses Boystown. He misses me. I blush and hold my breath for a moment, then he adds, "And Cecelia and all the girls at TransRising." I come back to earth with a jolt. This is juvenile of me, but the only fantasy I have about men is that Phil will someday find me the woman he can't live without.

We make small talk about who's doing what in the LGBT community, what it's like at the top of the CPD food chain. We order, make another toast to old times, sip the wine, a nice Washington State Cabernet. Phil leans forward, his elbows on the table, his face just a foot or two from mine.

"Bobbi, I need to say something to you. I'm way out of line, but I want to say it anyway, on the basis that I'm a friend and that's why I'm saying it. Okay?"

For a moment there, I thought he was going to proposition me, then he started with the friend stuff. I shrug.

"Bobbi, you made a bad mistake trying to get Detective Wilkins taken off the Strand case again."

I groan out loud. Five years ago, Wilkins tried to intimidate me during his investigation of the Strand murder. I called the LGBT advocate in the district attorney's office and complained about his bigotry—the bastard called us "tranny queers" and "butt fuckers" among other horrible expressions. She got him pulled off the case. I filed another complaint this week, but she couldn't help me this time. What happened in the salon didn't qualify as police harassment.

"Wilkins had been working the case on his own time, but since your complaint, he's gotten clearance to make it a full-blown investigation.

He convinced his captain that you filed it because he's going to prove you killed Strand."

My adolescent fantasies involving Phil evaporate. My heart beats against my ribs with the force of an iron fist. There is a pounding noise in my ears. "It's personal with him," I say. "Pure hate."

"It's more serious than that, Bobbi." Phil has a worried look on his face. "He thinks he can prove you set up that guy who got mugged in the alley where you were raped. He thinks that guy was connected to Strand. And he thinks he can link you directly to the Strand murder."

"Link?" I echo. "How?"

"Wilkins saw you finish that nutcase in your salon with an eye gouge. He has photos of the guy's eye and it looks a lot like Strand's eye injury. The coroner said his injury came from an eye gouge that was probably used to disable him.

"Wilkins also says there were synthetic hair fibers found at the scene, consistent with a short-hair wig, maybe a male toupee. That gives him a theory about how the crime could have been committed by a woman posing as a man. That's just a wild theory right now, but he thinks you could have passed as a man back then. And you were strong enough to overpower an adult male. He says he's going to tie you to the crime scene."

Like most transsexual women, it takes a lot to scare me. Phil's ominous message qualifies.

Wilkins is a mean and ugly brute who hates me even more than he hates all transsexuals because I stood up to his bullying the first time around. Lots of us complained, but I started it. This must have been festering in his nasty soul for years. I can see him manufacturing whatever evidence he needs to nail me, though he can destroy me without even bringing charges. Just leaking to the newspapers that I'm a suspect in a murder can send my salon's A-list clientele scattering to shops of better repute.

"How do you know this?" I ask when I regain control of my brain and tongue.

"He called me for background on you, Bobbi. He has the case file out. He's coming after you."

"He's going to plant evidence, isn't he?" I'm so filled with dread I can hardly say the words.

"No," says Phil. "Wilkins won't go that far. He's a tough guy, and he'll intimidate people to get them to confess, but he doesn't cross the legal lines. Don't feel too good about that, though. He's relentless and he hates you and he'll work like the earth on fire to make a case against you."

"I don't get it, Phil. I learned the eye gouge in a self-defense class. I'm sure hundreds of people in this city did, too. Maybe thousands. Lots of people know that technique. The only thing that puts me on his suspect list is that I'm queer." My tone has gone from fear to anger. I hiss out the word "queer" loud enough to draw attention from the table next to us.

Phil waits until the other diners return to their own conversation, then leans forward again. "Don't you ever use that word to describe yourself to me again, Bobbi." He says it sternly. "You are a beautiful woman and you have done great things with your life."

That stops me cold. For a second I think I see something in Phil's eyes, a romantic connection, maybe. But no, a closer look and what I see is a very nice man who said something nice to someone having a bad day. It's better this way. If he confessed his love for me right now, the waitstaff would have to mop the remains of my overwhelmed senses from the floor.

Our food comes. We make idle chatter with the waiter, a pleasant male who can't hide his attraction to Phil. Why should he be different?

When he leaves, Phil leans forward again, as do I. "Bobbi, I shouldn't have told you any of this. I'm asking you to keep it between us. I could get in trouble."

"Why *did* you tell me?" I ask.

"Because I care about you. And because I don't know what all is in the evidence book. Maybe they have blood samples or DNA or something. They have no legal reason to treat you as a suspect, no reason to get samples of your blood or DNA. Don't give them one, okay? And don't antagonize Wilkins anymore. Maybe he'd be a little more interested in other suspects if it wasn't so personal with you." He stares at me with an intensity I never thought he had. I always saw him as a sort of California surfer who blundered into police work in Chicago, thought it was a promising wave, and decided to ride it to the next coast in life.

"Okay," I answer. Inside, I'm still mulling the "I care about you" statement. My rational mind knows he cares about me like Marilee or Cecelia care about me, but I had a momentary thrill at the thought he cared about me the way a man cares about a woman. It was a brief thrill, measured in nanoseconds.

The rest of the meal is much lighter. Phil is a great conversationalist. He gets me talking about doing platform work at hair shows, models I've worked with, a celebrity actress who had me do her hair while they were shooting on location in Chicago. Another who was in town for a brief stay. He tells me about how the new police chief got his job, why the old one left, what happened behind the scenes in the investigation of a night club fire that killed dozens of people and involved all the key elements of a great Chicago drama—politically connected principals, racial tension, and a tragic event. I try several times to get him to talk about his personal life. I want to know if he's taken, and if he's gay or straight. Phil was very artful in keeping his personal life out of the conversation when he covered Boystown, and he still is.

After two hours of comfortable conversation, our meal ends. Phil settles the check, tends to my chair as I rise, and kisses me softly on the cheek. We hug the way friends hug, or maybe just a little tighter.

I can feel my breasts press against his chest and our abdomens meet flush against each other. I will play back this sensation many times in the nights to come.

We say our farewells at the door and go our separate ways, Phil completely oblivious to how eagerly I would have entered into carnal relations with him. I sigh. It's for the better. Men like him have their pick of women and even if he lost his mind and had a tryst with me, it would be over quickly. And I have enough on my plate without a broken heart.

*　*　*

TUESDAY, JULY 9

Like lines you can't forget from a movie you hate, this is all too famil-iar to me. Being vulnerable to a predator whom the law can't touch. At least, not until it's too late for me.

I'm soaking in my beloved oval spa and thinking. From a distant room the rich tones of Mozart vibrate into my steamy escape.

Usually my contemplations in this spa are romantic, sometimes erotically so. I think of people I know or have seen who are physi-cally attractive and imagine what it would be like to be intimate with them. My fantasies include both men and women. I'm glad I'm this way. It's like being an independent voter. I go for the person, not the genital party.

But my thoughts are light-years away from love and sex now. Now, the movie in my mind is playing a dark film set in alleys and bars, in shady places where light beams of social order and humanity can't penetrate.

I'm reliving my time in a jungle where a man murdered a trans-woman, maybe more than one, and got away with it. He liked to beat them up, too. Money and power put him above the law. Even the law of the jungle.

When the beast came after me, the other creatures in the jungle looked away. I was a pitiful prey. Trying to transition. Scared of the world. In my mind I was a woman, but when I saw myself through other people's eyes, I saw a man with tits and a dick. A freak craving acceptance and understanding.

The unfairness of it all came crashing in on me. I had started my transition days after a beautiful young transwoman had been brutally murdered. There wasn't a soul in the police department or the media who gave a damn. It wasn't Wilkins' case, but he wouldn't have cared anyway. We were vermin to him.

On the other hand, when a rich white guy like John Strand got himself murdered, all of a sudden cops like Wilkins were all over it. And Wilkins finally decided the dead transwoman was important—but only because she was a friend of mine and her murder a motive for me to take revenge on Strand. The injustice of it still raises my blood pressure.

I try to think of pleasanter things, but the weight of a crushing debt and the ominous shadow of Detective Wilkins keep drowning the sunbeams and lullabies I try to conjure. Most of all, I keep coming back to Phil's haunting message, that my complaint to the DA has enabled this ogre to stalk me night and day, until he gets what he wants. The irony. Five years ago I was being stalked by a murderer, now a cop is doing the same thing with the same intent. Wilkins doesn't want to kill me, but he wants to lock me up for the rest of my life, so what's the difference? I'm the meat in a big hate sandwich.

This will be a long, lonely night fraught with fleeting moments of sleep tormented by dark dreams, ending in wakeful restlessness. The night will usher in a morning filled with first aid to make my face look fresh and stylish for the salon. It's okay. I've been here before. So many times I couldn't count them all.

* * *

TUESDAY, JULY 9

Wilkins moves quickly from one to the next. He assumes they're all prostitutes. Some of them look like men and cruise for gay customers. Some are in various stages of trans female, looking for anything they can get. They disgust him. He has trouble establishing eye contact because looking at their faces makes him sick.

"Can you help me, here?" he says to each girl. "I'm a cop. I'm looking for anyone who knew this man." He flashes a photo of John Strand.

One after another, they look at him with a startled glance, then shake their heads no.

After a few refusals, he figures it out, and starts adding that he's not vice, he's not here to bust anyone or get anyone in trouble.

An hour later he gets lucky. A tall, thin African-American trans-woman nods her head yes. "He's that dude who got himself killed a while back," she says.

"You knew him?" Wilkins asks.

"I knew of him. I knew a girl he beat half to death."

"Can you put me in touch with her?"

The hooker shrugs. "Buy me dinner and I'll ask her if she wants to talk to you."

Wilkins starts to walk away. She's just trying to hustle him for a meal. Then again, he thinks, there was a shred of sincerity in her voice.

"Okay," he says. He passes her a twenty-dollar bill and his card. "Tell her to call me anytime. I just want to talk."

The girl nods.

"One other thing," he says. "You know this lady?" He shows her a photo of Logan.

The girl nods her head yes. "She has a fancy beauty salon. A friend of mine works there."

"What's she like?"

"Nice, I think."

Wilkins tries a few more questions. She doesn't have answers but maybe she'd pass his card on to someone who knew more. It is something, and it beats sitting in that shithole apartment of his.

* * *

WEDNESDAY, JULY 10

Cecelia rings my bell at nine a.m. dressed in a designer suit that has been tailored to flatter her flamboyant oversized body with the conservative elegance of a woman of means. She is looking chipper and energetic. The best-dressed six-four woman in Chicago, ready for another day of blitzing bigots and overpowering the unwilling.

Wednesday is one of my late-arrival days at the salon, and Cecelia often stops by for coffee. "Good God, Bobbi, you look like death warmed over," she exclaims as I open the door.

"Good morning to you, too." I turn and let her close the door.

"Aha! Did my anal-retentive sister worry her way through the night?" Cecelia says it in a teasing way as she throws her bag on the kitchen table and starts to work on the coffee. I have filled her in on the Detective Wilkins situation, along with all the other frustrations in my life. I sigh and sit in front of my makeup table again to finish applying a hemorrhoid cream to the bags under my eyes. The thought of putting something made for my ass on my face isn't a pleasant one, especially for someone who spent part of their life as a gay man, but it works. And it works better than cucumbers or anything else I've tried.

Cecelia sits next to me as the coffee drips.

"You worry too much, Bobbi," she pronounces. "But I've said that to you so many times you probably think that's part of my name. Cecelia Uworrytoomuch." She giggles at her own humor. I force a smile.

"My worries are a lot like when I was a woman with a penis—it's just not something you can get rid of right away."

Cecelia pats my hand. "Well, at least you don't have that old thing to worry about anymore."

She fetches the coffee in two steaming mugs, then pulls a notepad and pen from her purse and scribbles something on the pad, tearing off the sheet with great fanfare and putting it in front of me.

"What's this?" I ask, squinting at the wild cursive on the paper.

"It's the phone number for Jose Vasquez."

I groan.

"The man is an artist, Bobbi! Like you with hair. And he can get your mind off worldly matters."

We've had this conversation before. Only Cecelia would keep pitching it. Jose is an escort. A male prostitute. I haven't met him, but Cecelia has shown me pictures. She has also regaled me with eyewitness accounts of his sexual prowess that are so glowing and vivid I have sometimes felt myself flush with arousal.

Jose is a dark-haired, copper-skinned leading man with movie-star looks. Like Omar Sharif in *Dr. Zhivago*, but a trifle more dangerous looking. To hear Cecelia tell it, the only thing more remarkable than the thickness and length of his male member is his ability to become aroused, whenever, wherever, and as often as necessary.

Cecelia sees him once a month. He's on her calendar, like her hairdresser and her psychologist. It's like getting stagnant water out of the pipes after you've been gone for a long time, she says. Then she describes her wild orgasms, which, given her size and energy, must make the amorous Jose feel like he's riding a volcano.

I can't bring myself to hire a sex partner. Yet. It's not a moral issue, it's just something I can't settle for, though truthfully, I've fantasized about it a number of times, about being bedded by Jose and having one of Cecelia's wild orgasms.

The thought of Jose Vasquez stays in my mind all day. My endless fretting over a nasty cop and financial stress is shoved aside by a day-long sexual fantasy. I am so horribly repressed it's pitiful.

Late in the afternoon I have a ten-minute break and call Jose's number.

"Hi, I'm Bobbi Logan," I say when he answers. "Cecelia gave me your number."

"Wonderful!" Jose interrupts my canned intro. "She's my most wonderful client and she said she had a friend who might call."

I exhale a little. "So, how does this work?" I ask.

* * *

THURSDAY, JULY 11

The host at Café Matin leads me through tables of late-night diners and drinkers, and Jose Vasquez rises gallantly as we near him.

He smiles a warm welcoming smile. It doesn't matter that he's done this hundreds of times with hundreds of women. He makes you feel like you light up his life, like he's so glad to see you.

He takes the hand I offer and pulls me to him, kissing me softly on the cheek, an appropriate gesture in public made just a touch racy by following with a hug during which he exhales softly in my ear. He plays horny women the way great musicians coax heavenly sounds from violins and saxophones.

We have met here because I wanted to squeeze in a quick dinner after a long workday, but I'm so nervous I've lost my appetite. I'm feeling pathetic. A slut who can't get laid. If I was a real girl I wouldn't be doing this.

He senses my anxiety. It must happen a lot, even with genetic women. He initiates a conversation, recounting Cecelia's stories about what a fabulous hairdresser I am. By the time we get to the celebrities I've done, I'm aware of how prepared he was for this meeting, how easy he is to talk to, and how warm I feel when I look into his gentle brown eyes.

We finish hors d'oeuvres and Jose picks up his wine glass and proposes a toast to me. Then he asks what he can do to make my day perfect. I blush crimson. The perfect wine, his perfect gentlemanliness, the warmth of the place, the first time I've relaxed in ages . . . it all comes together in a flash. I make myself find ladylike words to respond, something to the effect I'd like to make love. But inside my transsexual mind, my thoughts are not nearly so ladylike. I'm thinking I'd like him to fuck my brains out. It will be my little secret, though I'm sure he's heard the expression before, from Cecelia if no one else.

*   *   *

Friday, July 12

"Well?" Cecelia's voice belies the smile she is wearing on the other end of the telephone line. "How was it?"

I don't have words in my vocabulary to describe how it was. All of my anxieties and fears and pent-up sexual fantasies were deliriously and deliciously exorcised from my body and soul over the course of an hour with Jose.

"It was just like you said," I reply.

"Oh no you don't!" Cecelia says. "I want a blow by blow. So to speak. Every golden minute."

I am drained and glowing and half asleep and still aroused. I'm still trying to believe that was me feeling those things, responding so recklessly. And I'm still feeling everything. It makes me smile and relax so deeply I feel like a puddle of warmth.

"Oh, Cecelia," I groan. "When I was a man I had no idea what a man could be. Good Lord, what a ride." Cecelia says she's glad I finally found God, chastises me for waiting so long. I tell her she was right about Jose and that I love her and I'll see her tomorrow. For once, she lets me go on the first try.

4

MARILEE'S EYES WIDEN as I tell her about my brush with Detective Wilkins.

Marilee is a psychologist, a wife, and a mother to three children—two she brought into the world, and me, whom she adopted years ago. Not formally, but she might as well have. We met when she was having marital problems and midlife crisis issues. I was in even worse shape, though I didn't actually realize it right then. I was trying to figure out what kind of queer I was—kind of tragic but also exciting—and I was trying to get over a divorce from a woman I still loved and who still loved me.

We have been each other's confessor ever since. Marilee is a practicing Catholic but only because she believes in God. She regards the clergy as meddlesome middlemen to whom the only thing she would ever confess is her contempt. I'm an atheist and a lifelong holder of secrets, so we end up in the same place. She knows everything about me. Every anxiety, every fear, every burst of egotism, every period of self-loathing and shame, every embarrassing thought I had as I evolved from an All-American boy with a ticket to the top of the business world to a conspicuous transsexual hairdresser.

I've shared things with some other, trusted people, but just some things. Cecelia knows plenty, even more than I tell her because she knows me so well, but she doesn't know the dark stuff, the stuff I wish weren't true, some of which keeps me up nights. And my transition shrink, the therapist who had to verify that I was ready for the permanent step of gender reassignment surgery, knew everything about my gender issues, including the fact that I was never really sure I was a girl, I was only sure I wasn't a boy. But no one knows everything except for Marilee. For some reason, I can tell her anything. Maybe because I know she'll love me anyway, and she never passes judgment, even when I do something stupid.

Like make a raging bully madder.

"Why is he so sure you killed John Strand?" she asks.

"Because he knows a lot of people in the community thought Strand killed Mandy, and because I'm big and ugly and he thinks I hate men."

"Stop with the big and ugly stuff, Bobbi. You don't think like that anymore."

"I don't, but he does." I shrug. I've been on hormones for seven years and my features have become more feminine. I've also made an electrologist rich and put a plastic surgeon's child through a semester or two of college with some feminization surgery. I still don't pass as a woman, but I'm kind of pretty and I have large boobs, so some of the stares I draw are lustful. But some are hateful, like Detective Wilkins."

"Okay," says Marilee. "I'll accept that. As for the man-hating thing, maybe you should tell him the same story you just told me." She smirks. I'd told her about my orgy with the male prostitute.

"But the big thing is, he saw me take down that junkie in the salon with an eye gouge. He says Strand had an eye-gouge injury, too." I say this with some anxiety. It's not like this is any kind of evidence against me. But he's the only cop who has ever linked me to that murder. There's no rational reason for it. It's just me being trans and refusing to cower before him. Hate like his is a powerful motivator, and I don't see him stopping until he has ruined my life.

I share this with Marilee and she nods in agreement. "Bobbi, it would be a good idea to retain a lawyer right about now," she says. "I can ask Bill which trial lawyer he hates the most. That would be a good recommendation."

Marilee's husband, Bill, is a cop. A decent guy who has even gotten used to me over the years. He used to be embarrassed when we met, sort of a macho guy not knowing how to be around a transsexual. Now we exchange polite hugs and hellos and life is fine. But I don't want the kind of defense lawyer he would hate.

"I think I'll go through Cecelia first," I say. "I don't need someone to get me off, I need someone to protect my reputation. Wilkins can destroy me just by starting a buzz."

I talk about my vulnerabilities, the huge debt on the salon, a big mortgage on my building, and business getting slower and slower since the big financial collapse. A little bad publicity, a nasty rumor or two getting passed around the city's elite—I could be broke and on the street in six months, leaving Roger and a lot of wonderful hairdressers in dire straits.

My angst must show. Marilee reaches across the table and squeezes my hand. Her touch is soothing. "You're going to be fine, Bobbi," she says. Her voice is soothing, like the soft, warm drops of a perfect shower. "You've been through this before."

So true. When I began my transition at work, the bottom fell out of my world.

"Do you ever think about who killed John Strand anymore?" asks Marilee.

Only two people know what I know about the Strand murder—Marilee and my transition counselor, a wonderful therapist who thought she'd heard everything until I finally came clean with her.

"I try not to," I confess. "I worry I might betray whoever it was if I knew. I also worry that it wasn't someone else. That I did it myself and the horror of it just sort of shocked it out of my memory banks."

"We've been through all that. It's highly unlikely."

As she says it, I flash back to the intensive sessions, the hypnosis, the endless hours on my own reliving each moment in Strand's apartment. I could even envision doing it, sliding the knife through his throat, seeing the blood. But I've never been able to recall actually doing it.

Marilee reads my silence as doubt. "You didn't do it," she says. "I'm a better suspect than you are."

I glance at Marilee with a startle. I never thought about her or Betsy or any other genetic woman. I consider for a moment if it could have been her husband. Killing Strand would have been child's play for a big strong cop. I drop the thought with disgust. He wouldn't do something like that for anyone but Marilee. For the millionth time the faces of my closest friends flash through my mind, and I can't conceive of any of them executing someone. I'm the only one I know who could do that and even though I remember not doing it, it seems like I must have. God, what a mind-fuck.

"Well, how was it seeing Phil again?" Marilee asks. "I haven't heard you mention his name in a long time."

I confess that he still makes me weak in the knees and that the eroticism I felt having dinner with him is probably what drove me to hire a male prostitute.

Marilee laughs lightly. "I love you, Bobbi. I love your passion and your candor and your wit and your sweetness. I wish we were all a little more like you. This world would be a lot more fun and a much better place to live in."

We exchange smiles.

"I'll tell you something else, Bobbi," she says. "I think your Officer Phil has a thing for you."

Her eyes are twinkling. I wonder if she knows something she's not saying. Her husband and Phil are cop friends. In fact, I first met

Phil at one of their parties. My heart cartwheels around in my chest. Wouldn't that be something?

* * *

SUNDAY, JULY 20

Cecelia stares at me like a raptor eyeing a rodent. I have asked her for an attorney referral, criminal court type.

"Is this about Wilkins?"

I nod my head yes. Her encounters with him go back as far as mine, though somehow he chose to hate me a lot more than he hates her. He tried to bully her during the Strand investigation, too, but she dismissed him like yesterday's garbage and got away with it because she's rich and connected and she's had a lifetime of practice putting pompous fools in their rightful places. All she got from him was a face full of bad breath and disapproval. He saved the rest for me.

"He still thinks you killed Strand?" She shakes her head in wonder, though I have no idea why. Wilkins suspected me from the get-go, and for that matter, Cecelia herself has generously shared her suspicions about me being the murderer several times. She sits back in her chair and thinks for a moment.

"Let's face it," she says finally, "You make a good suspect." I start to react. She holds up a hand, gesturing to let her finish. "Well, you knew Mandy. You were friends. You're a big, strong girl. You're very pretty and you have nice tits, but you are also big and strong, especially back then. And you did those kung fu classes all the time. It could have been you."

I sit mutely. What do you say when your best friend says she thinks you murdered someone?

"Don't get mad at me, Bobbi. I'm just saying. You know? It's not so surprising a cop would think like that."

"What about you?" I say. "You knew Mandy. You were the one who kept accusing Strand of killing her. You're big and strong. You're pretty and you have huge tits, but you're big and strong, too. You don't take self-defense classes, but that's because you don't need to. See what I mean?"

"Are you asking me if I killed John Strand?" she asks.

"No, are you asking me?" I respond.

"Heavens no!" Cecelia's hands fly to her mouth in horror. "I don't want to know that you didn't do it because I love the fantasy that you did. And I don't want to know that you did do it because the police might question me about it someday."

"You'd rat me out?"

"Of course not. But I'd rather not rat you out by telling the truth than by lying. Though I'm willing to do either."

She's trying to break the tension. I smile at her humor, but I keep staring at her face, looking for some kind of telltale. Cecelia is more than just a bold, outspoken woman. She was a very successful corporate politician for many years, so she knows how to run a bluff, keep her thoughts and opinions hidden, distract those getting too close to the truth. Talking about me as the murderer could be a ploy to keep us from talking about her as the murderer.

I stare too long in silence. Cecelia stares back, a questioning look on her face. "What?" she asks.

"Nothing," I say, dropping my eyes. "Sorry. I got lost in thought. Can you help me get an attorney?"

Cecelia nods, her face in a prune-like grimace as if to chastise me for even asking.

The waiter arrives with our salads. We exchange one more toast to each other's health, then begin our meal. We're in a tony café in the Lincoln Square neighborhood of Chicago, well north and west of the more famous Lincoln Park area. Lincoln Square still has remnants of its old ethnic roots, just like Boystown, where I was reborn. The buildings are low and many are old. The residences are two flats and brownstones, most rehabbed to immaculate condition. The stores and restaurants on the square are diverse, independent, lively.

Not many trans people live in this neighborhood, but one of the city's great independent bookstores, The Book Cellar, is located here and it draws people from all over the north side to the area, including LGBT readers. So we are not an oddity, two large transgender women having lunch in a nice café. We are noted, then ignored by our fellow diners. Just like everyone else.

Cecelia gives me the name of an attorney and promises to email contact information to me later, along with another name or two. Then she changes the subject to TransRising.

Cecelia and some other LGBT leaders launched Chicago TransRising three years ago to tend to the needs of the scores of dispossessed young transgender people living on the streets. They had been scourged from their families and their neighborhoods for being trans, and a lot of them turn to prostitution or drug dealing or petty crime to stay alive. They gravitated to the north side location of Chicago's LGBT Center because it's a safe neighborhood and they could come in from the cold there, during the day at least. But the Center couldn't handle all their problems. Chicago TransRising was organized to do more. The organization put together corporate donations and public and private grants to purchase a building that houses sixteen residents upstairs and classrooms and meeting places downstairs. Cecelia and her friends are working on funding for more space for residents, while TransRising administrators are working on preparing residents and walk-ins for winning jobs and leading successful lives.

"We have a go on Trans U," she says. It's TransRising's pet project, a set curriculum of practical lessons and support kids usually get in a family environment, everything from everyday survival skills like how to apply for a job, to traditional education initiatives, like getting enrolled in school and help with homework.

Cecelia got me to pledge money to the enterprise months ago, before I became a capitalist debt queen. I really don't need to be writing a check for $500 right now.

"I know you're worried about money," she continues. "So if you want to hold off on the contribution, you won't hear an objection from me."

"No," I say. "A deal is a deal. Besides, five hundred dollars won't move my debt needle a tenth of a percent." I don't know if that's true, but it feels true.

Cecelia raises a regal eyebrow and hands me a document. "The educating part is just as important as the money. Will you do a seminar on hair and makeup, Bobbi? These kids know how to look like hookers and Goths and all the teen stuff, but we need to prepare them for applying for jobs and fitting in at school."

I nod in mute acquiescence. Even if I could say no to the kids, I couldn't to Cecelia.

"One last thing," she says. I brace myself. Cecelia's last thing is always like getting hit by a train.

"TransRising has a committee working on plans for a fund-raiser. I'd like you to be on it."

I groan and make a face. Committees were bad enough in the business world, but they're even worse in volunteer organizations because so many people in the room are there for ego gratification.

"Why me, Cecelia?" I whine. "I donate money, I donate time, I do people's hair, I contribute to every cause under the sun. Isn't that enough?"

"Because you actually know something about marketing and strategic thinking, Bobbi. We have a committee full of young people who have entry-level jobs and think they know everything."

"I would rather bob for apples in a toilet than spend an hour with those snots."

Her face shrivels into a grimace. "They're just young. They need to be around some experienced people."

"Do you see the way they look at us?" I counter. "They start hormones in their teens. They never look like men. They look at us and see what straight people see—men with tits. I don't need any more angst in my life."

Cecelia is unmoved. "You're such a wimp! Stop whining. We need you on that committee. The only leadership right now is that girl Lisa."

I groan.

"Yeah," says Cecelia. "The prom queen. She's an assistant something at a downtown ad agency and thinks she's the second coming of Leo Burnett."

"I'd end up killing someone."

Cecelia smiles her smug, know-it-all smile. "You know you're going to do it, Bobbi. And you know it always turns out for the best when I make you do something you don't want to.

"I know," I reply. "But it's the only chance I get to whine."

5

NEWS MEDIA PEOPLE are calling it The Great Recession. I'm a believer. After the big financial crisis, business got soft but it wasn't like we were falling off a cliff. When I bought the salon, economists were still expecting a recovery in the near future.

Now, it's like we're falling off a cliff. Few economists talk about a recovery anytime soon, and people on the street are bracing for things to get even worse and stay that way for a long time. Beauty salons are supposed to be recession-proof businesses, but if that was ever true, it isn't anymore. The enormity of this economic disaster is touching everyone and everything. Millions of people are losing their jobs. Millions of houses are being repossessed. People who just a year or two ago were living the American dream are suddenly destitute. Buses and commuter trains are half empty, traffic is moving freely on the expressways, even in rush hour. You see working-age men and women at the grocery store in the daytime.

We're feeling it, too. Our bookings have plummeted. I'm explaining this to the entire staff. It's eight o'clock on Tuesday night, the end of a horrid day. They are much quieter than a roomful of hairdressers and assistants ever should be. There are many worried faces staring at me, from senior stylists who have families to feed, to our newest hire, who expects to be fired. She looks like someone just shot her dog.

I feel the same way. I made my payments on the salon in July by not paying myself. I paid my home mortgage and living expenses with savings. But my savings are very limited. I put almost everything I have into the purchases of my brownstone and this business.

"We're in trouble," I tell the staff. "I know you're worried about your own incomes, but the salon is having serious financial issues, too."

Like many salons, L'Elégance stylists get a commission on their work, not a flat salary. When times are good and popular stylists want to work hard, they can make very good money. When things slow down, incomes drop. Now, we're getting hammered.

I explain that our problems stem from two sources. Simple attrition is taking place because some of our customers are in households where one of the wage earners is out of work. They either quit going to the salon altogether or go to a cheaper one. Just as painful for us, many of our regular customers are still coming in, but at longer intervals. Our hairdressers are not dumb. Some of them are brilliant. And they are all very artistic. But simple marketing concepts like this are not part of their experience. What everyone knows is that corporations are responding to the downturn with massive layoffs, which is why many of our people are worried sick about getting fired.

"We have difficult choices to face," I continue. "We can downsize the business and try to move into a smaller space with fewer stylists and assistants and operate at a lower level of volume . . ." The frowns deepen in the room, especially on younger faces. The juniors and entry people who are the most likely to be let go.

"Or we can work as a team and work like dogs to bring in more new people." Faces brighten, even among senior stylists.

"How many of you would be willing to spend part of your days off and maybe one night a week promoting the salon?"

Curiosity fills the faces in front of me. Hands raise tentatively, held low.

"What would we be doing?" someone finally asks.

"Handing out promos in front of office buildings, at the El station, in front of apartment buildings. Doing styling demonstrations on the sidewalk while the weather's nice and hopefully in some office building lobbies when it gets cold . . . I'm working on that."

There is great interest in the styling demos. I explain that we'd get hair models from a Craigslist ad for a modest cost. The demo would require a team—a stylist, an assistant, and someone to distribute promos and chat up anyone who stopped. We'd do them right in front of the salon at first, then maybe in other places. Our promotion pieces would offer discounts to first-time customers and the discounts would come out of the pockets of both the stylist and the salon.

I tell them I'd like to try in-store demos on new cuts and colors every month or two. We'd set up some seating and some standing areas, have light hors d'oeuvres, wine, and coffee. One of the stylists would do a cut while another would do a color demo and a third person would do the talking and take questions.

A buzz grows in the room as people begin considering these ideas. I announce a break as pizzas are delivered. The buzz grows as people get food and beverage and scatter around the shop. They are a good bunch of people. Even the couple of stylists who might be prima donnas in a different salon are relatively contemplative here because of the culture. I know the staff will go along with the plan. They love it here as much as I do and we still have a chance to make good incomes if we're willing to go the extra mile.

When we reconvene, Barbara raises her hand. She is a beautiful fiftyish woman who was born in Australia and ended up marrying a Yank who brought her to Chicago. They have two teenage kids and she likes to be at home as much as possible. Promo time would be difficult for her.

"I think those are great ideas, Bobbi. Let's get going!" she says.

She is one of the most respected stylists in the salon, a brilliant cutter who combines the precision of a watchmaker with the art of a Rembrandt. Her embrace of the idea wipes out any lingering doubts among the staff. There is a murmur of assent across the room. I call for a show of hands. It is unanimous. People are laughing and smiling at each other. Nervous anticipation. Something completely new, but something that might be fun.

We tidy up the salon and as people leave I go into my office to shut down my computer. Our new hire, an assistant named Jalela, follows me in. Jalela is a transwoman, eighteen, African-American. Someone at TransRising suggested she apply for work here, figuring since I'm trans I'd be sympathetic. I wasn't. She came in looking like a street-walker, all mumbles and attitude. I didn't see any way she could fit in here. We're multiracial, but we're also snooty and we have a snooty clientele. Plus hiring someone just because we're both transsexuals is a good way to get an employee who doesn't think she has to work hard.

In the end, though, she seemed like a good kid who needed a break, so I took a chance.

"Will you have to fire me?" Jalela expects the worst, but she's able to look me in the eye without being confrontational. She has only been here a few weeks, but her evolution has been rapid and her motivation is off the charts. She loves working in a salon the way I did when I first got started. It would be a tragedy to lay her off.

"No layoffs of anyone, if I can help it, Jalela."

She ponders this for a moment. "How am I doing?"

I smile inwardly. Jalela is learning to be assertive in a positive way.

"You are doing great, kid." She is. She's quiet and conscientious and she never stops working, from the time she comes in to the time she goes home. I don't know how she manages to spend the day in high heels and bend that long, elegant frame of hers to do shampoos and scalp massages all day, but she does. I share these observations with her and she beams. She's heard them before, but the feedback is important. Her happiness makes me glow inside. Even though I'm sliding toward a financial cliff I may not be able to avoid.

That thought accompanies me as I make my way home. Robert Logan, business executive, workout king, and all-around hotshot—the former me, the male one—would be absolutely fixated and anguished over the business situation. He would have been able to think about nothing else. Bobbi Logan feels the pressure but still cares about the human things. In fact, most of the pressure I feel is in letting down Roger and the staff.

* * *

THURSDAY, AUGUST 7

In the middle of a blow-dry Samantha comes to get me. Very unusual that she would interrupt a service. She stands watch over the sanctity of our beauty emporium like a Knight Templar guarding Jesus' remains.

"Bobbi, you have a call. It's important. I'll get one of the girls to finish the service."

Sam's face is serious and puckered with concern. Not like her. Her tone is insistent. The call must be very important. I ask Jalela to finish the service for me. In my office, I pick up the phone and say hello. All I can hear is sobbing, I can't tell whose.

"Hello? Are you okay? Who is calling?" I try not to be impatient. Whoever this is has enough problems already.

More sobbing. I'm thinking this can't be a client complaint. Our mistakes produce anger but never bereavement.

"Can I help?" I say it softly, like an offer of a hug.

"Bobbi!" My name is spoken in a long, thin voice so filled with anguish it makes my eyes tear up. The voice belongs to Betsy. Oh God, I think, not Robbie!

"Betsy?" My voice cracks.

More sobbing and weeping, then the reedy, shattered voice again.

"Bobbi, he's dead."

It's not Robbie. I'm so selfish I rejoice for a moment. "Who's dead, Betsy?"

"Oh, Bobbi, it's Don. He's been killed . . ." Her syllables become muted by grief. I glean he was killed in a car accident.

My tears erupt spontaneously as I comprehend what she's saying. I get out most of a condolence before my voice breaks with a sob. I can't understand how something so horrible could happen to three people who are so good.

I get my emotions under control. I'm of no use to Betsy if I'm as brokenhearted as she is. "What can I do to help?"

"Bobbi, what am I going to do? This . . . this shouldn't happen. These things don't happen to people like us." Meaning, she's not prepared to lose her husband in the blink of an eye. Who is?

"He was such a good man, Bobbi. He deserved so much better." Her high, tinny voice gives way to sobs. I agree with her. There are a million or so outright bastards who should die before anyone like Don. Life isn't fair, and death is even worse.

I struggle to get information from her. She is having a hard time being coherent. Grief is numbing her brain and her senses. It comes out in bits. She got the call fifteen minutes ago. He had been taken to an Emergency Room in Evanston and was pronounced dead on arrival. Betsy has to do an identification, make funeral arrangements, break the news to her daughter, start her life as a widow with a small child. She can't will herself to move, to go to the hospital, to descend into the pit of heartbreak where the next day of her life begins.

I talk her through it. She will take a cab to the hospital. I'll meet her there. I'll be at her side for the formalities. I'll come home with her and help tend to Robbie, then help her call her attorney, Don's family, the funeral home. Whatever she needs.

* * *

Betsy's house is a sprawling, light-filled ranch on an oversized lot in tony Northbrook. It looks like a palace, with white stone floors and decorator walls and beautiful area rugs and modern art in blazing colors hanging on the walls. A million-dollar home before the recession. They picked it up for less after the real estate bubble burst, but they bought too soon. Betsy once laughed that they could have saved another quarter-mill if they had waited six months. That is proving to be more of an epitaph than a quip.

It is eerily silent now, with Robbie put to bed. Betsy sits across the table from me, red eyed, mourning the husband she lost just hours ago. Even with bloodshot eyes and dressed in black, she is one of the most beautiful women on earth.

We go over the funeral arrangements again. I offer to meet her parents at the airport and squire them to the visitation. It might get their minds off the tragedy that has befallen their daughter, seeing her first husband as a buxom transwoman. They were aghast when Betsy told them about my evolution. They would have been less bothered if I had taken up violent crime.

Betsy declines my offer. I ask if she would prefer that I not come to the visitation. She answers that she wants me there. I ask if I should make my stay a brief one. She says no. With Don gone, the only person between her and unbearable isolation is me. Her parents are decent people and they love her, but their relationship is based on judgment and advice, not nurturing and comfort. She has friends, but not the kind of friends you sob your heart out to.

I am her sole surviving soul mate. Since we reconnected during my transition, we have bonded like sisters, intimate, but not sexual, like our spirits have merged in an unending hug.

Which is why, even with my business sinking deeper every day, I will take time off to help Betsy get things done, and be there when she needs a shoulder to cry on.

She will need me in the weeks and months to come. I don't know how much insurance Don had, but it won't be enough for Betsy to carry on without some changes. She'll be going back to work full-time—that offer has been there since she went on leave to have Robbie. But her salary won't begin to cover the lifestyle she and Don had.

I get up to make hot chocolate. Betsy tidies some of Robbie's toys in the corner of the living room. It is like the FAO Schwartz of toddler playrooms. Robbie's corner is swathed in a deep plush carpet that's as soft as a cloud. The rest of the room is white marble with subtle throw rugs and modern furniture that manages to be beautiful and comfortable at the same time. An elegant fireplace graces one wall, chic chairs and a couch just in front, separated by a handmade teak coffee table.

They invited me here for Thanksgiving the year Robbie was born, along with Don's parents and some family friends. There was a warm fire in the fireplace, taking the edge off a frosty day. We had a lovely, quiet dinner and sat in front of the fire afterward, sipping wine, talking about babies and favorite Thanksgiving memories, the economy, sports, whatever came to mind. I got to hold Robbie for much of the time, making an ass of myself with baby talk and funny faces and tender kisses to her tiny forehead.

We were somewhere between mellow and tipsy when Betsy took the child to bed. Don and I were quiet for a while, then, out of nowhere, he said it.

"I know she named Robbie after you," he blurted out. Robbie's formal name is Roberta, which is the name I took when I stopped being Robert Logan. "I won't lie about it, I had a hard time with that . . . because, you know . . . it felt like she was cheating on me."

I told him she would never cheat on him, and would never do anything to hurt his feelings. I wouldn't either, but that wasn't important to him at the time. He said he understood, that he'd gotten over it. He never held it against me. He didn't let it stop him from giving me the full benefit of his business expertise, and he always welcomed me into his home.

For my quid pro quo, I will make sure his wife and child are safe and secure for as many years as I'm around. No matter what it takes.

* * *

SATURDAY, AUGUST 9

Our first outdoor demo is attracting a crowd. Our Craigslist hair model is tall and thin and sexy even though she isn't beautiful. She has chestnut-colored hair in great profusion and she sits erect on the stool we set up just outside the salon's front door. Maggie, a gorgeous young stylist, is doing the demo. She is wearing a short dress that flashes some cleavage and spike heels that show off her shapely legs. She is being assisted by Jalela who brings her own sultry flair to the tableau, tall and feminine, with graceful movements.

Maggie is trimming and shaping the model's length, then adding layers to create more shape and movement. She finishes by attacking the hair with texturizing cuts that produce short hairs among the longer locks, adding still more fullness. Maggie performs the technique theatrically, hair flying, shears flashing like the baton in a maestro's hand at the climax the *1812 Overture*. Passersby stop on the sidewalk to watch. More take in the show from a sidewalk café across the street. When Maggie finishes cutting, she does the blow dry with dramatic flair, the brush flying and rolling, the dryer swooping and diving, her body posing and flexing as she works the head.

By the time she's done, everyone who has seen any part of the demo knows this is a fabulous salon that combines beauty and pleasure with sheer artistry.

Samantha is working the crowd, handing out literature touting special discounts for first-time customers. She is a natural. She strikes up conversations easily, sings the praises of our salon with the sincerity of a preacher, establishes personal contact with each person, and doesn't get bogged down in serious flirtation. The last point is important. We are showing some flesh here, but we're marketing glamor, not a house of prostitution.

In the next few weeks we'll find out if the sidewalk demo got us any new customers. Whether it does or doesn't, we'll keep doing them here and maybe in other locations if we can. I'd like to do them in the subway station during rush hour, but the CTA is nervous about someone getting pushed on the third rail or maybe impaled on the stylist's shears, so for now we're just passing out the promo sheets.

* * *

SATURDAY, AUGUST 9

From the salon I dash to the visitation, which is like waking up in a foreign country. I'm surrounded by more straight white people than I've seen in one place in months.

Betsy sees me enter the room and breaks off her conversation with two well-wishers to come greet me. Her eyes are no longer red, but her lovely face is clouded in a weary melancholy. Her almond-shaped eyes that smolder with personality and sex appeal in normal times are beacons of grief.

She smiles as she approaches, but when we throw our arms around each other, she sobs. My hopes of an inauspicious North Shore outing are dashed, but it doesn't matter. What's important is my broken-hearted loved one.

Betsy thanks me for coming in a voice still trembling and raw. She recovers her poise. We face each other and smile.

"I should get the parent thing over with," I say. Her parents have been staring at us since she came to me. Her father's face is painted in disgust, lips downturned at the corners, jaws rigid, eyes blazing. His only child is showing love and affection for a transgender freak.

Betsy's mother tries to avoid eye contact when I glance in their direction. She didn't like me when I was a man. I'm sure the vision of me as a transwoman is just as disgusting for her as it is her husband. I walk toward them anyway, humming *Onward Christian Soldiers* in my mind. I get to the words *marching as to war* when we reach them. Timing is everything in life.

"Hello, Bob," her dad says, sticking out a hand for a handshake. It's pro forma, not a gesture of friendship. "My, you've changed." He says it sarcastically, like I'm a joke.

"Hi, Al," I reply, extending my own hand as daintily as I can. "It's Bobbi now." He shakes hands as if I am a man, tight grip, up-and-down movement. When I say my name his face wrinkles like he's sucking on a lemon.

The name and the male handshake are deliberate, of course. A way to put down someone you don't understand. Five years ago, such acts of bigotry were devastating to me, but time has eroded their effectiveness. Plus, Betsy's parents are not the kind of people whose approval I value. They hail from a small city in central Wisconsin and believe in whiteness and Christianity and think the only thing wrong with the Ku Klux Klan is that they desecrate crosses.

Betsy's mom averts her eyes when I turn to greet her. She extends a hand, her eyes locked on the floor, and murmurs a hello, no name. We exchange a feminine handshake, fingertips, no pressure, gentle squeeze from me, limp noodle from her. She will run to the lady's room soon and wash her hands, I'm sure of it. I'm not repulsed by her, but I still don't know how someone as warm and compassionate as Betsy came from the union of these two shallow stiffs.

The situation gets worse. Robbie returns from a snack break with two other kids. Betsy's mom squats low, arms outstretched to welcome the toddler and shower her with grandmotherly love and affection.

It's a socially acceptable way to avoid any further contact with me and to exert her superiority as a genetic woman.

Robbie begins an enthusiastic toddler run toward us, arms upstretched, face smiling. Five feet away it's clear she is ignoring her grandmother and making a beeline to me. "Aunt Bobbi!" she squeals.

As her grandmother teeters in a painful squat, the child wraps her arms around my leg and hugs me. Ordinarily, I would have caught her as she ran to me and lifted her in my arms for a big hug and kiss, but I didn't want to upstage her grandparents. She only sees her grandparents every couple of months, and I'm sure the time together is formal and cold. These people have the human warmth of a plastic Jesus.

Robbie and I hug. Betsy's mom struggles to her feet and walks off. Betsy's dad follows. Betsy and I make eye contact. I mouth the words, "I'm sorry." She shakes her head as if to say, forget it.

When Robbie and I finish our love ritual, I encourage her to give her grandparents a hug. I can't stand the assholes, but they are Robbie's family.

Robbie looks at them hesitantly. They're standing ten feet away from us, side by side in silence, two sourpusses having a bad day.

"You could make them very happy if you give them a hug and a kiss," I say.

Robbie looks at me, looks at them, looks at me. She smiles, eyes dancing. The fact that I'm watching seems to help. She toddles to them and lights up their lives with innocent affection.

I pay my condolences to Don's parents, who I know from dinners at Betsy and Don's place. I also meet several of Don's friends. They react like a lot of people do when they meet me. They are pleasant but uncertain what to say. I tell them that I was a friend of Don's and Betsy's and that Don was a consultant on my business venture. "We all lost something when that fine man was taken," I tell them.

They smile sadly. We establish eye contact. I offer a dainty handshake to each person in the group. Don's father and friends return it.

His mother and I exchange hugs. "He admired you, Bobbi," she says. "I don't know if you knew that, but he did. And he and Betsy used to worry about you when you were transitioning."

This is news to me. I knew Betsy was concerned, but I always figured Don's involvement was just supporting his wife's feelings.

I hang around for another hour, making sure Betsy is okay. I kneel in front of the open casket without looking at Don. This open casket stuff creeps me out. But this is for Betsy. She knows it's an act of love, as is the silent prayer I issue. An atheist's prayer wishing for Betsy and Robbie to have rich and full lives, and an atheist's promise to Don that I will do all in my power to make that happen and to make sure Robbie grows up knowing that her dad was a good man who loved her. I linger another few seconds as I wonder if Don's concern for me might have motivated him to follow me the night Strand was killed. I dismiss the thought as fast as it comes to mind. Don wouldn't have known anything about me and Strand. And besides, he was not a person who could kill someone, not unless they were a threat to his family.

I engage in a few conversations. It turns out that North Shore people are a lot like people everywhere else, just richer. Some let the trans thing throw them, but a lot don't.

A half hour before closing time, I make my farewells. This is a night Betsy will spend with her parents. Tomorrow, I will attend the funeral but stay in the background and leave when it is over. It will be easier for Betsy that way, and a lot easier for her parents.

* * *

SUNDAY, AUGUST 17

It's Sunday and Cecelia has pulled her Cadillac out of mothballs to drive out to Northbrook where we are babysitting for Robbie while Betsy has a session with a therapist.

We stroll to the playground, Robbie pushing the stroller that will carry her home when she wears herself out. We're an odd sight, a toddler with two oversized women. If anyone else used the sidewalk, we'd draw a lot of attention. But this is also a town where no one walks anywhere. What would be the point of having a Mercedes?

"I hope this means something to you, Bobbi," Cecelia mutters as we turn into the playground area. Two women watching over kids playing on the fixtures stare at us like herd dogs guarding lambs. "I am remembering why I live in the city. Good God, don't these people get out? Look at them stare!"

She pointedly waves and stares back at them until they avert their gazes.

"I'm glad you're here," I say. "I love it when you do that. Plus, when you're with me I get to be petite."

Cecelia mutters something but smiles. It's an old joke between us. I do love Cecelia's company. She reminds me to be proud of who I am and to regard those who disapprove as the limited human beings they are. Having her here frees my spirit to play with Robbie and not worry about the judgments of the other women. I help her climb monkey bars and slide down the baby slide. She loves the merry-go-round and the seesaw. Soon we are frolicking about in a game of tag. Cecelia is into it, too. It is good to see her laughing and prancing like a kid.

The North Shore matrons leave. Their body language says they were offended by our presence. My favorite t-shirt slogan flashes into mind: *Eat shit and die, yuppie scum.*

When Betsy gets back, she finds my note and joins us at the playground. She is trying to be merry and join in on the fun, but sadness radiates from her entire being. I ask her about it on the way home. It's nothing, she says. Just the usual. Which means she is mourning Don and she's fine, stop asking questions.

Back at her house, as Cecelia and I get ready to leave, Betsy asks if she and I can have a private word. Cecelia graciously sweeps Robbie away to her toys while Betsy and I retreat into the kitchen. We sit at the breakfast table and Betsy blurts it out with no fanfare or stumbling.

"Bobbi, I'm bankrupt."

"What?" I say. "How could that be?" Don was a numbers guy, a fiscal conservative. He would have had ironclad security for Betsy and Robbie.

"We put everything we had into this house," Betsy says. Her voice is quiet and thin, but she is dry-eyed. I think she is too overwhelmed with grief to express her profound heartbreak anymore. "All our savings, every cent we made from our other house. We could just barely make the mortgage payments along with everything else, but we thought we'd flip it when the market came back and use the profit to invest in something easier for us to afford. We figured the real estate market would come back in a year and if it took a little longer, I could always go back to work to help out. Get us over the hump."

"What about Don's life insurance?" Even $100,000 could give her a chance to ride out the storm.

"We dropped our life insurance policies so we could make the mortgage payments."

We stare at each other in silence for a time.

"Can you sell the house?"

Her lips tighten. "Maybe for about two or three hundred thousand less than we owe on it."

"Surely it has more value than that, even in this market."

"Not if you have to sell fast."

We lapse into silence again. I can't put together coherent thoughts.

"My parents want me to move in with them. They have good schools there for Robbie . . ." Her voice trails off.

I'm struggling to keep my selfish interests out of this, but it's hard. Her parents live six hours away. I could only get there by car and I don't own a car. And I would be as welcome in their home as a burglar. But even worse, I see them dominating their heartbroken daughter and trying to infuse Robbie with the social conscience of a Hitler Youth.

"What would you do there?" I ask. I put the emphasis on *you*. She would be much too far from Milwaukee or Madison to find a marketing job.

"What choice do I have, Bobbi? I'm going to lose my house, my car . . . everything. All we own are our clothes and the furnishings, and I don't have any place to put those things. I can't even afford a storage payment."

"But you can get your old job back, right? They practically begged you to come back after Robbie was born."

"They'll take me, but at a much lower salary. The profession has changed a lot. It's all websites and click-throughs, which I know nothing about. I don't have much value. By the time I paid for day care and rent, I don't think I could make a car payment and buy food."

"Then move in with me. Take your time figuring everything out." It just pops out, but it makes sense.

"I can't move in with you, Bobbi." She says it like it's a ridiculous idea.

"Why can't you?" I'm a little hurt, to be honest. Because of the way she said it.

"Because . . . you know." She doesn't want to say it.

"Because I'm a transsexual woman?"

"Because you're my ex-husband and a transsexual woman. People would talk. My parents would go ballistic."

"This isn't about people who talk or your parents, Betsy. It's about what's best for you and Robbie. Staying in Chicago is best for both of you. And who can you trust more than me? We're there for each other, aren't we?"

She reaches across the table and squeezes my hand. Her face is so sad and bewildered I want to throw my arms around her and save her from the world.

"Thank you, Bobbi," she says. "I have a lot of decisions to make.

I can't make them right now, but I appreciate your offer." There is a note of coldness in her voice. I have overstepped my bounds. She needs space.

I manage to shut up and nod, stifling what would have been a long rambling dissertation on what a corrosive influence her parents would be on Robbie, and how Betsy would suffocate in a small city, far from any metropolitan area, and how much I can add to her life and Robbie's. If she doesn't think those things herself, me saying them won't change anything. Plus, she doesn't need any more pressure. She's one or two proverbial straws away from a crushed spirit right now.

As we get up to rejoin Cecelia and Robbie, I say, "Promise you'll let me know how you're doing and what you decide."

She smiles grimly. "Okay, but promise me back you won't pressure me."

I tell her okay and we hug.

The drive back to the city is a long one for Cecelia and me. The Cubs have a night game and traffic is stacked up on the Edens as if the road is closed somewhere. We listen to classical music on the Caddy's great sound system.

"Do you think Betsy is okay?" Cecelia asks.

"No." I feel my eyes moistening. "She's mourning. And she says she's bankrupt." I tell Cecelia about our conversation.

She shakes her head from side to side and tears up. "That poor woman," she says. "That poor child."

We lock eyes. I see something in Cecelia I've never seen before. She has always projected an aura of defiance and independence that bordered on arrogance. Her face has a certain elegance despite her outsized proportions, large eyes, bright blue in color, feminine lips, surgically enhanced brows. She is pretty the way women who aren't supposed to be pretty can sometimes be. But her face has a hardness to it, and even as a woman, she has never been reluctant to dominate the meek. That's why we tangled so much before I began my transition.

Which is why the look on her face is so alarming. Her eyes almost ache with sadness. There is a softness about her. Her voice becomes delicate as she speaks of Betsy's financial problems.

"I just can't believe Don would leave them so vulnerable," I lament. "He was a careful man. He was careful with money. How could he not have a serious life insurance policy? I don't understand."

Cecelia puts a hand on my arm, a consoling gesture. "A lot of successful people handled money and risk that way in the run-up to the crash. The appreciation trend in real estate was so powerful for so long that people were making big money flipping houses. Don was a money guy. He'd have seen it as a great bet."

"A guy like him would go cheap on life insurance to get a bigger house?" I ask it incredulously, but as Cecelia lays it out I know that for someone like Don the potential for a big profit at low risk would be more seductive than a naked starlet.

"Lots of people just like him did that," she answers. "Banks are going to be repossessing houses for years because of it."

I usually try not to cry in front of anyone else because it looks so unseemly, someone as big and butch-looking as me crying like a schoolgirl. But my body chemistry is completely female now and tears come as naturally as curses did when testosterone coursed through my veins. The sadness of the moment, the day, the month, chokes my inhibitions and I sob in Cecelia's opulent Caddy as we start and stop our way toward home.

6

"Hi, I'm Detective Allan Wilkins." He says it like a syrupy politician asking for votes, trying to hide the fact that they make him sick. Two obviously gay men, walking down the sidewalk way too close to each other, chatting and chuckling like a couple of girls.

As he greets them, he holds up his shield and flashes a big smile, all white teeth and love. It's an integrated neighborhood, but getting stopped on the street by a burly black guy has the potential to scare the crap out of most white citizens. He doesn't want that. He wants trust and help.

The couple stops and returns the greeting with caution.

"I'm sorry to trouble you. I'm doing a follow-up on an old murder case. You may remember it. A few years ago? A man named John Strand was found dead in his apartment a block from here?"

The shorter man, pretty, with bleached blond hair and blue eyes, nods his head. "I remember. Tony didn't live here then, but I did."

Wilkins makes himself focus on the information he wants, choking off the mental image of this gay boy having different lovers every day or week like fags do.

Wilkins takes him back in time to when the murder occurred, reminding him it happened two days before the body was found. "It would have been a Friday night, very late. Saturday morning, actually.

Did you happen to see someone out walking between two and five a.m.? Someone not from the neighborhood?"

The pretty boy steps back slightly. Maybe a foot. It's his bad breath, Wilkins realizes. He tried to keep sucking on breath mints, but he ran out.

"Oh, Detective," the pretty boy sighs. "That was a long time ago. I don't even know where I was that night."

Wilkins nods. It was the answer he expected. "Let me share something with you," he says in a chummy, conspiratorial voice. He opens the portfolio tucked under his arm and removes a stapled set of papers. He pages through them quickly with the young man, careful to speak away from him to avoid another bad breath episode.

"These are news items about things happening in the city that night," Wilkins explains. "They might help you remember where you were, what you were doing, and all that. Take this home and take your time looking through it, okay? Let me know if you remember seeing anyone. And please show it to your neighbors and ask them to do the same thing."

The young man nods.

"This neighborhood isn't going to be safe until we find the killer, you know?" Wilkins adds. "It looked like a hate crime, so minorities are especially vulnerable." Trying to personalize the crime for the pretty boy by implying that the victim might have been gay without saying so.

"Was the victim gay?" the young man asks.

"We're not sure," Wilkins answers. "We'll know a lot more when we find the perpetrator. Right now, we need witnesses and leads."

"I'll do everything I can, Detective." He says it like a grade school kid talking to Officer Friendly. Wilkins would usually find that revolting, but right now he needs help. He smiles and wishes the couple a good day and moves on.

He has distributed dozens of his news packets in the neighborhood where John Strand got his throat slit five years ago. Not much chance anything will come of it, but at least it gets him out of that dreary apartment. And, who knows, he might get lucky with some of the seeds he's planted here.

* * *

MONDAY, AUGUST 18

I repeat Cecelia's counsel like a mantra as I enter the TransRising conference room. Keep smiling. Be pleasant. Greet each person you meet as if you are a parishioner meeting the pope. Be impressed with each person's amazing accomplishments. Don't talk about yourself.

The meeting is called to order by the Chicago TransRising president, a nice person named Danni. Danni is a genetic woman who presents as an almost-man who is both butch and feminine. She considers herself "gender queer," someone whose gender identity is fluid and whose presence in society causes even more distress than I do for people who insist everyone has to be either male or female. Danni is thirtyish, smart, and gifted at bringing groups like this together and getting them to accomplish important tasks.

After Danni's remarks and the requisite trip around the table sharing our names, professions, and years in the community, Lisa takes over. Lisa is a twenty-four-year-old transwoman who has been fully transitioned for five years and has lived as a female for a decade. She is slim and pretty and has the self-assurance of a homecoming queen.

She distributes copies of a conceptual brochure promoting a forthcoming benefit for the Center. It is to be a celebration of the fifty most influential transwomen in America. She and two of her friends, also twentysomethings, decided on the theme and will decide who the chosen fifty are.

The brochure is boilerplate. The most interesting thing about it is the message that the benefit is being sponsored by TransRising and by her website, *The Joy of Trans*. The website is supposed to be a celebration of happy, successful transwomen. It's a collection of self-written biographies of fifty or sixty young transsexual women whose homilies to their own self-discovery read like testaments from born-again Christians about the moment they found Jesus. The site is supposed to offer the public and the media a positive impression of the transgender community, but no one would read that stuff unless they had to.

As the committee members review the etchings, murmurs of approval and admiration flow freely from around the table.

"Any comments or suggestions?" Lisa asks, basking in the glow of adulation.

"What do you think, Bobbi?" asks Danni.

I squirm. There goes the low profile. I shouldn't be here. I don't like these people and I wouldn't go to this benefit if you paid me in nights with the amorous Jose. As soon as I open my mouth, my lovely sisters will start twitching like teenagers getting a sex lecture from an aged parent who couldn't possibly know anything about sex.

"It looks . . . fine." I almost said "okay," which is what it is, but that would be an insult to Lisa's genius.

"Pardon me," says Lisa. "You're a hairdresser, right?" As in, what could a stupid hairdresser know about marketing?

"Correct," I answer.

Danni fills in the group on my former career and circulates a copy of the latest promotional flyer for my salon. It's boilerplate, too. I'm not a creative genius.

"Not bad," says Lisa. "The sight line doesn't lead into the copy, and you could do more with the photo, but not bad."

I smile.

Danni follows up with me. "Bobbi, it sounded like you had something more to say."

If Cecelia were here she would jab me in the ribs and remind me to shut up. As combative as she can be, she gives these twits a lot of space in the interest of connecting our generations. Alas, Cecelia isn't here and Lisa's arrogance has gotten under my skin. Plus, I don't need this committee in my life right now, not with a failing salon and a loved one in severe emotional plight, a nasty cop breathing down my neck, and a social life so meager I have to pay a hooker to get laid.

"I just think we might talk about the strategy of having a Top 50 theme here. It's going to offend 90 percent of the people in the top 500. Plus if you've ever seen a botched list like this, they can be very damaging to the credibility of the sponsor. Do we feel like we have the expertise to pick the fifty most influential transwomen in America? Do we know who all the influential transwomen are?"

Lisa's face flushes. She is irritated by me in the same way a rich tourist is irritated by the supplications of a street person. Amazing that as timid and cowardly as I am, I somehow manage to set off people like this.

"Do you have a better theme?" she snaps. "Does anyone like Bobbi's idea better than mine?"

She looks around the table, a glare on her face, daring anyone to contradict her.

"We like the Top 50 theme a lot. Thank you for doing it," says one of the toadies. Several heads nod in agreement. Lisa glowers at me, demanding capitulation. I avoid a stare-down by writing a note on my pad. It's my resignation, addressed to Danni.

"Okay then," Lisa says. "Looks like we have a plan." She babbles on about the agenda for the next meeting, then Danni closes.

After the meeting two of Lisa's friends confront me. "So you hired Jalela, huh?" one says.

"Yes."

"Why did you make her apply at other places?" The question is a

hostile one. "Do you have a problem hiring transwomen?" As it happens, I had her apply at other salons so she could learn how to do it,
so she wouldn't be dependent on the largesse of other transpeople all
her life. I also helped her write a resume and coached her on how to
answer the standard interview questions. Not that any of this is any
business of the vacuous princess confronting me.

"I hired her and you didn't," I say pointedly. My decades of testos-
terone-driven male living give me the urge to add *you fucking moron*
to my statement, but I don't. "If you want to make hiring decisions,
get your own business. That's what I did."

I didn't swear once.

I brush past them to catch up to Danni before she leaves. This
committee is an ugly reminder of what it would have been like to go
through high school as an unattractive girl. The quality of my life will
go up several notches when I rid myself of this association.

Danni tries to talk me out of resigning. We have to learn to work
together, she insists. I agree but I tell her I'm not the right person to
bridge the gap, that an hour with those kids was enough to make me
wish I was a man again. A gross exaggeration, but it makes a point. I
assure her I will continue to support the center with donations as long
as I'm able, but no more promo committee. And I ask her to please
get my name off the committee roles before they issue the Top 50 list.
I do not want pioneers of the transgender community like Cecelia
blaming me for a list of juvenile twits whose greatest accomplishment
is winning Lisa's admiration.

* * *

WEDNESDAY, AUGUST 20

"Your news clippings got me to thinking and I went back on my computer to April 23, 2005, and there it was." The pretty boy is gesturing effeminately, but Wilkins doesn't mind. The man has information for him. "I went to a concert at the House of Blues that night. I remember the night very clearly.

"I went alone, something I never do, but I wasn't seeing anyone and I was getting stir crazy. And Bearcat Hogue was playing." The man's hands flutter with excitement. He is wearing a t-shirt and the hand gestures show off arms laced with tattoos.

"And the reason I remember all this is because after the concert, as I was leaving, I met someone." He rolls his eyes, sighs. It was a romantic liaison. Wilkins blocks the mental image, noting only that it's good the man has vivid frames of reference for the night. It would be impressive on the witness stand.

"So we went for a drink, then to a party, and when things started getting interesting, I invited him to my place. That's when he tells me he's with someone and has to get home." Pretty Boy makes a sad face, exhales. "He gives me a ride, though. I have him drop me at the corner. I start walking home. It's maybe three or four, and all of a sudden I realize someone is walking toward me. At first I'm scared. Punks beat up people like me just for the fun of it, you know? But this person doesn't even notice me. He passes under a street light, and I can see he's tall and cute. I remember because my next thought was, he's gay. Kind of shaggy hair and his walk was a little swishy"—he looks at Wilkins, smiles self-consciously and shrugs, acknowledging that he's a little swishy, too—"and I had this terrific urge to go introduce myself to him, maybe have a drink."

"I didn't. It was late and that can be so dangerous. But I thought about that moment a few times after that. It was kind of romantic, in a road-not-taken kind of way."

Wilkins reviews his notes with the man to make sure they're accurate, then starts filling in blanks.

"How tall would you say that person was?"

"I'd guess maybe six feet or so."

"Did you get his hair color, eye color, build? Facial hair? Anything like that?"

"His hair was darker in the streetlamp, not black but probably some shade of brown. He had a beard and mustache, sort of a Van Dyke. And I remember his hair was longish, at least for a gay man, if he was one. It covered the top of his ears and came down to his collar and it fell across his forehead." He gestures with his hands to show the hair length at different places on his own head.

Wilkins carefully works his memory for more details. The man was wearing jeans, a bomber jacket, hands in pockets. He looked fit. He had a cute ass, and the pretty boy said he wasn't the type to really notice such things. The comment didn't disturb Wilkins at all. His mind was fixed on how this description fit his theory of the crime. The tranny hairdresser gets dolled up like a man to do the deed. The only thing she can't hide is her prissy walk and that bubble butt of hers.

He hates that he noticed her ass.

"Did you see anyone else on the street that night?" Years of experience have taught Wilkins to ask and re-ask questions. You never know.

"No. It was deathly quiet that night. I remember."

"Not even someone walking their dog or going to the store for a pack of cigarettes?" Wilkins isn't pushing, just seeing if anything could jog the man's memory.

"The only other thing moving was a car that came by. I remember it now because its headlights helped me see that guy better."

The pretty boy didn't see the driver. The car was a black BMW, his dream car, but it was unremarkable otherwise. There were many of them in that neighborhood.

* * *

THURSDAY, AUGUST 21

"What kind of people did Mr. Strand entertain downstairs?" Wilkins asks.

The older man on the other side of the coffee table asks his wife to get them some cold lemonade. It was a cue and she took it, going to the kitchen to give them a few minutes of privacy to talk about things men talk about.

"I only saw a few of them and only one of them close up. They were women, but I don't think they were real women."

Wilkins raises an eyebrow as if he is surprised and confused. "Sir?"

"I think they were men dressed as women. Transvestites. Except the one I passed in the hallway had real boobs and she showed them off. She looked like a prostitute, a female prostitute, except she was big. Tall, big bones.

"The other two I only saw from behind. I can't be sure they were men, but since I saw the first one, that's what I think."

"So you think Mr. Strand was having encounters with transgender women in his apartment?"

The man makes a face and nods his head.

Wilkins takes the man back through his memories, digging for details as he goes. Gathering information that would probably be useless, but you never know. Plus it gives you an idea of how good the man's memory is, what kind of witness he might make.

Strand hadn't had the place very long. Less than a year, the man thought. You hardly ever saw him or heard him. He came and went late at night and early in the morning. The elderly neighbor thought he had sexual assignations there. No one ever saw or heard him in the place, not even a television set or sound system. His name wasn't on the mailbox, just the apartment number. He didn't get mail, except for junk mail. It was his honey shack. A pretty expensive one, too.

Wilkins scans his notes, thinking. "Anyone else in the neighborhood I should talk to?" he asks. The case file was sparse on input from the neighbors.

"You could try Crazy Ike," says the man, a smile playing his face. "He's the Neighborhood Watch guy. Has a place a few doors down. He's always reporting spies and terrorists. Crazy as a loon."

"Did he see anything around that time?"

"He reported a spy or something to the police around then, but he sees things all the time." The man laughs. "But give him a try."

At the end of the interview the building custodian is waiting to show him through Strand's apartment. It's occupied now, but the tenant okayed a maintenance walk-through. Wilkins carries the case file with him and reads about each room as he stands in it, putting the layout of everything in a three-dimensional picture in his mind. Where Strand was found hanging. The bathroom where strands of synthetic wig hairs had been found by the toilet, Wilkins thinking the perp might have barfed in the john after doing the deed. The back door where they entered, Wilkins doubting they came in hot and ready for sex, more like the perp had already disabled Strand. The garage where Strand's car had been found, the only fingerprints belonging to Strand, but the ones on the steering wheel smudged and smeared. The tech couldn't be sure why, but one possibility was the last driver wore gloves.

Wilkins kept finding things that supported his theory of the case. The perpetrator took down Strand using a tranquilizer delivered by syringe. Wilkins figured it happened somewhere else, so the perp knew about his love nest and how the garage worked. The investigator who took over when he got banned from the case considered the possibility that a transwoman did it, maybe a she-male Strand dumped for a new model. But he dropped the idea because it seemed too improbable. The motive had to run deeper than that. Fags and trannies go through partners every day without killing each other. Plus if it was a crime of passion there would be a different kind of crime scene, maybe genital mutilation, maybe a knife in the heart, some kind of signature of outrage. The investigator figured the murder had something to do with Strand's business dealings, a former client, maybe.

Wilkins never bought the jilted lover idea either, but he knew the murder had something to do with Strand's kinky sex life. Strand had been hung by his hands from the ceiling, then his throat was slit in a single movement. Not necessarily a professional hit, but it had some of the coldness. It was an execution. By someone strong and very determined. Wilkins figured the killer disabled Strand, drove to Strand's place in Strand's car, carried him into the apartment, strung him up, slit his throat, and walked away. Wore gloves the whole time, was methodical in making sure the crime scene was clean, no prints, nothing left behind. Used a knife from Strand's own kitchen and left it there, no prints, no leads.

The people who took over the investigation after Wilkins were never able to find a motive for the Strand slaying, but Wilkins knew in his bones it was the rape Logan reported a few months before Strand got it. The goons who did her had to have been working for Strand. The case was never resolved, so Logan took matters into her own hands. He can't prove it yet, but he would. Every discovery is advancing his theory of the crime. He is learning where to look for hard evidence. He just has to keep plugging away.

7

Betsy and Robbie and I are strolling through Brookfield Zoo. It's Sunday, late morning, and the place is starting to fill up.

My niece is having a glorious time. She is fascinated by the animals, especially the giraffes and the polar bears. And she regales in the freedom to run and scream and get picked up any time she wants by her mother or me.

The weeks since Don's car accident have been difficult for her. She's too young to comprehend death. She only knows that her daddy isn't coming home anymore. She tells me this every time I visit, which is frequent.

Betsy is grieving for Don and for her fatherless child, and she is terrified of what the future holds for them. The worst part of her grief is the occasional thought that she didn't love Don enough. She has poured her heart out to me several times and it always includes the confession that she didn't love him enough, that she took him for granted, that she didn't find him especially arousing as time went on.

These are not things I offer advice or counsel about, though my suspicion is that we all get to a point in a long relationship where we take our partner for granted to some degree, and I know for sure that sex changes a lot with familiarity. But when Betsy unloads, I just listen. The only assertive intervention I make is to insist that she was a wonderful wife to Don, and if he were here right now, he'd say so. I say this with the conviction of someone who can see two people who can't always see each other.

Betsy sees a therapist, but I'm not impressed with what she tells me about the woman. Her approach is very clinical, maybe even disinterested. I'd feel a lot better if she would see Marilee, but Betsy feels Marilee is too close to me. "It would be like asking my mother-in-law for help," she said.

We are making plans for next weekend. They will be coming into the city to stay with me overnight on Saturday. They'll go see the sights while I'm working, then we'll go to dinner and catch a set or two at Jazzfest. As much of it as Robbie can tolerate, anyway.

Betsy is actually excited about the idea. She loved living in the city and she misses it. We've been doing everything at her suburban castle and it's getting boring. Time to get back to civilization.

When I get home tonight I will start readying my extra bedrooms. Before I became the holder of a business debt bigger than Fort Knox, I managed to buy a roomy two-flat in Lakeview, not far from Boystown. I live in the first-floor unit and rent the other apartment to a tenant. The neighborhood is nice and the brownstone is to die for—solid brick, roomy, high ceilings, big rooms. It was rehabbed a year before I bought it, so it's beautiful. I have the ground-floor apartment, three bedrooms, a bath and a half, a space-efficient kitchen that is separated from a large living area by a breakfast bar. I use one of the extra bedrooms to do hair for friends. It has a twin bed that I have set up like a couch, plus a stylist chair, special lighting, large mirrors, and a portable beautician station bristling with my beauty tools and supplies.

The other extra bedroom is a guest room and office. It has a desk and my computer station, and a double bed and bedroom furniture.

As Betsy talks to Robbie about the tigers across the moat from us, I am thinking that I'll put Betsy in my bedroom, Robbie in the guest room, and I'll take the salon room. If Robbie has trouble sleeping in a new place, she can snuggle with her mom.

I share these thoughts with Betsy as we walk to the car an hour later. Robbie is sound asleep in the stroller. Betsy smiles and puts her hand on mine. I let go of the stroller with that hand, and we walk a few steps holding hands, exchanging appreciative small squeezes. I realize how much this time with Betsy and Robbie means to me. The wild dashes to the suburbs and back to work should be exhausting, but instead I feel a sort of exhilaration. Like I'm someone who is important to someone. It's different than having friends you love and a lot different than being successful in business. It's better. And it's addictive. I try not to think how wonderful it would be if Betsy and Robbie stayed. I try not to fantasize how perfect it would be for Betsy and I to raise Robbie to adulthood together, sisters bonded in love and a common goal.

It can't happen, but I can't help dreaming about it.

* * *

TUESDAY, AUGUST 26

Wilkins watches from a café table as his photographer friend joins the melee in front of L'Elégance across the street. The big tranny queer is doing a hairstyling demonstration on the sidewalk in front of the salon. Her tight black dress bulges with cleavage on top and leaves most of her legs exposed. Her hair sways and bounces as she works and falls like a curtain around her face when she bends.

She still disgusts him, but she draws a crowd. Her and the two women working with her. They're all in sexy outfits, selling the sizzle.

The photographer takes a position in front of the chair. He speaks to Logan. Wilkins can't hear him, but he knows the man is asking permission to shoot some photos. His cover story is that he's a free-lance photographer and hopes to sell the photos to one of the Chicago dailies.

The tranny queer smiles and nods her head yes, her hair bouncing and flouncing, making Wilkins sick. The photographer works the scene for twenty minutes, shooting different angles, working in close-up portrait shots of Logan using a zoom lens.

Later today, the photographer will begin Photoshopping the photos to give Logan facial hair and a male haircut and put that head atop a male body. The photographer will try to sell the originals to a newspaper, along with a short item about the plucky beauty salon using sidewalk demos to kick-start business. And Wilkins will have some photos of a male suspect to show anyone in Strand's neighborhood who saw a man walking the streets in the early morning hours after the murder.

* * *

WEDNESDAY, AUGUST 27

Lisa and her friends stop talking as Officer Phil and I enter the room. The buzz-kill is as sudden as if a switch had been flipped.

Phil is wearing an expensive, elegantly tailored suit that fits his athletic body like a glove, making him look like a movie star. His short hair is brushed back and glistens with a gel I recommended to him. He is ruggedly handsome and gentle at the same time. The hetero girls in the room are experiencing heart palpitations, like me, and even the lesbian girls must be wondering why a gorgeous hunk like Phil would associate with an ungainly old transwoman like me.

I keep my face neutral but give my brain permission to gloat.

Phil is here to talk to a congregation of young transsexual women at TransRising about interacting with the police department. He is masterful in the role, speaking without notes, encouraging spontaneous questions and comments.

Many of the young women in attendance have lived on the street and some still do. Their feelings about the police are complex and often negative. Several issue sharp criticisms of the Chicago PD and one is outright confrontational. Phil fields their barbs gently, his voice and face filled with compassion. The confrontational girl issues an obscenity-laced tirade about how the police treated her when they arrested her for stealing money from a john when in fact the first crime was the john stiffing her on payment after she serviced him. Phil doesn't point out that the first crime was actually prostitution. Smart. To a kid whose alternative is going hungry and sleeping in a doorway, prostitution is no more of a crime than breathing air or drinking water.

Instead, Phil talks about what sets off cops in those situations and how a citizen can conduct herself in a way to take the edge off. He tells cop stories about dealing with violent altercations and cops getting shot, stabbed, or beaten when they try to do the right thing. He paints a vivid image in our minds of what it's like to be a cop, walking cold into a confrontation, having no idea who is right or wrong, or who is dangerous, and trying to restore order without making an arrest.

At the end of his forty-minute presentation, most of the girls in the room are in love with him. God knows I am, but that's nothing new.

Lisa leaps from her seat to take control of the meeting. It had to be agony for her to surrender the podium to me to introduce Phil, but she didn't know him. She thanks Phil, asks him to wait a moment, then closes the meeting. She and her friends cluster around him, offering thanks, cooing approval for his presentation, batting eyelashes. I can't help thinking Phil is going to get laid tonight by the beautiful young woman of his choice.

After a polite period of time, Officer Phil thanks the girls, says he would love to do this again, says he is late for a date with a gorgeous redhead. As he says it he walks to me and offers me his arm. I am overwhelmed. He called me gorgeous. And even though he didn't mean it, he left several truly gorgeous young women standing there, watching me lace my arm through his and leave with the man of our dreams.

Phil takes me to a wine bar near the Loop. I thought he was just using me to shake free of my adoring sisters, but it turns out he had hoped I'd be available. Be still my heart!

We order glasses of red. I cross my legs as daintily as I can. We are sitting on stools at high tables and there is just enough room for a six-foot woman to get one leg over the other without dumping twenty dollars of red wine on her host. I try to pull the hem of my dress lower. I was doing sidewalk demos today so the dress is short, top and bottom. I'm showing a lot of leg and enough cleavage to make Phil's eyes roam. I know he's not interested in me, per se. It's that wonderful testosterone effect. Even gay men have to look.

After several minutes of small talk, I try to find out why we're here.

"You know you left a trail of broken hearts at TransRising tonight. When you walked out with me. All those beautiful young women."

Phil's eyes arch in feigned surprise. "Really?"

"Don't play innocent with me." I laugh. "You know every girl in that group wanted to leave with you." Phil is trying to be modest and polite.

"If you say so," he says.

"So why did you leave with me? You had your pick of younger and prettier girls." In the back of my mind I'm thinking maybe Phil is gay and just doesn't want to talk about it. That would explain his preference for me. I'm not insulted, but it would be nice if something about me made him crazy with desire.

"They are young and pretty and I like them all," he says. "But I . . ." He stops for a moment, searching for the right words. "I like your company, Bobbi." His eyes take an involuntary tour of my cleavage, then back to my face. He blushes a little.

I look at him and smile, then lift my glass for a silent toast. We are sitting side by side at a small round table, just large enough to hold our wine glasses. After we tap glasses and sip, his eyes rake over my exposed legs. I avert my gaze modestly only to see what seems like swelling in his crotch—he's sexually aroused, by me!

"What do you like about my company?" I ask it hoping for some ego stroking or maybe a confession of deep-seated desire for intimacy.

"You're smart. You're funny. You're easy to talk to. You're . . ." There he goes again, choking back the word he was going to say, looking for a different one. I would clean his house for a month to know what he was going to say.

"You're sexy." He says it in a rush and looks me straight in the eye.

He catches me off guard. My breath catches. For moment I don't know what to say.

"What does that mean, Phil?" My heart is pounding. I want him to whisk me out of here and into the nearest bed and have his way with me.

He stares at me. I can see that his mind is working a million miles a minute. He is trying to decide whether or not to take the next step. Seconds pass. He blinks, averts his gaze to the table.

"I want to tell you something, Bobbi." His voice and body language tell me the golden moment has passed.

"Feel free to talk dirty." I make it sound like a joke, but really I'm pandering like the village slut. I'd be disgusted with myself if I wasn't so aroused.

He shakes his head. "It's about Wilkins."

My erotic bubble pops and I'm back in reality. Shit.

"Oh?" I say.

"He says he's found people who saw a six-foot person walking in Strand's neighborhood in the early morning hours after he was murdered."

"That's like saying someone saw an oak tree in Oak Park, Phil."

"His theory of the crime is that the six-footer was a woman, a transwoman, disguised as a man. Wearing false facial hair, a male wig, male clothing."

I shrug. I try to seem nonchalant, but the truth is, this is scaring me. For a moment my brain conjures an image of me in court, my salon going bankrupt, losing everything even if found not guilty.

"Why are you telling me this?"

His turn to shrug. "Same old same old. I like you. I admire you. I root for you. I want to make sure you don't do anything to give him an excuse to get your fingerprints or DNA or anything. This man is relentless."

"Do you think I killed Strand?"

There, it's out. A direct question, finally. I dread the answer. So does he. He squirms.

"I'm a PR guy, Bobbi. What I think doesn't matter. Me, personally? I know you didn't. I know you couldn't. But let's just be honest here. If I didn't know you, I'd think it could have been you. You had issues with Strand, I don't know all of them, but I know you figured him for the murder of your friend. You're smart and strong and you have incredible willpower."

He stares at me when he says this. I drop my glance. As somber as this conversation is, I see myself asking him to bed me before they haul me to jail, kind of a transwoman spin on the young soldier asking the virgin to sleep with him before he goes off to war. Phil misunderstands my smile.

"I'm serious, Bobbi."

"I appreciate that, Phil. My mind just wandered for a moment."

We sip wine for another half hour making small talk, me wondering if maybe he just can't let himself have sex with a transwoman. Lots of men are like that. Gays because they see us as women. Straights because they see us as men. Maybe it's better that way. If gays saw us as men and straights as women we'd have so many romantic overtures we'd all be arrogant.

8

WILKINS SITS FORWARD and places a file folder on the coffee table. He swishes two breath mints in his mouth to make sure he doesn't alienate his audience. Opposite him is the bleached-blond queer and his boyfriend on the couch. They are holding hands, which would be disgusting if Wilkins let himself think about it.

"Thank you for seeing me," he says. "I want you to think back to the night you saw that person walking on the street, the night that man was murdered. I want you to think about what that person looked like, everything you can remember, every detail. Then I want to show you some pictures and you tell me if they resemble that person or not."

"Okay," the blond man says. "But it was dark, the light wasn't good."

"I know," Wilkins says. "And don't worry about that. I just want your reaction to the photos."

The man closes his eyes for several seconds, opens them, nods to Wilkins.

Wilkins produces an eight-by-ten black-and-white photo showing a man walking on a sidewalk in gray light. It is a Photoshop creation, Bobbi Logan as a man, seen from a short distance, wearing the clothing and facial hair Pretty Boy described to Wilkins earlier. The face is Logan's with a VanDyke, mustache, sideburns, and longish male hair. The body is Logan's but in male clothes, and without breasts.

"Does this look anything like the person you saw that night?"

The man studies the photo. "That could be him. I mean, it could be a lot of people, but it could be him."

"Do you see anything that doesn't look like him?"

The blond man looks at him questioningly.

"Look closely and tell me if there was something you saw that night that you don't see here, or something you see here that doesn't belong. The guy's too fat or too short or his head is too big or too small . . . like that."

The blond man studies the photo. "No, I don't think so."

"What specifically reminds you of the man you saw that night?"

The blond man blushes, nods his head yes, smiles self-consciously, holds his boyfriend's hand again. "It's his ass. The man I saw that night had a really cute ass. Not to be graphic, Detective, but not many men have curvy butts."

Wilkins should be revolted but he isn't. His adrenaline surges. It's not anywhere close to a positive ID. All he's done is keep Logan in play as a suspect. But he can feel it. He's right about this. He just has to keep digging.

"Thank you, sir," Wilkins says, putting the photo back in the file folder. "Just one more thing. Will you look at this photo and tell me if it looks like the person you saw that night?"

He produces another eight-by-ten photo, this one a portrait of Logan with a van Dyke beard and mustache, and male hair falling to mid-ear.

"That looks like him, I think, but I didn't see his face very well—just a quick glance. Although . . ." His voice trails off in thought.

"Although . . ." Wilkins coaxes him.

"Well, I'm pretty sure he had longer sideburns. There were a lot of shadows, but I thought his sideburns went to the bottom of his ear, maybe even lower."

Wilkins nods appreciatively and makes notes in his notebook, another on a sticky note that he attaches to the photo.

"Thank you, sir," he says to the blond man. "Thank you both." They shake hands. "You've been a great help to me and the department."

* * *

Friday, August 29

"Hi, Bobbi! It's Roger." He's calling from Florida. Probably baking his brains out in the tropical heat. I wouldn't live in one of those hot redneck states for anything. Well, maybe if Officer Phil was moving there and wanted to take me along as his concubine.

"How are you, dear?" he asks.

"I'm just fine, sweetie." I'm trying to master that cooing use of *dear, sweetie, honey,* and the rest of that saccharine lexicon that gay men and most other women employ so well. It sounds stupid when I do it though.

"How's business, honey?" The sweet references roll off his lips with the grace of an eagle riding thermals high above the earth.

I answer with platitudes, hoping not to get into the subject, but he presses me on it. I ask about Robert, his partner. Robert is fine, he says, but how is business?

"It's slow, Roger," I answer finally. I won't lie to him about it. "We're doing some promotional stuff to try to stop the bleeding, but we're off about thirty percent versus a year ago, and the people I talk to say this recession won't bottom out for another year or two."

"Oh, Bobbi, I was afraid of that." He issues a series of sympathetic clucks and groans. A normal American businessman would be asking about his money and I'm bracing myself for that.

"How are you meeting expenses?" he asks, finally.

"So far, by cutting my salary and not replacing one assistant who left. Plus a little belt-tightening in the color room, getting the girls to cut out waste. The usual."

"You're not paying yourself, Bobbi?"

He sounds like a comedian doing a Jewish mother routine. I almost laugh.

"I took partial payment," I say. "I'll get it back when things turn around."

"Bobbi, you can't do that. You are the key to the business."

We talk business strategies for a few minutes, then Roger says what he called to say.

"Bobbi, if you have to go light on your payments to me for a few months, you go right ahead. If we have to restructure the deal, that's what we'll do. I don't want you losing your building or living like a nun. You have to stay healthy. Robert and I are fine right now." He goes on but I don't really process his words. I can't get past the realization that this man trusts me enough to let me miss payments to him or change the deal entirely. I would never do that, but the offer makes my head spin. Five years ago when I was transitioning, most people wouldn't give me the time of day or an interview for a job or even deign to sit next to me on the El. Roger was the exception and now here he is saying "pay me when you can."

I thank him and promise that if the situation becomes dire I will call him and talk about his offer. We have that conversation again. Roger has too much time on his hands.

*   *   *

SATURDAY, AUGUST 30

Betsy walks into the living room and collapses on the couch next to me. She has just kissed Robbie goodnight. The child lasted one set at Jazzfest and we stayed for one more, admiring how she could sleep so restfully in a crowd. We walked part way home because it was such a nice night, shifting Robbie back and forth between us until we got too tired to carry her anymore and took a cab the rest of the way.

This is our first weekend sleepover at my apartment. It has gone well. I've been anticipating this event all week, planning every detail, cleaning, prepping the bedrooms, laying in enough groceries to feed the masses. And dreaming about being there for Betsy. Providing support and shelter while she gets her life together. Being the sister she can say anything to. Being a second mom to Robbie. All three of us going places together, shopping, beaches, concerts.

Betsy is still too burdened by reality to share my sisterly zeal, but she has enjoyed the day, too. She leans her head against my shoulder. I lower my head to rest on hers and we hold hands.

"Were you really surprised to see that policeman there?" Betsy asks.

Officer Phil saw us at Jazzfest and came over to say hello. As I introduced him to Betsy it occurred to me she might find him interesting when she started dating again. It would be nice to keep him in the family . . .

"Are you interested in him?" There is a tiny undercurrent of tension in her voice when she asks this. We haven't talked about how we would handle dating and sex yet. We're both healthy single women. It's going to come up, especially if we become roommates, but now might not be the time to get into it. If Cecelia were here she'd tell me to duck the question. This is America. Everyone gets weird about sex, even rational people.

But the answer to that question looms like a black shadow of fear in front of me. I can't have a real relationship with Betsy if I lie about who I am.

"Was it that obvious?" I answer. I thought I had done a good job of keeping my knees and voice steady when Phil chatted with us.

"Kind of. And he's obviously interested in you. Are you two . . ." She doesn't finish the sentence.

"No. And he's not interested in me. Not like that. Men like Phil don't dabble in transwomen like me. You don't want to see the kind of men who find me attractive." But in the back of my mind I'm thinking that Betsy is the second person to suggest this possibility. Her and Marilee. Two women who have a firm grasp on reality. Plus Phil's little erectile moment at the wine bar . . . It's enough to make my heart thump a little harder.

"I thought you were more into women. Like that lady from Indianapolis." My first romance when I transitioned was with a woman I met at a hair show. It was pretty torrid for a while, but the distance was a problem. Last time we talked she was dating a man.

I'm sensing that Betsy would be borderline grossed out by my sex life, not that I actually have one. Once again, I'm tempted to gloss this over. It would be devastating to have her think of me as some kind of degenerate sex maniac. But she might as well know what I am and decide for herself whether I'm human or alien.

"The truth is, girls like me don't get to be as selective about their lovers as girls like you," I say. "Not many people of either gender want to take me home to meet mom and dad. So I don't have a long list of qualifying characteristics to measure my suitors by. They have to be a nice person and there has to be a spark there. Beyond that, I don't care if they are male or female, black or white, tall or short, religious or not. I'd probably even consider a Republican, not that one would ask."

She's quiet for a while, contemplating what I've said and trying to figure out how to ask the next question. I know it's coming.

"You must have a very active romantic life." It's a statement, but it's a question. It's *the* question. Am I promiscuous? I sit upright so we are facing each other.

"I had the fling with Jen for a year or so. I've slept with a few people since then, but they all lost interest really fast. I don't know if that makes me loose or not, but I confess, it makes me desperate. The best sex I've had since Jen was with a male prostitute I hired to bed me. You probably think that's sick, but it was the best I could do."

Betsy's face goes through a range of emotions as I speak. She ends by smiling. It's a smile that is sympathetic and humorous at the same time. "You hired a hooker?"

"You make it sound like I found Jesus."

"You hired a stud to . . . to . . ."

"Service me."

Her face flushes. She founders for a moment.

"Bobbi . . ." She can't bring herself to ask the obvious question. She has too much class.

"It was great, Betsy. It wasn't love. There weren't any angels or heavenly music. It was just a good old-fashioned fuck and it made me feel like a million dollars. Which is close to what I paid."

"Really?" Her face is beet red and her eyes are the size of pancakes. This is not something Betsy would have ever considered doing.

"Well, not a million dollars. But a lot. He wasn't some guy on the street. He's an artist."

"An artist? Like Picasso?" She's laughing at me.

"More like a musician. He plays horny women the way Yo-Yo Ma coaxes beauty from a cello."

"How often do you do this?" She's enjoying my discomfort.

"Just the one time. It was Cecelia's idea. She has a regular appointment with him, like her hairdresser. I probably won't ever have the money to do it again."

She is captivated and maybe slightly repulsed by this revelation.

She asks how much I paid, where I got the name, what it was like. She alternately blushes and giggles. Genetic women are so practical about some things and so naive about others.

"I've tried to imagine what it would be like to see you with a lover. You know, coming to dinner or something." Her voice trails off. "It's weird. I feel a lot of things. Jealousy. I feel gladness for you. I worry about you, getting your heart broken or whatever."

"Jealousy?" I ask.

"Yes. I know, it's strange. I shouldn't feel that way but it's there."

I kiss her temple. It is a reflexive expression of love. She turns her head to me and kisses me on the lips. It is a soft, warm kiss and it absorbs me. I am aware of nothing else but our gentle embrace and the feathery currents of her breathing.

It lasts for just a moment. Not a lover's kiss, but close.

"I'm sorry," she says. She's embarrassed. "I shouldn't have done that."

"It's okay, Betsy. We can love each other." I'm pretty sure the kiss was a reflex from another time, years ago, when I was someone else who loved her.

"Not as lovers!" Her voice is quiet, but sharp.

"No, not as lovers. You're not gay. You'd have to pretend I was still Bob, and I'm not."

"What do you get out of this, Bobbi? What are you hoping for?" Her voice is soft, but this is the take-charge Betsy talking. She's creating some distance between us.

"I want to be there for you the way you have been for me," I tell her. "I want to have a sister who feels she can say anything to me and lean on me when she needs to. I want to have a sister and a niece I can love unconditionally and who love me back. I've had lovers, Betsy, but you're the only real family I've ever had."

She considers this for a moment. "Thank you for your honesty. Just please understand, right now I need some space in my life. I have a lot to work through."

We're quiet for a long time, each lost in her own thoughts. We don't get into the other question that loomed before us like a massive wall just before the kiss: How will our relationship fare when we start having romantic encounters with other people?

She breaks our long silence. "This has been a great day, Bobbi. I'd like to do this again."

Me, too. We hug. I dream of Betsy and Robbie moving in for good, having a day like this in the autumn, coming in with chilled faces, sitting down to hot chocolate. The three of us. A Terry Redlin scene glows in my mind, red cheeks on three loving faces clustered together in front of a fireplace oozing warmth, a womblike setting of smiles and love in a perfect world.

And in the dim recesses of my mind, it occurs to me that I want this too much.

9

WILKINS PLACES HER tea in front of her and sits on the other side of the small table, cradling his coffee. He hadn't expected her to order tea. In fact, there was nothing about her that he had expected. She was big and tall, obviously a transgender woman. But instead of a street person in stiletto heels and a miniskirt, she was conservatively dressed in a black skirt, pressed white blouse, ballet flats. Her hair was processed and curled into a fashionable bob. She looked like a young executive.

"I want to show you some photos and have you tell me if you know these people," Wilkins says.

"I can't do anything in court, nothing in public," she warns. Her name is Candice. She has the diction of an educated woman. Her vulnerability surprises him. He feels like he should touch her, pat her hand to put her at ease, but that wouldn't be professional.

"I understand."

"I'm just getting my life together, you know?"

"How so?" Wilkins asks, and immediately kicks himself. Never get personal with a witness, especially not someone on the fringes of the law.

"Look," she says, leaning toward him, lowering her voice. "We both know what I was five years ago. I've come a long way since then. I have a regular job. I'm finishing high school. I want to have a career. I want my past behind me."

"I understand." Wilkins collects himself and passes her a photo. "Do you know this man?"

"This guy's dead."

Wilkins nods his head yes. "He's John Strand. He was murdered five years ago. The case is still open. I'm trying to find anyone who knew him or knew of him."

Candice shivers with muted horror.

"What?"

The young woman's body shakes with tension. Her clenched jaw sends ripples of angst across her chocolate skin. Tears begin to form in her eyes.

"Did you personally know Mr. Strand?" Wilkins hears himself ask it gently. It's not his way, but it's not an act. It's like he's talking to his daughter, not that there's much resemblance. The tears, maybe. The heartbreak. Jesus.

Candice fights for her composure. "I knew him." She says it without trembling or crying. Wilkins is impressed.

"And?" he says.

"I'm not going to court to say this."

"No. Just tell me."

"He was evil."

There is something about the way she says it, Wilkins thinks. He'll come back to that.

"How did you know him?"

"I was new on the streets." Her tears start trickling down her cheeks. "He was a regular. He paid well."

"How regular?"

"Once or twice a week. A party once, him and his friends."

"He got rough?" Wilkins senses she wants to talk about it.

"Rough? Oh, Detective, I wish it had just been 'rough.'" Her tears come faster now. He hands her a napkin.

"Tell me."

"The first few times were okay, and he tipped big money. But after that it got like a horror movie. One minute he's all charm and smiles, the next minute he's a demon from hell. When I think of him, I see snakes in his eyes, wiggling, tongues out, fangs shooting venom . . ."

"What did he do?"

"He beat me."

"Bruises? Broken bones?"

"Yes."

Wilkins waits for her to elaborate, but she's silenced by the horror of her memories.

"Did he hit you with his fists?" he coaxes.

"Hit with his fists. Kicked with his feet. Squeezed with his hands, my breasts, my genitals, like he was making fun of me." She's openly crying. People around them are starting to notice. Wilkins puts a hand on her arm, gentle as a cloud, as he would if she were his own daughter.

"The last time was like all the hate in hell poured through his body and ripped mine to shreds," she says. "He broke my jaw, some ribs. My breasts were so sore I couldn't wear a bra. I thought I was going to die that night."

Wilkins lets her cry for a moment. "Did you file a complaint?"

"I was a junkie and a hooker and a transsexual. Who was going to listen to me?"

"A detective would have taken your report, checked it out," Wilkins says.

Candice looks at him with a dubious grimace. "And the next thing that happens is he comes and kills me."

"You never saw him again?"

"When I got back on the street, one of his goons picks me up. I don't know it. I think he's just a john. He roughs me up a little then tells me don't talk about 'The Man.' I say, 'Who?' And he grabs my throat and chokes me and says, 'You know who,' and I say, 'Okay.' He gave me some money and threw me on the street."

"What did that man look like?"

"He was white, ugly, pig eyes. About your size. Wore a Chicago Bears stocking cap, blue and orange."

Wilkins digs in his folder and produces a mug shot. "Do you recognize this man?"

Candice brings a hand to her mouth in horror. "I never want to see that piece of shit again."

Wilkins touches her gently again. "Not to worry, Candice," he says.

She dabs at her tears and sips her tea. Wilkins gives her time to collect herself. "Thank you," she says, finally. "Can I ask you a question?"

"Sure."

"You're not really trying to find the person who killed John Strand, are you?"

"Yes, ma'am. That's my job."

"That's the worst thing you can do, Detective. That man destroyed lives. He killed people, and the ones he didn't, wished they were dead. Don't let him take another good life. Let it go."

"I can't do that. I have to enforce laws equally. A judge and jury can decide the rest."

They sip their beverages.

"Why are you so nice?" she asks.

Wilkins tries to deny it, but Candice persists. "I have a daughter," he says finally.

Candice laughs. "I remind you of your daughter?"

"Yes."

"Is she an ex-hooker?"

"She's smart and beautiful. She's in college."

"That's not me," Candice says, a trace of regret in her voice.

"It can be," Wilkins says as they get up and start to leave.

"I'm just finishing high school. Twenty-one and just finishing high school. I work nights, ten bucks an hour. I'm HIV positive." Candice says it like a confession. It shakes Wilkins.

"I'm sorry," he says. He turns away for a moment and closes his eyes, stung by an impulse to hug the kid, wondering where in the hell that came from. A minute ago she was a man in a dress, a tranny queer. Now he wants to put his arms around her and urge her to stay strong. Damn.

She shrugs and smiles. "Sacrifices must be made, Detective. Prostitution got me out of a horrible home. Strand got me out of prostitution. Whatever happens, at least I get to die being me." She gives him a last fleeting smile and leaves.

As Wilkins watches her go, emotion tightens his throat. "At least I get to die being me," he murmurs. "My Lord."

* * *

TUESDAY, SEPTEMBER 9

This must be what it's like to be a doting wife to a husband experiencing a period of high anxiety. It's five thirty in the morning. I'm touching up Betsy's highlights, racing against the moment Robbie awakens and demands her attention.

We have been rustling around Betsy's Northbrook place since five. It is Betsy's first day of work and her anxiety is reaching seismic levels. I'm having my own anxieties. To do this for Betsy, I had to take the late shift at the salon, so my day won't end until nine o'clock tonight. I already look like a raccoon because of the dark circles under my eyes.

By nine o'clock tonight unsuspecting strangers will think I'm a zombie from hell.

I take her into the laundry room to wash out the color. Betsy maintains a constant monologue about the things that are worrying her. Especially Robbie's first day of all-day day care. She envisions the child sitting in the corner crying all day, feeling abandoned, traumatized for life. This is not rational. Becky has introduced Robbie to day care over several weeks and she loves it. Other kids to play with, doting teachers, new toys.

When she stops to take a deep breath, I point this out to Betsy. She smiles. This is a thank-you. But her peace of mind doesn't last long. As we walk back to the chair, she grabs my hand.

"Oh God, Bobbi. I've been gone so long. I don't remember anything about marketing. Everything has changed. It's all Internet now."

She rattles on as I comb her out and trim her bob. It won't be the precision masterpiece she usually wears, but she will look spectacular on her first day. As beautiful as she is, she would look spectacular in a fright wig and no makeup.

The noise of the blow-dryer wipes out conversation for a few minutes, and my mind selfishly gravitates back to my own problems. Surviving the day is one. I'm exhausted already. And trying to stay solvent is the constant problem. We are still running far below year-ago billings, though Samantha thinks we're stabilizing at that level. It's really too early to tell. September is a big month for our business and it has just started. We'll see.

Cecelia says I should sit down with my bank and see about modifying my mortgage payment plan. And she wants me to negotiate the same thing with Roger. I want to beg for mercy from a banker about as much as I want to wake up with body hair. As for leaning on Roger, I wouldn't do that until I was homeless and eating dog food.

Robbie toddles into the room as I finish the blow dry. She climbs into Betsy's lap and hugs her. She cuddles for five minutes as if charging her batteries, then launches into a full-speed assault on the potential of the day.

All toddlers are cute and she's even cuter than that. She has shoulder-length light brown hair, lively brown eyes, a pixie face, and an endless assortment of expressions that convey anything from anger to glee, but always with a mischievous glint.

She peeks at me from across the room. I mime a kiss. She blows back a kiss and smiles. When I finish Betsy's hair, she asks me to do hers. I lift her on the stool, brush out her hair, and do a quick round-brush blow-dry. She glows with pleasure. She loves getting her hair done. She loves dressing in her princess gowns, wearing lipstick, trying on her mother's heels. Or mine. She is so like me in that way it's almost as if we are genetically related.

For the millionth time, I think, if only I had had that acceptance and support. If only I had been born in the right body. But my next thought always puts an end to that fantasy. If I had been born a girl, or if I had been born trans to a family who accepted me, I would not be here now. Betsy and Robbie would not be in my life. I wouldn't change anything that would mean losing them.

* * *

TUESDAY, SEPTEMBER 9

Wilkins takes the seat offered to him, pops a couple breath mints, offers the packet to Ike Schmidt. He declines. Ike's wife brings them coffee while they settle in. Ike is an older white man, seventies, maybe, alert and brimming with energy. Wilkins figures him for the type who still hand-shovels snow in the winter. He is rambling on about neighborhood crime, Wilkins looking out the picture window, thinking Ike has a commanding view of the street.

When Ike's wife leaves, Wilkins gets down to business. "I understand you run the Neighborhood Watch committee here," he says.

"Someone's gotta do it," says Ike. "These people think nothing can happen to them, nice neighborhood like this, but that just makes us a target in this day and age."

"Your neighbors say you don't miss much."

"They think I'm crazy as hell, but it's true, I don't miss much."

Wilkins leans forward toward Ike. "Mr. Schmidt, I'm investigating a five-year-old murder that took place just down the street from here."

"Strand murder," Ike says. He goes to his roll-top desk and removes a file from a lower drawer. "Remember it well. Big shot lawyer liked to shack up with trannies and girly boys. And they call me crazy."

"I'm trying to find out if anyone saw anything unusual that night, or in the time leading up to that night."

Ike leafs through the file. "Well, every once in a while I'd see one of those lady-boys stroll through here. Gave me the creeps, goddamn queers."

"How did you know they were lady-boys?"

"Their size, mainly. Plus they seemed to hang around Strand's place."

Wilkins tries to keep it conversational. "They go in and out?"

"Some did. One I saw just kind of hung out on the other side of the street. Strange one. Couldn't tell if it was a lady-boy or a real swishy fag."

Wilkins' eyes widen ever so slightly. He passes Ike the doctored photo of the male Bobbi Logan. "Did he look anything like this?"

"Could be. Big shoulders. Prissy face. I couldn't say for sure. But it's possible."

"How long was he there?"

"Must have been fifteen minutes or so. I thought he was waiting for a cab or something," says Ike.

"Ever see him again?

Ike snaps his fingers. "A few times, now that you mention it. He'd just be walking down the block, slow like. Didn't really set off any alarms. I figured he had a friend hereabouts."

Wilkins returns the photo to his file. "Do you remember any others in particular?"

Ike smiles a little. "I saw a real beauty come out of Strand's building a couple of different mornings. Blond, great body, gorgeous. I figured her for a woman-woman until the news broke about Strand and his trannies. Boy, if they all looked like her, we'd all want one." He laughs. Wilkins laughs with him, trying to perpetuate the good mood.

"Do you remember anything else out of place around that time?" Wilkins leans forward again as he asks the question, letting Ike know it's important.

Ike goes through his file. "Seems like it, but it's not coming right to mind," he says. "Just give me a second."

"One of your neighbors said you reported a spy working in the neighborhood," Wilkins says, trying to prod the man's memory.

"You heard that from old Russell. He thinks I'm off my rocker." Ike pulls a sheet from the file. "Here it is, April 15, one a.m. I didn't think the guy was a spy, more like he was stalking someone, you know, a girlfriend, or maybe a guy he got paid to rough up. He was parked out in front of my place in the middle of the night when I walked the dog. Didn't look right. He sat there for a long time. I figured he might be up to no good, so I called it in. Of course, he was gone by the time the cops got here—only took 'em an hour or so. Good goddamn thing we didn't have some jihadi lunatic blowing himself up on the porch or something."

Wilkins thinks for a minute, trying to visualize what Ike saw. "Could it have been a police stakeout?"

"Not unless the cops are using BMWs for stakeouts these days."

"Ever see the car again?"

Ike scratches his head. "Can't say for sure. Lots of BMWs floated through here. Every yuppie sonofabitch in America had a BMW back then. Not so many today, though, eh? The ol' recession knocked a lot of those know-it-alls right on their asses."

"Did you see anyone or anything on the street the night Strand was murdered?"

"I was up around four that morning, peed, walked my dog just out front. I saw a man walking east down this street. Kind of odd. That's usually a dead time of night."

"What can you tell me about the man?"

"Not much. It was dark. Seemed youngish, a little spring in his step. Walked kinda like a fag."

"Long hair, short?"

"Longish, I think. It's been a while. Kind of like the early Beatles."

Wilkins scans his question list to make sure he'd covered everything, then stands and thanks Ike for his time.

"Always glad to help out," says Ike. "You want the license number of that BMW?"

"Is it in the police report?"

Crazy Ike snorts as he transcribes the number to a notepad. "No way. They never asked me about it. They figured I was crazy, but I'm not. He hands his note to Wilkins. "Just in case, Detective. Just in case."

* * *

FRIDAY, SEPTEMBER 12

It's Friday, and even though I have a full day of work tomorrow, I feel Saturday beckoning like a warm fire on a cold day. For one whole day, all I'll be doing is dressing hair. I hope. That prospect looms in my imagination like an erotic fantasy as I maneuver through the crowd on the El station platform with Robbie.

It is six thirty p.m. and I have been running between Chicago and Northbrook for two hours, since Betsy called, hysterical, wanting to know if I could get Robbie at day care. Her boss had just called an emergency meeting and warned that it would go late.

I only had one service left and my client was happy to reschedule. I took the El to the train station, the train to Northbrook, a cab to the day-care center, scooped up Robbie, and reversed everything. When I got to the day-care place—actually, they don't like that term, it's more like the Harvard of preschools—Robbie was the last kid there. She was playing happily, but my heart sank miles into the ground, weighted by guilt and a sense of failure. I never want this child to feel abandoned or alone. Of course, she doesn't, but when I saw her there, the last kid, I pasted my own fears and prejudices into the picture and have been running with an aching heart ever since. It goes with my acid stomach, but not that well.

I try to assuage my guilt by putting Robbie on my lap on the El so I can hug her and coddle her, but she isn't interested. In fact, she thinks the El is the coolest playground she's ever seen and spends her time making eyes at the various specimens of humanity who travel by that conveyance in our fair city. The suit people aren't much fun— bankers, traders, lawyers, and other members of the yuppie elite. A few of them do double takes. It's not every day you see a transwoman with a child, even on the El. But none of them want to play peek-a-boo with Robbie. Fortunately, the less pretentious people on board are far more accommodating, and Robbie has a great time on the run from the train station to the north side.

We duck into a grocery store on the way to my apartment so I can get food Robbie will eat. This was an impromptu call, and I had no time to get things ready for my niece and sister to come calling. I fed her a bag of pretzels on the train, but that won't buy much more time. I'm frazzled as I try to keep Robbie entertained and check off all the things I need to do to finish this day. Robbie is in a phase where she eats only hot dogs or bologna, chips, and cottage cheese. I snatch up these items and find a fish fillet for Betsy and me, along with a pre-mixed salad. On the way to the checkout I see a wine rack and select a nice red. I cradle it lovingly in my hands before placing it in the shopping basket; it is my lifeline to sanity.

At my place, I turn Robbie loose with a half dozen pots and pans and assorted utensils while I organize our meal. Thirty minutes later Betsy bursts into the apartment, face flushed after her brisk walk from the El station, her body radiating animation and anxiety. Robbie looks up from her meal, ketchup smeared from cheek to cheek, a happy smile on her face. It helps me that she's not drop-everything-ecstatic to see her mom. She was having a good time with Aunt Bobbi and not worried. Mom, on the other hand, is nearly frantic to hug and kiss her child and shelter her from the demons of the world.

When Betsy rises from the mother and child reunion, I use a damp paper towel to clean the ketchup from her lips and nose. She smiles and kisses me on the cheek and hugs me, venting a week's worth of pent-up emotions.

She brushes a strand of hair from my eyes, the kind of familiar gesture I love. "What's for dinner?" she asks. I take her through the menu and pour wine. We toast her first week back. Over dinner she tells me about the office. She's working as a staff person instead of a manager, but she's okay with that. It's a little harder taking supervision from someone younger than her, and her colleagues are a little standoffish, but she thinks things will be okay when the newness wears off.

It gets quiet suddenly.

"And . . ." I say, leading her.

"My boss. He's a little . . . I don't know . . ."

I gesture with my hands to keep talking.

"It's just . . . he's kind of touchy-feely, you know. He came up behind me at my desk once and put a hand on my shoulder while he talked to me. He calls me 'honey' sometimes, which frosts me."

The more I draw her out, the more the guy sounds like a creep. He's always smiling and syrupy, but it sounds like an act. He sounds like a small-dick alpha male trying to put Betsy in her place, or get in her pants. Or both.

"That meeting tonight?" she says. "I tore up your day and got a heart attack to make myself available for it, and it was nothing. Everyone else was gone. He calls me in his office, closes the door, and says he just wanted to know how my first week went, how I like the office, the other people, him. We could have had that conversation in the hallway in two minutes."

Just what I was thinking.

"He told me I was great this week, even better than he thought I'd be, and if I play my cards right I'll be getting raises and promotions." Betsy has a worried set to her mouth when she says this. "I'm really afraid that means he's going to want me to work late a lot."

I nod in agreement, trying to will myself to keep my mouth shut. I can't.

"I don't think it's work he has in mind," I say.

The anxiety on Betsy's face tells me she's thinking the same thing.

"I'll take care of it." She says it with a sharp note in her voice. I've gotten too close. She's telling me to back off.

10

"YOU WERE ALWAYS a stand-up guy, Pavlik." Wilkins locks eyes with Phil. "That's why I want to give you a heads-up."

Phil stares at the detective, not sure of what to say. Finally he shrugs.

"I've got a ways to go for an indictment in the Strand case," Wilkins says, "but it's going to happen pretty fast now."

"Congratulations, Al."

"It's not all good news, I'm afraid. Not for you. The way it's going to come down is, your girlfriend did it. Logan. There will be plenty of proof for an indictment and because she's a tranny it's going to get a lot of press coverage. You need to create some space between you and her. That's why I'm giving you a heads-up. You have a good future, Pavlik. The suits like you. The street cops like you. You look good on TV. You don't want to get splattered with any of the mud from this one."

"She's not my girlfriend, Wilkins, and you shouldn't call her 'tranny.' That's a bigoted expression. She's a transgender woman and she's my friend, not my girlfriend. And since you brought it up, I don't believe she did it. She's a nice person who's had a tough life. She thinks it's personal with you. Is it?"

"You're right. I don't like her," says Wilkins. "But that's not why I'm building a case against her. I'm after her because she did the crime. She assassinated that lawyer."

"You know that?"

Wilkins smiles. "I've got motive and opportunity. Motive: she was raped a few months earlier by men working for Strand. She got even with one of them by having him beat to a pulp in the alley where she was raped. He wouldn't talk about it then, but he will now. He's got nothing to lose. He's going to tell me he followed Logan into that alley. Someone else delivered the beating, but Logan set him up. He's also going to tell me he was working for Strand when he was following her."

"You know this?" Phil asks.

"I can feel it. I can tie her to the tranny prostitute who got murdered. Excuse me, *transwoman* prostitute. They were pals. Everyone knew that. And I'll be able to tie Strand to that prostitute pretty soon. It won't be long.

"I've got motive and means. She was smart enough to do Strand and she was strong enough to disable him and haul his ass into his apartment and string him up like a side of beef.

"I've got Strand entertaining trannies—excuse me, *transwomen*—at that apartment. It was his love nest for tranny fucking. Real women he took to his lakefront digs. Had to keep that kinky appetite out of the public view, right? So it makes sense that it was a *transwoman* who offed him there. Who else would know about the secret place?

"I've got a real good witness from the neighborhood who saw a man walking a block away about an hour after the time of death. Want to know what's interesting about the mystery man on the street? He's about the same height and build as your girlfriend, and even though he was dressed like a man, he has a big squishy butt that my witness thought was very sexy, and he walked like a *twink*."

Phil shakes his head. "Wilkins, you're way out on a limb here. You have a theory that only hangs together because you don't like Bobbi."

"Sergeant Pavlik, I have circumstantial evidence that provides a strong foundation for my theory of the crime. And there's a lot of it. Like, remember the eye gouge she used on that junkie in her salon? She used it on Strand the night he was killed. It could be a coincidence, but it's not.

"I've been investigating murders for twenty years, Pavlik, and I clear more of them than anybody. I'm good at this. And I know when a case has turned a corner. This one has. She's going to be going down."

"You're never wrong?"

"No. Not when the case turns. This is going to happen. Nothing can stop it now."

Phil shakes his head sadly. "What a waste. What a tragic goddamn waste."

Wilkins nods solemnly in agreement.

"Not just her life," says Phil. "Yours, too. Instead of hauling in one of the murderers in this town who kill for fun or profit, you take down a person who not only didn't do it, but owns a business, employs people, does good deeds all the time. How do you justify that to yourself, Wilkins?"

"If you do the crime, you do the time. That's how." He studies Phil closely. The man really has a thing for Logan, it's obvious. Jesus.

Phil shakes his head sadly again. "Thanks for the heads-up. I think you're way off base, but don't worry, I won't share this with Bobbi."

"Tell her anything you want. Tell her everything. It won't change anything. She did it, she can't undo it, and she can't keep me from finding the proof."

"You put her away and nothing is better in Chicago, it's just a little worse because there's one less good person out there." Phil walks away, his mind conjuring a vision of Bobbi Logan being led away from the courtroom in handcuffs, her red curls losing luster with each step, her strong body aging, her animated face taking on the gray pallor of prison, her bright eyes fading to lifeless orbs. It is too sad to watch.

* * *

TUESDAY, SEPTEMBER 16

It's not every day Martin Bancroft walks into your salon, not even every lifetime. But he walked into mine about twenty minutes ago, no phone call, no appointment, no warning. I had to keep him waiting while I finished my client, but he was fine with that. Sam got him coffee and offered him the sanctity of my office. She didn't know who he was, but she could tell he was important. Maybe it was the worshipful tone in my voice when I welcomed him.

Martin, being Martin, dropped his briefcase and umbrella in the office, then began touring the salon, station by station, sipping his coffee, watching each hairdresser work, asking questions. Professional questions. Where did you learn that cut? Who did that color? Have you ever tried a Denman brush for blow-drying that style? Only one of the stylists knew who he was, but everyone could tell he was some kind of hair god. And rich. He wears Armani suits and shoes that cost just a tad less than a Caribbean island. His tie is an elegant blend of violets and lavenders and purples, colorful, artistic, classy.

Martin Bancroft is the President, CEO, and owner of SuperGlam, and the hottest story in the beauty industry for the past decade. He was a mid-echelon manager at one of the big hair products companies before he took a walk and started his own line. He told me one night after we had all consumed too much wine that the key to his success was knowing he was only an average hairdresser but he was brilliant at seeing genius in others and still more brilliant at marketing it. He's not a modest man, but he wasn't boasting either.

His product line is pure elegance. It was one of the first organic lines and features natural ingredients and the lushest aromas in the world. But what really set SuperGlam apart was Martin's grand-scale teaching concept, calculated to win the hearts and minds of stylists and independent salon owners by making them better at what they do.

He gets to my station last. I am finishing an asymmetrical bob. He smiles his Hollywood smile, which tells me he is going to sell me a bridge. The only question is, which one.

"I see you don't have a specialized staff in L'Elégance," he says. "Why buck the trend?"

Many upscale salons have stylists who specialize in color and others who specialize in cutting and styling. The theory is, you do better work, faster.

I tell him we talked about it several years ago, but we all felt like we could serve the client better by not specializing. "Once you master the basics, it's not a question of how well you do the cut or the color, it's knowing the client well enough to know what she wants," I say. "Plus, none of us wants to work in a factory."

Martin smiles. "I like your thinking, Bobbi. It's easy to outsmart yourself in business. You get so focused on making more money you forget the only reason you ever made money was making the customer happy."

His face turns serious. "I'm sorry to barge in on you like this, but I was hoping we might chat for a few minutes. Would you have time to fit me in?"

"Of course, Martin. For you, anything!"

I wave Jalela over to do the blow dry.

"Who is that guy?" she asks before I leave the station.

"That is Mr. SuperGlam, but you and I can call him God."

Jalela's lips form the word "wow" as the noise of the hair dryer drowns out the word.

Wow indeed, I think to myself as I follow Martin to my office.

As we settle in, Martin apologizes again for popping in without notice. He wants me to work the Chicago show next month for SuperGlam.

I start to give him reasons I can't do it, but he holds up a hand asking permission to continue. I nod my assent.

"You don't have to do a lot of rehearsal. We want you teaching at our exhibit. Talk people through a technique, talk them through a style, let them know which SuperGlam products you're using, be your charming self.

"You'll like the pay and we'll provide a hotel room if you want, or a driver to pick you up and take you home. And you just work show hours—unless you want to cover the parties."

He names the daily fee. I should play hard to get, but I can't. I accept flat out. Then he tells me I'm looking very pretty, that owning a business seems to agree with me. I don't know if the accolade is just the reflex action of a career glad-hander, or if he actually sees something attractive about me. Either way, I'll bask in the compliment. It's not like they come along every day. They don't even come along every month.

* * *

WEDNESDAY, SEPTEMBER 17

"Have you gotten that lawyer lined up yet?"

Cecelia has a stern look on her face. We are sitting in the café across the street from my salon. We have a nice view of the salon's first weekday sidewalk demo. The demos have become a Saturday staple for L'Elégance and staff and it seems to be working on a Wednesday lunch hour, too. Office workers and sightseers and moms and nannies alike stop to watch for a few minutes, take our brochure, then move on. Some pause to chat, especially men, attracted by our sexily clad stylists and assistants. The scene is strangely serene, a weekday afternoon in the city, small groups of people constantly forming, then dispersing, then reforming. Like breezes rippling a field of grass.

"Not yet," I say. "Why?"

"Because that nasty detective is really after you, Bobbi. He's been talking to girls in our community."

"I heard he was showing photos to the street girls, but I heard they were pictures of guys."

"I don't know about that," says Cecelia, bending closer to me to lock in eye contact. "He's talking to people who know you. And he's asking about you and Mandy, and Mandy and Strand, and you and Strand."

"I don't see the problem." I shrug as I say it, even though my stomach is doing flip-flops. "It's no secret that Mandy and I were friends or that I met Strand a few times when I was with you. And you told the police about Mandy and Strand during the investigation of her murder, and not one of them gave a damn about it. Why should I be worried?"

Cecelia sips her coffee.

"Because, honey, he doesn't need much to indict and he doesn't need much to get a conviction. You're a transwoman. Most jurors are retired people who think transpeople are perverts. You could get convicted without a shred of physical evidence."

Her mouth forms a hard line. The bigotries that shape our lives make Cecelia's blood boil.

"Actually, he doesn't need to get a conviction to ruin my life," I say. "Just going to court would do that. The bad publicity, the court costs. My business would fail and I'd be as notorious as a serial murderer."

"So get the attorney lined up. Get smart, Bobbi. You have to get in front of this."

I nod. It's true. But my cash reserves are almost gone, I still can't pay myself for my salon billings, I'm struggling to pay my loans every month. The last thing I need is to be writing a check to an attorney.

I admit to Cecelia I don't have the money.

"I'll pay it," she says. Sharply. She is insisting.

"No. Friends don't borrow money from friends, not unless they want new enemies." It's true. Plus I will not be dependent on anyone. If I can't make it on my own, I'll fail on my own.

"This is serious. Don't be such an asshole, Bobbi."

"I prefer to be called a pussy." I'm trying to defuse the conversation with a little humor. "I have a lot more invested in that part of my anatomy."

"Don't change the subject," says Cecelia, suppressing a smile. "This is life and death stuff, Bobbi."

We are silent for a while. I know she's right. I'm trying to figure out where to get the money.

Cecelia breaks the silence. "I'll talk to him," she says, referring to the attorney. "I'll ask him to let you go cheap on the retainer. He'll do it, but you'll still have to come up with the money if he starts racking up hours on your case. Okay?"

I agree. It's the best deal I'm going to get, even though, if I think about it, the whole situation stinks.

After a brief silence I ask Cecelia a question that's been rattling around in my mind for weeks. "Why isn't he investigating you, too, Cecelia? You're big and strong and you had ties to Strand and your alibi for the night of the murder is no different than mine."

Cecelia locks eyes with me. "My doorman saw me come home that night and didn't see me leave again. I have a powerful attorney. He doesn't have anywhere near enough to justify pressuring me."

I see her point.

My spirits are dark as I set up for my sidewalk demo. I'm wondering if the salon will fail before Detective Wilkins arrests me, or if his revenge on me will be the final straw in my financial and social failure. The only thing that gets me through the afternoon is my demo, which is a big-hair up-do on a young woman of color, a friend of Jalela's. She has long, thick hair that curls and braids beautifully, and she wants to look sexy tonight. Soon I am lost in doing her hair, every part of me focused on bending and teasing and piling her hair into a presentation that will light the fire of every man who sees her.

As she glides away after the service, my worldly problems come back to me. Men on the sidewalk crane to watch her as she passes. I'm envious. She will get laid tonight, if she wants to, while I am getting screwed, whether I want to or not. You have to admire the irony.

* * *

THURSDAY, SEPTEMBER 18

In the twenty-four hours since my conversation with Cecelia I have reached a new pinnacle of success: I have an attorney on retainer. This, along with the mortgage on my brownstone and the colossal debt on my business are supposed to be signals to the world that this ugly, outsized transsexual woman has arrived.

It feels a lot more like I'm being buried.

The only good thing is, business isn't getting worse. It's not getting better either, but we're hanging in there. Our demos and shilling at El stations and office buildings seem to be helping. We're getting some new people each week and they seem to leave happy.

The dark cloud over everything is the stalking reality of Detective Wilkins and my financial vulnerability to even a hint of scandal. Not to mention the sheer terror of contemplating a life in jail. This aching worry has had all the repercussions on my personal life you would expect. I sleep poorly, I struggle to concentrate on anything other than hair, I seldom smile or laugh. It's had some unforeseen repercussions, too. In my idle moments today I thought about hocking next month's rent for another tryst with Jose, just to get laid while I still can.

Before I could work up the will to call him, Betsy called and asked if she and Robbie could stay with me tonight. I scuttled all thoughts of a fling and made a list of things to pick up on my way home. It occurs to me now as I carry my grocery bags into the kitchen that someday Betsy is going to stop by unannounced and find me with a man. Or a woman. It will be awkward, but we'll get over it.

Betsy arrives red-faced and straining. Robbie is tired and crabby. Betsy has their overnight things in a backpack. Between the pack and the child, she is carrying thirty or forty extra pounds after a hard week of work and parenting. The exhaustion shows on her face.

I pluck Robbie from her arms at the door and sweep the child into my kitchen, inviting her to help me cook and serve dinner. This delights Robbie. I give her a glass of wine to take to her mother as her first chore, asking if she can do that without spilling. She is sure she can. She's almost right. Aunt Bobbi chokes back the reflexive curse and we have fun wiping up the red drops together. I tell Betsy to relax and unwind while we get dinner. She collapses on the couch, gets up a moment later to feed music into the CD player, then collapses again.

Dinner is quieter than usual, just Robbie and I carrying on. Betsy is eerily silent. Something is wrong. After dinner, Robbie and I pack the dishwasher, then engage Betsy in a game of hide-and-seek. Though I have shed many of my inhibitions about being a large transwoman, this game reawakens my self-consciousness. As I crouch behind a chair, I feel like a hippopotamus trying to hide behind a flower. Of course, we're not trying to hide, really, so it's okay.

When Robbie has had her bath and three bedtime stories, Betsy staggers into the living room, flops on the couch, and curls into a ball. She looks at me, her soft brown eyes forlorn with sadness.

"What is it?" I ask.

She cries for several minutes. I hold her silently. Some things have to come in their own good time.

At length she sits up and faces me. "My boss has been making passes at me all week. Not just flirty stuff. He touches." She swallows, takes a breath. "He talks dirty. I try to ignore it, but he just keeps coming on."

I will myself to silence. My suspicions about her boss are coming true. He's a nasty little brute who gets off on dominating people. Somewhere deep inside my body my Y chromosomes are demanding that this cretin's knees be broken with a baseball bat. My gentler nature tries to ignore the chorus.

"Tonight he felt me up and tried to run his hand up my skirt. I slapped his hand and he laughed. He told me he wanted to . . ." Her voice stops for a moment. She can't say the word but she doesn't have to. I nod that I understand what she's trying to say and she continues. "I told him to stop and he just laughed more. He said I know I'd love it."

Her face grows taut as she relives the horror. Then her horror turns to anger. "I can't believe it! In this day and age? He thinks he can get away with that?"

She goes on for a while, expressing her outrage and her disgust for men. She feels dirty. She feels violated. And she feels impotent. There were no witnesses. It's just the new employee's word against that of a rising young star in the company.

I have some personal experience with these feelings. The people who raped me did it to put me in my place and to express their contempt for me. I felt what Betsy is feeling. Humiliated. Dehumanized. My anger rises to a simmering boil. If her boss were in the room right now, I would do my best to dismember him.

I try to collect my emotions so I can be there for Betsy. I put my anger in a compartment in my mind and close the door. I focus on

Betsy. I listen to every word. I murmur my understanding of how she feels. I confirm that she has every right to feel that way.

I ask if she's thought about taking this to the human resources people. "That would just get me fired," she snaps. She wants distance again. I shut up and listen, the good wife.

*   *   *

FRIDAY, SEPTEMBER 19

"She's a real b-i-t-c-h if you ask me," says Wilkins' dining companion between mouthfuls of eggs and pancakes. As if spelling the word made her seem more feminine. As if anything could.

"She's very hoity-toity. Like she's better than everyone else." The falsetto voice comes from an obese, middle-aged transwoman about five-nine and well over 250 pounds. Her lipstick is smeared. She wears a bad wig and too much makeup. Her dining style is primitive truck driver.

Wilkins keeps his revulsion hidden. He has become good at that from doing all the interviews. Some of the transwomen have been likeable, and some were okay, and some were like this slob who he wouldn't have liked even if she were presenting as a straight man. No matter. This one has issues with Bobbi Logan. If she knows anything useful, she'll share it. All for the price of a breakfast at Gay-HOP on Friday morning.

"Who are her friends?" Wilkins asks. He pops two more breath mints, just to make sure. Experience has taught him that his breath can be off-putting for some in the close confines of the Gay-HOP booths.

The woman chews and thinks. She rattles off the names of Cecelia and a couple of people at TransRising. "And anyone who pays her to do their hair," she adds with a malicious smile.

"Who does she date?"

More chewing and thinking. "I don't know," she says, finally. "I know she's hot for that cop who used to have this beat."

"Phil Pavlik?"

"Yeah. Officer Phil. Of course a lot of the girls were hot for him."

"Do you think they . . ." Wilkins wiggles his fingers, implying a tryst.

The woman snorts. "I sincerely doubt it. That man could have any woman he wants. I can't imagine him finding that cow attractive."

Wilkins produces a photo from his folder. "Did you ever see her with this man?"

As she looks at the photo, her eyes widen. "John Strand!" She looks up at Wilkins. "You think she—?"

Wilkins cuts her off. "I can't talk about an investigation in progress, ma'am." Next to free food, calling transwomen by feminine nouns or pronouns was the fastest way to rapport, he had found.

"Right now, all we're trying to do is see if they knew each other, and who else Strand knew in the trans community."

She chews and thinks. "They were both at a party at Cecelia's place once. I remember. It was after Mandy was murdered and Cecelia thought Strand did it. She was pissed that the police weren't checking him out so she invited Strand and Officer Phil to her afternoon tea.

"Phil didn't take the bait, but there were some interesting side plots. One was Bobbi Logan flashing her big tits in Officer Phil's face, not that he was interested. And I remember seeing Strand follow her out the door when she left. I thought it was strange because they barely talked at the party."

"What happened then?"

"He came back a few minutes later, so I don't really know."

"Anything else?"

"Not that I saw. I heard he went to her for a haircut once, and one of the girls saw her get in a car with someone who might have been Strand after a meeting."

"Was the haircut at her salon?"

She nods yes.

"Do you remember who saw her getting in a car?"

She chews and thinks. "No. But I'll keep thinking about it. If I come up with it, I'll give you a call."

Wilkins nods and smiles. Over coffee he asks if she ever saw Strand and Mandy together. She hadn't, but she says the rumor in the community was that Strand was the sugar daddy who paid for Mandy's gender surgery and her nice apartment.

Outside, he thanks her and asks if there is anyone else he should talk to about who knew Strand back then. She gives him some names, no guarantees.

11

Betsy is venting on the other end of the line.

This is becoming a nightly ritual. She holds it together all day, getting up at five thirty and getting herself and Robbie ready, dealing with an increasingly tense office situation at work, dashing home by way of the day-care center, putting together a meal, chatting up her exhausted daughter, reading bedtime stories, and the final goodnight kiss. She holds it inside for another five minutes to make sure Robbie falls asleep, then she calls me and as soon as I say hello, she starts to unload.

"I'm getting so much attitude from the other women." Her voice is tense. "They think I'm sleeping with that weasel."

She is referring to her boss and using an animal reference I haven't heard in a decade or two. I think of him as a bastard, or when I'm really angry, a shithead. Betsy always did have more class than me. Still, I keep thinking this might be a situation for unleashed testosterone. I keep thinking that society would be very well served by this guy getting his genitals pounded by an angry boyfriend or husband of one of his victims.

Or sister.

"Would you like me to have someone deliver a message to this bastard?" I ask. It slips out before I can squelch the thought.

"What are you suggesting?" Her voice is angry.

"He would be easier to work with if someone put the fear of God in him," I say. I'm upset, too, but not at her.

"Bobbi, keep out of this. This isn't your problem. It's mine and I'll handle it. I can't believe you'd say such a thing." Hostile, almost belittling. I know it's the frustration from her workplace getting directed at me. Because I'm safe. I won't fight back. We fall silent.

I ask her how her projects are coming and the mood lightens up a little bit. She loves the science of marketing, and she's one of the rare people who can apply the science creatively to the practice. I find it hard to believe her genius isn't appreciated by at least some of those around her, but then corporate environments can be snake pits and her department is defined by the depravity of her boss.

She is silent again. She is thinking about something and whether or not she wants to say it out loud.

"Bobbi," she says, "I'm losing the house."

"Already?" I thought those things took time.

"I work like a dog for fifteen hours a day to take care of us and keep my shitty job and the fact is, I don't make enough to pay the mortgage on this house, let alone the other expenses."

"Can't you draw it out for a while?"

"I don't want to live like that. I have to do something positive, get started again."

Betsy finally gives in to tears. "What am I going to do, Bobbi? I'm behind on the car payments, too. I have the worst job in the world and pretty soon I won't be able to get to it. I'm going to have to move in with my parents. Shit!"

"Move in with me, Betsy." All my vows to keep silent explode in a surge of anxiety at the thought of her wicked parents getting their venomous claws into Betsy and Robbie.

"Your parents would drive you crazy, Robbie, too. And they live in the middle of nowhere. Move in with me and you don't need a car. You can quit that shitty job and take your time looking for a better one. I can help with Robbie."

"I can't do that," she says. Her voice is firm. Resolute. To argue the point would be like trying to push a boulder up hill.

"Why?" I ask anyway. For transsexuals, pushing boulders uphill is part of an average day.

"Because I'm a mom. I'm supposed to take care of these things."

"You're moving in with your parents, for goodness' sake. How is that better than moving in with me?"

"They're family." Her voice is riddled with exasperation.

I swallow and try to recover. This hurts. I am far more loving and nurturing than those old turds ever were.

"I'm sorry, Bobbi. I didn't mean to hurt your feelings." She's sorry, but she's not taking it back, either.

"I don't believe that's the real reason," I say, finally.

"What do you think the reason is?" A challenge, like I couldn't possibly know.

"I don't know, Betsy. But we need to talk through it before you do something destructive."

"Moving in with my parents is destructive?" She's snippy, but I don't think it's because I've insulted her parents.

"You know it is. You trade your career for being a full-time fifties sitcom daughter and Robbie starts grooming for the life of a Stepford Wife." I let her hear a little edge in my voice, too.

"Move in here, Betsy. It's not forever. Only until you get your feet on the ground again."

We bat this ball around for another ten minutes. In the end, she agrees to think about it. I hang up thinking there's something else going on that she won't talk about.

As I tend to my evening chores, I reflect on the reality of my own mortgage and business situation. A good definition of "awful" would be both of us losing our houses and our jobs at the same time.

Not the kind of thought you want to take to bed with you, but this has been a long, dreary day and I can't muster the energy to do anything but tumble into bed and hope for a long, dreamless sleep.

* * *

WEDNESDAY, SEPTEMBER 24

Wilkins views the pathetic wreck in front of him, trying to hide his contempt, trying to appear sympathetic.

In his day, the man was a cruel, merciless brute. His sheet told the story of a man who made his living assaulting people and got his jollies off the same way. He had worked off and on as a laborer, but he also hired out as muscle. Strictly small-time, strictly freelance. Debt collecting, intimidation. Arrests for assault, most charges dropped. Did time for a weapons violation once, and serious time after a series of sexual assaults on both men and women.

His last arrest looked like he would be put away for a long, long time. He had raped a male prostitute and beat him to within an inch of his life. There was a witness. There was physical evidence. Then a high-priced criminal lawyer takes his case, the physical evidence disappears, and the witness can't remember things clearly anymore.

Where did the money for the lawyer come from? Wilkins figured that's when Strand entered the picture. A friend who knew how to make evidence disappear and witnesses forget. It must have seemed like a Christmas miracle to Andive, getting saved like that. Until it all went wrong five years ago.

Andive is a shadow of the hulking goon in his arrest photos. His beefy body has run to fat. He has trouble walking, leaning heavily on a cane and limping badly on both feet. His face is slack with sad, deep rings under his eyes. His cheeks fall in fatty folds. He sits heavily at the kitchen table, grunting in pain. Wilkins puts a twelve-pack of beer in the refrigerator and two cartons of cigarettes on the counter, the agreed-upon price of his audience.

He sits opposite Andive, popping a couple of breath mints in his mouth, offering the box to Andive who shakes his head no. Not much chance Andive would even notice his breath, the shape he's in, but no sense taking chances.

Andive's kitchenette apartment is as claustrophobic as a jail cell, white walls, white ceiling, broken white and red tile on the floor. A single room with a bed, a dresser, a television set, a kitchen table with three chairs, a sink half-filled with dirty dishes, a full garbage can scenting the air with the stink of bad food rotting. A place where animals come to await death. And Andive had been an animal in his day. Mean, stupid, no conscience. The kind of man where, after you arrested him, you wanted to go home and take a shower.

Wilkins stays focused on the job at hand.

"Thank you for seeing me, Mr. Andive." Wilkins is in strictly "good-cop" mode for this visit. Andive doesn't have to talk to him if he doesn't want to. It has taken weeks to get this far.

"I want to say again what I told you on the phone, Mr. Andive. I'm investigating the murder of John Strand and not any other crime. I'm looking for background information that you might be able to help me with. I'm not going to record this interview. You are not on record. Nothing you say can be used against you because it's not on record. If you have information that's helpful to my investigation, I may ask you at a later time to state that information for the record. That will be up to you."

Andive's eyes register some degree of comprehension. Wilkins repeats that he is not trying to make a case against Andive for anything. Andive nods.

Wilkins produces a photograph from his folder and puts it in front of Andive. "Do you know this man?" he asks.

Andive stares silently for several long counts, thinking about whether he wants to answer or not.

"I repeat, sir," Wilkins interjects. "This is not about you. I'm not setting a trap. I'm trying to learn some things that will help me solve a murder."

Andive nods. "I did know him. He's dead now. His name is John Strand."

"Thank you, Mr. Andive. Can you tell me how you knew Mr. Strand?"

"He helped me out when I was in a jam once. After that, I'd help him out when he needed things done."

"What kind of things?"

Andive shrugs. "Messages delivered. People watched. That kind of thing."

"What kind of messages did you deliver?"

"Mind-your-own-business messages. He liked his privacy. He didn't like people talking about him."

"What kind of people?"

Andive spreads his thin, tight lips in a malicious smile. "His tranny whores and lady-boys."

"What would they say about him?"

"Nothing after I paid them a visit."

"Why did he need you to see them?" Wilkins flashes a warm smile. "It's okay, this isn't about you."

Andive collects his thoughts. "He was a big shot. He couldn't have people knowing he liked getting it on with trannies. And . . ." His voice tapers off.

"And?" Wilkins coaxes.

"And he liked to get rough with them."

"How rough did he get?"

Andive shrugs. He's not going that far.

Wilkins reaches in his folder again and produces another photo. "Have you ever seen this woman?"

Andive's lips curl back in a silent snarl. He looks up at Wilkins, his eyes suddenly alive with rage. "What are you after?" he asks.

"I'm just trying to find out if this person and Mr. Strand knew each other and if they did, what the nature of their relationship was."

"Relationship." Andive smirks joylessly. He looks around the room, at Wilkins, away, his eyes darting and dodging as he weighs his words. "I've seen her around," he says, finally.

"Did you ever deliver a message to her from Mr. Strand?"

Andive's face breaks into an evil smile. "Might have."

"What was the message?"

"Don't talk about Mr. Strand."

"What was she saying about him?"

Andive shrugs. "Probably that he fucked her in the ass and pushed her around a little, but I don't know for sure."

Wilkins pauses, picking his words carefully so he doesn't scare the man quiet. "Can you share with me what the message was that you delivered?"

Andive's ghoulish smile would have made Wilkins gag if he wasn't so focused on what he needed to get done here. "'Be careful who you piss off.' That was the message."

Like the tumblers falling in a combination lock, Wilkins can hear a click in his mind. In Logan's rape file she claimed one of her assaulters said, "Be careful who you piss off, you fucking freak." He's tempted to ask Andive if he delivered the message with a gang rape, but resists the urge. Andive might say yes, but either way he might very well shut up and stop helping.

"Did she shut up after that?"

"I don't know. Strand had me and someone else following her around, letting him know who she talked to, where she went."

"Were you following her the day you got mugged?" There it was, the question of the month. The year maybe. Wilkins braces himself for an angry response, a demand he get out of the apartment and never come back.

Andive stares at Wilkins, his face angry, but not at Wilkins. At the memory of the beating that ended his life as a predator in a few minutes. "Yeah. I was following her. She knew it, too. It was a setup."

Andive's hatred radiates from his eyes and face.

"Why didn't you identify her to the investigators?"

"Strand wouldn't like it. He'd have had me killed. Plus that was the same place I delivered Strand's message to her. It could have gotten touchy for me, you know?" He smiles smugly. He just told Wilkins he raped Logan, but without saying the words. Sheer genius in his sick world.

Wilkins nods, trying to look sympathetic, trying to hide the revulsion he always felt when he got this far into the mind of a sick bastard like Andive.

"Do you really think Strand would have had you killed?"

Andive nods yes emphatically. "No doubt about it."

"Did you ever know him to have someone killed or to kill someone himself?"

Andive shakes his head. "Ain't going there, Detective."

Wilkins swallows his emotions, puts the photos back in his file, scans his list of questions. "You've been very helpful, Mr. Andive. Just a couple more questions. Do you have any idea who might have killed Strand?"

Andive nods yes. "That fuckin' tranny. No doubt in my mind. She might have had someone else do the dirty work, but it was her."

"What about your partner, the other guy following her?"

"He disappeared after I got mugged. He didn't have issues with Strand. Strand took care of him."

"Do you know the man's name?"

Andive shakes his head, no.

Wilkins thinks for a moment. "One last thing, Mr. Andive, do you know who Strand was seeing, if anyone, around the time of his death?"

"I heard he hooked up with a tranny hooker they called Barbi. I knew who she was. Everyone did. She looked like one of those Barbie Dolls, big tits, blond hair."

"What's her last name?"

"I don't know. Everyone called her Barbi Dancer. She was a stripper and a whore. She hung out at a tranny pickup bar in Boystown. Chicago Sizzle. She might still hang there. If she's still alive."

Wilkins packs his things, wishing he could ask Andive why he raped Logan when he delivered the message. Him and his accomplice. What were they thinking? Was it erotic for them? "How pure is a truth you find in a cesspool like that man's mind?" he asks himself. "Calling him shit is an insult to feces."

* * *

THURSDAY, SEPTEMBER 25

Danni and I make an odd couple sitting at a sidewalk table, sipping wine, watching commuters bustle home from work.

Me, born male, trying to look like a woman, clad in a form-fitting dress that shows off my legs and cleavage, wearing long, curly hair, painted nails, lipstick, and makeup. Danni, born female, dressed in male clothing, with a short, masculine hairstyle, genderless shoes, no makeup, not a hint of female breasts. I am a transsexual woman. She makes her gender choice day by day.

Today, by appearance at least, we are like two trains going in opposite directions.

"I thought the last committee meeting went better," she is saying.

I laugh good-naturedly. "The only way it could have gone worse is if someone got shot."

She smiles. "Really, though. I think the younger ladies are starting to accept you. And we need you on that committee."

We bat that thought around for a while. I'm not convinced that I bring much. "I have experience, but they have ideas."

"Not all their ideas are good ones," Danni says.

"Any idea that results in action is a pretty good idea," I answer. I tell her about the demise of the TransGender Association, the group that ushered me through my transition. TGA is dying under a tide of weak leaders, unable to change the group's traditional venues even in the face of a changing transgender world and steadily declining membership. New ideas are treated like alien conspiracies.

"What about the Top 50?" Danni gets us back on subject.

"If they had kicked it around more they might have come up with something better, but the truth is, the Top 50 is better than sitting around the table sucking eggs."

Danni shoots me a questioning look. "Are you just trying to shake free of the commitment?"

"No, Danni. But I have a lot on my plate right now and I'm trying to narrow things down to my vital interests and things I can significantly affect."

"You can significantly affect this committee and its work, Bobbi."

I don't believe it, but I ask her how I can affect the committee.

"In the first place, you can help keep a dialogue going across the generation gap. You are someone the young professionals can respect. You can carry on a conversation with them as a peer." I arch my eyebrows in doubt.

"Come on, Bobbi. You could have said something really snotty about Lisa's work. I knew it, you knew it, and she knew it. You chose not to. It meant something. You could have had an end-zone dance when that cop left the last meeting with you, but you didn't. You're teaching them who you are without giving them a reason to resent you. That's a lesson in itself, and it's also bringing closer the day when that committee can have an open discussion about things without anyone's ego getting in a bind.

"And the other thing is, you're showing them how to get along with the older generation of transwomen. You're someone they can respect, and when they do, it's easier for them to respect other women who transitioned later in life." Danni is good at this. She's talking about how hard it is for people to get past how we look, but she's not saying anything negative.

She takes a deep breath and locks me in eye contact. "This is important stuff, Bobbi. We're the smallest minority in Chicago. We need to work together. And we need to start getting transgender kids off the street. This is our chance. If we can turn around a dozen, fifteen, sixteen a year, get them through high school, into decent jobs or maybe college, if we can do that, people are going to sit up and take notice. People are going to figure out it's cheaper to save these kids and get them a decent start in life than letting them steal and suck men's dicks until they die of AIDS or get beaten to death."

I know she's right, about the need for unity and the need to start saving some souls. Okay, I tell her. I'll do my best. She extends a hand to mine and gives me a warm squeeze. It feels good. Having her respect is something to value, even if it means more endless meetings with Lisa and her goslings.

12

THE WORLD IS exploding. The earth beneath our feet quakes and rolls like a stormy sea. Nothing is solid. People are losing everything, almost overnight. First the job, then the house, then their self-respect.

It's not just the poor and working classes. In the shop we've heard horror stories of white-collar types who lost everything and are living with relatives, trying to make it on unemployment checks, praying for a job in a market that doesn't have any and probably will never again have any for people over a certain age. Fear of living on the street pervades all income groups.

People aren't jumping out of buildings, but there's a hum of panic just under the surface in our daily lives. You can't believe in anything anymore. Giant corporations have reneged on retirement benefits and laid off everyone over fifty and everyone else they can. Loud voices in Congress want banks and car companies to fail because it will be good for the economy. People who are heavily invested in the stock market have lost half of their net worth in a year; those who went heavy into higher risk stocks have lost even more than that.

A lot of stores have closed. Betsy tells me that even in Northbrook, the epicenter of the *nouveau riche* in Chicago, the strip malls are pockmarked with empty stores. It's like that in my neighborhood, too. We've lost restaurants. Dry cleaners. Novelty stores. Clothing boutiques. Even beauty salons, which once upon a time were supposed to be recession-proof businesses. No more. We became vulnerable to recessions when we started figuring out ways to make decent money doing hair.

Several nearby salons have closed. Their employees have come to us looking for their next jobs. I feel awful for them, and for the owners of the salons. The hairdressers will find work eventually, but it won't be easy. Some will end up in econo-shops, cutting hair factory style. They'll take a hit on earnings while they rebuild their client lists.

It makes for a nasty business all around. The shuttered salons in our area represent an opportunity for L'Elégance to pick up new clients. I feel like a vulture doing it, but we have been circulating our promotional literature intensely in the areas around those shops. Sam even taped our promos to their doors, right under the "Closed" signs.

It's not like anything we do is a silver bullet. We're still limping along. Sam tells me I should be grateful that our volume is steady, that the promotions are working, that we're doing better than most by holding our own as everything around us is melting. I wish I could feel good about that. I just paid my big bills for October and I don't see any hope for November. My savings is completely gone. I have no salary. I have to get through this month on tips and private customers I do at home.

As for November bills, my hair show gig will cover the mortgage on my brownstone, but I need the salon to generate enough profit to cover my business loan payments. The signs aren't positive.

What's unnerving is that even if everything goes well in the salon, I could go under anyway. If my upstairs tenant in the brownstone doesn't pay his rent, I can't make the mortgage payment even with the hair show money. If I have to write a check to a lawyer, I'll default on something. I feel like I'm living a modern version of that *Perils of Pauline* scene where she's tied to the railroad tracks and the train is bearing down on her. But in my contemporary vision, there is no villain. I just woke up on the tracks. And there's no hero to save me. I am going to die and the only thing that will happen after the train passes is someone will complain about what a mess I made.

Cecelia tells me to take out a couple more credit cards so I can gut it out for a few more months if it comes to that. Smart advice, but I hate credit cards. I have two that I got long ago just to establish a credit rating. I only use them for emergencies. I don't like owing anyone money. I won't take out more cards and run up more debt.

My worries somehow seem mild compared to Betsy's, though. She's still in mourning for Don. She feels like she's failing Robbie by working, but she lives in fear of losing her crappy job because it's the only one she can get, and she hates going to work because her boss is such a slime ball.

The stuff with her boss gnaws at me, too. I want to deal with him the way I dealt with one of the men who raped me back when. I shouldn't have feelings like this. I'm a lady now, or at least I'm trying to be one. I deal with my other frustrations like a woman, but if ever someone was just begging for a terrible beating, it is the arrogant slob who puts his hands on Betsy's flesh, pinches her butt, feels her up, and makes dirty innuendos.

To deal with my urges for retribution, I have turned to Thomas, my gay friend who looks like a brute himself, but has devoted his adult life to helping vulnerable people cope with bullies and other forms of human cruelty. We are the only occupants of a quiet chapel in the hospital where Thomas works. He doesn't like what he's hearing from me.

"If you threaten him or rough him up, he's going to make it harder on Betsy, I guarantee it," says Thomas. We haven't talked in ages, other than to say hi to each other at the gym. I really miss his company. I miss seeing the humanity that comes from a man who looks like an ogre at first glance.

"How could it be worse?"

"Guys like that are sneaky cruel. Maybe he starts a whisper campaign about Betsy's sex life, or he starts finding fault with her work, or he sets her up for something."

Thomas is no shrinking violet when it comes to dealing with people like Betsy's boss. He set up the retribution party for my rapist and I'm sure he's unleashed his Superman complex on more than a few of society's other predators. So when he counsels against action, I have to listen.

"What can I do then?"

Thomas shakes his head sadly. "I don't know, Bobbi. From what you say, it sounds like a bad situation with no solution. Even if she gets the boss off her case, does she really want to be there? It sounds like a toxic environment, especially for someone dealing with all the things she's dealing with."

We talk about that for a while. I try to come up with arguments for keeping the job, but they don't hold water. The more we talk the more I know I need to get Betsy out of that hellhole.

We drift on to other topics. Thomas is fully engaged in the battle for marriage equality in Illinois and fills me in on the struggle. They're making progress, but it's inch by inch. There's an irony here—I can marry a man under my new legal name and gender, or I could legally still be married to Betsy, because trans people are different than gay people with this insane set of laws. It just shows what mockery you create when you try to justify bigotry.

I tell Thomas I'm a capitalist now, but close to being a penniless bum. He tells me I should have bought a bank. A little bitter humor. The banks that triggered this crisis are getting bailed out by their victims while hundreds of thousands of small businesses are going belly up and millions of workers are losing their jobs.

Our conversation languishes for a moment. I fill the silence.

"Remember that cop who wanted to blame me for the Strand murder?"

Thomas nods.

"Well, he's back. He has reopened the case and I'm suspect number one. He thinks I'm a man-hating serial killer."

"Seriously?" he says.

I nod. "His name is Wilkins. He thinks I had something to do with that guy getting mugged in the alley and he thinks that's related to the Strand murder."

Thomas flinches a little. He didn't do the mugging but he used intermediaries to hire the goon who did the dirty work. He didn't like the idea of doing it in the same alley where I was raped, but it was vital to my self-esteem. It was a message—to myself and the people trying to intimidate me—that I was not going to play the helpless victim.

I asked one other favor of Thomas after the mugging. I asked him to use his resources to get me a tranquilizer that could take down a man in seconds. I didn't tell him who it was for, and he never asked me for details. He just got the tranquilizer and gave it to me in a syringe with the right dosage. We kept our distance after that. I didn't want him implicated if the police somehow tracked me down.

As Thomas and I speak in hushed tones in the silent chapel, I can't help wondering if he was the one who finished off John Strand. He sometimes followed me home from work in those days to protect me from Strand's goons. He could have followed me that night . . . I shake off the thought. I don't want to know.

"I want to forewarn you about Wilkins, just in case he gets to you," I say. "He'll never hear your name from my lips, but he's shrewd and he might show up on your doorstep someday. Just remember this— he bluffs a lot. He'll try to make it sound like he's got rock-solid proof you did something and the only way to save yourself is to confess. Don't fall for it. He doesn't have anything and he won't have anything and even if he did, you don't talk to him until you have an attorney to advise you. Okay?"

Thomas looks worried as he nods his head in the affirmative. Is he worried for me or for himself? My curiosity is raging. I want more than anything to ask him right now, right here, where he was that night. But I don't. Nothing good can come of knowing one of my friends killed Strand.

* * *

FRIDAY, SEPTEMBER 26

Betsy sips her third glass of wine. Robbie is sound asleep. We've waded through the awful memories of her week at work. Today her boss felt her up again and laughed when she cursed at him and said she was going to complain to HR. He told her to go ahead. They both knew it was fruitless. She is mad enough to kill and hurt enough to crawl into a hole and cry.

When she's out of things to say, I deliver the line I've been working on since I first raised the subject of her moving in with me. "Betsy, it's time for you to quit that sick job and move in here. On Monday. Quit in the morning, move in here in the afternoon. Spend a week just enjoying Robbie. Look for a preschool, go to a museum, walk along the lakefront. After that, settle up with your creditors as best you can and start looking for something you want to do. You don't have to work full-time. You don't have to make money. I can support us all just fine. You need time to recover and get yourself together. Your parents can't give you that. No one but me can give you that and I want to."

I'm aware that my financial situation is a lot more precarious than I let on, but transsexuals learn to not let grim circumstances intimidate them. I will make it because I must.

"That's nice of you, Bobbi, but I can't move in with you." She still says it like it's a silly idea.

"Excuse me, but why can't you?" I'm huffy.

She doesn't answer with words. She makes a face, like it's too obvious to say out loud. Now I'm angry.

"You're worried the neighbors will think you're a sick, tranny-loving lesbian and Robbie's schoolmates will tease her for having a transsexual family member. Come on, Betsy, say it."

"Yes." Her voice catches. Her face is grim. As hurt as I am, I can see the pain she's feeling. She feels like she's betraying me, adding another layer of stink to the manure-rich garden of my life. I shove my anger aside. I'll deal with it later.

"I know most of my neighbors and they know me," I say to Betsy in a measured voice. "They won't give two thoughts to our relationship unless someone wants to ask you out, in which case, they'll ask you. The ones I don't know I never see and you won't either, so why worry about them? Robbie's friends won't be into cruelty for several more years and by then you'll be back on your own.

"I'm not proposing marriage, Betsy. I'm asking to help when you need it. No strings. When you're ready to go, go."

We wrestle verbally for another half hour.

I break a moment of silence between us with a question that's been nagging at the back of my mind since we started talking. "Why is this coming up now, Betsy? Your aversion to who I am? Being seen with me? Having people know you love me? You've been there for me every step of the way, watching over me after my surgery, including me in your family life . . ." I go on listing the countless ways she has shown her love and affection for me.

"I've been thinking about that, too," she says, when I finally stop. "Before, it was me being the big sister. I was showing you the way, supporting you. It was all about me being a good person. But if I move in with you, you're the big sister. I'm the weak one, leaning on you. It's just so pathetic, you know? I'm so hopeless I have to go crawling back to my ex-husband who isn't even a man anymore. It just says so much about me, what a failure I am."

God, that hurts. She's not saying it to be cruel, that's why it hurts. She's speaking a truth that we both recognize: she and I can see me as the woman I am to the very depths of my soul, but others will see me as a dickless man, and see anyone who loves me as some kind of pervert. On a more positive note, we're finally getting to her real issues. She wants me to address them. Her resistance is weakening. She won't say yes, but she's close. I can feel it.

"Thank you for your honesty," I say. "I'm not crushed. I'm not angry. These are things we can always talk about, Betsy. We can talk about anything. We love each other. We must. Look how far we've come." Indeed, even as I say it, a sequence of images flashes through my mind, scenes from our life as a traditional male-female couple, scenes from my transition, scenes from the moments we've shared since Robbie was born. Betsy is having the same thoughts, her face a study in contemplation, her large brown eyes soft and misty.

"It's not about you or me, Betsy. It's about people being there for each other. You would do this for me and I would accept. You have been there for me; now it's my turn."

She nods ever so slightly, deep in thought.

"Good things will happen if you move in now," I say. "You'll get a great start to your new life because you'll have time to build a good foundation for it. And I'll get to feel a little better about my worth because I got to do something for people I love."

Betsy wraps her arms around me and hugs tight, our ears pressed together. I hug back. "I'll think about it," she says when we break. I dab at my eyes so I don't spoil everything with tears. Betsy's eyes are dry, but soft and loving. We have crossed some kind of threshold.

* * *

When Betsy awakens and sleepwalks into the bathroom, Robbie and I are just finishing a skillet full of bacon. Robbie calls her mother to breakfast, excited to be springing such a monumental surprise on her.

By the time Betsy has finished her morning bathroom ritual, the eggs and toast are done. We seat her at the table and serve her as if she were royalty.

"Is this going to be an everyday thing?" she asks.

"Does that mean you're staying?" Cecelia has taught me that you can cut through a lot of crap by answering a question with a question.

"Do you still want us?"

"With all my heart."

She's wearing a happy smile and her brown eyes have a light humor to them that I haven't seen since Don died. She's relieved. But I can read other feelings, too. Affection for me. Traces of anxiety. She still has mountains to climb in her life. And maybe that sort of stunned feeling people get when they find themselves in a moment they could never imagine would happen until it did. I'm feeling that one, too. Who imagines that one day they will be roommates with their ex-spouse?

13

WILKINS SIGHS. FOR every breakthrough in this investigation there have been endless days and nights of frustration. This night is looking like another disappointment.

The owner of Chicago Sizzle knows nothing. He's never seen Strand or Logan or the person in the doctored photo of the male Logan. So, of course, he knows nothing about Strand's girlfriend. Wilkins is sure he's lying about some of it. Logan had to come in this place once in a while. It's the hottest transgender bar in Chicago. He probably knew Strand, too. The man had an appetite for transsexuals and this was the place to find them. But Wilkins has no leverage on the guy, no way to make him talk. So he moves on.

He shows the photos to the bartender, trying not to notice two guys at the end of the bar kissing each other. The bartender is no help. He wasn't here five years ago and he's never seen any of these people. Wilkins sighs and puts the photos away.

"What about a tranny named Barbi? Barbi Dancer?"

"You don't want to be calling these ladies *trannies*," says the bartender. His face is serious. He's chastising Wilkins in a polite way.

"Oh?" Wilkins can't think of what else to say. What else would you call a man who becomes a woman?

"For them, being called a tranny is like you being called a nigger or me a fag. They prefer *transwoman*. Actually, they prefer *woman*."

Wilkins nods his head and thanks the bartender for the advice.

"The guy you need to talk to is Kong," says the bartender. "He's been a bouncer here for years. Works the party nights. Knows everyone, especially the transwomen."

"Does he play in that field?"

"No. He's strictly a man's man, if you know what I mean. But he likes the girls and kind of looks over them. A lot of the trouble he deals with is someone trying to cop a feel or saying something crude."

"And his name is Kong?"

"That's what everyone calls him. Like King Kong, you know? He's huge. Six-five, maybe two-eighty. When he tells someone it's time to go, they go."

"What's his real name?" Wilkins pulls out his pen and notepad.

"Don't know. But he'll be here tonight, and you won't have any trouble finding him."

Wilkins thanks the man. He walks a few blocks to Wrigleyville and finds a coffee shop where he can have a cheap dinner and wait without being surrounded by gay men kissing each other. They're okay to talk to, but he can't overcome the revulsion he feels when he sees gays holding hands or kissing, and in the bars at night he has to avoid looking at the videos playing on the TV screens showing nearly naked men bumping and grinding with each other.

At eight, he's back at Chicago Sizzle. The place is still almost empty, but Kong would have been easy to spot even if it were wall to wall. He looms like a giant spirit in the dim light of the club, a small head atop huge shoulders, towering over everyone else, his face ugly enough to be an ape's. He's engaged in tough-guy banter with one of the service staff, smiling and throwing out his chest, flexing and stretching his huge arms the way tough guys do when they're being nice to someone they could squash.

"Excuse me, sir, are you Kong?" Wilkins asks.

The man turns and evaluates him deliberately, head to toe. "Who wants to know?"

"I'm Detective Allan Wilkins with the Chicago PD." Wilkins shows the man his badge. "I'm looking for information about some people who might have been guests of this establishment five years ago. Your colleagues said you know everyone and might be able to help me."

Kong rolls on the balls of his feet like a big shot, his ego fully stroked. "What's it about? I don't want to get anyone in trouble."

"Nah, nothing like that," says Wilkins. "I'm investigating a murder from a long time ago. I'm trying to find a lady who might have known the victim, see if she can tell me something about him that might help get me going in the right direction. She's not a suspect."

Kong nods. "Okay."

They sit on two stools next to a small round table. Wilkins pops a couple of breath mints and pulls out his photos. "Ever see this gentleman?" He shows Kong the photo of Strand.

Kong rubs his chin. "He looks kind of familiar, but I'm not sure."

"His name was John Strand. He was the victim. He was seeing a transsexual woman around the time he was murdered. I've been told she hung out here."

"Her and every other trans-hustler on the north side," says Kong, smiling.

"Her name was Barbi. I'm told some people called her Barbi Dancer. White girl, blond hair, looked like the doll. Large breasts."

Kong smiles his wise man smile, like he just split an atom. "Oh sure, Barbi Dancer. Yeah. She used to be in here a lot. I haven't seen her in a while though. She might be working for one of the call-girl services. Her stock went way up when she got her boob job. I don't know if she got the rest or not, but if she did, she doesn't have to do fifty-dollar blow jobs anymore."

"Was that where she was five years ago?" Wilkins asks. "Backseat blow jobs?"

"Actually, I think she had a steady gig back then. That's when she got the boobs."

"Do you know her real name?"

Kong shakes his head.

"Any idea how I can find her?"

"Sure, ask the girls when they come in. They all know each other. If they know you're not going to bust her, they might help you out."

Wilkins thanks the man, puts the Strand photo back, starts to leave, then stops. "Just for kicks, do you know either of these people?" He shows Kong the photos of Logan as a woman and as a man.

"She looks a little familiar," he says, pointing at the female Logan. "Not a regular, but maybe someone who drops in now and then. He looks . . . I think I've seen him somewhere, too, but I can't place when or where."

"What seems familiar to you?" Wilkins asks.

"Well, good looking, nice body, athletic, but with that ass. It's almost girly. That's very rare. He'd turn some heads in my neighborhood."

Wilkins processes this information in two different compartments of his mind. One is registering the possibility that Logan was in this place in male disguise sometime around the murder. The other compartment is astonished at the attraction gay men have for other men's asses.

The first two transwomen he talks to are an education. They are wary, but after he sets their minds at ease that he isn't there to bust anyone, after they can see he respects them okay, they talk to him. They are a lot like regular women. Their voices aren't quite right, and if you look hard enough, you can see how they were male to begin with, but they are real people, and they care about helping out. They weren't around here five years ago and don't know anything about

Strand or the others. He thanks them and gives each of them one of his cards in case they hear something that might help. They continue chatting lightly, the girls waiting for a pickup, Wilkins for another transwoman to come in. The girls talk about their families, living on the street. Their dreams. One is trying to finish high school. The other wants to be a court reporter. It is hard to balance that with night work, she says. Wilkins is having his own balancing issues. He is enjoying the chat. He likes them. They are decent people just trying to survive. He wishes he could help them.

When girl number three walks in, they introduce him to her.

Rosa is her name. She's thirtyish, blond, tall, slim. Her face is pretty and feminine. Her breasts bulge from the top of her blouse like water balloons ready to burst. Wilkins' eyes dart to her chest several times, even though he tries hard not to look. When his eyes finally settle on her face, she is staring at him.

"I'm sorry," says Wilkins. "I meant no disrespect."

Rosa's face is still hard.

Wilkins shows his shield, explains what he's after, apologizes again for his ungentlemanly lapse, promises it won't happen again.

Rosa smiles, laughs lightly. "Don't worry about it," she says. "For a minute there I thought you were shaking me down for a freebee."

Wilkins shoves a couple breath mints in his mouth, offers the pack to her, she takes one, they sit down. He shows her the photo of Strand.

Rosa's eyes get a little rounder. She stares at the photo intently, looks up. "I know who this is. This is John Strand. He got himself murdered a while ago." She looks away, thinking, calculating. "Five years ago, I think."

"That's correct," Wilkins says. "How did you know him?"

"I didn't actually know him. I knew of him. He had a reputation in our little sorority. He was rich and he bought nice things for girls.

But he was rough trade. He liked to beat the shit out of a girl every now and then."

"Did you ever date him?" Wilkins asks.

"Date? Mr. Detective, you are the most polite cop I've ever met. What a nice way to put it. Thank you. But no, I never serviced Mr. Strand. He wouldn't have wanted me then anyway. I was too ugly for a big spender like him. A lot has happened since then." She gestures to her breasts and her face. "But even if he had, I wouldn't have gone with him. He was certified dangerous."

Wilkins draws her out. Her information is second or third hand, but graphic. Girls he beat bloody. Rumors he beat some to death. Bruises and black eyes on the girl Rosa said was once his main squeeze.

"He paid for her breast augmentation," she says. "And she thought he was going to pay for her GRS. He might have, I don't know, but even if he did, it wasn't worth it. He treated her so bad. He beat her, called her terrible things. And the way he made her feel about herself—like she was a freak and her only chance at being someone was getting that surgery and being his whore. Sick bastard."

Wilkins lets the silence hang for a few counts, looking at Rosa, deep in thought. "Was that girl's name Barbi?" he asks.

Rosa nods. Her face is solemn, sad.

"I'd like to speak to her, Rosa." He says it gently, as he would to his daughter. "She may be the last person who saw Strand alive. Other than the murderer. Can you help me get in touch with her?"

She looks at him for a long time. "I'll see if she'll talk to you. Where can I call you?"

Wilkins pulls out a business card. Under the department phone number he handwrites his cell number and hands it to her. "I'm out a lot, so go ahead and use the cell number anytime."

"Anytime? Detective, you're talking to a hooker."

"Anytime." He gives a sharp nod of his head to add emphasis.

As they stand up to leave, he scans the room for the other two women he spoke with. The club is filling up, and he can't see them. He leans closer to Rosa and says, "I don't see the other two girls I talked to, but I'm going to say this to you and ask you to pass it on to them. You all three have my card. I can't break the law for you, but if there's a time I can help any of you, call me. I'll do what I can."

Rosa stares at him. After a beat or two she leans forward and kisses him on the cheek. As she finishes she brings her fingers to the spot she kissed and touches his skin. Her touch is surprisingly soft, as if her fingertips were made of silk, as if she were petting a butterfly. Wilkins feels the need to say something but can't find the words. And then she's gone. He tries to understand what he wanted to say as he makes his way back to the stark confines of his empty apartment.

* * *

WEDNESDAY, OCTOBER 8

In the strange world of transsexual women, I feel like a fraud. In the opinions of the transgender thought leaders, we are supposed to be more like genetic women than genetic women. I don't pass the eye test, I have no feminine wiles whatsoever, and my personality is a strange blend of the man I was and the woman I want to be.

One of the awkward manifestations of my gender blending is how I respond to sexual attraction. I'm kind of feminine in that I don't have urges to engage in sex with someone I just met who looks nice. But when I have the hots for someone, I think my urge to act out is less inhibited than a genetic woman's would be.

Which is why I'm really glad I no longer have a male appendage. I'm cutting Officer Phil's hair in my home salon, and hard as I try to keep it strictly professional, inside I'm aroused. If I still had a penis it would probably be erect right now, and poor Phil would be horrified, never to entrust his person to my touch again.

He called for an appointment just as I was finishing my last client for the day. It was an emergency, he said, a big press conference tomorrow and his captain saying he looked like a hippy with the long hair and all. I told him I could do him at my home salon and spent the next several hours entertaining breathless fantasies about this service ending up in my bedroom.

Unfortunately, all that's on Phil's mind is a haircut and more brotherly advice for me to keep out of Detective Wilkins' way.

"It would be a good idea for you to have a lawyer on retainer, or at least familiar with what's going on," he says. "It's worth worrying about."

"Does Wilkins have photos of me gutting Strand?" I'm being sarcastic. Strand died of a slit throat, not a sliced gut. It was in all the papers.

Phil grimaces as I glance at his face in the mirror. "Very funny, Bobbi. What's not funny is, he's stacking up a lot of circumstantial evidence."

"What? That I hate men? That I thought Strand killed Mandy?" I'm acting flippant, but inside my stomach is churning. I know Phil means well, but I really don't need any more anxiety in my life right now.

"More than that, Bobbi. He says the guy who got mugged in the alley was following you when it happened, and Strand was the one who hired him to follow you. He says you had him beaten because he was one of the guys who raped you. He says the guy will testify."

My mind seizes in shock. I never thought that goon would incriminate himself just to get revenge on me. I stop cutting and stare into the distance. I can't fake nonchalance anymore. It's deathly quiet in the room. I can't think of anything to say and neither can Phil.

Actually, I can't even think about talking. All I can see is that train bearing down on me.

My brain thaws finally. "How does that man know it was me? I have no idea who that person is."

"He told Wilkins that Strand hired him to follow you. So he would have known who you were. And a jury would probably buy that, Bobbi. You're distinctive-looking."

"Yeah. Ugly chick. With a dick, back then, anyway."

"Stop that, Bobbi. That's not true and that's not what I meant. You're tall. You have red hair. Very red back then. And you're well endowed."

For a fleeting moment my mind skips away from fear and dread to savor his compliments. *Well endowed!*

"So you're buying that crap? The tranny did it?"

Phil winces. "I'm not buying anything. I know you didn't do it and I told Wilkins you didn't, you couldn't. I'm just telling you how Wilkins sees the case. And please stop with the 'tranny' references. It's an ugly word."

"Why is he telling you all this? Are you going to lose your badge for telling me? Are you violating some kind of secrecy in the investigation?"

Phil shakes his head. "No, Wilkins told me to tell you, told me there's nothing you can do about it anyway."

I try to finish the cut, but the tears come. Just a couple at first, then a stream. I stop, dab my eyes. The tissue comes away smudged with makeup.

Phil stands, puts his arms around me, hugs gently. "I'm sorry, Bobbi."

"You know," I say, when I can speak, "I work so hard. At hair. At life. At keeping people employed. I work to just get people to treat me like a human being. This isn't fair. It's just not fair. He's going to destroy me just because I'm transsexual."

As I sob, Phil strokes my back and continues to hug me. I can feel the warmth of his chest on my breasts, his flat stomach nestling against mine as our bodies meet.

"It's okay, Bobbi," he says. "Just have a lawyer ready and don't do anything stupid. He doesn't have anything a good lawyer couldn't neutralize."

"He doesn't have to convict me to destroy my life, Phil. If I have to spend money on attorney's fees right now, I could go under."

"Your salon?"

"My salon. My home. Everything I own. I'm right on the edge."

Phil's arms tighten around me. "Oh, Bobbi," he says. "I'm sorry."

I hug him tight. I can feel my arms tremble. I've buried my face in the nook between his shoulder and his chin. When we finally relax our grips on each other, I see eye shadow and mascara smeared on his neck. I dab at it with my tissue. The makeup comes off, leaving slightly reddened skin where I rubbed. Reflexively, I kiss the sore spot, as I would with Robbie.

Phil looks at me through sad eyes. I start to wipe my eyes with the tissue, but Phil brushes my hand away and kisses me on the lips, softly at first, then firm and warm, his arms squeezing me to him. Me squeezing back. Me rubbing my body against his, any sense of reserve or decorum forgotten in the moment.

And just like that, he breaks it off. He takes a step back, blushing. "I'm sorry, Bobbi. I don't know what came over me," he says. "I was inappropriate. I apologize."

A torrent of words and thoughts cascade through my mind, so fast and so mixed I cannot give voice to any of them.

"The only bad part was the end," I say finally.

"I'm not good with words—" He starts to say it, but I cut him off.

"I don't mean the words, Phil. I mean the kiss. We're adults here, right? We both know what I mean. I'm this close to begging you to seduce me." I show a small gap between two fingers.

He blushes beet-red. "Bobbi. That would be wrong."

"Wrong? Like fucking a tranny is against your religion?"

"No. Wrong because . . . because . . ." He stumbles for a moment. "Because I don't know if I'm sincere."

"You're going to have to explain that, Phil, because you felt pretty sincere to me."

He self-consciously arranges his male member so it isn't bulging so noticeably. "That's not what I mean." He struggles, looking down at the ground. "Actually, it is what I mean. Bobbi, you turn me on . . ." His voice trails off.

"Why is that a bad thing?" Says the girl who mostly provokes disgust in men. What kind of life is this, anyway?

"It's . . . I'm not sure why . . . I don't want to hurt you, Bobbi. I think the world of you."

It dawns on me finally. "You think maybe you just want to fuck me because I'm trans? See what it's like?"

Phil nods. His face is filled with shame. He glances at me and glances away. "I can't do that, Bobbi. Not to anyone, but especially not to you."

I take a deep breath and exhale. "Why on earth are you a cop, Phil? You should have been a priest or a rabbi. Or maybe an angel." I gesture for him to sit again so I can finish his haircut before I have a heart attack or begin compulsively masturbating.

"I don't want you to hate me, Bobbi." He glances up and we link eyes in the mirror. He looks like a puppy who just peed on the carpet.

"I could never hate you, Phil. You're the most decent guy I know. And just so you know, if we did it and afterwards you felt like you never wanted to do it with me again, it would be a lot like right now except I would have had a great orgasm to show for it."

If he blushed any redder, his capillaries would pop.

After he leaves, I prepare for a nice bath. I am experiencing a wide range of emotions. Unfulfilled, certainly. And wondering if it will ever happen for me, romantic love. And I'm feeling kind of pathetic. I was kidding with Phil, but I wasn't. I'd have been glad to be his tranny fuck tonight just to be the object of his desires for a moment in time.

Before I step into the bath I dig out a CD to put in the stereo. It's a digitized recording of an old Kingston Trio album a customer got me. I click forward to a song I'd been humming in my mind since Phil left. About a spinster woman so romantically hopeless her brother prays someone will take her out of pity.

14

Barbi Dancer answers the door to her apartment wearing a G-string and a tiny top that just covers the nipples of her breasts. Behind her, loud music plays on the sound system. Stripper music. Wilkins stares at her body for a moment after she opens the door. She is not at all put out. She arches her back a little to add to her pose.

"Come in, Detective," she says. She walks into the living room, her butt swaying provocatively. "Sorry about the costume." The tone of her voice says she's not sorry at all. She turns off the music. "I'm practicing a new number," she explains. She throws on a robe and sits down in a chair, gesturing for Wilkins to sit opposite her on the couch. The apartment is the second floor of a spacious brownstone in Andersonville. The living room has high ceilings, clusters of photos on the wall, many showing Barbi in various states of undress. The furniture is modern, new, in good condition. The colors are black and white, stark and modern.

Wilkins tries not to stare. She looks like she could have been the model for the original Barbie Doll. He's amazed at how perfect she is. He would never make her for a transwoman. Her voice is perfect, her feet and hands are feminine, her hair is Barbie-blond, and her eyes Barbie-blue. She has a tiny waist and a Barbie-perfect butt. She's maybe five-nine, five-ten.

"Thank you for seeing me," he says, popping a couple of breath mints in his mouth. He offers her the package. She declines.

"Rosa said you were a good guy, so I'm counting on that," she replies.

Wilkins goes through his standard introduction, then shows her the first photo. "Do you know this man?" he asks.

She looks at the photo of Strand the way a society matron would look at a dead rat on her living room rug.

"John Strand," she says. "I knew him. He's dead. His name is John Strand. Someone killed him five years ago."

Wilkins nods. "Thank you. That was just a formality. I understand you were seeing him? Socially?"

"I was his bitch." She looks away from Wilkins.

"Can you explain what you mean?" Wilkins says it gently.

"When he wanted to get laid, he came to me. When he wanted to get his friends laid, he came to me. When he needed to get his cock sucked, he came to me. When he needed to beat the shit out of someone, he came to me."

"Why did you see him?"

She looks at him, her hard-boiled veneer giving way to vulnerability for a beat or two. She shrugs. "He could be real nice. He was handsome and sometimes he made me feel like a woman. Flowers. Sexy nighties. You could say we were using each other. He paid off the bill for some facial surgery, and he paid for my breast augmentation. He promised he'd pay for my GRS."

Wilkins cocks his head quizzically. "GRS?"

"Gender reassignment surgery."

"How long had you been seeing him?"

"Oh, maybe six, eight months."

"What can you tell me about him?"

"That you don't already know? Well, mainly, he couldn't get it up with natal women. He tried. They were attracted to him, and he would try to make it with them but he couldn't stay hard. It made him crazy. He could only make it with transwomen. Pre-ops. I think he lost interest once a girl had GRS. I don't know that for a fact, but I do know he liked to do a girl in the ass. I always wondered about that, you know?"

"You said he beat you? What would make him do that?"

She shrugs, shakes her head, purses her lips as if reliving a bad moment. Wilkins registers surprise that such a hard-shelled person would show emotion, not that she wanted to. She fought it. "Anything," she says. "Nothing." She shakes her head again. "He liked to talk dirty in sex and sometimes he wanted me to talk dirty, too. But if I started talking dirty when he wasn't in the mood, he'd go crazy. Sometimes after sex he'd just lose it, like I made him sick. Whatever set him off, when he went off, it was like I was some kind of disease. He'd hit me in the face, in the stomach. Squeeze my nipples until I cried. Sometimes he kicked me. He'd kick anywhere, but especially in the crotch. Very personal. I had a penis then and a scrotum. Not much left, but enough so it hurt. I'd fall on the floor, and he'd kick me some more."

"How often did that happen?" Wilkins asks.

"Too often." She looks at him. "You're wondering why I put up with that. Because I'm an idiot. Because he'd always be really nice after that. He'd say he was sorry and he was working on his anger issues. And he'd give me nice things. The breast augmentation, the clothes. Money. I was a whore, Detective. I still am. I strip onstage, but I make my real money doing private gigs. I'm the girl who jumps out of the cake at a bachelor party and sucks a half dozen cocks. I'd rather be a brain surgeon, but you know higher education doesn't really recruit T-girls and the only way to get enough money for college is to do what I'm doing, so really, Detective, what's the point?"

Wilkins clears his throat. "I'm sorry," he says.

After a long silence, Wilkins speaks again, softly. "Were you with him on the night of April 27, five years ago?"

"The night he was killed?" She asks it rhetorically. "Yes. But I didn't kill him."

"I know that," he says quietly. "Could you just tell me about that last night? It might help me find out who did kill him."

"The person who killed him made the world a better place."

"Do you have any idea who might have wanted to kill him?"

"No."

"What about that last night. What happened?"

"He called that afternoon. Wanted to meet that night. I said okay, I was going to a club with some girlfriends, should I cancel? He said no, he'd be running late, that he'd call when he got there. We did this a lot, meeting like this. He didn't want to be seen with me, so he'd park nearby and call me, and I'd come running.

"So he calls me around twelve, and I come right away. He didn't like to be kept waiting, especially by a whore. I get to his car and the window is down so I say something to him, something like 'how about a fuck, sailor,' just being funny, you know? And when I get in the car he bashes me. Really hard. And he keeps hitting me." Her lips form a thin, tight line, her face clouds in anger and shame. She stops for a moment.

"He scared me. That night, I thought he was going to kill me. People said he killed girls before. So I grab the door handle and try to run. He tries to yank me back into the car, but I pull away and go sprawling on the grass. My nose is broken. I'm bleeding, I have a black eye. I'm thinking he's going to kill me now, right here, or maybe take me to his place and spend the night punching and kicking me. I scramble to my feet and try to run. I thought he'd catch me any second. I was in total panic. But I got away clean. I couldn't believe it. I looked back when I got to Halsted, and he was in his car, driving away."

"What else did you see?" Wilkins asks.

"Nothing, really. It was dark. The car was a half block away and moving in the other direction."

"Could you tell how many people were in the car?"

"No," she says.

"How many were in the car when you first got in?"

"Just John. I think. I didn't really look in the back seat, but I would have noticed if someone was back there."

Wilkins makes some notes in his book, then takes out another photo. "Do you recognize this person?" It's the photo of Logan as a man.

She stares at it for a moment. "Not someone I know, no. Cute guy, except he might be a girl."

Wilkins asks her to explain why she thinks that. She reads the facial hair as fake, the head hair as a wig, the butt kind of feminine for a male. Wilkins nods, impressed.

"How about this person?" He produces the photo of Logan as a woman.

"I don't know her, but I know who she is. Her name is Bobbi something. She's a big-time hair stylist and she's active in one of those transgender groups for older people."

"What do you know about her?"

"She's supposed to be nice. She does things for trans people. Contributes money to TransRising. Things like that."

"Was she ever involved with Strand?"

"Strand never mentioned her."

"No rumors?"

"Come on, Detective. We gossip about everything. Of course there are rumors."

"Like what?"

"Like she was the one who did Strand. But don't take it seriously.

There's a rumor that I fuck horses and sell the pictures and another one that the mayor has a boyfriend."

Wilkins reviews his notes. "Anything else you can tell me about that night? Did you see anyone else on the street? Someone walking? A car going by?"

She starts to shake her head, no, then stops, looks up at the ceiling, closes her eyes. "When I was running up to Halsted, a car pulled away from the curb just as I ran past. It scared the shit out of me."

"What do you remember about the car and the driver?"

"I never saw the driver, but I think the car was one of those expensive sedans. I think it was a BMW, but I had other things on my mind. It was black."

Wilkins studies her, surprised a girl under such duress would notice a car.

She fills the silence with her own thoughts, far from his. "BMW was my dream car back when I was a miserable queer everybody hated," she says. "I used to dream that I'd wake up a woman and meet the perfect man. We'd get married, and he'd buy me a BMW and treat me like Cinderella for the rest of my life, and I'd feel like Cinderella every time I drove that car somewhere. Stupid, huh? Bet you didn't expect to hear that from a whore."

Wilkins doesn't know what to say. Her sweet dream had descended into a bleak reality, even with the nice apartment. He thought of Candice, the ex-hooker he interviewed what, six weeks ago? A lifetime? Twenty-one and just finishing high school. HIV positive. Trying to make a life on ten dollars an hour, trying to break into the corporate world. Trying to get past a family that threw her out, an adolescence spent sucking men's dicks and sleeping in wretched places.

Barbi's life had more glitz, but just below the shine was the same grim truth.

"You'd look good in that BMW, Miss Dancer," he says, "but you need to get out of the sex trade. It's tearing you down."

"I can't make this kind of money waiting on tables," she says, gesturing toward her sumptuous apartment.

"You're smart. You can think of something." Wilkins stands as he says it.

Barbi is motionless for a moment, staring at him, a stunned look on her face.

Wilkins gives her his business card at the door. "Call me if I can help you sometime. I owe you one," he says.

Barbi puts a hand on his arm. "You don't look like it, but you're a good guy." She hugs him. "Thank you, Detective."

"For what?"

"You treat people with respect. It means a lot." Her eyes are misty. Words don't come to Wilkins so he nods to her as he leaves.

As he walks to his car, he gets back in cop mode. Black sedans keep coming up in this case. Logan didn't own a car, but what about her friends? His mind skips to the rich loudmouth transwoman . . . he pictures her in his mind, tall, blond, arrogant. Swenson. Her name was Swenson. She drives a black Caddie now. He'd see what she had back then. What if she and Logan did Strand together? They're friends. It could happen. Wouldn't that be something?

* * *

FRIDAY, OCTOBER 17

I flinch when I hear the quiet tap on the door. I'm in the bathroom, removing makeup and cleansing and moisturizing my face after a long day at work. I'm also naked, taking inventory of my body as I tend to my nightly ritual.

Before I can promise to hurry, Betsy enters. "Mind if I pee?" she asks, big smile on her face. She doesn't wait for permission. She pulls up her nightgown and plops on the toilet. A tinkling sound follows.

She looks up at me. I am still blushing and self-consciously trying to cover my bare breasts and womanhood.

She grins at me. It's her wise, big sister look, which has been missing for a long time. "Relax, Bobbi. Sisters do this."

The truth of what she says washes over me like an awakening. The sex fantasies that dominated my young male mind have given way to a rich variety of fantasies as a middle-age transgender woman. One of the most prolific genres is all the girl things I missed growing up male. Pajama parties, doing each others' hair, talking about boys, and having friends you could touch in an intimate but nonsexual way. The burgeoning subset of that genre has been fantasies of sisterhood with Betsy, of moments just like this, intimate, humorous, trusting. A warm sensation surges through my body and I smile at her.

"I just thought we need to lighten up a little," she says. The impish grin remains.

"Good idea," I say, my mouth dry. I slowly let my arms and hands fall to my side, exposing my bare body, as nervous as a young virgin. This wasn't in my fantasies. I was always clothed in my fantasies, nothing more risqué than a bra and panties. Try as I might, I remain self-conscious about my body and my femininity with Betsy since we became roommates. I keep my body covered whenever I'm in our shared space and I try not to leave my lingerie around for fear it will offend her in some way. This is completely irrational, but it's where I'm at.

"My goodness, Bobbi, your boobs are bigger than mine!" she exclaims. She is assessing me as I stand at the sink, blushing. I want badly to put on my nightgown or at least wrap myself in a towel. "And they're so perky." She's still talking about my breasts.

"You're a very sexy lady," she says. "But you didn't need me to tell you that."

I struggle to find something appropriate to say. "No one else is going to say it," I tell her. "Plus, when you say it, I can hear bands playing." I'm trying to be humorous. It's what I do when I can't be brave.

"Are you making fun of me?" Her smile widens. She knows I'm not. Her gaze falls to my pelvis. Her body language radiates curiosity. Straight people are obsessed with transsexual plumbing, even women. She wants to inspect it but is too much a lady to say so. I understand her curiosity. I understand that it's not sexual. I understand it is not because she is reviled. She's just curious.

"Why don't you take a look," I offer as I step toward her.

She blushes and sits back, protesting, apologizing.

"It's okay, Betsy. Sisters do this. If we had grown up together we would have compared body parts many times. Have a look. We'll get it over with and move on to other things."

Her impish smile comes back. She examines me closely, starts to touch, pulls her hand back as though singed by a hot flame. "It's okay," I say, and use my own hands to brush back pubic hairs and open my labia. This was never part of my daydreams, but I am surprisingly calm, perhaps because Betsy is so nonchalant. Her scrutiny lasts only a few seconds.

"Wow," she says, sitting back. I pluck my nightgown from its hanging place and put it on. Betsy stands, flushes, comes face-to-face with me. "You're beautiful, Sis."

"Does it seem anatomically correct?" I punctuate the question with my own smile.

"I think so," she says. "Really, though, unless you're a doctor, who ever gets a good look at an adult woman's vagina?"

I look at her questioningly.

"Well, I don't have a great angle to see mine, you know?" she says. "It's like, just because you own a car doesn't mean you know how to fix the engine."

She kisses me on the cheek and we leave together.

I hope this is one of those pivotal moments where everything that happens afterward is so much easier than before. Our first two weeks of living together have been good, but not easy. I haven't cohabited with anyone in a long time, and Betsy's marital years were far different than having a roommate. Not to mention the awkwardness of us having been spouses once. I have obsessed on anticipating every need, making sure the apartment is perfect at all times, and monitoring my every action to make sure nothing I do upsets, offends, or frightens Betsy. I think my inhibitions make Betsy nervous, and she's focused on being a good roommate, too, keeping out of my way, helping with stuff. I think our good intentions are the source of more stress and tension than if we were already at the taking-each-other-for-granted stage.

We're still establishing our routine chores like cooking and cleaning. Betsy wants to do everything because she's not working, and I want us to share everything because I want a sister, not a housekeeper. It's not the worst problem to have. We chat for a moment each night about the next day's schedule, who will be home when, who will cook, who will stop for food, what other chores need to be done.

We went back and forth on the rooming arrangements. I insisted she take the master bedroom because it wasn't practical for her or Robbie to sleep in the room I use for a hair studio, and because she would suffocate in that cramped room after all the nights she's spent in her Northbrook castle. I won the argument, but we are sharing the closet in the master bedroom. It was strange at first, hearing other noises, other voices in the flat, having to wait for the bathroom sometimes, planning a daily menu in advance. But I like it. I like all of it. I love feeling like I'm a part of something. When I lived here alone I seldom closed doors, but when I did, the sound of the closing door echoed through the apartment like a lonely song. The sounds of closing doors now are the sounds of life and love. I feel like an actual person with an actual family.

I have to remind myself constantly that this is just temporary, that Betsy and Robbie will be moving on in a few months. That I shouldn't get too attached.

* * *

WEDNESDAY, OCTOBER 22

Wilkins sits in the corner of the lounge, reading a newspaper like several others, looking up now and then to take in the scenery.

He has shadowed Logan to her gym several times, catching glimpses of her workouts, peeking through the window to watch her self-defense class. Her workouts are impressive. A reminder that he should be doing something. She lifts weights, does stretching and balance, runs. Some of her exercises make his body ache just watching. The running makes him breathe hard. He's not sure he can run a block anymore, so many days and nights of sitting, bad food, coffee. He has a physical coming up. It won't be pretty. They've been on him to get a regular doctor and dentist for years.

He shivers. He's been shot at, beaten, bitten by rats and dogs, he's walked into whitey bars, the only black guy in the place, he's corralled psychopaths, you name it, he's stood up to it, but doctors and dentists scare the shit out of him. Especially dentists. The sound of that drill goes right up and down his spine. Absolute torture. His dad used to whack him for whining and crying, but the sound of that drill made him whimper like a bitch and sweat like a pig. He ran out one day and never came back. Never made another appointment.

Logan comes out of the self-defense class and crosses the lounge, heading for the room with weights and aerobic machines. She's done this before. She goes in the workout room for a few minutes and comes back out, goes to the locker room, showers, and leaves. She isn't going in there to work out. It's something else. He gets up and stands at the threshold of the room to watch her. She's waiting at the edge of the free-weight area. A burly power lifter finishes a set of dead lifts, then walks over to her, big smile on his face. Hers, too.

Wilkins finds a row of plastic chairs and sits down. He can't hear what they're saying, but they have a lot of affection for each other. They touch several times, smile constantly. Logan gestures a lot as she talks, uninhibited. They hug. Wilkins makes for the lounge again so Logan won't pass directly in front of him on her way out. She breezes through on her way to the locker room, and he goes back in the workout room. He watches her burly friend lift. The man is superhumanly strong. Others in the area are deferential to him.

An attendant at the service counter checks people in and out. Wilkins approaches him, explains he's looking for a new personal trainer, asks if the burly guy over there is a personal trainer.

"Thomas?" says the kid. "Naw. Believe it or not, Thomas is a nurse. He just works out here."

"No kidding," says Wilkins. "Where does he work?" Like he's so amazed that a strong man would be a nurse.

"Memorial Hospital," says the kid. "They love him in the psych ward."

"I'll bet." Wilkins is thinking that Thomas could have easily busted up the hapless thug in the alley or handled Strand.

"I noticed he was talking to that tall girl when I came in. I was thinking of introducing myself to her, but if they're an item . . ." Wilkins lets his voice trail off in a question mark.

The kid laughs. "Naw. They're friends. Thomas has a partner."

It takes a moment, but Wilkins gets it. The scary looking ogre guy is gay. Jesus Christ, he thinks. Is anything in this world straight?

Wilkins says he wants to look around some more and leaves the workout area, then the building. He heads for the precinct, gets on a computer, looks up Memorial Hospital. It takes a while, but he finds Thomas' picture and bio. EMT credentials. Works emergency, psych, surgery. Experience in pediatrics.

Strong enough to break a bad man's bones. Smart enough to know drugs and how to get them.

He calls a friend in the Department of Motor Vehicles, has him run Thomas' name through the car registration database. It takes a while, but the man gets back to him. Thomas owned a 1998 Nissan Maxima in 2003. Probably used it as a city beater, his friend said. It was black. Cecelia Swenson was driving a new Seville back then, also black.

Wilkins looks at a photo of the Maxima on line. It looked more like a BMW than a Seville, but it wouldn't be hard to mistake either of them for a BMW if you were hysterical, scared out of your mind, running for your life on a dim-lit street. It could have been a Maxima or a Seville. It could have been a BMW. Or a lot of other cars.

15

FRIDAY, OCTOBER 24

WHEN I WAS transitioning, Marilee used to tell me that my adolescent urges to dress like a slut and constantly examine my body and fantasize about lovers just reflected the fact that as a female, my emotional development was that of a teenage girl even though I was well into my thirties as a human being.

This is one of those times where I think I haven't come very far. I'm doing hair in the SuperGlam stand at the Chicago Beauty Extravaganza. I have poured my muscular, oversized body into a tiny pink dress, stiletto heels, and fishnet stockings. One of the other hairdressers gave me a big sexy up-do, and I'm wearing heavy black eye makeup with false lashes big enough to squash flies. Most street walkers would consider my presentation too outlandish for humanity's oldest profession. It's especially gauche for a woman in her forties. I'd never dress like this in my personal life, not even in the edgy atmosphere of the salon. But it's the SuperGlam uniform of the day, and I'm luxuriating in complying with company policy.

I'm having a great time. I love doing hair in front of an audience, I love the theater of the show. People stop and gawk. I hear the occasional nasty remark and cruel laugh, but mostly I get silent appreciation and serious questions about my technique. I'm doing formal hair, and I'm worth watching.

The crowds on the display floor start to evaporate in the late afternoon as people head for a special show in the main theater. It's a welcome break. My feet and lower back are aching from wearing heels all day, two days in a row. We take a break. The models fade away to the other exhibits or watch the big show. The SuperGlam staffers do the same. I kick off my heels and enjoy the cloudlike sensation of walking on my bare feet.

I head for the exhibitor lounge where it's okay for me to sit down. I'm looking forward to getting off my feet, having a long cold glass of water, and maybe reading the paper or chatting with other show people. I am still deep in thought when someone overtakes me from behind and slides an arm through mine. As I look to my side to see who it is, she gives my arm a playful hug.

"Hi, cutie." It's Jen. My first lover as Bobbi. We met at a hair show when I was transitioning and had a torrid affair for a year or so. It was a long-distance relationship, and that was hard. She lived in Indianapolis, me in Chicago. After the novelty wore off, we sort of drifted into a friendship, then a distant friendship.

"Hi, gorgeous." I smile. Our familiar old greetings. I loved being called "cute" because I'm so self-conscious about my size and masculine features, and Jen loved to make me feel good about myself. She liked being called "gorgeous," too, because she knew I meant it, though when she presented in a butch outfit, I called her "handsome" with the same results.

Jen is in her thirties. She has a sultry face. Bedroom eyes, puffy cheeks, full lips. She has a cute figure, maybe a trifle overweight, but on her it's sexy. Large soft bosoms, curvy hips, graceful hands with beautiful long nails.

"You keep getting more beautiful, Jen." I gush like a groupie, but it's true.

"Not me, you. Bobbi, you look stunning." She smiles and hugs my arm again. I glow the way a cat purrs when you pet it. Jen examines my cleavage without a hint of inhibition. "My, my, Bobbi, the girls look very healthy." She adds a flirtatious smile.

I blush. Not so much because of what she said as what it makes me think of. She still turns me on. I'll feel guilty about that later, but right now I'm busy being aroused.

"I was wondering if you'd be here," I say. "I kept looking at the crowd but I didn't see you. I thought you might be home having babies by now."

"No. That didn't work out." Jen keeps smiling her seductress smile. This isn't a chance meeting. "I like men, but I don't want to make a habit of one." She laughs gaily. "How about you?"

"I don't have enough callers to limit myself to one gender."

The attendant in the lounge lets Jen come in as my guest. We sit in a private corner. I confess that my most memorable experience with a man involved a prostitute. Jen claps her hands in approval, her face lit up with humor. She believes in a life well lived and disdains societal norms that would drench sexual urges with buckets of shame.

"Unfortunately, right after that I bought my salon and became a capitalist pig and now I can't afford to pee in a pay toilet much less hire a stud to service me."

Jen laughs hysterically. She always loved my humor, just like I always loved her free spirit. We were good for each other.

I switch the conversation to her. She's not seeing anyone right now. The thing with the guy was fun for a while. The sex was good, but the rest of it got increasingly tense as time went on. "He was uptight about everything," she says. "But especially about me finding women just as sexy as he did. It made him sick to think about me making it with another woman. I couldn't ever talk about my girlfriends, even regular girlfriends that were just friends. He'd get jealous. He told me I was perverted. He wanted me to get *cured*."

There's an off note in her voice when she says this. She's trying to say it dismissively, but it hurts. It would hurt anyone.

"Like I'm supposed to wish I'd never made love with a woman when I could spend all my time with some jerk who farts and belches and smells like dirty underwear? I especially liked it when he breathed in my face after drinking beer and smoking cigars. The longer I stayed with him, the more I thought about how nice it was to make love with a woman."

Indeed. Even when I thought I was a straight man, I knew where she's coming from. I never really understood why most women are attracted to men. I still don't get it, even though I'm a woman and even though I find myself attracted to some men.

The time flies. We bounce to lighter topics, laughing and smiling, touching each other sometimes. When I have to get back to the SuperGlam stand, Jen pops the question.

"I brought a tuxedo. I was hoping you'd be my date for dinner tomorrow night." For our first date, Jen dressed butch in a really hot tuxedo, and I went all girly in an evening dress and up-do. It was one of the sexiest nights of my life.

"Oh, Jen, I'd love to," I sigh. I reach out and touch her. It's electric for me, always, touching her. "My situation is a little, uh, complicated right now."

"You're with someone?" she asks.

"Not that way. My ex-wife and her daughter are living with me. They just moved in." I explain about Betsy's recent losses. "I'm trying to be there for her, you know?"

"Are you two . . ." Jen makes a hand gesture. She's asking if we're lovers.

"No."

"Why would she be upset about us going out?"

I'm asking myself the same question. I don't know the answer, but

I'm pretty sure Betsy would feel vulnerable and abandoned. "Tell you what, Jen, let me see what Betsy's schedule is like and get back to you."

"Okay," she says. She scribbles her hotel information on a scrap of paper and hands it to me. As I glance at it, a lascivious smile plays at her lips, and she runs her fingertips up my arm. I get goosebumps.

"A girl's gotta live a little, you know?" She's trying to seduce me and I'm eager to give in. The story of my life.

* * *

FRIDAY, OCTOBER 24

The dentist sits back and tells Wilkins he can relax. He's wearing a mask. His eyes and forehead are wrinkled in an expression somewhere between concern and revulsion.

"Mr. Wilkins, your condition is way past my scope. You need to see an oral surgeon and you need to do it soon." He's a young man, white, imperious.

"What?" An electric chill passes through Wilkins' body. "It's just a few rotten teeth, some bad breath issues."

"Who told you that?" The dentist moves his stool back another foot or two and takes off his mask.

"The department doc." Anger creeps into Wilkins' voice, driven by fear.

"The one who *made* you see a dentist? For the first time in, let's see . . ." the dentist consults his notes . . . "maybe twenty-five years? That doctor?"

"Yes." Wilkins can feel the dentist's condemnation. "I just have this fear of dentists. Since I was a kid."

"I can see how anxious you are."

"I take care of myself. I don't smoke. I hardly ever drink."

The dentist writes a note in the file, not looking at Wilkins. "You don't take care of your teeth, sir. By avoiding regular dental exams all those years, small problems have become big ones. I hope I'm wrong, but I think you have oral cancer."

Wilkins blinks. "Jesus Christ! Is it life-threatening?"

"It can be, Mr. Wilkins. It can be very serious. I'm sending you to a specialist. You need to get past your phobias and get this diagnosed. It's time to be brave."

The dentist's attitude finally gets to Wilkins. "Don't sneer at me about phobias, you arrogant little pissant. I've been keeping twits like you safe for thirty years and I haven't missed a single day of work in all that time. I've gone hand-to-hand with the worst scum in civilization and never shirked my duty. Don't you worry about me. I'll do what I have to do. Just give me the name and get the hell out of my way."

The dentist stares at Wilkins in stunned silence. "My apologies," he says, finally. "No disrespect intended. And I hope I'm wrong about the cancer."

* * *

Friday, October 24

Betsy's face tenses up when I tell her about Jen. I ask her why this distresses her and she says it doesn't, that it's fine, that I should have a life.

"I do have a life," I say. "I have a life with you and Robbie. You're the center of my life. I also have friends. If it's going to be hard on you for me to go out with Jen, I won't go."

"No. No." She shakes her head. We're silent for a long while.

"You were lovers?"

"Yes."

"Will you be sleeping together?"

I wish I could lie. I wish I could say we were just friends, because Betsy is clearly troubled by the thought of me having a lover. We haven't talked about this part of our relationship yet. How do you start that conversation? But here we are, and I'm not going to lie. If Jen and I go out, we will probably end up in bed. "If it would bother you, I'll make sure we don't," I say finally.

She recoils slightly, crosses her arms, bites her lip. I move to her side and try to put my arms around her. She shakes me away. I feel like the husband again, unable to stem the sorrows of my beloved. I put one hand on her shoulder, slide it to her back, a half-hug.

"I'll call and decline," I whisper. This has been a pattern in our brief time together. Betsy has good days where she is her effervescent, self-assured self, and bad days when her mind and spirit sag under the full weight of her tragedy. I try to understand the swings and provide empathy wherever she is in the cycle.

As I start to get up, Betsy grabs my arm. "No! No, don't. I have to get over this. I have no hold on you."

"But you do, Betsy. I love you first, most, and always. I'm here for you as long as you need me."

She puts one hand to her lips and turns away. "I'm crazy, Bobbi. In my mind I keep seeing you fall in love and move to Indiana."

"I would never do that," I say softly.

"I know, but that's how I'm feeling. It's hard to see your ex . . ." She stops for a moment, not quite sure what to call me.

"Husband," I finish for her. "I was your husband. I'm a woman now. I passed inspection, remember?" I shouldn't use humor at a time like this, but I can't help myself.

"I feel like I wasn't woman enough for you. I feel like if I had been, you'd still be a man." She looks at me with bloodshot eyes. "And even now, I keep seeing you go in a bedroom with another woman because I'm not attractive to you."

"You are the most beautiful woman I've ever known." Even as I say the words I'm thinking they sound empty. I just don't know how else to say what's true. "I've always been attracted to you and I always will be. But, Betsy, you're not a lesbian. If we tried to be lovers, we'd lose each other. You need me as a sister, and I need you that way, too."

We hold each other for a long time, Betsy brokenhearted and lost, me guilty and inept. At moments like this I'm overwhelmed by how much it sometimes hurts to have people you love in your life.

*   *   *

SATURDAY, OCTOBER 25

Wilkins sits on a park bench where he can see the playground. He followed the three of them here as he has several times, Logan, the woman, the child. It's not part of the investigation. More trying to understand Logan, how she thinks, what motivates her. Catch an insight that leads to an insight that explains why she would murder John Strand. Hang him up by his hands and slit his throat. A ritual murder, gory, premeditated, and then some. Professional. A clean crime scene. Nothing out of place, no telltale clues.

There were the synthetic hair fibers, but a defense lawyer would shred that evidence in a minute. The guy liked diddling transwomen. Lots of synthetic hair fibers in that demographic. Wilkins laughs to himself, thinking of all the transgender women he'd met since he re-opened this case. He was getting so familiar with them he could spot a wig from natural hair before he said hello. He could read faces and tell where they had surgery.

The thing about Logan was, he knew she did it, but he still couldn't figure out why. The man-hating killing spree might work in court, but it was thin, and he didn't buy it himself. She definitely took her revenge on the thug, but it was a beating, not a killing. And she seemed to get along with men. God knows that pretty boy Pavlik had a thing for her. How about that? Handsome guy, women falling all over him, and he's got the hots for a half-male transwoman.

This case wasn't unfolding the way he thought it would. Not even close.

And now this family thing. Logan is shacked up with her ex-wife and her child. They do everything together, like they were married. He didn't see it coming. He had never heard of anything like this.

The woman is sitting on a bench near the swings. Logan is helping the child climb on the playground equipment. She squeals with delight when she reaches the top and jumps into Logan's waiting arms.

He's thinking of her as Logan, now. As a transwoman instead of a tranny or queer. And as "her" or "she." It has been a long, strange path. She still reviles him at times, especially when she gets dolled up like a whore to go to work, or when she hugs the woman, or when she kisses anyone on the lips.

He watches Logan and the child play. A few months ago the sight of a child being touched by a transgender woman would have made him feel queasy. The thought of the child being raised by lesbians would have made it worse. And yet, the little girl seems happy, and Logan and the woman seem considerate of each other. He remembers taking his own daughter to the park when she was a toddler, watching over her like a guard dog, smiling when she laughed out loud, her laughter riding on the air currents like the scent of spring flowers. He remembers holding hands with his wife when they walked to and from the park. They didn't do it enough. The job got in the way. And he got in the way, Allan Wilkins, the things he couldn't do, feelings he couldn't express, fears he couldn't climb over.

Wilkins sighs. Logan and the woman are walking back toward their apartment. The little girl swings gaily between them, holding their hands, leaping in the air as they walk so they can swing her forward. Her happy laughter haunts him. It is like an echo of his daughter's glee all those years ago. Logan stops at the edge of the park and picks up the girl in one hand and takes the woman's hand with the other. They walk away, the woman leaning her head sadly on Logan's shoulder, Logan bending her own head to console her. Like the poetry of a sad song, Wilkins thinks. What could have been.

* * *

SATURDAY, OCTOBER 25

I had hoped a trip to the park with Robbie would cheer Betsy a little, but it didn't. She's trying to be brave and supportive, but she is clearly miserable. We slog through dinner, me sitting in but not eating because Jen and I are going out to eat. Betsy tries to be conversational with me, but it's not working. I wish I hadn't invited Jen to come by and meet the family.

Jen arrives in time to say goodnight to Robbie. Robbie is intrigued with her. Jen cuts a dashing figure in her tuxedo, an intoxicating blend of male and female images. The slacks are masculine but don't hide her feminine derriere. The coat makes you think James Bond until you see the Marilyn Monroe cleavage bulging under the lapels. Her hair, an icy platinum blond, is slicked back on the sides and teased into curly spikes on top. If it were just us here, I would kiss her wildly and breathe hot sighs as I ran my hands over her feminine curves.

Instead, I greet her warmly and introduce her to Betsy and Robbie. Betsy smiles and nods. Robbie stares the kind of admiring stare that children do. Jen's face melts into a maternal smile, a dimension I never imagined she had. She kneels to the ground and extends a hand to Robbie. Her nails are long and exquisitely painted in black and red geometric patterns. Robbie grabs Jen's hand and examines the nails like a jeweler appraising a diamond.

"Momma!" she says. "Look! Look!"

Betsy blushes and bends down a little. "Very beautiful."

Robbie gushes, makes eye contact with Jen, smiles a shy smile.

"You're very beautiful," Jen says to Robbie. When she smiles her glossy lipstick makes her lips glow with femininity. She holds her arms out to offer a hug. Robbie steps to her and throws her arms around Jen. After a brief hug, Robbie pauses to stare at Jen's hair. She takes a lock in her fingers and examines it closely.

"Do you like the color?" Jen asks.

Robbie nods her head enthusiastically.

"Well, stay close to your Aunt Bobbi, and when the time comes, she'll fix you up."

Over Betsy's dead body, I think. Betsy is watching with a mechanical smile on her face. I'm certain she's playing images of Jen and me making out in her mind. Me, too, but I'm enjoying them and she's not.

Jen takes me to dinner at an Italian place in the north side theater district. It is the perfect Jen selection—chef-owned, gourmet cuisine, nice wine list, and virtually unknown outside its neighborhood. We start with wine and small talk about the hair show, the salon business, friends we share in Indianapolis and Chicago. Over the main course we talk about her stab at heterosexuality. It's humorous at first. She refers to her ex as Thick Dick and says when God was designing Richard—against all reason, Jen is a sincere believer—he decided to endow a man with the brains and the penis of a horse. Her tales of life with Thick Dick alternate between slapstick anecdotes about his stupidity and ribald accounts of his work as a stallion.

We stop for an after-dinner drink at a lesbian bar in Andersonville, a favorite of ours when we were lovers alternating visits between Indy and Chicago. We find a table in the corner and sip chocolate-flavored liquor. It's still quiet in the place. We talk in low voices. Jen talks about how beautiful Betsy is, how she can see why I was attracted to her. She asks if it's different now, as a woman.

"Yes," I say, not sure I want to go down this path. "I still love her, but it's a different kind of love. There's no sex. I need to be there for her and Robbie."

Jen pushes the issue. Wouldn't I really like to make love with her? I issue my standard answer, the one I give myself every time I have libidinous thoughts about Betsy.

"I understand what you mean," says Jen. "But still, don't you go to sleep some nights and dream about kissing those beautiful lips, how soft they must be?" She gets more graphic, what Betsy's skin must feel like, her breasts. She continues a sensuous tour of Betsy's body as she sits closer to me and starts touching and fondling. We kiss, hot and wet, our tongues coupling and rubbing. Her lips are full and soft, her breath sweet and damp and warm. Her cologne is delicate, like wild-flowers in the spring. It mingles with the scent of her hair, fragrant and delicious. It makes me picture us lying in a field of prairie grass and flowers, a gentle breeze wafting over our bare skin, birds singing, Jen's fingers bringing me to climax.

"Ready to go?" She says it dreamily, with a sensuous smile. She knows I am.

We go to her hotel and make love, cuddle, and talk, then repeat the cycle into the wee hours of the morning. We fall asleep in each other's arms.

I awaken to an overcast Sunday morning feeling equal parts guilty and fulfilled. Jen is still asleep, an angelic look on her face. It is impossible to imagine what an appetite she has for seduction and lovemaking when she looks like this. I rise quietly and ready myself to go home and change for work. The show must go on, even on Sunday. I rouse Jen briefly to say good-bye and leave. I dread facing Betsy when I walk in.

* * *

SUNDAY, OCTOBER 26

The apartment is as quiet as a tomb when I get home. For a moment I think they've left, moved out, then I see Robbie's toys in the living room, Betsy's coat in the closet. I hurry through my morning ritual and prepare for the day.

As I finish dressing and primping for the last day of the show, Betsy's familiar knock sounds on my bedroom door. I open it. Betsy looks tired, deep rings under her eyes, her skin shadowed in sadness.

"Did you have a good time last night?" Her voice is frosty.

"Yes." I'd prefer to lie because that's not what she wants to hear, but we have to get over this.

"Did you two fuck your lesbian brains out?"

I try not to be shocked by her language. Or her disgust. "We did what lovers do. You make it sound like bestiality. It wasn't."

"What is bestiality?" Betsy asks. She says "bestiality" with a scornful sneer.

"It doesn't matter. We made love. It was nice." I want to add that someday it will happen for her, too, but in her current state I think she would scratch my eyes out.

She glowers at me in silence. I step to her, my arms open to hug her, a tacit apology. She flings my arm away. "Don't treat me like one of your lesbian whores!" She says it in a harsh whisper, keeping her voice down so she doesn't wake Robbie, but charging her words with an anger that is unnerving. Her stare falls to the cleavage bulging from my SuperGlam dress. "Touching me with your boobs! Ugh! Do you have any idea how disgusting that is? Putting your arms around me? Were you going to feel me up? Kiss my tits? Oh God. Am I supposed to be turned on by that? You are disgusting, Bobbi!" She breaks down, sits on the edge of the bed, and sobs, her head in her hands.

Her words are shocking. They seep into my senses and find the place I store all the guilt I feel for all the hurts I've caused Betsy. Shame showers over me, followed by the overwhelming sense that I'm a misfit who doesn't belong in polite society, a familiar emotion that has walked with me since I quit denying my transgender reality. I push my issues aside and try to tend to Betsy. Her anger is real, but she doesn't mean her words. I put a hand tentatively on her shoulder. She continues sobbing but doesn't pull away. I sit beside her and put an arm around her. She continues sobbing, head in hands.

"Goddammit, Bobbi. I loved you so much! You were my everything. I needed you, and you had to go be someone else. I need you now, but you're someone else. You have tits and a vagina and you fuck other women." She rambles. I hardly hear her because I know what she's saying more clearly than she's saying it. Bob Logan was the one for her. Bobbi Logan is no substitute. She is expressing herself cruelly because it's the only way she can get it out. Knowing that doesn't really dampen the hurt, though.

"Do you think all this . . ." she struggles for the right word, gesturing at my girlie presentation . . . "this shit you've done to yourself makes you . . ." Her voice trails off. She doesn't need to finish the sentence. I get the gist of it.

I remove my arm from her and create a little distance between us. Being close to a leper isn't going to make her feel better.

"I'm sorry," I say.

"I can't live like this, Bobbi. This is perverted. You're my ex-husband, for God's sake. I have to move out. I'll find something tomorrow. This is over. This is over."

She lapses back into sobs.

"Would you like me to go?" I ask in a whisper. She nods yes without looking up.

"Okay," I say. "But you need to know, I'm the same person. I look different, but I'm the same person. No one will ever love you and Robbie more than I do. I hope some man comes along who will love you as much, but no one will love you more."

I give her a farewell rub on the shoulder and leave. I feel like the ogre in a children's story, ugly and cruel.

As I reach the sidewalk in front of the apartment, Betsy appears on the porch and calls me back.

"I'm sorry, Bobbi." It's cold out. She's shivering a little, her arms crossed. We are a few feet apart. "I'm upset. I didn't mean the things I said, but we have to talk. This isn't going to work."

"I understand," I say. "I have to get to the show, but I'll be home early. In time for dinner."

She looks into my eyes and nods her head. "Okay."

"I love you," I say as I leave. Her lips make a small, sad smile. Her head moves ever so slightly in a tenuous confirmation. There will be no more *I love yous* from Betsy. No more cooking for three. No more coming home to an apartment filled with voices and life.

* * *

SUNDAY, OCTOBER 26

Robbie is at a neighbor's home, playing with a friend when I get home. Betsy is making a simple vegetarian spaghetti meal. She greets me in a civil voice and makes one of those almost-smiles. I kiss her on the cheek. I've thought about this in the nooks and crannies of my day, the moments when I didn't have to concentrate on my work. I don't believe Betsy hates me. I don't believe she is reviled by me. I think she just wishes I were still her leading man. It would fill a hole in her heart and it would make her feel more secure.

I share her wish. I wish I could be all that for her and still be me. She was the one for me, too. I'll never love anyone as much as I love Betsy. It's ironic when you think about it.

When I'm done taking off makeup and changing into soft, comfortable, dowdy clothes, I join Betsy in the kitchen.

She stops stirring the sauce and gives me a gentle hug as she apologizes. "I'm sorry for the things I said. I didn't mean them."

"No apology necessary," I say. I have more to say, but she cuts me off.

"It is necessary. No one should ever say things like that, especially to you, Bobbi. You are the best person I know. That's why it hurts so much. Losing you."

We grow silent. I know better than to challenge the notion she's lost me. This isn't the time, even though I think I'm an even more dedicated partner to her now than I was as a man.

"I understand how you might think I mutilated myself," I start. "And I know I'd make you feel more secure if I was a man and we could be husband and wife."

She's shaking her head no. "I don't think you mutilated yourself, Bobbi. I understand you and I accept you, maybe more than you do. You're a sweet, kind woman, and I love you. But I can't help it, you were once the man I loved, and I can't get past that. When you have dates, I'm always going to feel like you're cheating on me, like I'm not woman enough. That's why I have to get out on my own."

The sauce starts to boil over on the stove. Betsy doesn't notice. She is completely focused on our conversation. I reach over and turn off the burner. "I'd like to have a sex life and I'd like you to have one, too," I say. I'm not going to bring up the fact that she has no job, no money, and no immediate prospect for independent living. It would only add to her frustrations.

"Let's give it a few weeks, a month. It's not like I have a social life anyway, and if I do, I won't ever be distasteful, and I won't ever do anything provocative in front of you and Robbie." She is listening thoughtfully.

"You've started applying for jobs, we have Robbie in preschool, let's see what happens." As I say it I realize that it makes sense. It also quiets my inner feelings of despair at the prospect of living without them.

Betsy looks at me for a long moment. "Okay," she says softly. "But just until I get a job."

We dine quietly, then fetch Robbie. I'm waiting for Betsy when she finishes the tucking-in ritual with Robbie. I lead her into my bedroom, seat her in my styling chair, and begin a luxurious scalp massage. They taught scalp massage techniques in my beauty school, and I became masterful at them practicing on Betsy. It's the one thing in cosmetology where having big, strong hands is an advantage. Betsy is groaning lightly with delight. I should have thought of this before. This will be a regular ritual in our house, as long as we share a home, anyway.

* * *

Friday, October 31

"Are we talking on the record or off?" she asks.

They are sitting in a quiet corner of a downtown Starbucks in the middle of the afternoon. Her law offices are in a high-rise a block away. Wilkins has just asked her about John Strand.

"I'm not a reporter," he says.

"I know. You're a cop. Things that are said on the record you expect to be repeated in a court of law. What I'm willing to say on the record is a lot less than what I'll say off the record. What's your pleasure, Detective?"

He appraises her. Just the kind of attitude you expect from a litigator, especially if you're a cop. Tough. Confrontational. She's also attractive but she plays that down. He could see how her attractiveness might have come later in life. She is tall, strong looking. Not like a transsexual, but somewhat similar. Attractive facial structure, high cheek bones, blue eyes, short blond hair in a contemporary style. Good dresser. Probably bigger than the boys in grade school, gawky, shunned. Somewhere in college or law school she emerges as a swan.

"I'm just looking for some background here, Counselor. How about we start off the record. If I need you to speak on the record, I'll ask you about it later."

She nods her approval. Her cell phone beeps. She glances at it, clicks a button, puts it in her purse, and looks at Wilkins.

"You worked with John Strand for several years."

"Yes. Until 2002. He was my mentor."

"What was that like?"

"Why are you asking me?"

"Because you left the firm. The women who are still there won't talk about him."

She nods, knowingly. "Same reason I don't want to talk on the record."

"We're off the record."

She nods again. "Okay. He was a very sharp attorney and a great fixer. He knew every judge, every politician, every department head in the city, and a lot of the same kinds of people in Springfield. He could get a lot done, in court or out. Very smooth. Being his protégé was a first-class ticket to the fast track in the firm."

"But . . ." Wilkins bridges her silence.

"But he was inappropriate with women. With me."

"How so?"

"At first it was just innuendoes and talking dirty and talking down to us. Like we were stupid. I was a lot more upset by the talking down than the innuendoes, to tell the truth. But it got worse. He'd come up behind me when I was working and kiss me on the cheek and hug me. Once he stuck his tongue in my ear. The year I left, he'd cop a feel now and then and laugh like it was a big joke. It didn't feel like he was doing it to get laid. It was more like he was showing me who was boss. That he could hump me or fire me any time he wanted.

"Thing was, I think he was impotent. After he was killed, one of his corporate clients, a woman, supposedly told someone in the firm he was a stud lawyer but a gelding in bed."

"Did you ever sleep with him?"

She makes a face. "Never."

"What else did you know about him?"

"Nothing in the way of hard facts."

"What did you hear?"

"After he died, a lot of stories started making the grapevine. One was that one of the assistants was tending the entrance to the firm's big Christmas party and this transvestite or transsexual person shows up, asking for John Strand. She gets him and Strand blushes crimson. He whisks the transperson away, comes back a few minutes later, and tells the assistant it's a pro bono client he's helping off the books, a charity case, doesn't want anyone to know because of complications it would cause in billings and hours and all that."

Wilkins nods.

"Here's the eerie part. A few weeks later the assistant reads about a transsexual prostitute found beaten to death. The story was in a neighborhood paper. North side, where the body was found. No photo, but the description of the girl could have been the one she saw at the party."

"Do you believe it?"

She shrugs. "Do I think John Strand could have beaten someone to death? Yes. He was really artful in disguising it, but I got this eerie vibe from him. I don't think he had a conscience and he hated women. Plus, I think he loved to dominate people. It made him a killer litigator." She pauses a moment, realizing the significance of her word choice. "I think the only person in his universe was him and it was a violent, cruel universe."

She pauses as she stares at the tabletop for several beats. "Speaking as an attorney, I have no proof of anything. Speaking as a woman, I think he was a creature from hell. I'd be surprised if he only had one victim."

"Who do you think killed him?"

She shrugs again. "A vengeful ghost? A guardian angel? A lightning bolt from heaven?"

"No remorse from you, then?

"None. The world is a better place without him."

"Where were you the night he was killed?"

"I was on vacation in California. Lots of witnesses. Class reunion."

"You weren't a suspect anyway. Just some cop humor."

* * *

SATURDAY, NOVEMBER 1

Halloween is one of the biggest days on the transgender calendar, which is why I spent much of my day at TransRising helping do hair and nails and makeup for legions of young transwomen preparing for a night of colorful parties. I did get a selfish benefit from it, though. Two volunteers from my salon gave me a Halloween look—something

I've never had before. I'm going as my favorite Disney princess, Ariel, she of long red hair.

As Betsy and Robbie and I head for Cecelia's costume party, I don't look much like Ariel, but temporary color has given me flaming-red hair and theatrical makeup techniques have provided a regal and kind of exotic look.

Cecelia's parties are always tasteful events, which is why we are taking Robbie with us tonight. We won't stay long. She'll pass out by nine. But that works, too. Betsy and I are easing back into some kind of compatibility after things bottomed out last weekend.

Betsy has curbed her anxiety to get moving. She's mulling a job offer from a nonprofit group that lobbies for LGBT rights, and I think she's going to take it. It's time. She's still mourning for Don, still spends parts of her days in sadness. She is sometimes withdrawn from me, sometimes close and familiar. I can see both sides of her on the same day sometimes. I try not to let the distant Betsy leave scars on my always fragile ego, and I try not to rejoice too much when we share moments together the way I have dreamed we would.

Betsy threw herself into getting Robbie and herself into costume. She is going as a sexy witch, something she pulls off by being beautiful, no prurient display of tits and ass necessary. Robbie is going as her kitty. They are both dressed in black. Betsy has a witch hat she crafted from black construction paper. Robbie has two sets of cat whiskers; the ones made from plastic bag ties fall off in the cab on the way to the party, but the ones that are painted on with eyeliner hold firm. She's completely enamored of herself and her new identity. She walks up to everyone she sees and meows at them until they acknowledge what a beautiful cat she is. Then she tells them her mommy is a witch and her aunt is the princess Ariel.

Our cat introduces us to everyone at the party.

Betsy relaxes as the party gets under way. Her smile is the smile I remember, warm and light. Robbie is happy and well behaved. The people are friendly. Cecelia has a vast spread of finger foods placed on tables throughout her designer apartment overlooking Lake Michigan and the Chicago River. It's an older, professional crowd. The costumes are tasteful. I would be the most outrageous exhibit but for Cecelia, who is presenting as an Amazon Queen, tottering around in heels the size of stilts. She's wearing an enormous wig that's teased so high and wide it seems impossible for her to make it through a doorway. Her bosom is padded to the size of a couple of grapefruits, and her dress shows off her royal legs to great advantage.

People float from one table to another, drift in and out of groups, glide from room to room getting different views of one of the world's great cities from high in the sky. I bring a glass of wine to Betsy and tell her I'd like to take Robbie for a while so she can mix and mingle. She looks at me with a twinkle in her eye and an easy smile. "Okay," she says. "But go easy on the sweets."

I heap different foods on a plate and lead Robbie into the kitchen. The caterers are bustling in and out, but I find two chairs on an un-used side of the kitchen table for us. Robbie picks through the food, unwilling to try much of it, not liking the rest. The head caterer sees the dilemma. He asks her if she likes hot dogs. They are one of her three current food groups. He is back in a few minutes with a plateful of tiny wieners wrapped in a puffy bread dough. Robbie eats four of them, dipping them in ketchup, and drinks a glass of milk.

When we go back to the party, Robbie immediately hooks up with an older couple who marvel at what a cute kitty she is. She takes each by one hand and brings them to the floor-to-ceiling windows in Cecelia's living room. She fearlessly steps to the glass, her nose smashed against it, and encourages them to do the same so they can see the street below. As in, thirty-some stories below. I get dizzy just watching from the middle of the room.

As Robbie and her friends entertain each other, I look about the room. Betsy is in a cluster of people, chatting back and forth, at ease, engaged. She holds the wine glass near one shoulder. She has not consumed much of it. Her eyes drift to Robbie. Her smile widens. She finds me next, a few steps from Robbie. Her eyes sparkle. I feel my whole body glow. In that moment, I realize that she is having a good time because we're here together, because she can trust me with her daughter. And because, underneath her misgivings about me being a woman now, she knows I am the terra firma in her life, the one place she can step where the earth beneath her feet won't crumble away. That's what makes me glow. That, more than anything in my life, is what I want to be. Though I wouldn't mind having a lover, too.

When Betsy takes Robbie to the bathroom to get ready for our trip home, I take a leisurely stroll through Cecelia's condo. I have a lot of memories here. Many great late-night talks with Cecelia. Meeting various people at her parties, corporate honchos, attorneys, politicians. I go into her bedroom to retrieve our coats. As I walk in a man exits from her private bathroom. It produces a flashback I don't want to have. Another Cecelia party, long ago. Another man coming out that door, a very handsome man who makes several passes at me that night. Me, the half-formed transsexual woman, weak kneed by the attentions of such a handsome man. Him, the good John Strand. The seductive John Strand. The fake John Strand.

16

SHE DIDN'T WANT to meet for lunch, so they're in a coffee shop in a hip north side neighborhood popular with liberal Yuppies. Wilkins was relieved she didn't want to do lunch. He's having trouble eating solid food because it hurts his teeth and gums. He can handle soup, but it drives him crazy watching someone else eat real food.

Wilkins places a mocha latte in front of her and sits down catty-corner to her with his bottle of water. He offers her a breath mint. She declines. He pops a couple. He thanks her for meeting him. She nods and tends to her drink.

She's a young white girl, early twenties, hot like a lot of hairdressers are, cute in a cuddly way. Soft cheeks, big eyes, sexy hair. Swollen red lips. She dresses like a hairstylist, a short skirt and tight, low-cut top.

"Can I call you Brenda?" he asks. She nods her assent.

"I'm investigating a couple of incidents that occurred at Salon L'Elégance," he begins. I believe you were present at the one last spring involving the estranged boyfriend of one of the stylists, a Trudy Dunbar. Is that correct?"

She nods.

He goes through his standard good-cop intro. This isn't about her, she's not a suspect, he's just gathering background information so the district attorney can evaluate evidence. She nods her understanding, sips her latte. He produces the photo of Logan in a dress and makeup.

"Do you recognize this person?" he asks.

She nods, full lips curling into an unattractive sneer. "Bobbi. That's Bobbi. She owns the place."

"It seems you don't like her."

"The bitch fired me because I wouldn't take shit from a client."

Wilkins knows that already. It had taken some careful field work to find an ex-employee who might have a less rosy impression of Logan than the current staff did. What surprises him is how quickly young Brenda goes from a pouty sexpot to a foul-mouthed shrew.

"What is she like to work for?"

Another face. A deep breath. She crosses her legs imperiously. "She's a mean bitch. She thinks she knows everything about hair. She's always criticizing everything you do, if you're young. She leaves the old ones alone because they don't need her shit, and they'd just tell her to go fuck off. She's got rules for every fucking thing. You can't go to the bathroom without breaking a rule. That's why there aren't any young people there. It's all old farts plugging away. Anyone with any life gets out of there."

Wilkins jots some notes in his notebook. He won't bother reading them. He does it to make people like Brenda feel important. It does something to their egos. Makes them say more than they might otherwise.

"Can you think of anything about Ms. Logan that would precipitate the kind of violence that has taken place there?"

"Have there been other incidents?" she asks. There's an eagerness to her question. She's looking for dirt.

"I can't really talk about the investigation," he says. "I'm just trying to find out if there is more to these things than meets the eye. What can you tell me about Ms. Logan I might not know?"

She smiles, not a pretty smile, a sarcastic smirk. "Well, she ain't no lady, for one thing." The smile gets wider. "She's a *he*. A tranny. Had his wee-wee whacked off. Fucking degenerate queer." When she says it, she finishes by leaning toward him and raising her eyebrows, waiting for him to be surprised. He wonders how dumb she is.

"Is she violent? Does she make others violent?"

"Well she sure messed up that poor bastard who came looking for Trudy, didn't she? And in the salon she's always giving orders and telling people what to do because she's a fucking football player in a dress. Don't let the big tits fool you, Detective. That's not a woman."

Wilkins winces a little. Her spiteful assessment of Logan sounds a lot like his, but it sounds ugly and unfair coming from her.

Wilkins asks a few more questions but learns nothing new. Brenda doesn't like Logan, has nothing good to say about her. The bullying accusation might be more interesting if anyone else corroborated it, but the character stuff on Logan was coming in positive. Brenda wouldn't do his case any good, cussing like a mule-skinner, full of transphobic bile. She would be a field day for a hyperaggressive defense attorney.

Still, her assertions have some value to him. At the appropriate time, he might reference the bullying testimony in a list of particulars to intimidate Logan, get her saying things in denial that can be used against her.

* * *

WEDNESDAY, NOVEMBER 12

I walk in the door, and heavenly aromas waft into my senses. Betsy greets me as I cross the threshold, sharing her beautiful I-love-you smile. She has a sumptuous dinner prepared and a nice bottle of red open and breathing. There's a gleam in her eye, and she has enough energy to make me feel like a sloth.

She's back! My heart turns a couple of cartwheels. I wish I believed in God so I could thank someone. Instead, I kiss her cheek and hug her and pelt my innocent niece with a torrent of kisses and hugs. Dinner is a slow-roasted pot roast rubbed with herbs and spices, surrounded by carrots and potatoes and onions and peppers.

When Robbie excuses herself to resume play in the living room, Betsy and I sip wine and lapse into that kind of languid, easy conversation people have when everyone is feeling mellow and no one wants the mood to pass. She talks about her day. She has been working for the Equal Rights Council for a week. Today, they asked her to start working on a position paper on marriage equality. She's floating on clouds. She talks about the issues and her research with the passion of a missionary. Her beautiful face is flush with color. Her wide, oval eyes are filled with excitement. Her hands gesture and flow like a flag in a spring breeze.

She tells me about her coworkers. They are congenial, respectful of each other. They are committed to idealistic things. They are glad to have her on board because no one wants to pitch the position paper to the dailies and the radio and television stations. She apologizes for talking so much. I tell her I feel like I'm at a great concert and I don't want the music to stop. She pooh-poohs me, but it's true.

She asks me what I've been up to.

Perhaps because we've talked so little in the past month, perhaps because I'm giddy over her mood, or perhaps because I've had two glasses of wine, I tell her some of my truths.

"Well, the good news is that business seems to be improving." I give her my theories: that our promotions are working, that we're getting some business from salons that went under, that America is getting used to the idea of the recession and starting to resume some activities that were dropped after the financial catastrophe.

"What's the bad news?" She asks it playfully.

"I still can't afford to hire my male prostitute."

She giggles. "Okay, I asked for that. But really, you've seemed very tense a lot of the time. What's going on?"

The person who is the sun and stars in my life is sitting across the table from me aglow for the first time in weeks. I could never tell her that most of my anxiety was about her and about my ability to be there for her.

"Oh, just frustrations at the salon and things like that."

"You're dodging me, Bobbi. Don't do that. I'm not a child."

"There's a whole list of things, Betsy. If you knew them all, you'd never respect me again."

"Like what?"

"Like I want Officer Phil to sweep me into a dark room and make wild, passionate love for a night. And another. And another."

"What about that woman? Jen?"

"Her, too." I should never admit these things to anyone but Marilee or Cecelia, but the wine has my defenses down. I expect Betsy to be repulsed, but she laughs out loud instead.

"Bobbi, you have this so wrong. You were so restrained as a man and so wild as a woman. It's supposed to be the other way around."

I blush. "Not really. I don't actually *do* anything. I just have fantasies."

"Join the female race." She pours the dregs of the bottle into our glasses. "Now, stop dodging the question."

I swear she has been getting shrink lessons from Marilee. My illicit sex fantasies were a painful confession, but of course not the biggest cause of my anxiety. I try blaming it on business worries.

"Come on, Bobbi. We're supposed to be sisters, right? Sisters tell each other things. Things they might not tell a lover or a parent."

"Do you think we're there now? Sisters?" It's a question I have, but it's also a good way to steer the conversation away from dangerous topics.

"Do you think we aren't?"

"Well, you're hell-bent on getting your own place."

"Most sisters who love each other don't live together, Bobbi."

I have to concede the point. Betsy still wants to know what I'm holding back. I'm out of excuses for not telling her.

"There's a detective investigating a murder from five years ago. He would love to charge a transgender person with the crime. The victim was involved with transwomen. The cop would like to implicate me because he hates me even more than he hates transgender people in general." I tell her about my run-in with Wilkins five years ago, getting the DA's office to pull him off the case, him getting his hands slapped for being a bigoted shit-for-brains.

"He's back on the case," I tell her. "The murder victim was someone important, and the city wants the crime solved, so they've turned him loose, and he's bugging me."

Betsy looks puzzled. "You would never kill someone." She thinks for a moment. "Would you?"

"I haven't yet," I say. I'm being coy but not lying. "But he can make it hard for me anyway. He can bring charges and make me spend thousands of dollars to defend myself. That would really hurt. Money is tight right now, and the publicity would be bad for the salon."

She bites her lip, thinking.

"I have retained an attorney, just in case," I say preemptively. "He has advised me not to discuss this with anyone but him. That includes you, Betsy. You can be subpoenaed and forced to testify and a good prosecutor could turn the most innocuous statement into something that appears to corroborate wild allegations from someone else. That's the gist of what he said."

Betsy digests this, deep in thought. "I don't understand."

"I can't explain our legal system. I'm just asking you to let me take my attorney's advice."

"It feels wrong," she says. "I don't like us having secrets, especially when Robbie and I are so dependent on you."

"I don't either, Betsy," I reply. "Sometimes there's just no right answer."

"That's too slick, Bobbi," she says. Her face is angry. "I tell you everything, you tell me nothing. You kept your transition a secret, your lovers . . ." She goes on about my lovers for a while, not really fair, but I get her point. I didn't tell her about my transition because I was terrified she would find me repulsive. I'll share that with her at some future time. She's not in the mood to hear it now.

"Do you really think I'd betray you to the police?" she asks. Her face is flushed. I have hurt her deeply.

"I don't want to put you in a position where you would have to choose between lying and betraying me," I answer.

"And I want to make my own decisions. Do you think I'm so pure I haven't lied for someone I love?"

Actually, that's what I was thinking.

*　*　*

FRIDAY, NOVEMBER 14

Every night this week, I have been wakened by tortured dreams. They're always some variation on the police crashing into the apartment, hauling me away in cuffs, Betsy and Robbie sobbing with terror, me rotting in a cell, my salon closing, my loved ones taking shelter with Betsy's parents in the village of malicious trolls.

The bitter irony is that to overcome the telltales of sleep deprivation, I have to get up a half hour earlier each morning to do battle with the rings and creases in my face.

Fortunately, things are going a little better in the salon. We're still struggling financially, but the staff is upbeat. We haven't had any blowups or incidents. And everyone has been very nice to me. I know that sounds stupid. I'm the boss. But I'm endlessly vulnerable. I can keep going in a shitstorm of setbacks, but life is so much lovelier when I am surrounded by people with warm hearts and glad smiles.

My legal problems still bother Betsy, but she knows I'm not a danger to society or to her or Robbie and she has gotten on with her life.

Tonight I have joined Betsy and her coworkers for drinks and dinner at a nice restaurant in the north Loop area. There are four of them from the office, plus Betsy. They are a nice group of people and they have welcomed me. I can't help feeling like this is the event where the new employee introduces everyone to her husband or boyfriend, except Betsy is substituting her ex-husband who has gone through some changes. No one else seems aware of it, and I have been made to feel at home from the moment I entered the restaurant.

Her colleagues are two gay men and two lesbians. There are another half dozen people who log time regularly at the office, a mix of gay, lesbian, and straight people, and one transgender woman. They rave about the transwoman, whose contributions are limited because she is active in so many transgender groups. As they talk about her, I realize the woman sounds a lot like Lisa, the young leader at TransRising. I make a note to myself to tell Betsy not to mention me when she meets this lady. It will go much better for her.

After dinner, we stroll down to a small jazz club on Dearborn. It's a cold night, but the door is open and the lush tones of a saxophone drift out onto the street, telling the story of Billy Joe with a drawn-out bluesy sadness that is unspeakably beautiful.

It's a classic Chicago jazz/blues club. Small, dimly lit, a semicircular bar in one corner ringed by maybe fifteen stools, a small stage in the middle of the back wall, elevated a couple of feet above the floor, the rest of the room filled with small tables and hard, functional chairs. There's a five-dollar cover, and only serious drinkers and people with iron buttocks will make it through more than a couple of sets.

A trio is performing on the stage: piano, sax, and bass. It's early so there are lots of chairs open. We sit at a table near the stage. The group goes into one of their original numbers, upbeat, bouncy, filled with adventure and promise. There are close to two dozen people in the chairs and another ten or so at the bar, but more are arriving every minute. We order drinks, and I settle back to let the music wash over me and enjoy the eclectic crowd.

As the musicians finish their set and take a break, I feel a strong hand on my shoulder, followed by a voice in my ear. "What's a nice girl like you doing in a place like this?"

It's Officer Phil. When I turn my head, our faces are inches apart. For once, my first impulse isn't a mental orgasm. It's a self-conscious impulse to hide my mental orgasm from Betsy and her friends. I try to act like Betsy would have acted if I approached her like that back in the day. I smile, say hello, introduce Phil to Betsy and her colleagues. We exchange small talk for a few minutes, then Phil gives me a friendly hug and retreats back to his own table. There are two other men at his table, and three women. Two of the women seem to be in their fifties, like the two men. Probably the wives of the two men. The third woman, Phil's girlfriend, obviously, is younger, maybe thirtyish, and beautiful. Not quite in Betsy's class, but way beyond mine. Slim, cute figure. Long, honey-brown hair cut in long layers so it swirls with each turn of her head. Beautiful eyes with naturally long lashes, light brows, the facial structure of a model. I feel like an idiot for entertaining fantasies about a man who has his pick among women this beautiful.

Our group rises to leave, which is fine with me. I need to get my mind on something else. As we make our way to the door, Phil comes over and asks if he can buy Betsy and me a drink. Betsy thanks him but says she has to get Robbie from the babysitter.

"But you go ahead, Bobbi," she says. She's trying to be nice, but the thought of spending close-up time with Phil and his lovely date is not at all attractive to me.

"I don't want to intrude on your date," I say. "Some other time, Phil." I say it kind of frostily. I'm a little insulted by the offer, to tell the truth. It's insensitive.

He blinks and does a double take. "My date?"

I start to point to the pretty lady at his table. There is a young man sitting in the chair Phil had occupied just a moment ago.

"Her?" he says. "She's not my date. She's with my brother. Pete. I'd like to introduce you."

I feel the usual arousal starting, but shake it off. "Thanks," I say. "I'd love to but I need to get Betsy home. Another time?"

He nods his head yes, but Betsy interjects. "You don't need to see me home, Bobbi. I'm with friends. They'll drop me. You go have a good time." She kisses me on the cheek and whispers in my ear, "You're not my husband. You're my sister. Go have a good time."

"Okay," I tell Phil. "But I can't stay long."

He introduces me around. The two couples are his cop colleagues and their spouses. His brother Pete is a rising star with Boeing, staying an extra day after a meeting at corporate headquarters. Millie is his fiancée. She loves Chicago. They're having a great time. They're thrilled to meet me. Phil told them that I am a rock-star hairdresser. Millie wishes we'd met sooner. I tell her whoever did her hair did a great job, but it would be fun to do her next time she's in town. I give her a card.

When the combo comes back onstage, I tell Phil I need to get going. I have to work tomorrow. More than that, I'm just uncomfortable. Millie isn't Phil's date, but other Millies are. If we were just pals, it would be fine, but for me, it's more than that, and I just can't pretend to be a beer-drinking buddy.

"Okay," he says. "Let me take you home."

I try to decline, but he insists. The others at the table say goodnight as we leave.

Phil's car is some kind of upscale sporty sedan, one of those understated elegance models that look kind of common on the outside, but inside it's all plush and comfort. It's so quiet you can hear every nuance of the music and voices on the sound system with uncanny precision. When he turns off the sounds, it's the same with his voice, his hard consonant sounds clear as a bell, his speaking voice resonant and rich. As we drive along, chatting away, I begin to feel like a girl on a date instead of Bobbi, the transwoman, wondering what it would be like to be a girl on a date.

When we get to my brownstone, he finds a parking place on the curb and turns off the engine. He reaches over the console and takes one of my hands in his.

"I'm really worried about you, Bobbi. Wilkins is not going to stop coming after you. He's deliberately telling me what he's finding. He *wants* me to tell you. He's that sure of himself."

I shrug. What can I say to that?

"He says the girl who was dating Strand identified you and said Strand talked about having a relationship with you. He says he has people who say you're a bully. He says he's got a friend of yours who's strong enough to carry a piano up a flight of stairs by himself and has easy access to anesthetics and tranquilizers. Bobbi, when you put that together with the guy who got mugged saying he was working for Strand and following you when it happened, it looks bad. Really bad."

My mind is racing as he speaks. It does look bad unless you know that lots of it is complete bullshit. Strand wouldn't talk about me to anyone. Thomas does not have access to anesthetics. I've never been any kind of bully. He may have found people who don't like me and say bad things about me, but I'm not one to pick fights or intimidate anyone.

"I'm sorry it sounds so bad to you, Phil. Here's the truth. I'm a good person. I live a good life. I love doing hair. I love making people feel good about themselves. I love wearing dresses and feeling girly. That's who I am. I can't keep someone like Wilkins from hating me or thinking bad things about me. All I can do is live my life as well as I can. And that's what I'm doing."

As I finish babbling Phil leans across the console and kisses me. It's not a friendly peck, it's hot and deep and in a trice we are struggling awkwardly to embrace each other over the console. After several minutes of panting and groping, I ask if he wants to come in.

He sits back, puts both hands on the steering wheel, thinks. "You know I do, Bobbi. But let's not. It could get too complicated."

"Right. You mustn't get a reputation as a tranny fucker." I'm hurt and more than a little frustrated.

"I just introduced you to my brother and two of my best friends."

"Not as your lover, Phil. As a friend you saw in a club."

"It's not that, Bobbi. I've already told you." He mud-wrestles through another rendition of how he wants to make sure his motives are pure. "Plus," he says, "if Wilkins brings a case against you . . ." His voice tails off. He doesn't have to say it. It could get ugly for both of us, but especially for him.

"I understand," I say finally. I bend across the console and kiss him again. "I don't want any more warnings or updates from you, Phil. If you want to see me, call me for a date. You don't have to take me to bed. We can be friends. Or we can be lovers. But I don't want to hear about Wilkins anymore."

He looks at me in silence for a moment, then nods his head. "Okay, Bobbi." He puts two fingers to his lips, then to mine. "Sleep well."

Nice sentiment, but the only question about tonight's sleeplessness is whether it will be caused by erotic fantasies or visions of doom.

* * *

FRIDAY, NOVEMBER 14

Wilkins sees her come out of the club on Pavlik's arm. It still blows his mind. He wonders if Pavlik is balling her.

They walk past him, unaware of a man sitting in a car in the shadows, intent on whatever it was they were saying to each other. Damn, thinks Wilkins. He's fucking her. He's fucking a transsexual. How about that.

Moments later a dark sedan glides past. He can see Logan in the passenger seat. The car stops at the corner and the street lights silhouette the back of Pavlik's head in the driver's seat. Wilkins shakes his head. A great career going up in smoke. Wait 'til the suits find out he's got a taste for transwomen. Well, Wilkins thinks, it won't be him who says anything. Pavlik's appetite for women might be kinky, but he's a stand-up guy.

* * *

SUNDAY, NOVEMBER 15

Cecelia wrinkles her nose as the waitress sets the food in front of us. We're in an organic food restaurant on the far north side. We've ordered salads for lunch. We are in a virtual state of fasting because Thanksgiving is coming up, with all its dietary excesses, and after that, Christmas and New Year. We have both labored too hard, too long to keep our bodies trim, such as they are. So we're eating tangled masses of green hay and vines and other things you probably wouldn't even step on let alone eat if you saw them in a field somewhere.

The people at the next table over have been staring at us since we came in. We're used to it and usually just ignore it, but Cecelia sometimes can't help being Cecelia.

"Would you like some of this for your goat?" she asks one of the women.

The person she addressed blushes and turns back to her own plate. Her dining companion laughs, though. "Are you sure it's safe for goats?"

We start a good-natured banter between tables based on the proposition that one could run afoul of the Anti-Cruelty Society for feeding food like this to defenseless animals. When they leave, I decide to get my business with Cecelia done.

"I need to ask a favor."

"Of course," she says. "How much do you need?"

"No, not money." I lean a little closer so I can speak in a low voice. "Betsy wants to know more about my situation with Wilkins, and I can't talk to her about it." I explain about my attorney insisting that I avoid any conversations about it with Betsy or other family or friends. "I know her. At some point she's going to insist on knowing. I'd like you to tell her."

"Why me?" Cecelia asks.

"Because you already know the stuff I want you to tell her. You can tell her about the lowlife bastard who got mugged, and you can tell her about the Strand murder. You can tell her that Wilkins suspects me because I'm a big, strong girl who has been known to fight back and because he hates trannies, especially me."

"I don't understand why you can't tell her that," says Cecelia. She's not objecting. She's curious.

"Because I can't answer her next question. If I tell her, she has to ask me if I did either of those things, or both of them. No matter how I answer that question, if I answer it, she can be a witness in a trial. I don't want her to have to do that."

"And me? What about me, Bobbi?"

"When she asks, you can truthfully say you don't know. And that's the end of it."

"What if I *do* know?" Cecelia opens her eyes wide, emphasizing the point.

That stops me short. "*Do* you know?" I ask.

Cecelia is too artful to answer a question we both know shouldn't be answered. "Have you considered that maybe you should trust Betsy and tell her what she wants to know? She loves you. You want her to trust you, right?"

"What I know could end up being a curse for her, Cecelia. She could be forced to testify, or she could be forced to lie. I'm going with the attorney's advice. He already has the last of my savings. If I have to start writing checks again, I'll go under." I let that sink in for a minute. "So will you tell her?"

Cecelia looks lost in thought for a minute. "You need to understand something, Bobbi." Her tone is ominous. "Wilkins is asking around about me, too."

My shock must be obvious. Cecelia nods her head up and down. "Yes," she says. "He thinks I'm a big, strong girl, too. I don't mind being a suspect, but I find his description of me insulting." She feigns indignation and we share a laugh. But even as I laugh, I ponder the significance of Wilkins sharing my curiosity about Cecelia's potential for murder. He's a bigot and a cretin, but he's a chillingly good detective.

Cecelia turns her gaze to me, and we lock eyes. "There will be a day in time when this is over, when Wilkins goes on to pursue actual crimes against humanity. When that happens, I want you to tell me what you know about that goon getting rolled in the alley, and what went on with you and Strand." She pauses to sip some water. "Until then," she says, "Betsy is going to have to live without all the answers, just like the rest of us."

17

SWEAT POURS OFF Wilkins' body like he's being drenched by a hose. He mops at his brow with the last of the tissues the receptionist gave him. He can feel sweat flow down his neck and along his spine. It drips from his nose to his chin. His arms are dripping wet. His hands are so clammy he's afraid to touch anything.

The place is as quiet as a morgue and just as antiseptic. His mind supplies the sound of a saw cutting off the top of a corpse's head in a postmortem. The sound is a lot like a dentist's drill, which is even more terrifying to him.

He shouldn't be such a coward. This is just a sit-down-and-talk session. But he's sweating because he knows the news won't be good. The needles and drills, the pain, the terrifying, brain-stabbing pain is just starting. His mouth is so sore he can barely eat soft food anymore.

The young oral surgeon enters the office and sits down, smiles at Wilkins, a smile of forced sympathy, the kind he hates.

"Mr. Wilkins, I'm afraid I have bad news for you," he begins. "We have found oral squamous cell carcinoma in your lower jaw, your gums, and your tongue. That is a serious form of cancer. I want you to see an oncologist I work with at once so that we can confer. He may want you to see an Ear, Nose, and Throat specialist and if he does, the same thing applies. Do it sooner rather than later. Your cancer looks advanced, but I want a second opinion, and if you want to get other opinions, I'm fine with that.

"I don't want to scare you, but you need to know this is a serious condition. I understand from your history that you have a fear of dentists and doctors, but you need to overcome that now and let us do our work."

The rest of it is like elevator music to Wilkins whose reeling mind goes in and out of the present.

"Do you have any questions?"

Wilkins snaps back to the here and now. The foreboding reality of his shitty life. He shifts in his seat, trying to recall what the man had said, what he was thinking while the man said it.

"Is this life-threatening?" he asks.

"I'm afraid so, Mr. Wilkins," says the surgeon. "It's very serious. We have to move fast."

Wilkins sits back in his chair, stunned, numb. This is impossible, he thinks. He hears a voice. It's the oral surgeon. He's lost track of time and place. The man is standing up.

"I understand this is quite a shock," says the doctor. "Take as long as you need. I'll have someone look in on you in a few minutes to see if you need anything."

Wilkins doesn't hear him leave, just stares at the wall, thinking about his son, his daughter, his ex-wife. His parents. They flash through his mind like dancers on an old Soul Train, just smiles, no lines. But then they don't have to speak. They tell a story just by being there. His story.

He should go get rip-roaring drunk, but it actually hurts to drink now, too. Maybe he should ask for a shot of some kind of painkiller, or a magic pill—or just put the Glock in his mouth and check out.

* * *

THURSDAY, NOVEMBER 27

In my youth, Thanksgiving wasn't really festive, but it wasn't as glum as the other holidays because my mother loved to cook and making the big meal put her in a good mood. That seemed to lift my sister out of her continuing gothic misery into something approximating a fun mood, too. And my dad would lose himself in football games and not look bitter and angry for most of the day.

That was as close to happiness and bliss as we ever got in my house.

Thanksgivings were better during my years with Betsy even though I was struggling with identity issues. After we split, during my coming-out years, it became a lonely day for me. I started enjoying the day again when Betsy and Don began inviting me to Thanksgiving dinner. It was fun getting dressed up, helping with the dinner, getting treated like a woman. Fortunately, Betsy's parents were always in a warm vacation spot for the holiday. Don's parents often joined Don and Betsy for the Thanksgiving feast, and they were warm, accepting people who added luster to the occasion.

This is already my best Thanksgiving ever. I spent the morning doing hair and nails at TransRising, getting my transgender sisters ready for the big Thanksgiving dinner at the LGBT Center. Betsy and Robbie stopped by to lend moral support. Betsy hasn't given up on our relationship, and I never will. Then my nemesis, Lisa, stopped in, and after I complimented her on her beautiful hairdo—a very chic high ponytail with lots of curls and flair—she worked alongside me for an hour, styling hair and doing nails. She was actually quite pleasant, though most of our conversations were with our clients.

Now I'm off to the Thanksgiving dinner with Betsy, Robbie, and Don's parents and their friends. Dinner's at my place, we all know each other, and we'll have a warm and leisurely celebration marked by good cheer and sumptuous food.

* * *

SATURDAY, NOVEMBER 29

As much as I treasure sharing my life with Betsy and Robbie, I've been looking forward to having this night to myself. A hot steamy bath, a chance to collect my thoughts, to reflect on life, to contemplate the future. A leisurely glass of wine. A good book.

Betsy and Robbie are out with her in-laws at a children's theater presentation followed by dinner. I was invited, but the grandparents will get more lap-time with Robbie without me, and they deserve it. Plus, I could use the rest. I'm feeling jangled by the pressures of my business and my personal life.

Unfortunately, this is not to be a quiet evening at home. Moments after my loved ones leave, Phil calls. A friend just gave him two tickets to *Blue Man Group*, a raucous theater production that has been playing to rave reviews and full houses in Chicago for years. If it were anyone but Phil, I'd have said no. I should have said no anyway. This relationship is getting weird, the physical attraction, the friendship, Phil's struggle to accept me and to accept himself wanting to be intimate with a transwoman.

I say yes because he is a nice man and I like him. If it were just the sexual attraction, I'd have said no.

Blue Man Group is a fun show, even though I'm not in the mood to be out. Phil's tickets are third row center, which would be fabulous at a jazz concert, but at *Blue Man Group* the seats come with sheets of plastic and the advice that we should use them to protect our clothing. I prepare myself for a pie fight.

The blue men are apparently here from another planet and they explore ours through a combination of mime and pounding rhythms that lead to sight gags and a paint fight. The paint fight is where the audience gets involved, at least those seated in the front rows. We are splashed with a fluid that looks like paint. It's not that serious, we're told. The colored liquid easily wipes off the skin and washes off clothing. So we laugh even as we are besieged by fluid-flinging aliens.

When the show ends, Phil invites me out for a drink. I have drops of blue on my clothing, and even though I've rinsed my face and hands, I feel like I'm still wearing whatever it was they were splashing up there. I beg off, explaining my desire to change and wash up. He understands.

When Phil pulls up to the curb in front of my apartment, only the outside light and the entry light are on, which means Betsy has gone to bed. I thank Phil for a great time, kiss him on the cheek, and get out of the car. He gets out and walks me to the door.

It's a cold night. Plumes of condensation form with each breath we release. We get to the door, and I thank him again. As I try to plant another kiss on his cheek, he guides my lips to his and embraces me. It happens to me again. I lose all control. First my body, then my mind. We make out like a couple of teenagers under the glow of my porch light.

I break the clinch, my hands on his chest, pushing him back lightly. "Let's not, Phil. We've been here before. Nothing's changed."

Sane, smart words. But the voice saying them is panting with desire. And the man I'm saying them to has opened my coat and pulled me to him. I can feel his hands on my butt, pressing us together, and he is breathing heavily in my ear.

He whispers. "I can't help it, Bobbi. You're all I think about. I want you. I want to be with you. I want to feel your bare skin, your body . . ." His voice drifts into the vapors. I'm focused on my own desires. I've never made love with a man I loved, or even one I knew well and liked. I haven't made love with anyone at all in weeks. Months maybe, though this is not a time for me to do calculations. I am so aware of his body, his hands, his erection, his lips, I really can't think of anything else. In the dim recesses of my mind I know this is a mistake. There will be regrets. Deep, dark regrets.

But there's an answer echoing, too. *Face down your fears.* I want him. I've wanted him for years. It's time to do this and find out where it ends.

I lead Officer Phil silently into the apartment and to my room. I close the door and turn to him in the dark. I peel off my coat and step out of my dress while he wrestles his clothes off. Our naked bodies find each other, his skin impossibly warm, his erection hard against my pelvis. Five years of post-op fantasies begin playing out on a dark, cold night in late November. When he mounts me, when he penetrates deep into me and his body covers mine, I feel like a petite blond homecoming queen, a young woman who has always been a woman, being seduced for the first time by a sweet young man, two innocents giving in to natural desire, a man and a woman bonded by interlocked body parts. I try to control my moans and gasps as he brings us both to orgasm, try not to wake Betsy with my wanton behavior.

Surely she will forgive me, I think, just before my mind is consumed by sensations that block out all other reality.

* * *

SUNDAY, NOVEMBER 30

Regret doesn't come all at once, like an avalanche descending in a wall of nightmares. It evolves slowly, hour by hour, as I wait for a phone call from the man to whom I gave my body and soul last night.

It's pathetic that someone who has been through as much as I have would be so naïve. I was convinced when he left my bedroom last night that he would call this morning or surely this afternoon to express his affection and maybe even rave about what a hot-blooded lover I am. The illusion was nice while it lasted. I woke with an all-over glow, body and mind purring with contentment. I fantasized about his call coming at work, me taking time from a service to pick up the phone, hear Phil greet me with sighs and kisses, ask if we can do it again tonight.

But the call never came. By five, I knew it never would. By six I realized that he called me last minute for the *Blue Man Group* because his original date cancelled late. Who better to call as an emergency fill-in than the perpetually unfulfilled transwoman. Ugly, but easy. And it gives you a war story to share with the guys, the night I fucked a tranny. I try to remind myself that I was willing to risk this rejection just for one night with him, but it doesn't remove the sting. It makes it worse because it highlights what a desperate fool I was. Am.

This is a workday for me, so some of my shame is diluted by working on clients and talking to people. Until I go home. Betsy treats me with icy distance and tells me she and Robbie have already eaten. I deduce that while humiliating myself with Phil, I also made enough noise to wake Betsy and leave her permanently disgusted with the image of her ex-husband getting laid in the next room.

I microwave a frozen dinner. I'm still picking at the meal when Betsy finishes putting Robbie to bed. She sits across the table and stares at me with intense eyes. "Did you have a good time last night?" It's not a question. It's a condemnation.

I stare back, so conflicted in what I want to say that I can't say anything. Yes, I got laid and it was beautiful. No, the day after was worse than dying. I got to feel like a woman for twenty minutes, and the price is feeling like trash for maybe the rest of my life. Mostly I just want to beg her not to join the unseen mob pummeling me right now—every person who has ever made me feel bad about myself is beating me with baseball bats made from the judgment tree.

When no words come, I burst into tears. They pour down my face. I push my chair back from the table and lean forward, face in hands, and sob. This is the final humiliation. I have made myself repulsive to Betsy.

Her face softens, but she stays on her side of the table. When I stop crying and sit up again, she asks another question, her voice still icy. "Who were you fucking? Or is that none of my business? I'd just like to know you weren't putting my child's life at risk by bringing in some kind of prostitute or maybe a drug dealer or a porn star."

"I would never do that." My voice is just above a whisper and shaky.

"I wish I could believe that, Bobbi. I'm scared out of my skull right now. You don't say a word about going out or having someone over or anything. I come home and you're not here, then in the middle of the night I wake up and hear you banging and moaning. For a minute I thought you were being raped." Her face is severe, her disgust obvious.

"It was Phil." The tears start again, but I refuse to sob anymore. "You weren't in any danger. He's a cop. And other than never wanting to see me or touch me again, he's a nice guy."

"What?"

"I got laid by I guy I really like. I've been hot for him for years. Last night he notched up a tranny on his been-there-done-that belt and I'll never hear from him again. Because I am a stupid, ugly slut and no one will ever want me as a woman. I'm sorry I grossed you out, but could you give me a day or two before you tell me what a piece of shit I am?"

I get up and go to my room. I can't take any more. I know we need to talk this out, but I can't do it right now. I strip, put on my bathrobe, and trundle to the bathroom. Betsy has gone to her room, the light glows from beneath her door. I draw a bath and slide into the heat and bubbles and stare at the ceiling light through the refracted vision of my tears.

18

It's eerie looking around the room and realizing I'm the oldest person here. Good grief, I'm only forty-three.

My assistant Jalela has hauled me to this meeting in the basement of the TransRising building. The upper floors house the live-in residents, while the basement provides classrooms and a meeting area for the residents and dozens of other transpeople who come here for support services. This meeting is the kickoff to the TransRising's mentoring program, and Jalela wants me to be someone's big sister. She has some girls in mind and introduces me to them. We sip cider and nibble on cookies and work the room. The diversity of the gathered transwomen is mind-boggling, even to me. There are about two dozen of us. We run the gamut from mid-teens to ancient me. We are tall and short, heavy and thin, pretty and not pretty, feminine and masculine, and we are everything in between.

Some of us are socially gifted, able to chat easily with each new face. Some of us are not so gifted and spend much of the social hour in mute silence. After years of doing hair, I fall into the former category. Making small talk is not my favorite thing in life—I much prefer serious topics—but this isn't the place to discuss brain surgery or atom splitting.

After an hour of mingling, Lisa calls the group to order and explains the program.

"We put the mentoring program together to fill one of the black holes many of us step into when we start living as our true selves," she says. "Many of us lose the family and friends and role models we would otherwise have to help guide us into adulthood and into careers and relationships.

"A lot of us, left to our own devices, start focusing our lives on body parts. I need to get breasts. I need to get rid of body hair. I need GRS.

"Natal women and men grow up thinking about their bodies, too, but most of them also focus on other things. Sports. Grades. Going to college. Getting a good job. Having nice friends.

"We want the mentor program to help our girls develop fuller lives, to help them realize that it isn't body parts that define us, it's many, many things. Are we people of good character? Can our friends trust us to do the right thing? Can our employers trust us to work hard and be loyal? What skills define us? When someone asks you, 'Who are you?', what do you say? 'I'm a transwoman'? No, that might be *what* you are, but *who* you are must be more complex.

"I'm young and my identity is still evolving, but if you ask me who I am I would say things like, I'm a graphic designer and a transgender activist and someone who works really hard without complaining. I'm smart and competent. I'm a woman and I want to have a family someday.

"I could go on, but you get the idea. A vagina and breasts will not make you happy in this life. You need other goals. All of our volunteer mentors have been successful in their careers. They have all transitioned and lived to tell about it. And they work every day to foster the kinds of interpersonal relationships we all need to have a full life." She is articulating things that I agree with completely, and I am left to wonder again why we are so uneasy with each other.

Lisa eventually introduces each of the prospective mentors in the room, and each of the ladies who have not yet been assigned a mentor. The mentors include a corporate executive, a saleswoman, an engineer, a mechanic, a doctor, two attorneys, and me. I'm feeling dwarfed by the accomplishments of the others, but she introduces me with great fanfare.

I smile and wave a hand to acknowledge Lisa's praise. Fortunately, I don't have to say anything. I'm so off balance from her introduction I wouldn't know what to say. I always assumed she thought I was an airhead hairdresser, not to mention old and ugly.

The flattery is especially welcome in this dark period of my life. It has been four days since I offered up my body as a hole in the fence for Phil to rub against. He did finally call, but all he said was he had been busy and would call again when he had time to talk. No need. That said it all.

And Betsy still keeps a lot of distance between us. She no longer has me take Robbie to preschool on my late mornings, and they manage to eat before I get home each night. She is applying for paying jobs so she can get her own place. I feel lonely already.

After the formal program is over, I work my way to Lisa to thank her.

"We appreciate you coming forward, Bobbi," she says.

We stand awkwardly facing each other, both of us, I think, wanting to take this moment of goodwill another step forward. For the life of me, I can't think of anything to say. Neither can she. We finally exchange faux hugs and move off in search of easier conversations.

* * *

TUESDAY, DECEMBER 2

Wilkins shifts and fidgets, staring at the walls of the waiting room, too nervous to pick up a magazine, too bored, too uncomfortable, too engulfed by life's shit storm to do anything but sweat.

Perspiration pours down his face and his upper body. His palms are wet. His mouth hurts. It even hurts to swallow fluids now. He should just get up and go back to his dreary apartment, put a hollow-point in the chamber of his Glock, and blow his brains out. The only thing that's going to happen here is they're going to tell him he's going to die, but he'll have to wait in this torture chamber for an hour before they get to it. And they won't just let him die, they'll make him do other things, painful things that mean coming into doctor and dentist offices all the goddamn time.

He should just go home and eat a bullet and get it over with.

But he has things to do first. He has to try to fix things with his kids. He's got to get his case files in order for whoever takes over. He has to close out the Strand case. No one else would put in the time. No one else would risk the bigotry tag he got for liking a tranny for the crime. He snorts an ironic laugh. How the world has changed. How many times he was called nigger by rednecks and John Birchers and expected to take it, even though he had a badge and a gun. Life was so screwed up sometimes.

Doors slam inside the oncologist's office. The receptionist leads Wilkins to an office. Three physicians stand to greet him with handshakes as he enters. The oncologist is a wiry, fiftyish white man with a Russian name and a light accent. The internist is an African-American woman in her thirties with large eyes and a kind smile. The oral surgeon is the same young white male who started everything, a clinician who looks at a patient and sees a specimen, not a person.

There are four files on the table, one compiled by each of them and a fourth from the ENT who specializes in cancer diagnosis and treatment.

The oncologist speaks first. "I'm afraid we have bad news, Detective." There is regret in his voice, but he makes eye contact and gets right to the point. Wilkins appreciates that. Let's get it over with so I can get out of here and breathe again, he thinks.

"You have extensive cancerous tissues in your mouth. There are squamous cell carcinomas on the left side of your mandible, your lower jaw. The cancer has spread to your gums and your tongue. I'm afraid it is too advanced for routine treatment. When we catch these lesions early enough, we can treat the patient with a relatively simple surgery and/or radiation therapy.

"Unfortunately, your cancer has advanced far beyond that stage. Radical surgery is required—"

Wilkins feels his world shake. It's about what he expected to hear, but somehow, hearing it rocks him. The oncologist defers to the oral surgeon to discuss the surgery, but Wilkins is barely aware of the change in voices and speakers. The surgeon's technical dissertation passes far beyond Wilkins' comprehension.

The oral surgeon stops speaking and looks at Wilkins expectantly. "Do you have any questions?" he asks.

Wilkins blinks, shakes his head slowly. "I don't really understand . . ." He wants to say what he doesn't understand, but he doesn't understand any of it. He doesn't understand why his life has come to this. An early death, alone. A life trying to make the world safe for others coming to an end in a sterile office surrounded by strangers.

The internist speaks softly. "Detective Wilkins? Can you hear me?"

His mind comes back to the present. His eyes focus on the internist's sympathetic face. He nods yes.

"To save your life, we are going to have to do a mandibulectomy and a glossectomy. A mandibulectomy is the surgical removal of part of your lower jaw. It is a disfiguring operation even with reconstructive surgery. The glossectomy is a partial removal of your tongue. It will affect your speech. You may have difficulty being understood by others when you speak. You may also need to undergo radiation therapy and maybe chemotherapy, too, after the surgery."

She lets him absorb her words, then continues. "There are several other serious side effects that can result from this treatment. You may suffer from fatigue. You may have swallowing difficulties. Some people experience memory loss and dizziness. You may have to depend on a feeding tube for hydration and nutrition—"

Wilkins almost passes out from shock. The kindly internist is describing a nightmare, a vision more hideous than anything he could ever imagine.

"Detective Wilkins?"

He gradually becomes aware of the doctors again. The internist is saying his name. He focuses on her. She watches him expectantly. They all do. He has missed something. He's supposed to say something but he doesn't know what.

"Do you have any questions, Detective Wilkins?" She says it gently. He deduces that was her original question.

He collects his thoughts. "Survival? What are my chances?"

The doctors defer to the oncologist. "It's hard to say. The odds are pretty good that you can extend your life by a year or two. The five-year prognosis is less promising. There aren't good numbers for cases as advanced as yours, but I'd guess we're talking one chance in four, maybe less, that you'll live five years."

Wilkins calculates what a year or two could mean. Patch things up with his kids. Close the Strand case. He tries to think. There was something else he wanted to ask. Something he heard before he zoned out.

"Disfigurement," Wilkins says. "What does that look like?"

"We have some photos of others who have undergone a mandibulectomy," says the oral surgeon. "But I have to warn you, they can be very shocking. You might want to take a day or two to digest everything before we get into that."

Wilkins shakes his head. "No. Let's get this over with."

The oral surgeon opens a medical text to a marked spread and pushes the book across the table to Wilkins. A half dozen photos jump off the pages of gray text. Four show vile growths in people's mouths. The other two show horribly disfigured faces, scarier than any Halloween mask, their mouths tiny circles, their faces caved in on one side like a rotting jack-o'-lantern. Monsters.

"Sweet Jesus!" Wilkins gasps. He sits back in his chair and looks at the ceiling as if struck by a fist. Tears come, then sobs. He leans forward. He vomits. He cries uncontrollably. His mind fills with the sight of his son and daughter recoiling in horror from the sight of their father, his ex-wife hiding her eyes at the sight of him. The photos are the end of his life. He will never get his family back. He is no longer human.

* * *

THURSDAY, DECEMBER 4

I spend the morning pouring my heart out to Marilee about everything, but especially about my relationship with Betsy. She counsels patience and she's convincing. I leave in the lightest mood I've had in days, but that evaporates as soon as I get back to the apartment.

Betsy greets me with a scribbled note and a demand. "We need to talk." The note is a phone number and a name: *Detective Allan Wilkins.*

We sit at the kitchen table. I realize it's quiet in the place. Robbie must be playing with the neighbor. Betsy has been expecting me.

"Who is this man?" she asks, tapping her finger on the note in front of me.

"Didn't he tell you?"

"Don't be coy, Bobbi. I don't know if he's investigating you or if he's your latest cop lover."

Her hostility makes me wince. "He's the cop I told you about. He's investigating a murder that he'd love to charge me with. I'm not going into the rest of it because it can only get you in the middle of something you don't want to be in. Here's all you have to know: I didn't kill anyone."

"There's more to it than that, Bobbi. There has to be. If you aren't willing to trust me with what happened, how can I trust you?"

"I've told you everything I can about Wilkins. I'm sorry. I can't do more."

"You have too many secrets." She grimaces. She rattles off a list of secrets I've kept from her, from transitioning to my promiscuous sex life. "Good God, Bobbi, is there anything or anyone you won't fuck? One day it's a woman, the next time it's a man. Now it's a murder you can't talk about. What am I supposed to think?"

I'm at a loss for words, but she's not ready to hear me anyway.

"I need some truths here, Bobbi. Who are you? How are you involved in this murder? I need to know if my daughter is safe here. I need to know if you're going to be a bad influence on her."

She stares at me, seething with anger that borders on hate. I don't know where to start or what to say. She glowers at me, silently demanding a reply.

"I don't know what I am, Betsy. I am trying to be a good person. I've had sex three times this year and I've never killed anyone."

"How do I know you're telling the truth?"

I blink. Good question. "I don't know," I say. "Maybe you just have to take it on faith. Like how you believe in God."

"You're comparing yourself to God?"

"No. I'm saying the truth about me is a lot easier to see than the truth about God. You just have to make up your mind. Am I a person who goes to work every day, cares about people, loves you and Robbie? Or am I a closet nymphomaniac axe murderer?"

"You don't have any other lovers?"

"I don't have any lovers at all. Jen has a new heartthrob, and Phil doesn't want to see me or talk to me. I think he's pretty grossed out by having fucked a tranny."

"Do you think that's all it was for him? A conquest?"

It hits me then, what really makes it hurt. "No. I think he actually likes me and I think he found me attractive and when we made love, we made love. It was after that, when he realized he had feelings for a transsexual, and what that meant about him, that's when he started thinking of me as a barnyard animal or a venereal disease."

For all her anger and suspicion, Betsy's face softens.

"There are some things I'm never going to have, Betsy." I say this to her, but really to myself. "I'm never going to have children of my own. I'm never going to have a deep, passionate, long-lasting love. And no one will ever see me as an actual woman. Not even me."

We sit in total silence for a long while. Betsy rustles in her chair. "Are you going to call him?" She nods toward the message.

"Yes."

"Are you ever going to tell me what happened?"

"I need some time," I tell her. That secret chapter of my life is becoming a wall that surrounds me and it's getting higher every day. With every fiber of my being I want to tell her everything right now, but I can't get past how dangerous it would be to us both.

* * *

THURSDAY, DECEMBER 4

"I need to talk to Stephen." Wilkins tries to say it nicely, but thirty-plus years on the force makes everything come out in the clipped staccato of a tough street cop. A man who fell into the role of the "bad cop" because he looked the part and stayed there so long he was the part.

"I'll see if he wants to talk to you." Her reply is just as clipped. She hates him. Crazy. The divorce was her idea. He didn't fight her on anything. Gave up everything he had, even his kids it turned out. They decided he was the bad guy. The only way to deny it was to say their mother was wrong, which he couldn't do.

"It's important," he says. "I wouldn't bother you if it wasn't very, very important."

"Hang on." The phone clicks as she puts it on hold.

Several minutes later, the phone clicks and his son's adolescent voice comes over the airwaves. "Hello." Flat and cold.

"Stephen!" He tries to greet his son with enthusiasm and energy. "Good to hear your voice, Son." He waits a moment for Stephen to respond, gets a mumbled syllable.

"Something's come up and I need to see you, Stephen."

"What about?"

"Well, I don't want to get into it over the phone. How about we go for a walk after school one day this week?"

"I don't know. I have things to do." His son is mumbling, his words barely distinguishable.

"How about setting aside an hour, say, Thursday. I won't bother you again."

The boy says he has to check with his mother. He puts a hand over the mouthpiece of the phone and has a short conversation. "Okay," he says when he comes back.

Wilkins sets up the meet for Lincoln Square. Near the kid's school. Scenic neighborhoods. Nice cafés.

*　*　*

FRIDAY, DECEMBER 5

"Wilkins." Even on the phone, when you can't see him, the guy sounds like a mean prick.

"What do you want?" I don't bother saying who's calling.

"Thanks for calling back, Logan." I almost faint with surprise. A thank-you from a troll. And he used my name instead of calling me Cinderella or Queenie.

"I want to sit down and talk to you," he says.

"How stupid do you think I am?"

"I don't think you're stupid. I want to talk to you about the case, what I've got. All off the record. We can meet anywhere you want."

"Why? What's in it for me?"

"After you hear me out, I'm going to offer you a deal. If you like it, you take it to your attorney, and I'll take it to the DA. Maybe we can get this closed by Christmas."

"If you think I'm a murderer you have to think I'm a liar, too, so what kind of deal are you offering me?"

"The best deal you're ever going to get."

"Why? Why would you offer me a good deal? You think I'm vermin and I murder men because I hate them."

"I have my reasons."

"Give me one."

"I've learned some things, okay?"

"I don't believe you. Give me another."

"I want to close this case before Christmas."

I laugh sarcastically. "Detective Wilkins, there is nothing attractive to me about you closing this case before Christmas."

"You have nothing to lose. I won't tape the conversation, no bugs or listening devices, just you and me. Take it or leave it."

"I'll leave it."

"You can pick the place. I'll get your boyfriend to check me for wires before we sit down."

"Phil? Detective, poor Phil isn't my boyfriend and he wants nothing to do with me."

"He told me he'd do it."

"When?"

"Today. I talked to him before I called you."

We go back and forth for several minutes, like a tennis rally, on my safety, his promises. I ask if he'd be willing to put in writing his guarantee that nothing said between us is ever used in court. He is. He agrees to bring a signed statement to the meeting.

"Okay," I say. "When?" We jockey back and forth and settle on a weekday evening. He asks where and I tell him to call me at the salon on the day of the meeting. I've read some spy books.

His call lingers in my mind like a bad dream. The end is near for me, I can feel it. He's going to give me a choice. I can wait to be indicted and go through $50,000 in legal bills and a year or two of litigation and having my reputation and the image of my salon shredded in the news media. Or I can plead guilty and get some kind of reduced sentence, something that would put me back on the street when Robbie is having babies and people are flying space ships instead of driving cars. I can see the faces of Betsy and Robbie as my failure leaves them abandoned in a failed economy, at sea in a country that equates personal financial failure with immorality and people hope you die badly as a result.

I can see Betsy never ever again trusting me for failing her now. Why would she? Could I start over? A transwoman in her sixties or seventies, alone, trying to make new friends? Trying to do hair? I can't bring myself to commit suicide, but it would be the best option. My life is essentially over. I got to be a woman for five years and an aunt for three. That's something, I guess.

19

Cold winds laced with rain and sleet force a change in plans. Wilkins can no longer tolerate the cold. He arrives at the café a few minutes early, but Stephen is already there, sitting at a window table staring at his smartphone.

The teenager looks up as Wilkins approaches. His handsome face goes from recognition to an uncertain frown in a blink or two. Wilkins takes off his coat, drapes it on a chair, offers a handshake to his son. Stephen shakes hands without standing up. His eyes are frozen on his father, his face painted in shock and consternation.

"Are you okay, Dad?" he asks.

Wilkins savors the moment his son calls him "dad." It doesn't happen much anymore, only when the kid forgets himself, forgets he's supposed to hate his dad for divorcing his mother. That moment of happiness is blotted out by the greater realization that he looks like shit, even to his son. Especially to his son. Jesus Christ, imagine how the kid would have felt if he walked in here with a monster face and feeding tubes sticking out of his body.

Wilkins takes a deep breathe to regain his composure.

"I have some health problems, Stephen. That's why I wanted to talk."

"What kind of health problems?"

"I have oral cancer. I need surgery. It's risky. No guarantees. So I want to talk to you about a few things in case I don't make it."

Stephen leans forward, his arms on the table, his head dropping. "Damn," he says. He breathes deeply. He looks up again.

"I've written down some things for you," Wilkins says, pushing an envelope across the table. "You can look at them later. It's a rehash of what I'm going to say.

"First off, you need to know this cancer is my own fault. I've always been scared to death of dentists. So I haven't seen one in many years. I'm telling you this in case you inherited my fear. If you did, go anyway. Think about what I look like as an incentive."

"But you're going to get better." The kid says it, but it's a question, a statement of hope that he wants to have confirmed.

"Not really. I can extend my life, but I won't ever look any better. I'll never be able to eat solid food again. I will lose body mass and strength. I'll have a lot of other problems, too. That doesn't matter. The important thing is, you take care of yourself. Don't make the mistakes I did. Will you promise me that?"

Stephen nods.

"Good. Now, your mom thinks I betrayed her and you and your sister. She has every right to feel that way. I was a piss-poor husband and father. But not because I was unfaithful or anything like that. It was because I put the job first and I wasn't there enough for her or my kids. I want you to know it wasn't because I didn't love you, or her, or your sister. I just didn't know how to be a husband or a father. I did what my father did. I just worked. Don't do what I did. Take classes or read books or do whatever you have to do, but don't do what I did. Do you understand what I'm saying?"

Stephen nods, his face frozen in sadness and shock. A waitress stops and takes their beverage orders. When she is gone, Wilkins shifts his gaze from his son's face to the table and nods a few times, as if agreeing with himself.

"Okay. I want you to know that if I don't make it, you guys will still be okay financially. Your mom has money in the bank, and she'll get my pension benefits. I have some savings, too. Everything will go to your mother, and she'll make sure you both get through college, get a good start. It's all in my will. If I don't make it, my attorney will contact your mom and get things going. The main thing is, you and your sister and your mother will be just fine. Okay?"

Two tears trickle down Stephen's face. "It sounds like you're going to die, Dad."

"The odds aren't good, Stephen."

Stephen covers his face with his hands for a moment, then wipes the tears from his cheeks. "What can I do? Can I do something?"

Wilkins smiles and nods. "Yes, Stephen. There are two more things you can do for me. "

"Okay. What are they?"

"First, tell your sister I didn't have this conversation with her, too, because she's away at school, not because I love her less."

Stephen nods.

"Second, in your envelope there is a card with my address on it and a key taped below. If you get word that I died, I want you to go to the apartment and take care of clearing it out. Take your mom with you. You can have anything you want in the place and throw out the rest.

"I'm going to mail you a package. I want you to open it some place private. You can share it with anyone you want after you've been through it."

"What is it? Mom won't let me have your gun."

"I wouldn't give you a gun. I'm selling mine to another cop. I never used it anyway."

"Really?"

"Really."

His son is surprised. Even his family thought of him as a mean cop. Another mistake. "I became a cop to protect people from violence, not to be violent," says Wilkins.

The boy nods his head up and down for a moment, absorbing this new knowledge. "What's in the package, Dad?"

"My legacy."

"What do I do with it?"

"You'll figure it out."

Wilkins fends off Stephen's attempts to learn more about the mystery package and eventually steers the conversation to how Stephen is doing in school, how his sister is doing in college, what they want for Christmas. Forty minutes later they stand, shake hands and hug, Wilkins thinking his son must really love him to do that, to have physical contact with his emaciated father. Wouldn't it be sweet to have that every day for another twenty years? See his kids grown up, be successful. Maybe get their mom to talk to him again, invite him for Christmas dinner?

He watches his son walk tall and strong out into the storm, and a reality as bleak as the winter sky descends on Wilkins. There will be no magic moments with his kids, no reconciliation with his wife. He will never get better than this. He will only get worse.

He sits down at the table again and dials Logan's number. One more thing to do today.

* * *

SATURDAY, DECEMBER 6

Officer Phil walks in just as I'm just finishing my last client. He comes to the reception desk, nods at me, looks to Samantha. She escorts him to my office. We exchange glances and I smile at him. He smiles back.

For the first time in years I receive his attention without any emotional fluttering. Whatever feelings I had for him are diluted in a sea of tension about this meeting with Wilkins. My sleep has been even more tormented than usual these last two nights as I play through various ways tonight's scenario might play out.

All of the scripts in my dreams end badly, with me losing everything, Betsy hating me, the salon boarded up, me never seeing Robbie again.

There have been a half dozen times at least where I was on the verge of calling Wilkins and cancelling. I can see no possible benefit for me and all kinds of risks. On the other hand, I keep thinking that what makes MBAs so stupid is they only believe in things they can measure. Their knowledge becomes a fence around their intellect. They can't grow beyond it because they think that's the edge of the earth, there is no more. So we will meet. Wilkins will talk. I might learn something I didn't know before. It might help me deal with his unrelenting pressure.

Wilkins enters minutes after Phil. Samantha escorts him to my office. I finish my client and Barbara is just finishing the only other client in the place. In a few minutes, everyone will be gone. Wilkins and I will have our meeting right here, the one place I know he couldn't bug beforehand. I know that's ridiculous, but we can laugh about my cloak and dagger foolishness later.

When I enter the office, both men stand up. We exchange terse hellos. Wilkins looks awful. Shockingly awful. Like a cadaver. His skin seems gray in color, his face is drawn, his clothes hang like bags from his withered frame. If he were gay, I'd figure him for full-blown AIDS. I start to ask him if he's well, then choke it back. This is business and he is not someone whose health I should care about. Indeed, my life would be much better if his life were over.

I ask Phil to check Detective Wilkins for a listening device. He has Wilkins assume the spread position against the wall and frisks him.

"He's clean," says Phil.

"Detective, will you please open your shirt?" I ask. "No offense," I say to Phil. But really, why should I trust him? Do I really know whose side he's on?

Phil nods. Wilkins opens his shirt. He's clean. I thank him.

"Phil, did Detective Wilkins plant a listening device in this room?" I ask. Phil says no. "Would you tell me if he had?"

"Yes, Bobbi, I would," he says. "That was what he asked of me, that I represent your interests. He's clean. The room is clean."

I thank Phil and tell him he can go now. He nods, gives me a faux hug, and leaves.

"Can I get you coffee or tea or a cold drink?" I ask Wilkins.

"No. Thank you," he says. Wow. Manners. What's the world coming to?

Samantha calls out a good night as she and the last hairdressers leave. I wish them well, then ask Wilkins to follow me into the salon. I've set up a conversation area at my workstation. I gesture for Wilkins to sit in the service chair. It looks like he could use the comfort. I sit in a folding chair directly in front of him.

He opens his briefcase and removes several file folders. "I won't take much of your time. I want to review where the case against you stands right now and, like I said on the phone, I want to put a deal on the table for you to consider."

I listen but do not comment. He says it started with the murder of my friend and client Mandy Marvin, six years ago. I got disgusted with the police investigation and started poking around on my own. That led me to Strand, who was rumored to be Mandy's sugar daddy and a man with a history of hurting and maybe killing transwomen. One thing led to another and Strand had two goons beat and rape me, then I set up one of the goons for a mugging in the same place I was raped. Then I finally kidnapped Strand and executed him in his love nest. Wilkins recites evidence he has to back up most of his points.

"Ms. Logan, I have motive—he had you raped, he was going to kill you. I have means—you're strong and you have self-defense training. And I have opportunity—you can't account for your time after eleven o'clock that night. You say you were home alone, but you could have been anywhere."

He establishes eye contact with me. "I'm going to meet with the DA to initiate an indictment. We can save everyone a lot of time and money by reaching a deal beforehand, something that lets you plead to a lesser charge in view of Strand's aggression toward you."

He waits for my response. It's slow in coming. His theory of the crime is so close to the truth I'm dizzy with dread. I struggle to regain my poise.

"My, my, Detective Wilkins. Why would you do such a nice thing for me?" I ask. "This is the very first time we've exchanged words when you haven't called me a queen or butt-fucking twink or, oh, let's see, there was fag, queer, girly boy. Shall I go on?"

Wilkins nods his head in little movements, like he's agreeing with me and thinking about it at the same time. "I apologize for those indiscretions," he says. "I was wrong to say those things. I was expressing what I felt, but that wasn't professional. Neither what I said nor what I felt. I've learned some things from this investigation."

"Like what, Detective?"

"I learned that Strand was a bad man. I can't prove it, but he probably murdered your friend and he may have murdered others. I've learned that people don't choose to be transsexual, that's just how it happens. And I've seen how hard that can be for someone. I—" He halts for a moment. "I respect you. What you've done with your life."

I have to focus to keep from falling off my chair in wonder. Never in a million years could I imagine him saying those things. But I block it all from my mind and tend to business.

"Did you learn that Strand wouldn't have been murdered if the police had conducted a proper investigation of Mandy Marvin's murder?" I should tone down the insolence in my voice, but I can't.

"We failed to do our job." His concession is disarming. I didn't see it coming. Still, he's the enemy. I pull myself together.

"So now you want to cap it all off by sending me to jail?"

Wilkins shrugs. "I don't make the laws and I don't get to pick which ones to enforce. What I can do is work with the DA to make it as easy as possible on you. I'm sure they'd take murder-one off the table, I'm not sure how much further they can go. There's a self-defense element to this. Strand had already shown his bad intentions and the testimony of the rapist suggests Strand was getting ready to do something again."

"How nice. The goon confesses to raping me and you let him off in return for testifying against me for some other crime? Can you imagine what my attorney would do with that?"

"Ms. Logan, I have no idea what kind of cross your attorney would muster with that or any other witness. More to the point, none of us, your attorney included, has any idea what a jury or a judge will take away from any witness' testimony. Trials are a crapshoot."

"Trials can't be any worse than police investigations. I got raped by two men and no one gave a damn. The so-called rape specialist at Chicago PD told me I deserved it. And now you're going to let the rapist off so you can put me in jail because you think I did what you wouldn't do—bring the murderer of a transsexual woman to justice. Fuck you, Detective. Fuck you and your whole rotten department. Fuck the DA, too."

Wilkins' eyes flash for a moment. I expect him to come out of his chair and get in my face with that awful breath of his. But he catches himself. He takes a deep breath, gets his composure back.

"I understand your anger, Ms. Logan. The rapist isn't going to get 'off', but he will get some kind of deal. I think he wants to go to prison. He can't function anymore.

"But more to the point, I'm offering you a chance to come clean. The memory of that murder must surely haunt you. You don't have to live with that. You can tell your story and get a reduced sentence. I hope a very reduced sentence, maybe a year or two with the rest suspended. Something like that. But a clear conscience."

I grimace. "I have a lot of problems with your proposition. The main one is, I didn't do it. And I won't confess to it. Period."

Wilkins looks at me with a sad expression on his haggard face. He shakes his head slowly, side to side, like he's saying no to something. "That's the first lie you've told me, Ms. Logan. I'm surprised. I really am surprised. That was the last thing I expected from you. I've learned a lot about you. Most people who know you, like you. They respect you. You're straight and fair with them, and honest. They all say that about you."

"Well, Detective, you surprised me, too. I never expected you to be civil. But I think we've said all there is to say."

We rise from our chairs. At the door he turns to me. "Goodnight, Ms. Logan. Do yourself a favor and talk to your attorney about what we discussed."

Very artful of him, especially for a career "bad cop." He says it like he's got my best interests in mind.

"I will think about that, Detective. And here's something for you to think about. What if that gorilla had raped your daughter or your wife instead of me? Think about what kind of deal you'd give him or the man who hired him."

*   *   *

SUNDAY, DECEMBER 7

Since I began working at Salon L'Elégance all those years ago, the first week in December has become one of the most joyful periods of my year. That's when we officially begin the holiday season in the salon. Because I never had much family life, the salon's celebration of Christmas and Hanukkah and Kwanza was the first time in my life I felt the joy and light of the holidays, the music, the colors, the hustle and bustle, the smiles, the sense of something special taking place. It has been like that for me ever since.

We decorate the salon ourselves, part of it according to a coordinated plan, and part just the inspiration of any given individual at any given moment. Given our collective penchant for colors and shapes and pushing the boundaries of convention, the process is wildly creative and fun.

Most retail businesses do this after Halloween and they hire outside specialists to do it, but the people of L'Elégance share an aversion to such blatant commercialism, some for religious reasons, others because it seems dehumanizing somehow, the way pornography dehumanizes sex. The funny thing is, I think we get some commercial benefits from not commercializing the holidays, starting with the fact that decorating the place together just puts us all in the holiday spirit. And it lasts all the way to Christmas. We smile and sing and hum and greet our clients with real enthusiasm.

This year we're adding to the mood by giving gift bags to customers. Regular customers get a beautiful bag containing four sample-size SuperGlam products. First-time customers get a beautiful bag with two products. The bags are festooned in bows and ribbons and they include a holiday greeting card from the salon staff. It's costing some money, but this has been a hard year, and it's important to say thanks to the people who have helped us survive.

For all that, I'm straining emotionally to get into the mood of this day. It's hard to shake off the unnerving message from Detective Wilkins yesterday. It's one thing to hear about his investigation in bits and pieces, where each brick in the wall is a crumbling lump of clay formed from biased interpretations of circumstantial evidence. It's quite another to hear the whole thing strung together. All of a sudden Wilkins' flights of flimsy start hanging together with a structural strength that seems impregnable. I start hearing the jury foreman pronouncing my guilt.

I am stalked by images of the gray void of prison, the pallid skin, the lifeless gazes, the monotony. A life without color or form. A space of straight lines and rules, where circles are erased and free form is illegal. In my images it is a slow-motion walk to death, an endless, monotonous trudge through nothingness. It is silent and barren. There are no faces, no music. Dark turns to light without consequence; there is still nothing to see. The sound is a blend of industrial noises that bang and hum and grind into a single, dark rumble, gloomy and perpetual.

I can barely stand to look at Betsy and Robbie because the aura of doom that stalks me stalks them, too. I cannot fathom how I will live with the knowledge that their lives will be shredded even more than mine when I am charged. When my fragile world comes apart. I will meet with Cecelia soon to see what I can do to leave something for them to have when they start over again, but it's hard to imagine what I might be able to provide. My beautiful salon is doomed. It will fail within a few months after I'm charged unless Roger drops everything and comes back to save it. My money for attorney's fees will disappear in a trice. My apartment building will last longer, maybe a year or two, because repossessions take a while. But I can't sell it, not for what I owe on it. In a year, my defense against charges brought by a prosecution apparatus that includes an army of attorneys and paralegals will be a single public defender, chosen at random from a pool of public defenders, some of whom have never won a case.

Because of the dark tunnel I am entering, I strain to compartmentalize my bleak prospects and focus at times like this on the poetry of life as it exits right now. I breathe in the holiday colors and rhapsodize with the music. I look upon the work of my colleagues with the appreciation of an art lover; the perfect tones and textures and contours of what they do make my heart beat faster. This is magic, this blending of form and light and passion that celebrates humanity in a way no other art form does.

Tonight, when I go home, I will do the same thing with Betsy and Robbie. I will ignore the cliff looming a few steps ahead in my life and focus on what a beautiful person Betsy is, what a miracle it is that she loved me and loves me still, how lucky my half-life has been. I will immerse my being in Robbie. I will hear her voice and memorize her perfect innocence. I will record the sound of her laugh in my mind, along with pictures of her movements and mannerisms that express the freedom and joy of early childhood. I will relish these moments now and preserve them so that I may play them in the theater of my mind in the future when my reality is no longer tolerable, when all that's left is an old movie of my brief second life.

* * *

MONDAY, DECEMBER 8

Betsy's eyes are closed and her body is limp. She is in the midst of a scalp massage, and we are at the midpoint in our spa day. Betsy's attitude toward me has softened. She still wants answers, she's still not really certain about me, but she's still trying to be there for me just as I am for her.

I declared Spa Day to celebrate Betsy's completion of a large project at work. It was received with fanfare by her colleagues, and she is feeling a resurgence of self-worth and relevance. There may be a chance for a paid position down the line, and even if there isn't, Betsy has gotten her confidence back, and it won't be long before she starts pulling down a salary somewhere. Her mood is heightened by the fact that Robbie loves her preschool. The guilt she once felt about "abandoning" her daughter for portions of each day has morphed into a shared excitement for the world our beloved toddler is experiencing.

Despite the demons that follow me everywhere I go, I'm feeling a little festive myself. A lot of it is seeing Betsy's spirit rise from the ashes, but some of it is selfish. I haven't done the books yet, but the salon has been busy from open to close since the week before Thanksgiving. We are attracting many new customers from our promotions, we are retaining quite a few of the new people who came in last summer and fall, and some of our clients who quit coming in at the onset of the recession have begun coming back.

This is pleasing on several levels. I didn't destroy the business; I may have even made it better. It will survive the recession if we continue to do the things we've been doing. And, if the worst happens to me, Roger can come back and take over a viable business. He won't have lost his investment. He can keep it going until he finds a new buyer, a more worthy one, I hope.

Betsy and I started our day at a massage spa a few blocks from L'Elégance. We had side-by-side deep massages that left us as limp as overdone pasta and so relaxed it took forever to dress afterward. We are doing hair at the L'Elégance, of course. After her shampoo and scalp massage, Betsy will get the most elegantly crafted graduated bob in the city, courtesy of Barbara. I will be getting a cut and color from Bobby. He's a young, flamboyantly gay hairdresser who has a wild, uninhibited genius for color. He has convinced me to let him decide the colors without discussing it with me. "I want it to be a surprise," he says. This from the colorist who has sent heads of bright orange, shocking purple, hot pink, and sky blue out our doors in the past couple of months. If my immediate future was a sit-down with a banker or some other stuffed shirt, I probably wouldn't have agreed to it.

But the thought of the police taking me away in a Christmas coif of green, red, and white hair has a certain charm to it. In my mind's eye, I could see a judge looking down at me from the bench and saying to the prosecutor, "You're charging this Christmas fairy with murder?"

When we finish here, we will go to the nail salon a few doors down for a mani-pedi with holiday colors.

Bobby foils my hair with nimble fingers that seem to travel at the speed of sound and while my color is developing, he and Betsy and several stylists carry on a running dialogue about how I'm going to look in my wild new hair, which is said to be hot pink, platinum blond, and a custom shade of purple. What purple hair shade isn't custom, I wonder.

Bobby and Jalela work together to remove my foils at the shampoo bowl. There must be fifty of them at least. He has colored nearly every hair on my head, but he used foils to interweave four colors. Four is a lot, more like an Impressionist painting than a traditional hair coloring service. After the shampoo, Bobby insists that I sit with my back to the mirror while he trims and blow-dries my hair so I don't see it until I can get the full effect of his masterpiece. Betsy and Jalela hold their hands to their mouths in mock shock as he works. Everyone is having fun with this, even me. I'm thinking what a great figure I will cut wearing a hot pink up-do into Cook County Jail when the gendarmerie come to take me away.

In the end, it's kind of a letdown when Bobby spins the chair and I behold myself in his mirror. There is no hot pink, no purple, nothing outlandish at all. Instead, I have the most beautiful red hair I've ever seen on a woman, a tasteful, complex blend of multiple shades that looks both natural and evocative. As I turn my head from side to side, light shimmers and dances from my curls and emphasizes the graceful movement of my hair. The mix of colors and shades adds depth and mystery to my hair and makes it look fuller.

It's brilliant work. My hair looks feminine and sexy, but I also look like a professional woman who would fit nicely into a corporate conference setting or negotiating loan terms with a bank officer. I'm not sure how the other inmates will feel about me in jail, but the guards will have no trouble seeing me at a distance.

Betsy and I head for the nail salon. Another hour of fun and fantasy. The real world will still be there when this one ends.

* * *

TUESDAY, DECEMBER 9

Cecelia gets weepy as she talks about her ex-wife, now in hospice care.

We are having a quiet lunch in her castle in the sky so that I can ask her for great favors. Before we get to my business, I ask her how she is holding up.

It's been hard for Cecelia since she received the news that her ex-wife has an advanced stage of breast cancer. I'm astonished at how deeply moved Cecelia is. Every anecdote I've heard about their marriage suggested that Mrs. Swenson was an egocentric, materialistic opportunist with the heart of a vampire and the sincerity of a politician.

Apparently there was more to her than that, at least to Cecelia who cries long and hard. She had always held out hope for reconciliation, she said. Like with Betsy and me. If anyone ever deserved it, it was Cecelia. But even now, she mourns from a distance. Mrs. Swenson has no interest in seeing her ex-husband in a dress and makeup.

When we finish our salads, Cecelia pours coffee and gets to the business of things.

"So, what brings you to my parlor today, Bobbi? Please tell me this isn't about Wilkins."

"I'm afraid it is," I say. "It's about that and how it will affect everything in my life."

Cecelia sighs with regret. She signals with one hand for me to continue.

"Wilkins has strung together enough circumstantial evidence to charge me with Strand's murder. My attorney doesn't think it's a strong case, but just being charged will ruin me, and I'll be leaving Betsy and Robbie in a terrible position."

Cecelia's large blue eyes are troubled.

"I wanted to see if you could help me make sure the salon goes back to Roger if I'm going to default. The business is still viable. We're starting to do pretty well, actually. And I wanted to see if you could figure out a way for me to put something, cash or assets, in Betsy's name so she will have some kind of equity if I go away."

"Jesus, Bobbi," says Cecelia. She stares at me for several counts before responding to my request. I can't help wondering if the horror on her face is the realization that I'm going to the gallows for a murder she committed. The thought passes. She couldn't have done it.

"Sure, I can help you," she says finally. "I have a few ideas."

"And there's one other thing, Cecelia. The worst one. I want to tell you what happened so when the time is right you can tell Betsy." I have to come clean with this. It's killing me.

Cecelia shakes her head no. "Not a good idea, Bobbi. Don't forget, Wilkins is looking at me, too. I don't want to know what you know. Not until that hound from hell goes on to other things."

Cecelia's eyes are wide. I read her face and body language, looking for some hint that she knows more about this than she has ever let on. Nothing. I try to picture her slicing a knife through a defenseless man's throat. I can't make it work.

I shrug. "It's complicated, isn't it?"

Cecelia sits back. "Isn't it?" She wears both a confused look and a bemused smile on her face. I can't tell if she knows something she's holding back, or if she thinks I know something I'm holding back. Or both. Our "someday" talk is going to be a doozy.

* * *

TUESDAY, DECEMBER 9

As we wait for members of the holiday party committee to straggle in to the TransRising building, someone turns on the television set in the conference room.

Like a practical joke played by a malicious deity, Officer Phil's image blinks on the screen and glows in living color across the room. Several of the ladies at the table recognize him.

"Hey, isn't that your boyfriend?" says one. She's actually trying to be friendly. She rolls her eyes a little to express her approval of what a hunk he is.

"Friend," I reply, trying not to betray my emotions. "We're friends. He's still available as far as I know."

The table talk diffuses into other subjects. I can hear bits and pieces of what Phil is saying. He's standing at a lectern studded with microphones. Cameras flash nonstop. Light from the television crews makes him blink. I can't tell what the event is, but he is a picture of suave decorum, serious, sincere, not a bit defensive. The Chicago press corps has to love him.

I had almost gotten him out of my mind, during my daylight hours, anyway. I've been so preoccupied with Wilkins and his investigation. Every day I get up and expect to be served with a warrant or notification to appear before a grand jury. Every day I try to compartmentalize my dread and enjoy my freedom and participate in the festive mood of the season.

Seeing Phil is like getting stabbed in the heart. I see his kind, handsome face holding court, the lips that once kissed mine answering questions with aplomb, his tapered body completely at ease in a perfectly tailored suit. Thousands of women are watching him right now and thinking how nice it would be to go out with him tonight. When he walks down the street, dozens more will think the same thing. And they will all be prettier, more feminine, and far more respectable than I.

Bobbi Logan was never going to be the girl who got asked to the dance by the prom king. A quick tryst in the back seat of a car maybe, but no hand-holding in public, no long, warm embraces each night, no poems or flowers, no breathless "I love yous."

The television set is snapped off, stopping my pity binge. Lisa calls the meeting to order. We have been convened because the band contracted for the big holiday party fund-raiser has cancelled due to illness. This news is received with great regret by the other members of the committee. Apparently the band was highly regarded. I had never heard of them, or the other bands that were being considered. I'm a generation older than the next oldest committee member and woefully out of touch with pop culture.

Lisa has located several bands that are available for our date. She plays recordings supplied by each one and opens the meeting to discussion. After twenty minutes of give-and-take, opinions begin to coalesce around a group with a contemporary rock sound. The twentysomethings think the sound is sophisticated and will be great for dancing.

"What do you think, Bobbi? You've been very quiet over there," says Lisa. She's patronizing me, but in a friendly way. She's trying to acknowledge that more than half the people who come to the Holiday Ball are middle-aged and older transwomen, a group I represent, by age at least.

I blush crimson and defer to the group's wisdom about things like this. Scrambling to say something intelligent, I ask if a few members of the group could play holiday music during cocktails, to add to the festive ambience.

There are several groans, but Lisa puts the idea up for discussion. A consensus grows that it would be nice for mood, for the young as well as the old. They elect to hire the band; if they can't do the holiday music, we will play CDs. I volunteer a choice of my salon's mixes.

The meeting adjourns, all parties happy. Lisa thanks me for my contributions as we leave. The wiseass in me wants to ask her if this means she will come see me in jail, but instead I thank her for undertaking so much. It's a more sincere response.

20

BETSY ANSWERS THE phone in the living room and brings it to me in the kitchen. It's my night to cook.

As she enters the kitchen, she points to the phone, mimes a word I don't understand. I shake my head in question. She moves one hand to her crotch and makes an obscene gesture to indicate a giant erection. Very funny. Her spirits are rising each day while mine are sinking.

I take the phone and grimace at Betsy. We really are like sisters. I say hello.

"Hi, Bobbi." It's Officer Phil. The big dick. I almost snicker at the inside joke.

"Hi Phil," I respond. "Hey, I saw you on television yesterday, holding court with the press. I couldn't hear what you were saying, but you looked very composed."

He says it was a press statement about the latest CPD scandal. Nothing serious. He asks how I am. I ask him to wait a moment, then ask Betsy to take over the meal. I drift into the living room.

"Well, other than having a mad-dog detective trying to put me in jail and trying to make payments on my business and my building in the worst economic crisis in seventy-five years, things are pretty good. Oh, wait, did I mention that the man of my dreams fucked me and never talked to me again? No, wait, let me rephrase that, it sounds too pathetic. What I mean to say is, on top of everything else, my love life is pitiful. How are you?"

"I've missed you, Bobbi." Silence.

"Is this where I gush about how honored I am?"

"I don't blame you for being mad. I'm . . . I'm trying to work out some things. Personal issues. Failings, really." He's silent again. I have no idea what to say. I'm not even sure what he has said. It's hard to pick up a train of thought from him.

"I was hoping you'd see me again, Bobbi. Will you have dinner with me?"

I think about this for a minute. My adolescent self wants to say yes. The mere sound of his voice sets off fireworks in my senses. My wicked adolescent self wants to say yes and get laid again. But my forty-three-year-old self, the person who has been living under a cloud of doom for months, is having none of it.

"I don't think so, Phil," I say. "I have too much on my mind right now to help you decide if you can handle a transwoman." I'd like to say more. A lot more. I'd like to tell him what it feels like to be felt, fucked, and forgotten. I can handle the one-night-stand thing, but not being shunned by someone who cares about me but can't get past the trans thing. I'm not human, even to him. But I don't say any of these things.

"I wish you'd reconsider," he says. His voice is sincere. A mental image pops into my mind of him standing in front of the microphones and an army of media people. Cool, poised, patient. I can hear the same things in his voice now and it angers me. He's giving me the professional Phil and that's not what I want. I want the human one, with vulnerabilities, humility, a sense of humor when things aren't so heavy.

"Thanks for saying so." Silence. He wasn't expecting that response. I let the silence grow and fester.

"Okay," he says, finally. "Uh, well, if I can ever be of any help to you or you just want someone to talk to, uh, you know, please call me. Anytime."

"Thank you, Phil."

"Goodnight, Bobbi."

I say good-bye and hang up the phone. Betsy looks up as I come back in the kitchen. "Dare I ask?" she says.

"He asked me out."

"And?"

"And I said no."

Betsy widens her eyes in surprise. "I thought you really liked this guy."

I nod, trying to suppress my sadness. She glances at me, expecting more. "He sleeps with me then stays away for weeks because he's not sure how he feels about fucking a tranny." The tears come full force. Betsy hugs me.

"I'm a little surprised," she says when I get myself under control.

"You wouldn't be offended if it happened to you?" I ask.

"Of course I would," she says. "But you're the girl who hired a hooker to get off with. What's the difference?"

She's partly joshing, partly trying to get me to put this in perspective.

"Expectations. All I wanted from the prostitute was an orgasm and good manners. Phil had me thinking about love songs and holding hands. Doing things together. You're right, it was silly of me. A girl like me should be happy for the orgasm and just look for the next one."

"That's not what I meant and you know it." Her voice is a blend of humor and reprimand. "Welcome to the world of women. You don't think this happens to the rest of us? Being a woman isn't just body parts and clothes. This is part of it. You make yourself as attractive as you can, then men size you up and decide if you pass muster. Men

who stink and make you shudder to look at them, they size you up.
Nice ones size you up. Everything in between. Every day all kinds of
men decide if you're cute or fuckable or a pig."

"You get to make the same judgments on them," I point out.

"Not really. When I reject a man, it's because I'm a bitch. When
he rejects me, it's because I'm ugly or I'm flat or I'm not passionate
or my boobs droop. I don't make these rules, Bobbi, and I try not to
live by them, but this is how it is in our society. Male privilege is real.
They can make you feel like crap and it makes them feel like studs. We
make them feel bad and it's because we can't control our emotions or
we're irrational."

"I can't believe Don was like that," I say.

"He wasn't like that. That's why I married him." She pauses, then
adds in a soft voice, "That's why I married you, too."

That takes me aback for a moment. I had never seen any likeness
between Don and me other than maleness, back when I was one. "We
were practically twins, I guess."

Betsy laughs.

"I wouldn't have expected you to see any similarities between us." I
blurt it out. I'm a little hung up on the thought.

"Why, Bobbi?" She's surprised.

"Because Don was a real man and I was a fake one. I mean, I know
he was a very nice man and you appreciated that about him, but surely
it was also a pleasure to make love with a man who liked being a man."

"I liked making love with Don. I liked making love with you, too."

"But surely it was more frequent with him . . ."

Betsy laughs. "You still have a lot to learn as a woman, Bobbi. It
wasn't any more frequent with Don than with you. Just because someone is a hetero male doesn't mean they want to stand stud every day.
Life gets in the way. Business, travel, meetings, worries. And there's
the Virgin Mary syndrome . . ."

I cock my head in question.

"When you're dating, an interested man can't wait to get you in bed. After you get married and the novelty has worn off, they don't think of you as a sex object anymore. You're more like the Virgin Mary. They love you but they don't have wild sex thoughts about you anymore. You have to work through that with them."

I nod. I know what she's talking about. I lived it from the other side of the gender divide, but I thought it was just me. What has grabbed my attention, though, is that she's addressing me as a woman, a less experienced sister. We are talking about sex like two women, like adult siblings. It makes me feel so authentic. I glow all over.

I wonder if I will find a friend like this in prison. Not a lover. A soul mate who will accept me as a woman.

* * *

Wednesday, December 10

Wilkins leafs through his murder book. He has been working on it day and night. He can't sleep anyway, and the department has put him on medical leave, so there's nothing else to do.

It is the most thorough murder book he's ever assembled. He has added extra touches to make sure nothing slips through the cracks if he dies before the case is prosecuted. There's the boilerplate stuff, like his theory of the crime and the relevant factual documents. And added features. He has created an appendix that profiles each person he believes could have had a role in the run-up to Strand's murder. Each profile has a photograph of the person and hard data that will make locating them easier a year or two or three from now when this thing comes to trial. Drivers license number, phone number, social security number, current address.

After the facts he writes a narrative about each person. Who they are, what they do, how they figure in the murder.

The murder book is as thick as a Russian novel and has just as many characters. He's proud of it. It's his last work as a cop. He wants to go out right. Maybe they'll use this as an example in training young detectives in the future. That would please him.

He is focused on the investigation all the time. Everything else in his life is too depressing to contemplate. He wonders if he will live long enough to see Logan's trial. Probably not.

He thinks it's a decent case, which is far more than any other detective could have achieved. No smoking gun, but months of hard digging and creative analysis have produced a powerful inventory of circumstantial evidence. Plenty of proof to indict, probably enough to convict. But it would be better if he had even just one piece of hard evidence linking Logan directly to the crime. DNA or a hair sample from Strand's apartment. An eyewitness. A confession.

A confession. Wilkins sits back in his chair and thinks about the confession. He thinks Logan is one of those people who wants to confess. People with a sense of decency have trouble living with a crime like this, knowing they murdered someone. They are plagued by guilt and fear for as long as they hold it in.

Wilkins has that trait, himself. That's one of the reasons he never shot his firearm except at the range. His son will learn that about him in his journal, the one he's been keeping just for Stephen. *Stephen*, he says, *don't own a gun and don't shoot anyone. Even when it's legal, it's hard to live with.*

Logan has a conscience. She has to be plagued by nightmares and remorse. He thought she might have come forward by now. He could sense that she wanted to when they talked. She wasn't on the edge, but she was close.

He wonders if maybe she's protecting an accomplice, if that's what's holding her back. She could be the type. He couldn't come up with anything on an accomplice, but that doesn't mean there wasn't one. The weight lifter was at work that night. The Swenson woman didn't have a great alibi for the time of the murder, but the doorman at her building saw her come in before midnight and didn't see her leave again.

As much as he poked around for information about other possible accomplices, nothing else had turned up. Just Barbi Dancer's recollection of a black sport sedan driving by at around the time Strand was being abducted, but that went nowhere—no license plate, no driver identification, not even an indication the vehicle had anything to do with Strand's abduction and murder.

He pictures Logan in his mind, how she looked when they talked in her salon. Yes, he thinks, she was close. She wanted to tell him. It's worth asking her again. He would ask, not bully. He'd be respectful, courteous. He'd give her a last chance to redeem herself, free her soul, catch a deal from the DA.

He tries to scuttle the next thought, but he can't keep the image out of his mind of Logan being hauled off to jail in handcuffs, another victim of a murderer the police should have caught. It's the law, he thinks, but it's not fair. Logan was right about that. If CPD had done a better job with the Marvin investigation, none of this shit would have happened.

He pushes the thought from his mind. His job is to enforce the law. A judge or jury will decide what's fair. But as he thinks it, he knows better. Trials are about laws and evidence. She'll take a beating if it goes to trial.

Call or meet in person? His appearance is so off-putting that he has been avoiding in-person contact when he can. Even walking down the street is embarrassing, people gawking at him, doing double takes. Jesus, wait 'til they make my face into a monster mask, he thinks. The medical text photos flash into his mind, rotting jack-o-lantern faces crushed on one side, hellish fiends with puckered mouths and desperate eyes. People will wince and gag.

But maybe not Logan, he thinks. She sees strange-looking people every day. She mothers them. Maybe seeing Wilkins' pathetic appearance will break down some of her defenses.

He dials her number. It's not like he has anything else to do. It's not like he has anything to lose.

*   *   *

FRIDAY, DECEMBER 12

"You should come, too," says Lisa. "I can get you a ticket. Free."

She is sitting in my chair at the salon. I am prepping her for an up-do. She has a formal party to attend tonight, a black-tie fund-raiser for the LGBT community. The mayor will be there, congressmen, bankers, stockbrokers, the hoi polloi of Chicago. The big thing is, she came to me for the 'do. The olive branch has been extended.

I smile and study her face and hair in the mirror. When we meet at community functions I see her differently than I do now. What I notice when we meet out there is her femininity—her face, her actions, her voice most of all. I notice that she is pretty, but as a transwoman myself, her attractiveness is less significant than the fact she looks and sounds like a woman. Many of us don't, me especially.

In the salon, a different image appears. Now I look closely at her face shape and skin tone, the symmetry of her facial structure, the relationship between her head and the rest of her body, the color of her hair, her best features. It's no longer about her transsexuality or mine. Here, she is just a woman wanting to feel beautiful tonight, and I am a hairdresser who wants to help her get there.

"I think society events like the Mid-Winter Ball are best left to the Cinderellas among us, Lisa," I answer. "But thank you. That's a generous offer." Indeed it is. The tickets go $250 apiece.

"You're as much a Cinderella as anyone else," she says as I work her hair with my hands, feeling the texture, looking at how her face changes when I move the hair to different positions. "Here's an idea. Get your boyfriend to come, and I'll get two tickets."

This is a very nice offer, but I'm feeling like the main point here is, she can get two tickets, just like that. And she thinks Officer Phil is a hunk.

"I'm afraid Phil and I aren't an item."

"You broke up?"

"If you can call it that."

I begin sectioning Lisa's hair. "What happened?" she asks.

This is where I change the subject with clients. I don't talk about sex or politics during a service. But Lisa isn't a regular client. She's here as a one-shot deal, and we know each other outside these walls. And we aren't friends, so there's nothing to lose.

"Basically, he's not sure he can handle life with a transwoman, but I don't think he'd have that issue with you or one of the other cute girls. I'm just too big and masculine. Oh well . . ." I try to say it with nonchalance, but even I can hear the edge in my voice. It still hurts.

"Don't say that. You're a proud, beautiful woman, Bobbi."

Yay rah. It's nice of her to say something encouraging, but this is strictly pro forma script in the trans world. Everyone is proud and beautiful. Lisa means well. She's motivated by her Lincolnesque humanity. She's here to save the wonderful people of transgenderland and some of them are somewhere between ugly and embarrassing to look at. Being patient with us is part of being a savior.

She tells me that I'm a role model for several of the girls at TransRising. "Especially the bigger ones." As she says it she realizes her social error. "You know, I mean the taller ones. They see in you that they can be tall and sexy and have great careers."

Good recovery, Lisa. Just for that I won't dry your hair with a blowtorch.

We talk about the TransRising ladies while I wrestle with her hair. It's long and straight, not a hint of curl, and as slippery as satin. That makes it very attractive when she wears it down. It moves with silky grace and gives off a healthy shine. But it's hard to work into formal hair because it resists back-combing and curling as if each hair were coated with Teflon. I cover the base of her locks with a hair spray that sets up like Krazy Glue, then tease like a hairdresser possessed by the devil.

Lisa is talking about the girls at TransRising. She remains calm as I turn her head into a ball of cotton candy. She is interesting and insightful, much as I wish she weren't so I could feel better about my misgivings toward her. She knows each of the TransRising residents on a personal level, their histories, what they like and don't like, what they want to achieve with their lives, where they are in their transitions and education. What they need to accomplish to be accepted as women in polite society.

For all my doubts about her motivation, Lisa is invested in the dispossessed people of TransRising in a way that no other volunteer is. The hours and energy required to accumulate the knowledge she has goes far beyond anything the rest of us would even contemplate. Even if I'm right about her motivation, her work for disenfranchised Chicago transwomen is Mother Theresa–worthy.

Lisa has given me carte blanche on this service because she's never had an up-do she likes, and I'm getting into it. I carefully sweep the hair from the back half of her head into a series of graceful arches that rise upward over her crown then bend forward toward her face. I make the same arc with sections of hair on the front half of her head and intertwine them with the ends of the back hair. I continue to arc sections back, up and forward, and secure them in an intricate pattern that's really just a loose, puffy two-strand braid. The height of the hair decreases as it comes forward achieving the silhouette of a classic twist, but with a lot of texture and complexity. A few inches from her face, I stop braiding and feather her ends into long bangs that descend to her eyebrows.

She is elated and I am jealous. She looks like a red carpet celebrity. The bangs bring more oval symmetry to her face, the high-piled hair in back gives her an aura that is equal parts royalty and sexpot. When she combines this with a low-cut gown, she will leave a trail of male desire wherever she goes.

"Bobbi," she exclaims, "you're a genius."

She's gushing like a schoolgirl who's just been kissed by Elvis. I look at her and see youth and beauty and the arrogance that comes with it, but when she looks at herself she looks through the prism of her own vulnerabilities, just like the rest of us. She got a princess moment right here in my chair and she can't stop glowing about it. I'm gushing, too—this is the kind of client joy I live for.

As I show her what she looks like from the sides, the rear, and standing up in a full-length mirror, I wonder what it's like to be Lisa, to be young and beautiful and smart and ambitious and to look and feel like a woman. There is joy on her face.

I will never know that joy. When I look in a mirror I will always see someone who doesn't look at all like the *me* inside. I will always see the masculine features where a Lisa-like princess is supposed to be. And I fear that someday in the not-too-distant future I will be seeing these things in a prison mirror, if they have mirrors in prison.

* * *

SUNDAY, DECEMBER 14

The magnificent jazz singer Lou Rawls once likened Chicago's winter winds to "a giant razor blade blowing down your spine." My analogies are running more to a naked plunge in the Arctic Ocean as Cecelia and I play tag with Robbie while Betsy kneels at Don's gravesite. The exercise gets our blood pumping again, though it's too late for my fingers and toes, which will probably never recover the sense of touch.

When Betsy's mourning ends, I scoop up Robbie, and the four of us head to the car. We are arm-in-arm, Cecelia on one side of my grieving former wife, me on the other. In the car, I direct Cecelia to a restaurant a few miles from the cemetery. It's nearly empty on a Sunday afternoon, the other patrons gathered in the bar to watch football and drink. We get a table overlooking the river and order hot drinks and soup. Robbie is fascinated with the electric fire glowing in the fireplace and Cecelia takes her for a closer look.

"How are you holding up, honey?" I ask Betsy.

She shrugs. "I'm okay. I just wish—" She stops, shrugs again, stares at her soup.

"What do you wish?"

She stares me in the eye. "I'll tell you my worst secret if you'll tell me yours."

"Let's not do that."

We fall silent. Betsy stirs her hot chocolate, eyes downcast, for a long minute. She looks up.

"I was a poor wife to Don," she says. I've never seen eyes so sad. "I wasn't really honest with you before, when we talked about sex. He . . . he . . . wasn't a very good lover. Especially after my miscarriage. He had trouble getting . . . aroused. I could do it, but . . ." Her voice trails off. "But it was difficult for both of us. It was a lot of work, and sometimes he still couldn't do it. And then he didn't want to kiss me because, you know . . ."

Yes, I know. Men are so neurotic about sex. You pleasure them and all of a sudden you have germs.

"Everyone has those kinds of issues sooner or later," I say.

"I don't know about everyone. I know Don was crushed. He felt awful that he wasn't a better lover. He even asked me once if I needed to take a lover."

"Did you?" I withdraw the question immediately. It's not my business. I only asked because I didn't see why she should feel responsibility for their sex life.

"No, of course not." She answers anyway.

"So why the guilt?"

"Because when he offered to get Viagra, I told him not to. I said I preferred it natural, even if it was just sometimes. But, Bobbi, the truth was, I just wasn't interested in him sexually. I loved him, but I didn't enjoy making love with him. So he died unfulfilled. And it's my fault."

We join hands across the table. I look into her eyes. "He would never say that, Betsy. He did not feel that. You were the highlight of his life. I could see it with total clarity. Anyone could."

She shakes her head and looks down again. "I wish I could feel that way."

"I think if you talked about this with a therapist they would tell you that you're turning your grief into guilt. They might even know why that happens."

Actually, I don't have much more faith in psychologists and therapists than I do in a kind and interactive deity. About half of the ones I've met had the intellectual depth of a Fox News commentator.

"The best sex I ever had was with you." It just bursts from her lips, quiet, but as shocking as if she had screamed it in a crowded room. I have come to think of my former penis as a sort of dildo with nerve endings that was distributed to the wrong person. I enjoyed the male climax and getting aroused, especially in my younger days when testosterone coursed through my veins as if I were a real boy. But I never really thought of myself as male, not even at climax. And as our marriage matured, the frequency of sex slowed down a lot. I always assumed Betsy just forgave me for being a crappy lover. Her revelation leaves me speechless.

"It's okay, Bobbi. You can talk."

"I feel like I lost the last set of car keys." This is unintentionally funny. I was thinking that my lost penis was the engine that made us "go" in bed. Betsy snickers.

"Well, Cecelia has the keys," she says.

"Yes." I nod. "But not the one you want."

We exchange juvenile laughter.

"If you let me set you up with my hooker, he'll make you forget my missing member in an hour or so. He is a genius and I was a fraud."

Betsy's face is bittersweet, part smile, part sadness. "It wasn't just the physical part, it was the love that made it sweet, Bobbi. I can't get that from a hooker."

I understand what she means, but the thing about being a transsexual is, you learn quickly you'll never have it all. Your life becomes a matter of getting what you can. I'd love to be Officer Phil's official full-time lover, but that's not going to happen. Actually, it's not going to happen with any nice man. An erotic session with a professional every now and then isn't my first choice, but I got a lot of pleasure from it and it beats watching television.

* * *

SUNDAY, DECEMBER 14

"Wilkins." His tone is curt, to the point. His voice is deep, and carries into my auditory canal like a declaration of doom. I shouldn't be returning his call. I am completely out of my mind for doing so.

"This is Bobbi Logan, returning your call." I say it with all the femininity I can muster, my voice an octave higher, a pronounced sibilant lisp. I know he hates me for what I am and I am being defiant. Plus, of course, if he starts insulting me, I have a good reason to hang up on him, which I should do anyway.

"Thanks for returning my call, Ms. Logan."

His civility is disarming until I realize he's just doing his good-cop routine. My defense mechanisms fly into the ready.

"I wanted to ask if we might talk again, now that you've had a chance to think about what I said."

"That won't be necessary," I say. "I have nothing to confess. If you can make a case against me, please do."

"Ms. Logan, I am turning over this case to the district attorney shortly. I would really appreciate one more opportunity to speak with you about it. I will be respectful."

I politely decline his request.

"If you change your mind, call me any time, day or night, okay?" he says.

I agree but assure him no call will be forthcoming. When we hang up, something about the conversation nags at my mind. Partly his tone. He was polite and businesslike, but there was an undercurrent of something . . . sadness, maybe. With a touch of urgency. And the other thing . . . he had led me to believe he was taking the case to the DA days ago. Something is going on . . .

21

I'm watching Jalela do foil highlights for one of her TransRising friends. Jalela has blossomed in her short time with us. She's observed and assisted on so many color services, she's already close to a New Talent in her foiling abilities. Plus, she'll be starting cosmo school next month, and she's getting a nice head start here.

Jalela finishes the last foil and sets the timer. Her foils are exquisite. There is no other word for it. They are precise and neat, uniform in appearance, snug to the scalp, perfectly formed. There's not a drop of bleach anywhere on her apron or the client's cape. Many of us do excellent highlights without being anywhere near so precise, but the great ones tend to be like this.

In my peripheral vision I sense movement at the reception counter. I glance over and see Samantha leading someone to my office. It's Officer Phil. It's rare that Sam would put anyone in my office without talking to me first. Something is astir. Probably something unpleasant. Good grief, I wonder if something has happened to Betsy or Robbie.

Samantha walks quickly to me. "Sergeant Pavlik—Phil—says he needs to talk to you for just a moment. I put him in your office," she says.

"Is something wrong?" I don't try to hide the alarm in my voice. "Are Betsy and Robbie okay?"

"I don't think it's anything like that," says Sam.

I let my mind briefly flirt with the thought he has come to declare his undying love for me and to beg me to move in with him and wake up in his arms every morning. Then I erase the thought. I'm not in a place in my life where I can be entertaining schoolgirl fantasies. And if that was his message, this isn't how he would deliver it.

I ask another stylist to oversee the rest of Jalela's service and head to my office.

Phil stands as I enter. I extend a hand for a handshake, preempting any thought of a hug or kiss. It turns out I have some pride.

We sit.

"This is unexpected," I say.

"I've been working the north side today," says Phil. "And I heard something a little while ago that I wanted to share with you."

"You have my undivided attention." I try to say it in the haughty tone of a wronged woman. I think I succeeded. It feels good.

"Bobbi, Detective Wilkins is on medical leave. Apparently he is very sick. The person I spoke with thought it might be cancer, but he didn't know for sure."

I blink and sit back in my chair. My mind goes back to our last meeting, the shock I felt at Wilkins' appearance, gray and emaciated. Yes, cancer would be a good guess. A flurry of new thoughts streak through my consciousness. Might he die before bringing a case against me? I feel remorse that I have many times wished bad things for him and now that he is ill, I realize I didn't really mean it, or shouldn't have. An arcane puzzle pops into mind: What if the heavenly baritone of an all-seeing deity poured down from the heavens to say Wilkins would live if I confessed to my crime. Would I give up my life to save his? The heavenly voice would have to be very convincing.

My mind meanders back to the here and now. "Why are you telling me this?" I ask.

"Because it might be important information for you," Phil answers.

"How?"

Phil shrugs. "I don't know, Bobbi. I just thought you should know."

He can't say it, but he's thinking that this case might go away if Wilkins dies or retires, that I shouldn't confess to anything or make any deals. He can't say it for legal reasons, and I don't want to think it because I don't want to think of myself as someone who would celebrate someone else's tragedy. Still, it occurs to me that I might survive all this after all. Brief visions of a happy ending flash through my mind until I regain my senses and stop the thought. This is not a guarantee of a happy ending. Indeed, I'm recalling the sense of urgency I heard in Wilkins' voice when we spoke on the phone. He's trying to finish this case before he's incapacitated. I could be arrested any hour now.

"Thank you, Phil," I say.

Silence engulfs the little room as he searches for something to say. I wait. I have this part of womanhood down pat.

"Just thought you should know," he says, finally. He stares into my eyes. He starts to speak once, twice. Stops. He wants to tell me he misses me and I want to kiss him on the lips when he does. But we can't go there anymore, either of us. He stands. We shake hands across the desk but instead of letting go, he bends at the waist and sweeps my hand to his lips. I can feel their warmth and softness. Resisting the urge to throw myself against him and have him envelope me in a full body hug is almost more than I can bear. But I do.

I smile at him and lead him to the entry. He turns to face me one last time at the door. To keep from kissing or hugging him, I button his overcoat and run my hands along his arms. I try to say thank you again, but I'm overcome by sadness. My eyes mist, I nod my thanks. He nods back like he's agreeing, brushes my cheek with a gloved hand, and leaves.

Sam hands me a tissue as I pass the reception counter. A few tears roll down my cheeks like a gentle dew. Not a sobbing, brokenhearted adolescent, a woman in mourning. Progress, I guess.

* * *

Friday, December 19

"You've got poor Stephen worried to death." Her voice is angry. Wilkins couldn't remember it any other way, though early in their marriage it was always soothing, like a massage of the soul after a long day or night of dealing with society's vermin.

"Are you really sick or are you just playing games?"

Wilkins is tempted to tell her to mind her own business, to ask her if he ever played games about anything, or made excuses, or was ever anything but dead honest. But he doesn't have the energy for such things anymore, and it doesn't really matter anyway.

"I have cancer. I have to have an operation. It might not do the trick."

"What kind of cancer?"

"Oral."

"Are they pulling teeth? What kind of surgery are you having?"

He sighs. "They have to take out part of my jaw and part of my tongue."

She is silent. "Will you—?" She can't finish the question.

"The surgery is *disfiguring*"—he says the word sarcastically—"that's how they describe it."

"Disfiguring? What does that mean?"

"It means I won't need a mask at Halloween."

Another long silence. She is shocked, he can picture it.

"Please don't share this with Stephen. I've told him that the surgery is risky but not anything about what I'll look like afterward. We can

get into that if I survive. If I don't, I'm leaving instructions to be cre-
mated. Please don't let anything happen to prevent that."

"Okay." She says it in a quiet voice.

"I wrote a lot of things down for him," says Wilkins. "He'll share it
with you. I'm leaving what I have to you. I gave him a key to my apartment in case I don't make it and I told him he can have anything he
wants in there. I'm sending a few personal things to Anita at school
with a letter, and I'm sending a box of things to Stephen."

"No guns!"

"No. No guns. My dad's pocket watch, some pictures. Some awards
I won. My scrapbook. Things like that. I'm sending Anita my mother's wedding band and some jewelry. I have a few more days to put
everything together. It will all be in order in my apartment. Stephen
has a key. I suggested he take you with him when he comes."

Silence. "Allan, I don't know what to say."

"There's nothing to say. I just have to play out the string."

"Can I do anything? Can we do anything? Your kids love you, you
know. I love you, too. It's just—" She can't complete the sentence.

"I know," says Wilkins. "Thanks for the thought. We'll see what
happens after surgery."

After he hangs up, Wilkins leans back in the chair and raises both
hands to cover his face. He sees himself after the surgery, a face like
a horror monster, his mouth in a permanent "O" like some fiendish
ghoul, his tongue no longer able to make speech sounds, using a tube
to eat. Too weak to climb stairs. What the fuck is he going to do with
himself then? What kind of life is that?

* * *

Friday, December 19

This is our holiday party night at the salon. The party starts when we close at six, but the festive atmosphere builds all afternoon. Each of us brings a dish, and we exchange small gifts. We could go out to a restaurant or have a meal catered in, but for as long as I've been here, the salon culture was to invest a little of ourselves in the celebration.

After we eat and chat, I ask for the group's attention. In years past, Roger delivered a brief benediction, thanking God and karma for the bountiful year that was and hoping the new year will be good, too. The staff gathers expectantly. A new voice for an old script. They clap and smile as I stand before them.

"In the great tradition of the finest boss I've ever had—that being Roger, but Samantha is catching up"—general laughter—"I want to thank all the fates and deities and friendly prayers that got us through the roughest year we've ever had at Salon L'Elégance," I start. More applause. "And to all of you who prayed, and to all of our collective gods, please do what you can for us next year." More applause and smiles.

"I won't drag this out, but I have a few announcements . . ." Several people emit mock groans. I play along, promising to be brief if they will just give a moment more of their valuable time.

"First, let me say that because of everyone's hard work promoting our business at all hours of the day and night, I am pleased to tell you that Salon L'Elégance has returned to profitability!"

People clap and cheer. We're all invested in this place.

Barbara comes before the group, standing beside me, and raises her wine glass. "Let's drink to Bobbi and Salon L'Elégance!" A boisterous salute ensues. I blush crimson, to the delight of my colleagues.

"It is I who should salute you," I say when the noise dies down. "I don't know of any salon where the staff would do the things you have done to keep the business afloat. And I can tell you for sure that we wouldn't be here if we hadn't done what we did." I raise my glass and we toast again.

"One final thing," I say. "The senior management of Salon L'Elégance has experienced a moment of fiscal insanity and elected to thank each of you for your love and sacrifice with a small holiday gift. This is not something we can do annually, as you know, but this is a special year, and you are special people and we need a special moment together."

As I speak, Sam distributes envelopes to each person. Each envelope contains a check for $100. Not the kind of money investment bankers throw around, but a tiny miracle in our business where the house profit margins are modest and bonuses are rare because ours is a business that operates on commissions and tips.

Around the room, the reaction is electric as people open their envelopes. In my corporate days I saw white-collar types swear angrily at receiving "only" a $5,000 holiday bonus. My colleagues aren't like that. People smile, some clap, one stylist holds her check to her chest and closes her eyes. I think perhaps her child will get a Christmas gift that wasn't within reach a moment ago. That thought makes me giddy. Jalela is holding check and envelope to her face and beaming with happiness. She comes to me, arms outstretched, and embraces me.

"You're the best," she says. "I love you!"

"I love you back," I answer. We hug and rock.

After many minutes of bedlam and celebration, Samantha calls the group to order one more time. "Bobbi," she says. "On behalf of the Salon L'Elégance staff, I have an honor to bestow on you. Please come forward."

I turn crimson again, which pleases everyone.

"On behalf of the greatest staff of hair professionals in all the world, and the most dedicated Bobbi Logan groupies anywhere, it is my pleasure to present to you the first ever Mistress of the Lethal

Curling Iron Award." As she says it she pulls a carved-wood likeness of a curling iron, true to life in every detail except for the arrowhead on the end. My name is inscribed on the handle, along with the words, "Supreme Order of the Lethal Curling Iron." I can barely read the inscription for laughing so hard.

A tiny voice deep inside me wonders if I could ever find this kind of joy in prison. I answer that myself. I'm lucky to have found it here.

* * *

SATURDAY, DECEMBER 20

Betsy and I face each other in our living room. Robbie is playing at her friend's house next door. We have an hour to ourselves. Betsy is still pressing for full disclosure on my involvement in the Strand murder, but she takes it gracefully when I again decline.

I switch to the more important point.

"If they arrest me, Cecelia will handle things here. You and Robbie will have this place to live in as long as you want, and you'll get living expenses for at least a year."

Betsy makes a face. "I don't want your money."

"I know you don't," I say. "I want you to have it. I want you to have time to make some choices. Good choices, not panicky ones."

"You aren't my husband." Her face is puckering as she says it.

"This isn't marriage. It's love, and you'd do it for me."

Betsy stands, grasps my hands, and makes me stand. She wraps her arms around me in a soft, melancholy hug. "You are such a good person, Bobbi," she murmurs. "It breaks my heart you went through so much alone. Don't do that ever again." I can feel her tears on my skin.

* * *

SUNDAY, DECEMBER 21

Betsy pretends to act surprised that Phil happens to be shopping for toddler girl clothes at Macy's at the very moment we are in the same department picking out gifts for Robbie.

She walks right up to him and says, "You're busted, mister. Betraying the ghost of Marshall Field!"

"What about you?" he says.

"I was forced to come here by you-know-who." She points at me.

"Hi, Bobbi," he says. I return the greeting. We stand in awkward silence for a moment.

"Do you have a niece or daughter I don't know about?" I ask, finally, nodding to our surroundings.

"No. I, uh . . ." It's obvious he's trying to make something up. He blushes. "Okay, Betsy said you'd be here about now, and I was hoping to talk to you."

"You could have called me."

"I tried that."

Betsy is smiling sheepishly at me and nodding. She wants me to chat with him. We seem to have crossed some kind of threshold. "Why don't you two go have a coffee or something? I'll catch up to you in a little while," she says.

I make a face at her, then take Phil's hand and tug him in the direction of the Walnut Room, one of the last vestiges of the old Marshall Field's store. Field's was a Chicago institution until the conglomerate that owns Macy's bought it and converted the Field's stores, even the sacred one on State Street, into Macy's stores. The city is still outraged. Bad enough to lose our own landmark to a lesser brand, but worse that Macy's is as New York as Field's was Chicago. There are still protests every year under the old Field's clock tower. Personally, I would rather have Field's still there, but I can't see taking sides in the silly games of giant corporations.

Macy's has continued the Walnut Room Christmas tradition. It is more Christmasy than Santa's spread at the North Pole and more festive than all the suburban lights rolled into one display. It's even moving for an atheist. Coffee and cinnamon and lovely aromas I can't identify fill the air. It's like a great feast just breathing here, and the decorations and music massage your senses like a soft guitar. I try to stay mad at Phil, but as we sit over our hot drinks, old feelings come back. I gaze at him and fantasize about riding in one of the horse-drawn carriages outside, cuddling against him under a warm blanket, vapors of breath streaming into the frigid air as we glide through the magnificent canyons of downtown Chicago.

"How have you been?" he asks.

"Busy. Happy. Getting along. You?"

"I'm okay." He bobs his head up and down like there's more he has to say, but he doesn't say anything. I choke back the temptation to fill the silence with small talk. This isn't my meeting.

I'm getting better at this.

"Bobbi," he says, looking at me now, "I miss you." He stares at me. I have absolutely no idea how to respond.

"The trans thing...I..." He stops and stutters several times. "I'm still trying to deal with it." He says it with a rush, like I'm going to shoot him between the eyes as he says it and he wants to get it all out. "I know that's offensive to you, but it's not about you. It's about me. I have to grow a little."

About him? I want to ask how it's about him when I'm the one he can't handle.

"The thing is, I can't get you out of my mind. I like being with you."

"Well, that sure makes a girl feel good. At least you think I'm a good lay."

"I didn't mean it that way," he says. He's beet-red, his voice a little chippy. He's getting tired of my little gibes. He recovers. "I meant I like to be with you. Like this. At a club. In a restaurant. Any place."

I knew that's what he meant but I felt like being cruel. I feel like I'm making a point in a very feminine way—no snarling anger, no loud voices, just a little dig that he can explain away if he wants to.

"I'd like for us to go out on dates. As friends. Maybe it becomes something else, maybe it stays friends. I'm good either way."

"You know I'm crazy about you, Phil. But I'm not desperate. I'm not going to invest myself in someone who is too ashamed of me to introduce me to Mom and Dad or take me to the policeman's ball."

"We don't have a ball," he says. He's trying not to smile.

"Well, your turkey shoot, then. Or your bad guy shooting range, whatever you guys do to entertain your significant others."

"I will introduce you to my parents next time they visit. I will proudly take you to my favorite cop bar and introduce you to my friends."

I can see how this might work. He would be introducing me as his friend. It's not as edgy as introducing a transwoman as your lover. It gives everyone a chance to get used to the idea. I tell him I'm okay with that and try to smother the impulse to ask if we might make one little exception to the just-friends rule and run over to my place and make mad, passionate love. The urge passes, but it lingers just below the surface. Probably will always be there until he walks away for good, which, realistically, is where this is headed.

We make small talk until I check my watch. I tell him I need to get back to Betsy and Robbie.

"Just one other thing, Bobbi," he says. "Our friend Allan Wilkins called me yesterday—"

I sit back, raise my hands in protest, and cut him off.

"No, no," he says. "Hear me out. It's not what you think."

He waits for me to calm down.

"He asked me to see if you'd talk to him one more time. He's having surgery in a few days and he's trying to get closure on some things in case the surgery doesn't go well. I told him I'd relay the message, but I also told him I didn't think it was a good idea for you to do that. He just thanked me and said you'd understand. Frankly, I don't."

Phil wants to know what Wilkins meant. I don't want to get into it with him. But Wilkins is right. He has read me perfectly. I would like to tell him. I'd like to confess to him and to Betsy and get free of this suffocating weight. For five years, the quiet moments of my life have been tormented by little film clips that pop into my mind from nowhere. They run for a few seconds or a minute, but like a bad aftertaste, they cloud my world for hours. They are scenes from the Strand murder, a blend of what I did and what I wanted to do, and haunting dreams about how the murder played out. Some scenes are starkly real, some gruesomely exaggerated. Some clips show the knife slicing through Strand's throat, the blood gurgling out, his eyes wide with shock, his jaw slack. Another shows his choirboy look when he was trying to convince me to let him go. Of course, it was an act, a moment of fraud sandwiched between a display of his vicious animal nature and his arrogant, do-my-bidding-you-tranny-scum routine, but guilt and horror often block those mitigating images.

The vision of Strand's throat being slit is so vivid I still sometimes wonder if I actually did it myself, if my recollection of leaving him strung up alive is just the fabrication of a mind too racked with guilt to accept reality. In my lucid moments I know I didn't murder him, but that realization doesn't reduce my guilt at all. I made it easy for someone else to do the deed.

I lose sleep over normal things, too, but they come and go. The kidnapping and murder of the murderer John Strand is with me forever. I have accepted it as part of my normal life. Losing one or two nights' sleep every week is the price I pay for continuing to live.

Maybe it's time for one last meeting with Wilkins. A last chance for two tortured souls to find some sliver of peace.

* * *

MONDAY, DECEMBER 22

Wilkins arrives at the coffee shop a few minutes after I do. He sees me in the corner in an overstuffed chair that faces another one across a small table. He approaches, his gait slow and weak.

His appearance is frightening. The ebony skin of yesterday is as gray as a corpse and hangs in deep folds that weren't there just a month ago. His eyes, always shining with intensity, now view the world with the dimness of a dying flashlight.

"Can we move to a different table?" he rasps when he gets to me. He points to a conventional table with two traditional wooden chairs. I agree. As he settles into his chair, I ask if I can get him something. My shock at his appearance must be obvious.

"No," he says. "I can't eat solid food and I have to be careful what I drink. That's why I look like shit. That's how I got this cold." That's why we're sitting at this table, I realize. His raspy voice wouldn't carry across the void between the stuffed chairs.

"I'm sorry you're ailing," I say. I really am. This has to be more than a cold.

"We all have our crosses to bear," he says. A segue into my confession. "What's your cross, Detective?"

He starts to wave me off, but stops. He stares at me, nods, and reaches into his portfolio. He places tear-sheets from a book in front of me. They have photographs of people with horribly mutilated faces.

"I have oral cancer," says Wilkins. "I have to have an operation. If I'm lucky, I'll die on the operating table. If I survive, I'll look like this."

The world stops turning. Everything seems frozen in place, including my lungs. I stare at the photos in horror. I can't take my eyes off them. I should pretend like it's no big thing, but the images are horrifying. I make a little moaning sound and gasp. I would not wish this fate on my worst enemy. I wouldn't have wished it on John Strand.

I can't help myself. I lower my head and cry.

"What can I do?" Those are the first words that come to my mind that I can say. He would have been offended if I had voiced the other words, *you poor man, I feel so awful for you.*

He reaches across the table and puts a hand on my wrist. "You can tell me what happened with Strand."

The thought jolts me out of my mourning. "What?" I stare at him, trying to see if his horrible appearance is some kind of act, a miracle of makeup and modern plastics. "Is this some kind of joke?"

He shakes his head slowly. "No joke, Ms. Logan. I have very little time to finish up what I'm going to finish up. Your story, your true account of what happened with John Strand is the most important thing on my agenda. I'd like you to tell me what happened, your words, your perspective. You can tell me now, no witnesses, no tape recorder, so I'll at least know the truth. After that you can decide if you want to make a statement for the record."

He recites again how good it will be for my conscience to unburden myself and come clean with my society, and how he can still intercede with the DA to get me special consideration.

"Believe me when I tell you this offer is only good for one more day," he says. He smiles a little, a sad, ironic smile.

"You don't expect to survive your surgery?" I ask.

"Even if I survive it, I won't be able to talk for months, maybe never. I won't have the strength to go to the DA's office or even meet you here. My clock's ticking."

My eyes drop from his eyes to the table, to the pictures of mutilated people. Even as I'm consumed by grief, I am overwhelmed by a sudden understanding of this man, this relentless pursuer. He is a cop. That's what defines him. Closure on his life requires closure on his last case. He is going to die a worse death than John Strand, worse than any murderer or rapist or child molester, even though he has given his life to the protection of others. I feel myself letting loose. This is the time and place.

"Okay," I say. I take a deep breath. "Most of it is just like you figured. I had been trying to track down the man who beat Mandy Marvin to death. I was obsessed by it. It was bad enough he did it, but what got me was, no one cared. It was like, transpeople don't matter . . . I don't matter unless I can bring that bastard to justice.

"Strand was easy to find. When he figured out what I was up to, he wanted me to know he did it so he could toy with me . . . a psychopath tearing the wings off a fly. He seduced me, then abused me, but that just made me more determined. I should have backed off after his thugs raped me, but they started following me again. I knew it was just a matter of time before they killed me, so I put together a plan. It started with a little sweet revenge. I led one of the goons into a mugging of his own . . . as you guessed. I wanted the revenge, but I also needed to strike back at them successfully, just to know I could. I never really believed I could succeed against Strand, but after I pulled off the mugging, I felt a little empowered and that maybe I could at least scare him."

"What about the other thug?" Wilkins asks.

"I never saw him again. I think Strand sent him away and put the A Team in the game."

"What happened next?"

"After that, I started planning Strand's death. I assumed a male disguise and followed him around and got to know his patterns, where he picked up his girl, where he went. On the night it happened I had trouble getting up the nerve to take him, but he made it easy when he started smacking his girlfriend around."

Wilkins rubs his chin. "He was a strong man. How did you take him down?"

"I surprised him. He was getting out of his car to catch his girlfriend who was trying to run away. I used an animal tranquilizer and the eye gouge to disable him. I drove him in his own car to his love nest and I trussed him up and hung him by his wrists from the ceiling."

"Was he awake?"

"He came to after I strung him up. He was disoriented at first, but he came around, and we had a nice little chat. I told him about the dreams I had after I was raped, especially the one where I cut off his testicles while he watched. He actually got scared for a moment . . . followed by a psychotic rage, of course. When he quit twisting and kicking, I went behind him and put the knife to his throat . . ." My voice trails off. I'm transported back to that moment.

". . . I could feel the honed edge of the blade on his throat like it was an extension of my fingers. I could picture the little trickle of blood starting on his windpipe. I could see in my mind's eye how the blade would slice cleanly to his jugular in one clean swoop, and a force of pure evil would leave this world."

I lock eyes with Wilkins. "In my mind I was saying 'Yes! Now!' The moment had come. But I couldn't do it. I stood there and commanded my arm to slice the blade through his throat. I swear I could feel the nerve impulses moving from my brain to my arm to my hand. My mind was screaming, 'Kill this murdering bastard!' Every rational thought I had was about how he'd kill me if I didn't kill him right now. But I just couldn't do it. I couldn't make myself do what needed to be done. It will haunt me to my final breath. I couldn't kill the devil."

"What?" Wilkins is astonished.

"Really," I say. "I threw the knife on the floor. I ran to the bathroom and vomited like a teenage girl on her first drinking binge. When I could stop heaving, I washed up and left. I took his car keys so he couldn't beat me home and kill me right away. I knew he'd come, and soon, but I hoped I might see him coming and get lucky, maybe kill him in self-defense. A reflex action instead of premeditated murder. It was a fantasy, of course. I hated myself for being so weak, giving my life to an animal like that.

"... Next thing I knew, there's a newspaper headline that someone slit the bastard's throat."

"Damn you say!" Wilkins sits back in shock.

"Yeah, I can hardly believe it myself."

"So who did it?" Wilkins asks.

"I don't know," I answer. "And I don't want to know."

"You're saying someone came in after you and offed him?"

I smile weakly. "Either that or there really is a God who works in mysterious ways."

"That person would have been following you that night."

I nod. "Or following Strand."

"Why would he have been following Strand?"

"Because Strand was a murderous, evil, motherfucking bastard?"

"He was all of that," says Wilkins. "And you have no idea who finished the job?"

"I don't even want to guess. It's bad enough that I'm going to pay the price for stopping Strand. Let's not add to the body count."

Wilkins sighs.

"What now?" I ask.

"I'll file my report," says Wilkins. "Eventually, someone will read it, and the DA will send someone over to take your statement. You can refer them to your lawyer, and she'll ask for a deal. I'll recommend leniency, but if you don't like the deal, just deny you ever said anything to me about Strand."

We're quiet for a long while. The earth has shifted for both of us, and it takes some getting used to.

"Do you have a family, Detective?" I ask.

I should be running home. I should be rethinking my rash decision to confess. I should be getting away from these hideous photos in front of me. But I can't leave. I feel so sad I can't stand and walk out of here. Not yet.

"Ex-wife and two kids, nineteen and sixteen."

"Will they be there for you?"

"Sure." He nods his head up and down, but his body language says he's facing this on his own.

"Can I visit you in the hospital? If I'm not in jail?"

"No," says Wilkins. His voice is firm. "I don't want anyone to see me like that."

We are silent for a long while.

"You should reconsider that, Detective." It's my turn to reach out with a comforting hand. "You can learn a lot from a transsexual about dealing with other people's perceptions of how you look."

His eyes come slowly into focus on mine. They are sad eyes, but there's still life in them and a glimmer of something. Realization, maybe.

"There's how you look and there's who you really are." My voice is sympathetic. So is my heart. When you've walked this walk, you hope no one else ever has to again.

"John Strand looked like a movie hero but he was evil. Whatever you look like now or next week, you're a good person."

He nods slowly. "Thank you," he says. "That means a lot coming from you."

My eyes widen in surprise.

"I guess we both learned some things," he says.

* * *

TUESDAY, DECEMBER 23

Marilee registers several emotions as I tell her what transpired between Wilkins and me. First comes the sad-eyed visualization of a dying man making his last wish, then wide-eyed shock that I would confess, and finally her mom look.

"You're too good for your own good, Bobbi," she says. "I wondered how long you'd be able to live with that terrible secret."

"You've kept it, too," I point out. "How did you do it?"

"I've kept worse secrets than that," she says.

After a long silence, she asks me if I'm going to confess on the record.

"Should I?" I ask.

"That's a choice only you can make."

I knew she would say that.

"What would you do?" I ask her.

"Oh, Bobbi," she sighs, "my answer would have no weight. It's a hypothetical question for me. For you, it's real. If I confess, it's about morality and principle. If you confess, you spend the next twenty years in jail."

"So you see it as a moral dilemma?"

Marilee thinks for a moment. "No," she says. "Not to me. If you were a hit-and-run driver, or you had hurt an innocent person, then yes. It would be a moral dilemma. You took hostage someone who wanted to kill you. A murderer who had no conscience. I don't see that as an immoral act. You just did what you had to do. The question now is whether or not you can live with it."

Marilee was the first to hear my confession after I kidnapped Strand and he was found murdered. She knows about the tortured dreams I've had ever since, dreams of guilt and dread.

"Somehow, I don't think confessing and going to jail will make the nightmares go away. In fact, it seems like it would be worse because

I'd also have the guilt of abandoning Betsy and Robbie in their time of need."

Marilee nods her head soberly. She won't say it out loud, but that's what she sees, too. The only rational act is to deny everything. I shouldn't even be thinking about it, but I hate lies. I hate living my life that way. My life as a male was a lie, at least after I figured out who I was. Having come clean, having survived being cursed and spat upon and gawked at and abused to emerge on the other side of the tunnel as a person, a person I like, I don't want to go back into the dark with another lie.

I say all this to Marilee.

"Of course," she says. "But you don't have to lie. You can refer the police to your attorney who can tell them you refuse to answer questions that might tend to incriminate you." She's been the wife of a cop for several decades.

"That would satisfy the legal code," I agree, "but to me, it's like lying without saying the words."

I wonder how Wilkins would handle it. By the book, no doubt. Let the chips fall where they may. Live with the consequences. Honor the honor code.

Of course, who am I to think about honor? I'm a felon. And if I do the honorable thing, many of the people I hold dearest will suffer. Betsy and Robbie. The L'Elégance staff. Roger. Cecelia won't cry herself to sleep nights, but there will be a hole in her life.

It's the perfect mind fuck: a real-life problem with no right answer.

22

Tuesday, December 23

Wilkins stares at three packages on his kitchen table. One is for his daughter, Anita, at her college address. Along with his mother's jewelry, it contains the gifts he got her for Christmas and a letter explaining his illness, how much he regrets the distance between them after the divorce, how much he loves her. How, if there's an afterlife, he'll spend his looking after her and her brother and her mom.

Another box is addressed to his son, Stephen. It contains Christmas gifts, along with his mementos and his journals. Medals, citations, newspaper clippings from some of his big cases. The half dozen journals he kept off and on over the years. The last journal has a lot of soul searching about his cancer and how it feels to see death standing in the doorway.

He stares at the third package, the one containing the murder book for the Strand investigation. It is complete, right down to the identity of the person who finished off Strand after Logan left. It took him an intense day and night to figure it out, but it's there. His last case is done.

He can deliver it to the DA, something he has put off for days because he felt weak and tired and wasn't sure he had the energy to deal with one of the snot-nose assistant DAs. Truth be told, he also had misgivings about fucking up Logan's life. She's a decent person who just got trapped between a rock and hard place. She was right about some things. None of this would have happened if they had investigated the transwoman's murder right.

And she was right about Andive. If that wretched piece of shit had raped his daughter or his wife, they'd be digging up his body parts for the next thousand years.

And now there's another life at stake. The murderer. Who wasn't a murderer, but more a lifesaver. Someone who wanted to make sure Logan survived. Someone who knew Strand would add her to his line of victims as soon as he could. Two more lives ruined because the department couldn't bring Strand to justice. A bad exchange.

He tries to change his line of thought. Even when you see that justice won't be served by following the law, there won't be justice for anyone if cops start making the calls themselves.

His mind wanders. This is his last act as a detective. A legacy in its own right. It's all about how you handle yourself when you're at the end of the line. Do you stay disciplined and professional or drown in self-pity and go through the motions? Allan Wilkins would be a role model for his son. Stephen would be facing all kinds of challenges in his adult life. Allan Wilkins might not be there with him, but he could leave a legacy that the boy could draw on.

Which got him thinking. What would Stephen think? Would he be proud if his old man stayed true to the oath and put away someone he didn't want to put away? Or would he see Logan as someone who got screwed by a system that wouldn't protect her from a killer but will prosecute her for defending herself?

Wilkins sighs. In twenty-four hours, give or take, he'll be a monster, wishing he were dead, afraid to show his face in public, a prisoner in this miserable apartment.

* * *

WEDNESDAY, DECEMBER 24

Wilkins finishes writing the letter, folds the pages, slides them in the envelope. He doesn't seal the envelope, just pushes the flap inside the V.

It's lunchtime, but he doesn't eat anymore. Even the liquid crap they give him hurts to swallow. Now there's no point in putting himself through that pain. He stands, puts on his coat, slides the letter in one pocket, his meds in another, and grabs a water bottle from the refrigerator on his way out.

An elderly couple shares the elevator with him on his way down. He's seen them before. They say nothing when he gets on, just look at the floor. That's how most people react now, and he hasn't even had the surgery. He can see them standing in a puddle of their own pee if he got on wearing that monster face . . .

At the ground floor he strides out to the street and walks half a block to his car. The effort exhausts him.

It's cold. Chicago cold. Noon on Christmas Eve day and it feels like maybe twenty degrees, enough wind to chill you to the bone. He's shivering and his hand shakes a little as he unlocks the car. It's a department vehicle, unmarked. The captain pulled strings to let him use it, at least until his surgery.

Well, he's already an hour late for the surgery. The phone has been ringing for the past half hour. Some rich surgeon is missing a payday on the last day before Christmas. Poor guy. Wilkins has problems of his own.

He settles into the seat behind the steering wheel, fires up the engine, dials up his favorite music station on the radio. He reclines the seat back to an easy-chair angle, then fishes the meds out of his pocket. He takes a sleeping pill first, just one. It usually knocks him out in about five minutes. He checks his watch, then lays back and enjoys an old Aretha Franklin song on the radio. He gazes out the windshield at the trees, the gray sky, a lamppost draped with holiday decorations. He closes his eyes and rests. He opens them and looks at the headliner of the car, feels the comfort of the seat, thinks how nice it was of the captain to let him use the car. Which is why he's going to do this with pills, not his Glock, which is the way a cop should go out. The more he thought about it, the more he could see the captain getting burned for breaking the rules and the department ending up with a blood-spattered car that they'd have to write off.

Wilkins sighs. He opens the other bottle, a concoction of sleeping pills and pain pills. He starts downing them, four or five at a time. It hurts to swallow. He wants to get it done as fast as he can. If he ends up having a lot of pain in his gut, he'll just have to deal with it, but not for long. Hopefully, the first sleeping pill will knock him out, and he won't feel the rest.

He hopes his wife and daughter forgive him for all his failures. He hopes Stephen finds something to love about his memory. He hopes someday there won't be so many people robbing and killing other people.

Johnny Hartman sings slow and sad about an affair that was almost like a song, but much too sad to write.

Amen, Johnny, Wilkins thinks. Saddest song he ever heard. In a movie about white people in Iowa, for goodness' sake. The blues is for everyone.

It is the last conscious thought of his life.

* * *

WEDNESDAY, DECEMBER 24

This is insane, but no one can refuse Cecelia when she gets like this, not even Betsy, not even when we all know what she's doing is completely and totally insane.

Which is why Betsy, Robbie, Cecelia, and I are spreading a blanket on North Avenue Beach at one o'clock in the afternoon on Christmas Eve day, even though the air temperature is somewhere south of twenty degrees. There's a steady wind blowing, but mercifully, Cecelia has put us in a protected spot. She acts like she just invented Florida.

"Look, we're completely out of the wind, Bobbi. Stop whining," she says to me. Big smile on her face, as much as I can see of it with the furry hood of her arctic parka snugged around her face leaving only her nose and parts of her mouth and eyes exposed to the raw air.

"Oh this is nice," I say. "I'll just get out of these awful clothes and get some sun." I try to effect the sarcastic voice of a latter-day Valley Girl. I'm pretty close.

Robbie thinks this is the greatest adventure ever. She is puffed up like a snowman in a white snowsuit and white boots. She's wearing enough layers of insulation to herd arctic caribou and she has the pent-up energy to run them to exhaustion. She dashes off, an unleashed spirit free at last of the bottle she had been living in. She looks like a powdered donut rolling across the beach. I trot after her hoping to get warm, worried that icicles are forming in my lungs.

Cecelia calls us in a few minutes later, sits us in a circle on the blanket, and distributes goodies from her bag. Sandwiches, chips, cookies, and cups of hot chocolate. No need to blow on the hot chocolate to cool it off.

It's really cold.

"You're probably wondering why I've called this meeting," says Cecelia as we finish eating.

Betsy nods her head and smiles with blue lips. I mutter an obscenity under my breath, but smile.

"One, just to get out and shake off the cabin fever," says Cecelia.

"We could have done that at a nice warm café," I object.

"But it wouldn't have felt as good when we went home," she counters. Point taken, assuming we survive to make it home.

"Second, we can't let the cold weather own us. We have to get out in it and have fun. This is very European, you know. You go to Copenhagen, Stockholm, Munich, anywhere in northern Europe and you see people having picnics in nice public places, even in the winter, even now."

"That's old Europe." More sarcasm, echoing the words once used by an American politician trying to dismiss European leaders in an international debate. Cecelia smiles and ignores me.

"Third," she starts. I'm listening closely now. Cecelia's third things always knock you on your backside. "Third, we're gathered here because it's Christmas Eve day and even though my beloved Bobbi is an atheist"—she mocks indignation—"this is a special day and tonight will be a special night, and it's my Christmas wish that the two of you sit right here and think about how special it is that you have each other. I want you to be able to hug someone you love tonight and tomorrow. Take it from someone who has no one, I know how special that is."

"Why don't you spend the night with us, and we'll hug you instead of each other," I say to Cecelia. It just slips out. A look of shock flares on Betsy's face until she realizes I was just trying to be funny.

Cecelia laughs merrily. "I'll let the two of you have a frank and open discussion while Robbie and I go beachcombing." She engages Robbie in the idea of looking for princess tiaras and other treasures on the frozen tundra of the Lake Michigan shore.

As they trundle off, Betsy looks at me with a blank face. "What does she think we should be talking about?"

I shrug. "I have no idea." My attempt at speech is muted by chattering teeth and numb lips. Betsy's lips are as blue as mine. I scoot over to sit beside her and pull the blanket over us. We giggle like kids in the darkness.

"Bobbi," she says when we settle down. "I don't know how I'll cope if they take you away."

"You'll be fine," I say, rubbing her back with one hand. "You're smart and tough. You're ready to go out in the world. I'm the one who'll have to find a way to cope."

"I'm not worried about making a living, Bobbi. It's losing you again."

I tell her I'm flattered, but she'll be moving on with her love life soon. There will be a new Mr. Right.

"That's not what I mean," she answers. Her voice catches. She's having an emotional moment. "Bobbi, you're my greatest love, whether you're a man or a woman. I love you like I love Robbie . . . forever, no matter what. We won't always live together, but we'll always see each other. But it would be more fun if we could meet at a restaurant or shopping mall rather than at some jail." She starts the sentence in a somber voice, but something about it strikes her funny bone and mine at the same time. We snicker and the snickers turn to laughs.

"Maybe you could bring a male prostitute to brighten my spirits and clean out my plumbing, as Cecelia would say." Betsy doubles over with laughter, her voice rising higher. I laugh so hard I can't breathe.

She tilts her head up so her face is inches from mine. I can feel her breath on my face and see the redness of her cheeks and the fullness of her beautiful smile. She's grinning like a child on Christmas morning. "I love you," she says. She throws her arms around my neck and pulls us together in a cheek-to-cheek hug. It is warm and perfect.

I try to breathe in every molecule of air Betsy exhales, I memorize everything, her scent, the angle of the sun on her face, the warmth of our bodies crushed together, my arms around her, her hooded cheek against mine, Robbie's excited footsteps as she jumps on Betsy, making us both grunt. Cecelia kneeling beside us and putting her arms around us all.

This is a movie that will play in my mind for all the years I have a mind. It will bring light and sound wherever I am, whether it's a prison cell or a beauty salon.

23

Robbie is sleeping and our fingers are finally warm enough to wrap presents. Lighthearted banter fills the room.

Cecelia stops wrapping and stares at me. "You're in an awfully good mood. What's going on?"

"Lots of things." I talk about feeling good about the salon, and the outlook for Betsy and Robbie, and the joy of the Christmas season. "And also," I add, "my soul is free. I confessed to Wilkins."

Cecelia and Betsy gasp. Betsy's face is stricken with fear, Cecelia couldn't be more flabbergasted if the FBI were bashing in the door.

"What?" says Cecelia.

"But you told me you didn't do it," wails Betsy. "You murdered that man?"

"I didn't murder him, but I abducted him, and I confessed to that. Someone else did the murder."

"You confessed to Detective Wilkins?" Betsy exclaims. "Why didn't he arrest you?"

"It was off the record," I explain. "When he turns in his report, the DA will send people to take my statement."

"Thank goodness," says Cecelia. Her relief is palpable.

"I'm going to tell them what I told Wilkins," I say.

Cecelia explodes. "No! Are you crazy? Refer them to your attorney,

that's why you have her. You don't have to give self-incriminating testimony. It's in all the television shows."

"Please listen to Cecelia," says Betsy.

"You were right, Betsy. Back when you said I have too many secrets.
Some of my secrets were just lies I hadn't told yet, things about myself
I don't want other people to know. I can't do that anymore. I lived
with a secret about myself for most of my life because I was ashamed
to admit I was a woman. When I finally came out, it was like being
born. It was horrible and wonderful at the same time, but even in the
darkest moments, I was finally me. It was wonderful. Almost perfect.
Except for the Strand murder.

"I'm not living with that secret anymore. I kidnapped him because
he was going to kill me, and no one could protect me. I didn't kill
him, but I kidnapped him with that intention. I'm going to tell my
truth to the DA and let the chips fall where they may."

Cecelia glowers at me. "You're having an attack of suicidal insanity.
Let it pass."

Betsy takes my hand. "Let's think about it for a few days. I'm sure
nothing will happen until after Christmas."

"Amen to that," says Cecelia. "Bobbi, jail is cold and gray and mean.
What would a softie like you do in a place like that?"

"At least I'd go as a woman," I answer. "And I'd still be able to do
hair. Wherever there are women, there are women who want their
hair done."

We wrap gifts in a funereal silence. Betsy and Cecelia both pause
now and then to dab away tears. I feel awful for casting such a pall on
the party.

The buzz of the doorbell jolts us all. Officer Phil is standing at the
threshold, a box in his hands. I open the door and invite him in.

"Hi, everyone." He waves. Betsy and Cecelia manage welcoming
smiles. He hands me the box. "This was at your door."

I offer him a libation and Santa cookies, but he has a serious expression on his face.

"Bobbi," he says, "I have some news about Wilkins. Can we talk privately?"

"We've just been talking about him," I say. "You can share your news with everyone."

Phil is uncharacteristically flustered at my response. Incredible. A guy who talks to the media every day gets tongue tied with an audience of three? "Okay," he says. He pauses, like he's working up his courage. I feel like the Chicago PD riot squad is going to come barging in any moment.

"Wilkins is dead," says Phil. "He killed himself this morning."

I feel like I've been hit in the chest with a sledgehammer. "Oh that poor man." Tears come streaming down my face. I keep seeing the distorted faces of the oral cancer survivors. "Suicide?" My voice squeaks. Phil puts a hand on my arm. I bury my face against his shoulder, and he hugs me while I cry.

"My goodness," says Betsy. "Oh my goodness."

When I stop crying and look up, Cecelia locks eyes with me. "It's a sign," she says.

"What kind of sign?"

"A shut-up sign!" Cecelia is emphatic. "The investigation might die with him."

"That's what I came to say," says Phil. "I'm not sure what happened to his evidence book. It wasn't at the station and it wasn't in his apartment. Just sit tight and let's see what happens."

"Thanks for your concern," I say to Phil. "But, I have my own ideas about these things."

He smiles a little. "If you ever took my word for anything I'd have to arrest you for impersonating Bobbi Logan. But Bobbi, remember, if you come forward, you could affect the lives of other people who might have been involved in that case."

"Like who? What do you know you're not telling me?"

He asks Betsy and Cecelia if he can have a private moment with me. I take him to the kitchen.

"Maybe Wilkins told me more than one person was involved in the crime," he says.

Phil is being too coy. "Maybe?" I echo. "Did he or didn't he?"

"Just think about it," he whispers. "It's not just about you. If the case dies with him, maybe you should let it."

I gape at him. It's one thing for Cecelia to counsel silence, it's quite another when a cop does. I wonder who he's protecting. When words finally come to me, they aren't profound. "Well, thanks for thinking of me," I say.

"I've never stopped thinking of you." His eyes are soft and sincere, his face serious and handsome. A tingle of arousal stimulates my need to break the somber mood in this place.

"Hey, big boy," I say, trying to effect a Mae West voice. "If I end up in prison, will you drop in on conjugal visit day?"

Phil stays serious. "Don't even think about prison," he says. "Fate has intervened. Accept it."

Betsy intervenes, calling us all to the table for hot chocolate laced with a chocolate-flavored liqueur. It is more delicious than chocolate cake and probably more fattening. We engage in sporadic, lazy conversation about nothing, a moment of limp bodies and peaceful minds. When the moment passes, Phil excuses himself, then Cecelia.

Betsy and I tidy up the kitchen, change into nightgowns, and share the bathroom to do our nightly routines. We finish with a hug, a little tighter and longer than usual, and we share the melancholy thought that this may be our last Christmas together for a very long time. As I start for my bedroom, Betsy takes my hand.

"Please hold me tonight, until I fall asleep?"

My answer is a kiss on the cheek. We pad down the hall to her room, slide under the covers, and spoon, my front against her back, my arm around her, my face nuzzling against her neck. As I drowse toward slumber, I'm recalling the song about making this moment last forever.

* * *

THURSDAY, DECEMBER 25

Christmas morning begins when Robbie climbs on my body and pries one of my eyelids open.

"Are you awake, Aunt Bobbi?" she whispers.

I laugh out loud, my body shaking, my mouth trying to muffle the noise. This has to be the oldest and sweetest tradition in Christendom, the wondrous child rousting the slumberous adults on Christmas morning with the old eyelid-peel maneuver.

I am still in Betsy's bed, we are still spooned, my left arm still embraces her. My movement and noise has stirred her, but not to wakefulness.

I kiss Robbie and gesture for her to snuggle between Betsy and me. Her face lights up. Robbie's snuggling is laced with wiggles and giggles and eventually wakes Betsy. She rolls onto her back, a Mona Lisa smile on her face. She kisses Robbie and hugs her for a long moment, then reaches over to touch one hand to my cheek. "I love you," she says softly. She's saying it to both of us. We turn to face each other, Robbie in the middle, and share a group cuddle. It's like the perfect dessert at the end of a perfect meal.

The moment passes quickly. Robbie is anxious to behold Christmas morning, to see the tree, start the music, open gifts, put the popcorn out for the animals, and to express herself the way children do, with movement and laughter.

Before we follow her into the living room, Betsy puts her arms around me and kisses me on the lips, a sister kiss. "Thank you for last night," she says. I hug her tight. I feel like I am part of a family, a real one where we love each other, even when we disagree, even when we disappoint. Another first, in a season of firsts.

* * *

THURSDAY, DECEMBER 25

Cecelia arrives at nine, laden with a group-sized container of Starbucks coffee and a huge shopping bag filled with presents and a half dozen cinnamon rolls, each one a gooey, eight-hundred-calorie assault on the waistline.

We open gifts and dine and sip and trade Christmas stories, then talk about our favorite Christmas movies. I talk about *A Christmas Story*. I was a lot like Ralphie as a little boy, so I could identify with him. But deep down inside, I wanted to be his mom. She was beautiful and sexy in an earthy way and selflessly loving. Everything I wished I could be as a woman. And I loved her curls.

At midmorning we pile into Cecelia's Caddy and do our Christmas rounds. We stop at Marilee's house and drop off small presents, have a cup of coffee, and enjoy Marilee's homemade rolls. Robbie engages Marilee in a game of hide-and-seek, always hiding behind their beautiful Christmas tree, always delighted to be found. At noon we head for the TransRising building, stopping at a catering firm on the way to pick up a Christmas dinner for twenty people—the residents and their friends. This is just part of Cecelia's holiday largesse. When the residents opened gifts this morning, each of them got a card with five crisp twenty-dollar bills in it. The cards were signed "Santa" but the elf in charge was Cecelia. The old softie.

We return home in the early afternoon to start preparing our

Christmas dinner. Cecelia leaves to complete her rounds of friends
and causes. Her holiday giving list is deep and varied. I remember
the first time I became aware of her generosity it was like a slap in the
face. I had always thought of her as a self-absorbed transwoman at
war with the world. That was before we became friends. Discovering
the real Cecelia was one of many lessons I've had about judging others. My harshest judgments are so often wrong.

Phil calls just as Betsy imposes thirty minutes of quiet time on
Robbie . . . and by extension, on the two of us, too. Phil wants to drop
by for a moment. I'd rather not break the spell of the day. Nothing
against Phil, but the sight of him often turns my thoughts to his body
against mine and this is a day for family. But there's no fair way to
turn him down. Fifteen minutes later he's at the front door. I don a
coat and meet him on the front steps. We go to his car, double parked
in front. The car is warm, holiday music plays on the radio. He hands
me a shopping bag with the gifts in it, a princess doll for Robbie, a
book by a woman whose husband became her sister for Betsy, an an-
thology of music by the great jazz saxophonist Sonny Rollins for me.
I thank him and kiss him on the cheek. His gifts are very thoughtful.

He fills me in on the latest about Wilkins. "He left a note," says Phil.
"He said he just couldn't see any reason to go on living. Apparently
the surgery he was scheduled to have was disfiguring."

"You can't even imagine," I say. "He showed me the pictures. I
wouldn't have wished that on Adolf Hitler."

"You know," says Phil, "sometimes you think you know a guy
and you don't really know anything about him. I always thought of
Wilkins as an honest cop, but hard, a man with no softness anywhere.
He leaves everything to his ex-wife. How many people do that? And
in his suicide letter he thanks his captain for letting him use the department car and says he hopes he doesn't mess it up by dying in it,
but if he does, he leaves another note asking his ex to pay for damages.
Jesus, who thinks of things like that when they're planning a suicide?"

We sit in silence for a while, paralyzed by the thought of that tortured man.

"Want to hear the kicker?" says Phil. "We all think of Wilkins as a bone crusher, and he was pretty fearless in taking down people who resisted arrest. But one of the guys who knew him told me the man never fired his firearm except on the range. Said he didn't believe in it. Can you imagine that?"

Actually, I could. But the realization came too late for me to acknowledge his human qualities to his face. Maybe it wouldn't have meant anything to him, coming from me, but maybe it would. I really have a long way to go as a human being.

"Still no word on the status of his investigation," says Phil.

"He said he was taking it to the DA the day before yesterday," I tell him. "I expected to get a call from them, or maybe a visit. Maybe even get arrested and charged."

Phil doesn't know what to say. Me either.

"Thanks for telling me, Phil," I say at last. "And thanks for the gifts." I lean over and kiss his cheek again. He squeezes my hand.

"Merry Christmas, Bobbi."

"Merry Christmas, Phil."

24

AFTER ROBBIE SETTLES in for the night, I collapse on the couch and Betsy tidies up around the Christmas tree.

"Oh!" she says. "You forgot to open this one." She's holding the package that came yesterday. It got pushed behind the tree, somehow, maybe by Robbie who constantly sorted the gifts by color and size in the lead-up to Christmas. A plain brown box wouldn't rate very highly in her systems.

"It's addressed to you," says Betsy, handing it to me.

The return address is a north-side apartment number and street, no name. I open it, joking to Betsy that I hope it's not a bomb.

There's no holiday wrapping inside, just a very thick book, like a photo album, but something much more businesslike. It takes a moment to understand what I'm looking at.

"Oh my God!" I exclaim.

"What is it?" There is alarm in Betsy's voice. I must have frightened her.

"It's from Detective Wilkins," I say. I try to keep my voice normal, but my mind is on fire. I'm pretty sure I'm looking at Wilkins' investigation, what he called his "murder book." It's a thick, three-ring binder notebook, brimming with pages and dividers. I open it and leaf through the pages.

"I think he sent me a duplicate file of his investigation," I tell Betsy. I'm thinking it's a nice gesture. My attorney and I will see everything the DA sees and we won't have to wait for it while the prosecutor plays court tricks.

As I flip through the collection of photos and reports, diagrams and maps, an envelope falls out. There's a note inside. I read the first page.

Ms. Logan—

I decided you should have this. You've been through enough. I could have destroyed it myself, but that would have left you in doubt. You can destroy it and know it's gone. And you need to destroy this. If you don't, two good people will be destroyed by John Strand—you and the person who wouldn't let him kill you. I'm not saying you did the right thing, but Strand's destruction has gone far enough. Find a better way next time.

"Oh my God!" I exclaim. I read the page again and keep coming back to the sentence, "You've been through enough."

"What is it, Bobbi?" Betsy comes to my side this time, deep concern on her face.

"It's a message from the grave."

"What?"

"It's Wilkins' murder book. The real one. All the evidence he put together on the Strand murder."

"Why is it here?" she asks. "I don't understand."

I'm struggling with the concept myself. Slowly, I look at Betsy.

"He didn't file it. He doesn't want me to confess."

"I thought he was supposed to be a heartless bigot." Betsy isn't being funny. There's real confusion on her face.

"This is unbelievable," I say.

I leaf through the pages and pull out some of the photos. They all have names on the front and copy on the back about the person. I show Betsy the photo of me. It's not very complimentary, but girls like me don't photograph well. I turn the photo over and read the text to Betsy. "Roberta 'Bobbi' Logan, owner of L'Elégance Salon, pursued Strand for the murder of Mandy Marvin, a transwoman beaten to death in 2003."

I pull out another photo showing a strikingly beautiful woman, blond, stacked, perfect. I show it to Betsy. "Meet Barbi Dancer," I say. "Strand's last victim. The girl he beat up the last night of his life." I stare at her photo, wondering what it feels like to be so incredibly beautiful. "Can you even imagine what it's like to be someone like Cecelia or me?" I say to her image. The copy on the back of the picture tells me that Ms. Dancer is employed in the sex trade and she called Strand "a demon from hell." Amen, Miss Dancer.

A few pages later I see an image that chills my soul. I show the photo to Betsy. "He's one of the men who raped me. His name is . . ." I read the copy, "Andive." I look at his ugly mug for a moment. "It's better I didn't know your name back then," I murmur. "You, I could have killed." Wilkins' caption says Andive knew I set him up in the alley. Good.

I keep turning pages in mute astonishment until I get to the one that slaps me in the face. It's Officer Phil, wearing an expensive suit, addressing the media, handsome and hauntingly sexy. I turn the photo over and read Wilkins' note. "A BMW sedan with license plates registered to CPD police sergeant Phillip Pavlik was reported as a suspicious vehicle a few doors down from Strand's apartment a week prior to the murder. On the night of the murder, Ms. Dancer saw what might have been a black BMW pull away from the curb as she fled Strand's car." My mind is racing. Phil? Are you kidding?

As I put the photo back in its plastic sleeve, I glance at Betsy. She's holding Wilkins' note and looking at me in a strange way. "Is that Phil?" she asks.

I nod yes. She hands me the second page of Wilkins' note. "Read this," she says.

I'm convinced you didn't know it, but Sergeant Pavlik followed you many times after you were raped, including the night of the abduction. He entered Strand's residence after you left to make sure no evidence was left behind. He found Strand alive. He knew the man would kill you as soon as he got free, so he took it upon himself to clean up your mess. I'm surprised he had it in him. He's not that type. He must think the world of you. For his sake, destroy this book. Let the rest of Strand's secrets die with him.

I lose all strength in my legs. I sit heavily on a chair and stare gape-mouthed at Betsy. Can this be true? The things I've said to Phil? The names I've called him? The man who can't let himself love me, but he does this?

And Wilkins? To me, he was always a tranny-hating bigot. Now he gives me back my life.

I rock back in the chair, my mind trying to comprehend the mean-ing of this. Can this really be the original report? The only copy? I leaf through the book again, looking for original material. Everything from the old investigation files is a dry copy, of course—the summary of the original Strand investigation, the report on the alley mug-ging, the brief summary of Mandy's murder. As for pages relating to Wilkins' current investigation, it's impossible to say what's an original and what isn't. The pages and photos come from digital files on a computer somewhere.

I'm spinning between competing emotions: elation at the thought that I may not be going to jail or even to trial, and profound sadness that my freedom was the last act of a dying man. A man who was much better in life than I ever gave him credit for. A man I never got to thank.

You've been through enough.

Wilkins' words echo in my mind. I try to picture him writing this note. I try to understand why he decided to let me off, and when he made the decision. The package is postmarked December 24 by a delivery service. The day he was supposed to have his surgery. The day he committed suicide. I guess the surgery was a journey he just couldn't make. I don't think I could have made it either. It's one thing to look awful to other people and be regarded as a freak. I know about that. You can learn to deal with it. But he wasn't going to be able to talk or eat regular food. He was going to be weak and emaciated. He was going to die slowly. A proud man living on an umbilical cord to modern science, his spirit housed in a small, dark place awaiting death.

I keep leafing through the investigation book as I ponder the Wilkins enigma. It's hard to recall the man I feared and loathed, the angry bigot who called me every horrid name you can call a transsexual. Something in his investigation changed him. Or maybe his illness. Whatever it was, he became civil and respectful, and in our last meetings, it was hard to dislike him.

The apartment is as silent as a graveyard. My mind careens wildly through the revelations of Wilkins' work. Not just the facts and speculation in the book, other things, too, maybe more remarkable. His journey and, to a lesser extent, mine.

Betsy squeezes into the chair and puts an arm around my shoulders. "Are you okay?" she whispers. I nod, too numb to speak. She kisses my cheek.

We thumb through the final pages of the notebook together. There is an eight-by-ten photo of a dark BMW sedan, its license plate circled with a highlighter. A caption below says it's the car used to stake out Strand's apartment in the days before his murder. It looks familiar, an older vintage BMW than most of the ones you see on the street.

On the last page there are images of several 2005 license plate registrations. One is Cecelia's, for a black Seville. One is Thomas', for an ancient Nissan. The third has the same plate number as the one on the BMW photo and the complaint report. It's highlighted. So is the name of the license holder. Phillip J. Pavlik.

Wilkins' warning rings in my ears. *And you need to destroy this. If you don't, two good people will be destroyed by John Strand. You and the person who wouldn't let him kill you.*

* * *

WEDNESDAY, DECEMBER 31

I've been doing hair since seven o'clock this morning. Everyone but me has left for home. I would love to go home, too, but I have one more thing to do.

Stephen Wilkins, the teenage son of Detective Allan Wilkins, knocks on the salon door at exactly two thirty, our appointed time. He greets me as Ms. Logan and extends a hand. He is a tall, handsome young man and his hand is huge. I hug him instead of shaking hands and tell him I'm sorry for his loss. His face is sad. I think I did the right thing, even if a hug from a white transwoman wasn't exactly what he was hoping for today.

I usher him to my workstation, offering him a soft drink on the way. I gesture for him to sit in the styling chair where his father sat just days ago. He's a polite, quiet young man with little physical resemblance to his father. He is lean and angular. He has a lot of structure in his face, prominent cheekbones, wide eyes, a chiseled jaw and chin line. Young Stephen will leave a trail of brokenhearted women in his wake if he chooses to, but the first impression he gives is that of a considerate and serious kid. He's certainly showing me a great deal of deference.

After we get settled, we look at each other uncomfortably for a moment, neither sure what to say. I'm the adult, so I break the silence. "Do you know why your father wanted us to meet?"

Stephen shrugs, his face a question mark. "I got a package in the mail with some of his things in it . . . that he wanted me to have. There was a letter to me about a lot of things. One was to call you and see if you'd talk to me."

I blink. It's my turn to shrug. "I'm not sure what he had in mind," I say.

"Were you . . . you know . . ." Stephen is asking if I was his dad's girlfriend.

"Oh, no, Stephen," I say. "Your father and I weren't social acquaintances. Far from it."

He exhales, with relief, I think. We look at each other in silence again.

"How did you know him?" Stephen asks.

Good question. Detective Wilkins didn't have enough hair to be a client. I pause a beat or two, trying to decide how to answer. Wilkins has left me no choice though. I owe him. This is what he wanted to happen.

"Your father was investigating me for a murder that happened five years ago." No more lies. For some reason, Wilkins wanted his son to know about this. I tell Stephen it's going to take a while and ask again if he wants a soft drink. He accepts.

When Stephen is comfortable, I tell him the story of the Strand murder and investigation, including his father's treatment of me, my actions against him. How he reopened the investigation last summer. How he started to change, and how I started to change, too. When I get to the part of him calling me "Ms. Logan" instead of a queen or a queer I start getting an idea of what Wilkins wanted his son to learn from me.

"I think your dad wanted you to know that he changed. He made a powerful case against me and decided to drop it. He figured out everything, even though there was no physical evidence. To do it he interviewed dozens of people. A lot of them were the kind of people he hated. Transwomen. Gays. Prostitutes. And, Stephen, I think what happened was, somewhere in there, he started seeing people like me as people instead of things. He started treating me with respect, and I don't think it was an act."

Stephen absorbs this information quietly. "He left everything to my mom," he says. "In his will." I remain silent. I can't think of anything to say. "She couldn't believe it. She's been mad at him for a long time. A long time."

"I didn't know your dad, Stephen. But at the end, I think we learned things about each other, he and I. Your dad believed in service, that was the most obvious thing about him. He believed he was on this earth to do good, to make people safe."

"He told me once he was too much about the job and not enough about his family," says Stephen.

"I can see him saying that," I reply. I can.

We sit quietly for several moments. I'm thinking about Stephen and his father, and me and my father. "Your father had a spiritual makeover, Stephen." I'm treading on dangerous ground here, butting into someone else's life. But I feel like I need to say this.

"The case file he gave me, it could have ruined my life if he gave it to the DA. It went against everything he stood for, not following through. I'm sure he never did that before in his life, never took a bribe, never failed to do his duty. I keep asking myself, why now? Why me?"

I glance up at Stephen to see if I'm boring him. He is a rapt audience.

"I think he was making a statement—to me, but more to himself and to you. It was a statement about compassion, and how it can come into conflict with duty, and how there are no easy answers when that happens. He let compassion win this time and he wanted you to know it. I guess so you'd have that to think about when you have to confront hard choices."

I resist the temptation to go further with that thought for fear of turning this into a lecture. We sit in silence until Stephen starts talking about his father. He rambles a little, painting pictures of his father teaching him to hit a baseball, throw a football, defend himself in a fight. Talking about obeying the law, respecting others, having good manners, treating his mother with absolute respect. He talks about the gulf that grew between his parents, the separation, the divorce, his mother's lingering anger, his father's attempts to reach out to him and his sister. Stephen is lost in those memories, reciting them without being aware of where he is, spilling his heart out to a hairdresser felon he just met.

He comes back to the here and now with a jolt. His eyes blink, he shifts his body in the chair nervously. "I'm sorry," he says.

"Don't be." I start to say that this is just what his dad wanted, that by us talking together we both learned more about him and about each other. But I don't say it. Stephen is way ahead of me.

We sit in silence again, mourning in different ways a man we're just now getting a full picture of. This wasn't how I wanted to start my New Year's Eve, but now that we're here, it's hard to think of anything else.

Stephen stirs. "I've kept you too long," he says.

I assure him that it's been important for me, too, to understand the full depth of his father. "I feel like I owe you for what your father did for me," I say.

Our meeting ends with a somber hug at the door, probably the last contact I will have with anyone from Wilkins' family. I feel strangely empty as I watch him disappear down the street.

EPILOGUE

It's Memorial Day in America, a day for the faithful to celebrate our fallen soldiers and everyone else to recreate. For me, it's a day of contemplation. I always visit my parents' graves and spend at least a few minutes thinking about my father. My mother said the war made him the angry man I knew, so I always wonder what my life would have been like if he hadn't served. I try to imagine him accepting his queer second-born as a child to love and support, but I can never get there. It's okay, there are lots more things to think about, and many of them are pleasant.

Betsy and Robbie are visiting Betsy's parents in Wisconsin, a long weekend cooking bratwurst on the grill and looking up old high school friends. We weren't conflicted about me staying back here alone. We've gotten past that. We're sisters who are living together temporarily. We love each other and we love Robbie. The living arrangements are going well. It will be hard for me when Betsy gets her own place, and when she falls in love and marries again, but it won't be heartbreaking. She'll never shut me out of her life, and I will rejoice at every golden moment in her life and Robbie's.

I think her next life will be starting soon. She is a different woman than the fragile, shaken person who moved in with me last fall. Her volunteer work has relaunched her career. Her marketing genius has

asserted itself in a nurturing environment. She's had several interviews for a salaried gig, and she'll find something good, even in this
wretched economy.

We've come so far in these few months, Betsy and I. Learning
about ourselves. About each other. I think we've learned a lot about
love. True, deep, transformative love. And the bruises that come with
it. And the rainbows.

Maybe it's a good thing I've been through all the things that happened this past year. Knowing that everything can fall apart in the
blink of an eye keeps me from getting arrogant about how well things
are going now. The salon has turned the corner. We're as busy as we
ever were and we're taking a nice profit.

The one lavish gift I've purchased with my profits is a scholarship
for Jalela. I haven't told her about it because then it would have been a
tribute to what a good person I am and what a big ego I have. Instead,
I funnel money into a special scholarship account at her school. Each
month she does well, her tuition is paid. All she knows is, she's getting
a scholarship that's conditional on earning it. She will, of course. She's
the best student they've had in years.

Phil and I still see each other. It's casual—a jazz club date here and
a dinner there. He took me to a police bar once and introduced me
to all his friends, but it wasn't like he was getting ready to propose or
anything. It won't ever come to that. I think somewhere along the
line he'll meet a genetic woman who floats his boat and he'll get married, or else it will never happen for him.

We often end our dates in bed. The sex is fabulous. I think he gets
a kinky rush from making it with a transsexual. For me it's sort of a
cocktail of beautiful music and soft lights and the most erotic porn
I can imagine. I just have to keep from wishing he was someone who
would want to share a life with me. It used to bother me, knowing that
could never happen. But gradually I realized it's not going to happen

like that for me with anyone. The best I can do is find someone who is really good in bed and treats me with respect the rest of the time. Which is the perfect definition of Officer Phil.

I haven't told him about Wilkins' final revelation to me. I think it would be awkward, and it really isn't important to talk about it. My worst fear is that he'd be afraid I'd rat him out if he quit seeing me. Whatever I get from him, I want it to come from his heart.

I've looked at him many times, trying to picture him killing Strand. It's hard to visualize because he just isn't a violent man. So when I look at him I see a man who loves me, and a man who can't permit himself to love me unconditionally. I think I understand. I'm his forbidden desire, like the woman a celibate priest obsesses over, like the slave girl her gentleman master can't be known to lay with. But he loves me and his passion runs deep. Deep enough to kill a man in cold blood so that man could not kill me. Deep enough to risk his career, his conscience, his freedom. Maybe someday we'll speak of these things, but not now. This is a time to enjoy being alive and to savor the humanity of others.

I'm lucky in many ways, and one of them is Cecelia. She is the best best-friend I've ever had. I told her this recently and added that it was hard to believe I used to avoid her because I thought she was loud and vulgar. "Well, honey," she said, with that flare that only Cecelia has, "that's because I was loud and vulgar . . . and I still am, you just love me for it now."

It was good for a laugh, but the truth is, she's changed a lot in the years since Mandy Marvin's murder brought us together. She is quieter now and more dignified. She's still willing to disembowel, figuratively speaking, the unsuspecting bully who has the poor judgment to target her or anyone close to her, she just does it with the withering grace of a powerful woman. She says I've made her more feminine. I don't know how that could have happened, but the opposite is certainly true: she feminized me by insisting that I express who I am and cast aside concern for what others think.

Sometimes when I think about Cecelia and how I judged her years ago, I think about other people I've misjudged. Jalela. Detective Wilkins. And I realize there must be many others I judged wrongly but didn't get to see the parts of them that were invisible to me. It makes me realize I need to keep out of the judgment business whenever I have the choice.

I don't know what the future holds. I could get hit by a bus tomorrow, or stricken with carpal tunnel so I can't do hair anymore, or develop breast cancer, or any of a thousand other things that can slam the lid on life in a hurry. I'm putting aside money with the faith that I will live to be an old woman. I can't imagine what that will be like, but I've started taking mental notes on how mature women I admire handle themselves.

But most of all, in quiet moments like this, sipping wine and soaking in a hot tub, Brahms playing in the other room, most of all I think about how fortunate I am to have been given this second life.